RUNYON

FROM FIRST TO LAST

containing
all the stories written
by
DAMON RUNYON
and not included
in
"Runyon on Broadway"

the
publishers are
CONSTABLE
Orange Street London WC2

LONDON
PUBLISHED BY
Constable and Company Ltd
10 ORANGE STREET WC2

First published August 1954
Reprinted   November 1954
Reprinted   November 1957
Reprinted   May 1961
Reprinted   September 1964
Reprinted   December 1968
Reprinted   July 1972

ISBN 0 09 451730 4

PRINTED IN GREAT BRITAIN
BY COMPTON PRINTING LTD.,
LONDON AND AYLESBURY.

PUBLISHER'S NOTE

The contents of this volume have been gathered from three collections of Runyon material originally published in 1947, 1948 and 1950 (and for the most part now out of print) with, in addition, a novelette and five stories never before published in book form in Great Britain. The collections—*Runyon à la Carte Short Takes* and *All This and That*—were not exclusively collections of *stories*; and in order to create a second omnibus volume of Runyon fiction to range with the first omnibus *Runyon on Broadway*, we have arranged in more or less chronological sequence all the stories not contained in *Runyon on Broadway*.

Herein will be found the first stories Runyon ever wrote; also the last; also an intermediate series of miscellaneous tales headed by the short novel *Money from Home*. As a postscript is reproduced a group of eight short sketches written during Runyon's final and grievous illness, which will surely survive among records of human courage in the very shadow of death.

RUNYON FROM FIRST TO LAST

RUNYON
ON BROADWAY

containing
all the stories published
in

MORE THAN SOMEWHAT
FURTHERMORE
TAKE IT EASY

the
publishers are
CONSTABLE
Orange Street London WC2

CONTENTS

7

CONTENTS

THE FIRST STORIES

I. THE DEFENCE OF STRIKERVILLE

T HE squad-room conversation had drifted to the state militia, and everyone had taken a verbal poke at that despised arm of the military resources.

"Onct I belonged to the milish," remarked Private Hanks, curled up luxuriously on his cot and sending long, spiral wreaths of smoke ceiling-ward.

"That's what I thought," said Sergeant Cameron. "I recall the time you first took on—Plattsburg, '97, wasn't it? I had an idea then that you came from the state gravel wallopers."

"I'm kiddin' on the square," said Hanks. "I was an out-and-out snoljer with the milish two years ago out in Colorado. I helped put duwn the turrible rebellion in the Coal Creek district."

This statement was received with obvious disbelief.

"Lemme tell you about that," said Private Hanks, sitting up. "Lemme relate the sad circumstances of J. Wallace Hanks' enlistment in the Colorado State milish, and if you all don't weep, you haven't got no hearts.

"They was a bunch of us discharged from the Fifth, in Denver, in 1904. We all has a good gob of finals, and of course none of us were going back. You all know how that is," and Private Hanks looked suggestively at Private William Casey, who had just re-enlisted that day for his fifth "hitch", after a fervid declaration of a week before that he was through with the service for ever; Private Casey at that moment being seated disconsolately upon his cot, red-eyed and dispirited.

"It takes me about a week to get ready to back up into the railroad building to hold up my right hand and promise Recruitin' Sergeant Wilson and Uncle Sam to love, honour, and obey, or words to that effect. The rest of the gang was no better off. They was scattered up and down Larimer Street, stallin' for biscuits, and doing the reliever act with them nice new citizens they'd bought in the flush of their prosperity.

"We all see another three year trick sticking up as conspicuous as a Chinaman in church, but none of us is dead anxious to go back so soon. We don't want the gang out at the fort to give us the big tee-hee after all them solemn swears and rosy air-castles we'd regaled them with when we departed. We'd like to lay off awhile until the novelty of our return wouldn't be so strikin'.

"Most of us is too sick to even think of looking for work. We'd maced about everyone we could think of, from Highlands to the fort, and we're done, that's all. We're about twenty-five strong, take us altogether, and there wasn't forty cents. Mex in the layout. Things is certainly looking fierce, and we're all standing around on the corner waiting for the first guy to say the word for a break to the railroad building.

"I happens to pike at one of the signs in front of an employment office to see if someone ain't looking for a private secretary or a good manager, and it reads like this:

" 'WANTED!—Able-bodied men for the State militia of Colorado. $2 a day and found.'

"I leaves the rest of these sad-eyed dubs standing around where they are and stalls up into this employment office.

"There's a plug sitting behind the desk looking as chest as a travelling man, and I nails him.

" 'What's this gig about militia?' I asks him.

" 'Strike-soldiers wanted—two dollars a day and found,' he says, short-like.

" 'Well, that's where I live,' I tells him. 'I'm the original soldier; all others are infringements.'

" 'You gimme two bucks,' he says, 'and I ships you for a soldier.'

" 'Say, mister,' I asks him, 'if I had two bucks, what d'you reckon I'd want to soldier for?'

" 'That's my bit,' he says. 'If you ain't got it, of course I can't get it. The noble State of Colorado, she pays me just the same, but when I can get it out of rummies like you, I ketches 'em coming and going. See?'

"I did, all right, and it looks to me like it was pretty fair graft. This guy explains the milishy business to me. There's a big strike on in the Coal Creek district. The milishy is out, but there ain't enough men, so they gives this employment guinea orders to pick up all he can. He's just the same as a recruitin' sergeant, only different.

"I tells him about the rest of the bunch, and he agrees to take 'em all. Then I went back and told the gang, and you'd oughta hear the holler they sent up. Milishy! Nix! Not for them! They'd starve first, and a lot more dope like that.

" 'Come out o' it!' I tells them. 'Here's a gee hungerin' to slip us two bucks a day and all found, and you hams standing around with wrinkles in your bellies, side-stepping like a bunch of mules in the road. He takes this on while it lasts and gets a stake. The State's good for the money, or ought to be. Come along, children, before the boogie man sloughs you in the skookum for mopery!'

"Course they comes! Why, this is duck soup for us all. Think of two cases a shift for snoljering! We're there stronger than father's socks when we lines up in that employment office.

"The gee I talks to sends for an officer from this milish, and he takes charge of us. He ain't a bad feller, only he's a kid and don't sabe the war business much. He asked me if I'd ever seen service, and when I flashes about half a dozen parchments on him, he liked to had a fit. At that, he's a nice little feller and don't mean no harm. Some of the guys were trying to kid him, but I made 'em cut it out.

"This officer shoos us down to the depot and loads us up on a train for Coal Creek. He asks us what we wanted to join, and of course we're all out for the cavalry. It seems that was just what he wanted. They had a troop up there that was away shy of men, and a bunch that can ride fits in mighty nice. And so a slice of the first squadron of the Fifth goes into the milishy business.

"I'd hustled the bunch right through the preliminaries, and they don't get much chanst to ponder over it until they was on the train. And then they was sore at themselves and also me. They breaks up into little squads in the smoker and sits looking gloomy-like out the window. Every onct in a while some guy would sigh and say:

" 'S'posin' ole Bluch would see us now!' meaning Cap. Bluch Baker.

"This kid officer was mighty nice on the train, but he finds everyone but me mighty unconversational. We pulls into Coal Creek late that night, and then he suddenly gets all-fired preemptory.

" 'Get out and line up on the platform!' he bawls at us, and, seeing we're there, we do it.

"There's a lot of guys in uniform standing around and looking us over some curious, but we're pretty tired and don't mind. This kid officer gives us right forward, and we climbs hills for the next hour or so until we comes to a bunch of Sibley tents, and a rooky challenges us.

" 'Halt!' he says. 'Who is it?'

"What d'you think o' that? 'Who is it!' But that's what he says, all right.

"The kid officer tells him it's Lieutenant Somebody with a detachment, and the rook yells for the officer of the day. We're finally passed, although all hands looked at us some suspicious, and I don't blame them. Another big gang is standing around rubbering at us as we drills into camp, and they makes a lot of fresh remarks. I'm pretty glad my bunch is tired, or there'd been remains to clean up. We're assigned to tents, and a sergeant comes along and gives us a couple of skinny blankets apiece. The tent has floors, so bunking ain't so bad as it might be, although it was colder'n a banker's heart.

"A kid making a stab at reveille on a trumpet gets us out in the morning, and this same sergeant of blanket fame issues us mess-kits. It had snowed a few feet during the night, and we're none too cheerful when we lines up at the mess-shack for breakfast. We didn't have no roll-call, because we hadn't give in our names. The camp is laid out pretty well, as we see it by daylight. The company streets were laid out in rows on a hillside, and there was a big stable for the cavalry horses at the bottom of the hill. We weighs up our comrades in arms as we sees them at the mess-shack, and they're mostly kids. A few gees with very suggestive-looking shoulders and shame-faced expressions is scattered among them.

"The breakfast ain't so bad, what there is of it, but I could tell by the wise look on the mugs of some of the gang that came with me that there'd likely be a minus in the ranks before long.

"Later in the morning, the captain of the troop lines us up again, swears us in, and takes our pedigrees. I listened mighty intent, but I failed to hear anyone kick in with their right name excepting me, and I had to do it because that kid officer had seen my discharge. Then they issues us clothes.

"Say, you orderly-bucking stiffs, I wisht you could see them clothes right now! Most of them was second-hand, and I take it that our predecessors in that troops had put in their time in civil life serving as models for ready-made cigarettes. I never heard such a holler as went up from my gang since the canteen was abolished. They cussed the state milishy, the State of Colorado, the governor, and all his hired hands, and they wound up by cussing me for getting them into it. They was the worst-looking lot of rookies I ever saw in my life, and they was all the madder because I drew a pretty fair outfit myself.

"After clothes, we were sent down to the stables to draw our mounts. I have mentioned that those clothes caused pretty much of a holler, but it was simply a soft guffaw to the muffled roar that the gang let out when they saw them gallant steeds. I think the State of Colorado robbed the hack horse market of Denver when they sent out the milish, and they copped the whole crop of the previous generation of horses at that.

"Skates? Say, they wasn't horses. They were hat-racks! They were shadows of horses—visions—dreams!

"The bunch was sore at first, but the funny side finally struck them, and they commenced picking out the worst mutts they could. There wasn't much choice, but the lay-out my delegation drew was certainly a fright. They had all kinds of fun kidding with them horses and with the rest of the troop. They'd put their saddles on wrong side before, and all such foolishness, to make the troops think they was awful rookies.

"But if the clothes and other things were jokes, that soldiering wasn't. Nix! No play about that. I've monkeyed around in the war business a few days myself, and I never struck anything any harder than playing soldier in Colorado. You works right straight through from reveille to taps. Post duty around camp; patrol mounted, and guard down in them mines where they'd drop you in a cage so fast you had to hang on to your hat with both hands to keep your hair from flying off. When you got down a mile or two, they'd throw you off with your little gun and tell you to stick there and shoot anyone that batted an eye. Fine business, that!

"It seems that my bunch was about half of this cavalry troop we belonged to. In addition there was a whole regiment of foot-shakers in camp, a battery with one of them old-time Napoleon fieldpieces and a Gat, and another big troop of cavalry. They called this last lay-out the Denver Light Horse, and it was a bunch of swells. Most of them looked to me like they might be calico rippers in civil life, but they sure laid it on there. They had good horses, and their uniforms fitted them. We looked like a bunch of volunteers fresh from the States, lined up alongside of them.

"The clothes and horses let 'em out. They weren't there with anything else, and most of them had something to say about running the troop. I give it to the guy that had command of us. He was a captain named Pard, and I finds out afterwards that he was a boss machinist or a boiler-maker in Denver when he wasn't working at this tin snoljering business. He was a silent sort of plug, but he was strong on the tactics. He knew what ought to be done, anyway, and when he told you to do anything, you had a hunch he meant what he said.

"This Light Horse outfit weren't for us a-tall. The second night we were in camp, a large delegation comes yelling down to our streets, and when we looks out to see what the trouble was, we finds they had come to toss us in blankets. Get that? Toss them old heads from the Fifth in blankets!

"They didn't toss. Not any to speak of. We turned over four tents coming from under them, and when the hospital corps arrived, there was ghastly bleeding remains scattered about. Naturally, we didn't get popular with the Light Horse.

"This Captain Pard was wise to us in no time. He got hep that he had a crowd of the real things under him, and he didn't try any foolishness with us. The rest of the camp had to drill every day. He gave it to us just once. Then he sorter grinned, said something about us appearing to be pretty well instructed already, and that's the last drill we had. He had to take us out every day for a stall, but we put in our time laying around smoking cigarettes in some shaft house.

"Them strikers we were hired to suppress were already pretty much suppressed, as we found it. They was mighty sore at the milishy, and I don't blame 'em, but our fellers got acquainted with a lot of 'em and found 'em pretty decent at that. There's about 'steen little towns in this Coal Creek district, from one to six miles apart, and our troop did patrol duty on the roads between 'em. The strikers were peaceable enough, although they didn't have no use for scabs. They never started anything with us, so we let 'em alone.

"They was especially sore at this Light Horse outfit. Them guys would go tearing through the streets on their horses, paying mighty little attention to life or limb, and they cut up rough with the strikers whenever they got a chanst. They had a big place downtown called a bull-pen, and these Light Horse snoljers were everlastingly throwing someone in the pen, and it made the strikers pretty hot.

"When they finds out we're 'tending strictly to our own business and not minding theirs, the strikers got sorter friendly with us and told us their grievances.

"The mining companies owned the houses where the strikers lived and when the strike comes on they just naturally throws them strikers out of house and home. So the strikers go to living in tents in regular camps and making out the best way they could. The biggest camp was located about two miles out of town and was on our patrol. We had to stop there every night to see if things was quiet, and it wasn't long before our gang was mighty friendly with them strikers. The women in the camp always had hot coffee for us, and generally a bite, and we got to thinking quite a few of them.

"This camp I'm telling you about is on a hill, and there's only one road to it that's anywhere near decent for travelling. We calls the camp Strikerville.

"We'd been doing this play soldier act for about three weeks and was just sighting for a pay-day to blow, when a striker comes to us one day and tells us that the companies is going to give them the run from where they are camped. He says he has it pretty straight that the deputies will do the job and that this Light Horse outfit is in on the play. The deputies and the milishy are to raid the camp at night and start a row; then the next day the milishy will run the strikers off altogether, on the ground that they are a menace to public peace.

"It seems, according to what this guy tells us, that if the strikers could be chased clean out of the district, scabs could be gotten without any trouble, and the mines put to work again. He says the milishy's part in the deal ain't to be recognized at headquarters, but the snoljers are to go along with the deputies like they was doing it of their own accord; same as the time a bunch of deputies and soldiers wrecked a union newspaper office over at Cadence. The headquarters hollers afterwards about 'disorganized mob,' and making a rigid investigation to discover the guilty parties, but it was always noticed that the guilty parties was never caught, and the office stayed wrecked.

"Well, this feller tells us that the gang was going to pull down the tents and wreck the whole camp. He was mostly worried about what it might do to the women and children, because there was a lot of 'em in the camp, and it was colder'n blazes, with two or three feet of snow on the ground.

" 'A girl baby was born to Mrs. McCafferty just to-day,' he says, 'and it will go kinder rough with her and the kid.'

" 'Why don't you put up a fight?' asks 'Dirty Dick' Carson.

" 'Fight? What with?' the feller asks. 'They took up every gun in the district when martial law was declared. If we could only put up one scrap, it would put a stop to this thing of sending these disorganized mobs, as they call 'em, around doing the dirty work.'

" 'I got a scheme,' says Dick to me, after the feller left, and he outlines it with much joy. It made a big hit with me right off the reel, and in stables that evening C Troop, as represented by the former members of the Fifth Cavalry, has a quiet meeting, and Dick and me talks to 'em long and earnest. When we gets through, we had a hard time keeping them from yelling their heads off just to show how pleased they are.

" 'It's all for that McCafferty kid,' I tells 'em. 'Think how you'd like it if you was just born and got throwed out of house and home into the snow. Also think of Mrs. Mc-Cafferty's coffee.'

"The bunch got so excited with sympathy, I was afraid they would tip it off to the rest of the camp. To carry out our scheme, we had to heave the first sergeant of the troop in. He made up the night patrols and assigned the other sergeants to command. Dick and me went to him and has him down to our tent where half a dozen of the old heads is gathered. It just happens that this top sergeant was a guy that had been with the volunteers in the Philippines, and he thought he was an old soldier. Along with it, he was pretty decent, and when he hears our scheme he kind o' grins and falls for it right away.

"There were two patrols made up of about ten men, each under a sergeant, and they worked from dark until early morning riding the roads. At roll-call that evening the top reads off the names of the men on patrol, and although everyone of my bunch had been on duty the night before, our names is included in the list. In addition to that, he increases each patrol to eleven men, so as to take in all us fellers, and he says:

" 'There's going to be non-commissioned officers' school this evening, and I want all my regular non-coms there. I'll appoint Private Hanks to command Patrol No. 1, and Private Carson to command Patrol No. 2. They'll report to me for instructions.'

"That looked regular enough. The rest of the troop was tickled to death, because they thought the top was throwing it into our gang for double duty. It had commenced to snow again heavy, and no one wanted to ride roads that night.

" 'Serves them old stiffs right; they think they know so much,' I heard one of the rooky kids say, as we scattered for our tents.

"In the meantime, I sends one of our fellers through the lines just as soon as we was saddled and ready to start out, with orders to ride to the strikers' camp and put them next. Then Carson and me went to the top for orders.

"I've always had a hunch that when we was talking to him in front of his tent, I saw a pair of eyes gaping through the flap, and that them eyes looked mighty like Captain Pard's, but I couldn't prove it if I had to.

" 'Don't let anyone get hurt now,' was what the top had to say, and we falls in our details and rides out of camp.

"As I'm going past No. 1, the sentry hollers at me:

" 'More H Troop?' H Troop being the Light Horse.

" 'Nope! Cavalry patrols; C Troop,' I told him.

" 'I didn't know; most of H Troop seems to be out on mounted pass to-night,' he says, and a sort o' chuckle runs through our bunch.

"It had started in to snow like the dickens, and you could hardly see your file leader. We were all pretty well bundled up, so we didn't mind. The patrols were supposed to take different roads about a mile from camp, but we all headed straight out towards Strikerville. I sent out a couple of scouts to Handley, where the deputies hung out, and told them to hurry up and bring back a report.

"When we climb the road to the strikers' camp, and you had to do it pretty slow on account of the rocks and not being able to see very well through the snow, we finds a big stir going on. There's a light in every tent, and camp-fires are burning all around. The women and kids are huddled over the fires, and the men are scattered about in little bunches, all talking at once.

"This guy I sent ahead had scared the life out of them. The president and half a dozen other leaders of the union who lived in camp met us, and I made 'em get busy right away.

"As I tells you, this camp is on a sort of flat plateau on top of a hill, and there is only one road to it. I made them put the women and kids in the tents furtherest away from the head of the road, leaving the lights and fires burning only where they could be seen from the bottom of the road. Then I gets every man jack and every kid of any size in the camp rolling snowballs. It was a wet, mushy snow and packed fine.

" 'Put in a few rocks, if you want to,' I suggests, and I guess they did.

"I posts one of the men at the bottom of the hill, and I

puts the rest of them to work throwing up breastworks across the top of the road, to avoid accidents. There was a lot of loose rocks laying around, and a fine trench is up in no time.

"Pretty soon my scouts from Handley comes in, their horses dead beat.

" 'There's about twenty deputies and twenty-five of them H Troop guys over in Niccoli's saloon,' they tells me. 'They're getting pretty drunk, and someone's liable to get hurt. They won't start until about midnight, and then they're coming a-hellin'.'

" 'Any non-coms with the troop?' I asks, and they says 'No.' None of them had their carbines, either; nothing but six-pistols. That was to divert any idea that they was out on anything but mounted pass and a hunt for joy.

" 'Them deputies are making a fierce talk about tar and feathering some of your guys,' one of my scouts tells them labour leaders, and it didn't quiet the agitation which was stirring them none.

"I had the snowballs stacked along the front of the trench as fast as they was made, and it wasn't long before there was enough to fill an ore waggon. I kept everyone hard at work just the same, because I didn't want to run shy.

"All we could do was to wait and watch, and it was pretty cold work. The snow stopped along about midnight, but it stayed pretty dark. My fellows loafed around, smoking and talking and visiting the McCafferty kid. None of the women folks went to bed, although they had no notion of what was coming off.

"It must have been about one o'clock when I hears, away off, the pound of horses' feet on the snow and a jumbled lot of talking and laughing. I hustles my men together and lines 'em up back of the breastworks where them strikers are still rolling snowballs like mad—good hard ones, too. I had ten of the fellers load the carbine magazines, and the rest I bunched with all them strikers, carefully instructed.

"Pretty quick, my outpost comes running up the hill.

" 'They're stopped down below,' he says. 'They're going to come with a rush to surprise the camp. All of 'em are half-stewed.'

"I looked over my arrangements with a critical eye and didn't see anything lacking. My friends was lined up back of the breastworks, them with the carbines in the middle, and the strikers and the rest of my bunch on either side with arms full of big snowballs. We could look right down on the roadway, shining like a streak of whitewash across a coal pile. Back of us a few dying camp-fires were sputtering, and lights burned in a few tents. It was as quiet as a graveyard. Then a sudden yell splits the air, and here they comes!

"They was all mounted, and they was trying to run their horses up that steep, slippery road, yelling like crazy people. Some of them starts shooting in the air. They was riding without any kind of formation, and you couldn't tell soldiers from deputies.

"I waits until they are right below us in the road, and then I fires a shot from my carbine and hollers, 'Halt!'

"They stopped right in the middle of a yell for about a minute, but it was long enough. It brings 'em to a stop just below us, and I screeches:

" 'Ready! Aim! Fire!'

"My carbine gang tears off a volley, and the rest of the gang behind the breastworks launches about a barrel of snowballs on top of the bench in the road.

" 'Fire at will!' I commands, and they does; the fellers with the carbines shooting at the nearest fixed stars, and the others whaling away with the snowballs.

"Say! I've seen crowds suddenly jimmed up in my time; like the old Thirteenth on the Warren the time of the fight, or the gang at Zapote bridge the night the head of Carabao charged us, but that delegation in the road skinned 'em all a Salt Lake City block.

"They was just naturally stood on their heads. They yelled in dead earnest, but they didn't do no shooting; they didn't have time. I hadn't thought about there being any danger until I see that bunch milling around in the road; the horses rearing and snorting and kicking, and everyone trying to go in the same direction at once. I was leary someone was going to get killed. If any one of 'em had gone down in that muddle, it would have been all day with 'em. The language them men used wasn't scarcely fit to eat.

"All the time my crowd was slamming big snowballs down on the heads of the enemy and firing carbines, and some of the yells that rose out of the cloud of snow in the road sounded real painful. The firing squad was working them carbines overtime between laughs.

"The women and kids in the camps came running up to the breastworks to see what was going on, and they gets next to the game right away and commences to fire snowballs too, screaming and laughing.

"At what I judges is the psychological moment, I hollers:
" 'Charge!'

"Then all of us sets up an awful yell and loads and fires snowballs faster than ever.

"Them in the roadway that had their horses turned right didn't hesitate. They went down that road with a disregard for their necks that made me nervous. Them that couldn't get their horses turned right slipped off and went on foot. Pretty soon all you could hear was echoes dying away in the distance and the screaming and laughing in the camp.

"We didn't wait for them strikers' thanks. We got our horses and got out of there almost as fast as the enemy. I separated the patrols and sent one out one way and took the other direction with my squad. We rode off a couple of miles and then went racing back. We got back to the foot of the hill considerably blown, right after old Major Kelley, Captain Pard, all the headquarters' officers, and some of H Troop came tearing along. Back of them Carson and the other patrol was whooping it up along the road, and away back a company of infantry and a Gatling squad was kicking up the snow as fast as they could.

"They had heard the shooting at headquarters, and an H trooper had buzzed into camp with an exciting tale about the strikers' massacring harmless soldiers and deputies.

"Now, of course, they knew something about this frame-up to attack the strikers' camp at headquarters but they hadn't figured on it turning out but one way. Only that lone H trooper had returned, and the major seemed to sort o' expect to find many gory bodies scattered around.

"I reported having heard some firing, but no signs of excitement. The whole works climbed to the strikers' camp, many hunching up as close to the major as possible. I saw Captain Pard occasionally glancing at me with a funny look, as he took in that mussed-up roadway; but the major didn't seem to notice anything. The camp was as dark as bats, but in answer to our yells some of the strikers came out looking mighty cross and sleepy. No, they hadn't heard anything. No fighting; hadn't heard any disturbance, and it was getting colder all the time, and the major was sleepy himself, it ended in thim telling Captain Pard to instruct his patrols to make a thorough investigation. Then they all went back to headquarters.

"On the roads, before daylight, our patrols picked up fifteen H troopers, most of them bunged up about the head or face where them rock-loaded snowballs had landed, and we turned everyone over to the guardhouse for overstaying pass limits. Sore! Oh, no! That's a mistake! I think they had commenced to tumble, because our fellers kidded 'em a good deal.

"When I was turning in that morning, an orderly comes to me and said the major wanted to see me at the officers' mess. I was scared stiff for a minute, thinking the old man was wise, but I went over.

"All the officers of the camp were there eating breakfast. Captain Pard was sitting with an H Troop officer on either side of him, and he looks at me like he wanted to laugh.

" 'Private Hanks, did you learn anything about the occurrences of last night?' asks the major, looking stern.

"I saw right away that none of them was on, excepting maybe Captain Pard, and they evidently had been turning it over among 'em and trying to get at the right of it.

" 'Sir!' says I, saluting, 'as near as I can make out, a gang of H troopers got gay around the strikers' camp, and the women snowballed them away!' "

2. FAT FALLON

"**A**LL soldiers go to heaven when they die," said Private Hanks as he sat on the steps of one of the barrack halls out at Fort Logan, carefully fishing what he called the "makings" of a cigarette from his blouse pocket. "I bases that opinion on my own dope," he continued. "I got it figured out that the Lord wants people in heaven who appreciate their surroundings, and after the army a soldier is sure able to do that.

"There's one man I'd like to meet up there. He's down in Arizona now, commanding a penny-ante post on the desert, and I don't suppose he's got much show of getting to heaven from there; but if he does I'd like to be on the reception committee to meet him and say: 'Come in, Fat; here's a harp and some wings, and the gang's all here waiting for you.'

"Flash Fat Fallon's the man I mean—the whitest man I ever knew. I take off my hat to Fat, and so does everyone that ever soldiered with him. He's a captain now, and I hope he'll live to command the army.

"Fat commanded B Troop back in them days when the war business was doing well over in the islands. That was before we lead with our jack and caught Mr. Aguinaldo's ace, and when everybody worked but Otis.

"We had one squadron of cavalry there to about ten thousand infantry and artillery, and that one squadron gave the finest imitation of one man being two different places at the same time you ever saw. We were out ahead of every flying column; we did a little rear-guard duty for provision

28

trains; a little outpost duty; a little reconnoitring duty; a little barrack duty, and a little everything else that nobody else could do.

"Say, I went into B Troop weighing about one hundred and fifty pounds, and as soft as mush. I came out weighing one hundred and twenty-eight, but I was like cold steel all the way through. I was so tough my face hurt me. We had them little native horse for mounts; and you got so strong that you'd get off and carry your horse once in awhile, to give it a rest.

"Flash Fat was a lieutenant then, just from the Point, and nothing but a big, good-natured kid. He was the only officer we had with the troop, and he was all the same private out in the field. He slept with us and ate with us and joshed with us and belonged to the family generally. I'm telling you right when I say Fat used to go out and stand outpost in his turn just like the rest of us. The troop always worked separate from the rest of the squadron; in fact, the whole squadron wasn't together for over a year.

"Flash got the name of Fat when he was a kid and used to be that way. We tied the 'Flash' on him just to be doing. He was a kid always, and I'll bet if you dropped in on him down there in Arizona right now you'd find him out playing ball with the gang, or up to some other stunt like that.

"When he was in barracks in Manila, before the gugu blow-off, Fat was captain of our ball team and played catcher. We led the Eighth Army Corps league, too.

"I've seen that bunch of huskies playing 'run, sheep, run,' 'duck on rock,' 'old sow,' and things like that, with Fat right in with them, busier than a man with four hundred dollars and a thirst. If it was too rainy to be outdoors, like as not you could happen in our barracks and find Fat and a crowd playing miggles on the floor of the barracks. They used to act like a bunch of school kids at recess all the time, and at headquarters they called us Fallons Failings; but they had an all-fired healthy regard for us on the firing line.

"You couldn't tell Fat from a private out in the field. He never wore any mark to show any difference, and he was just as ornery-looking as the rest of us. He carried a carbine, and was always right where the guns were going off. Fat was one of the few officers I've seen who ever gave a private credit for doing a little thinking for himself.

"In them days a troop or company commander didn't always wait for orders from headquarters before he made a move. The troops was pretty much scattered, and the officers had to use their own nuts.

"B Troop was a rough, tough outfit, recruited in a hurry in 'Frisco for the war, and Fat didn't have no snap at first. He made his hit with us one day in barracks, when he called down a big stiff named Devaney for something. Devaney got mouthy when he thought Fat was out of hearing and was telling us what he was going to do to Fat when he got out of service. Fat heard him and steps up, quiet-like, and says:

" 'You needn't wait until you get out, Devaney. If you think you can trim me, come back of the barracks and try it. If you do, I'll see nothing's done to you for it.'

"Devaney couldn't renig. A big bunch of us heard it, and he couldn't side-step talk like that. He'd been posing as a fighter ever since he came into the troop, and he had most of us buffaloed. So he went back of the barracks with Fat, and for some five minutes there was the prettiest scrap I ever see. They was about the same size and heft, but there wasn't nothing to it from the minute they put their hands up.

"Devaney never laid a mitt on Fat. He never had a peek-in. Fat stalled him for awhile, just cutting his face to ribbons with jabs, until he got him good and bruised up, and then he put him out cold.

"There wasn't anyone else in the troop wanted any doings

with Fat after that, and Devaney was one of his best friends.

"It was a picnic out in the field with Fat, from one way of looking at it. A hike with us was one long josh. We kidded each other, and we kidded everybody that came along. We went into a fight like it was all a joke, but I've seen Fat sit down beside a guy that'd been bumped off and cry like it was his own brother.

"One time in October we was in Manila, resting up for a few days after a hike down Imus way, when we gets orders to take part in an expedition up the lake—Laguna de Bay. They was going to clean out the town along the lake. B Troop was the only part of the cavalry to go along, but there was a lot of doughboys, so we figured we'd mostly guard wagon trains.

"Fat comes up that night with his eyes bulging out.

" 'Say,' he says, 'we're not cavalry any more. We're hoss marines. My orders is to load you on a casco, and we're to be towed up to the lake by one of the army gunboats.'

"And that's what happened, all right. We left our horses in Manila and loaded up on one of the big, pot-bellied cascoes that'd hold a regiment. Then a crazy old side-wheel steamer that they'd fitted up with a field gun and called a gunboat hitched on to us. They was a bunch of jackies from the Olympia under a lieutenant on the side-wheeler.

"Fat told us that we was to cruise around the lake until the troops attacked a town from the land side, and then we'd go after 'em from the water side—catch 'em coming and going, you know.

"It wasn't bad on the casco, because they was only about sixty of us and they was lots of room, but the idea of cavalry-men being turned into hoss marines give us a pain in the neck.

"We took it like we took everything else, though, as a big josh. Going up to the lake, we had a picnic playing sailors.

We'd stand on top of the casco and hail all the boats that passed, like regular sailors, and I guess we made them jackies on the tow-boat pretty tired.

"Fat knew what town we was to hit first, but his orders was to cruise off and on until we heard sounds of firing from the land side. Laguna de Bay is what you might call a young ocean, strayed away from its ma, and you can do a lot of cruising round without hitting land, if you want to.

"We knew we'd have to monkey around that lake two or three days, anyhow, before the troops got up, so we made ourselves right to home on the casco.

"Away down in the hold some one found a lot of old pumpkins, or squash, that the owners of the casco had left there, but they wasn't no good to eat, so we didn't disturb 'em.

"The first night we was out on the lake, just trailing along behind the tow-boat and smoking and talking, Fat says:

"'Fellers, when we get back to Manila again, you know what I'm going to do? I'm going to organize a football eleven and play these college dubs in the volunteers. I hear 'em around the English club telling how they used to play back in the States, and they're figuring on organizing elevens when it gets cooler. We skinned 'em playing baseball, and we can skin 'em at football. I used to go some miles at that game when I was at the Point. Anybody know anything about it?'

"Not many did. Some used to play it when they was kids at school, but that was so long ago most of them had forgotten it. But we was for football if Fat said so, and we talked over all kinds of plans before we went to sleep.

"'Say, loot,' says big Peterson, 'ain't that the game where they has yells?'

"'Sure,' says Fat. 'I've been thinking over a lot of hot ones for us, too. We'll have yells, and don't you forget it.

FAT FALLON

Here's one I thought of the other day. It's part Spanish, part Filipino, and part United States:

> " 'Zooput! Zooput! Masama—
> Cosa est, no soledad—
> Razzle, dazzle, sis-boom-ah!
> B Troop! B Troop! Rah! Rah! Rah!'

"Fat had a voice like an army mule braying, and it wasn't no manner of music that came from his throat when he turned it loose; but it sounded good to us. The jackies on the tow thought we was bugs for true. You couldn't see land on either side, you see, so there wasn't no danger of the enemy hearing us.

" 'Here's a good one, loot,' says Corporal Benson, who was quite a poet, but all right at that:

> " 'Doughboys, doughboys,
> Haw! Haw! Haw!
> Cavalry'll eat 'em
> Raw! Raw! Raw!'

" 'Fine,' says Fat. 'Let's all practise them two.'

"And with him leading us, we sat on top of that casco just churning up the water with them yells. The jackies on the tow had the field gun trained on us in case we started to board 'em. We kept up until we was all hoarse, Fat and Benson making up new yells until we had about a dozen.

"Next morning the blamedest storm came up, and in about ten minutes we was shy a tow. The rope busted, and the side-wheeler went chasing off by itself, leaving us limping along by our lonely.

"They wasn't no danger. That old casco wouldn't founder and it couldn't tip over, so we didn't care a whoop.

When I woke up I heard the fiercest sort of a racket on top of the casco, and I could make out Fat's voice. He was hollering:

" 'Lower away the capting's gig!'

" 'Port your helm, Mister Johnson.'

" 'Ladies first in the life-boats.'

" 'Toss me some light preserves.'

"And a lot more like that. When I lamps on top to see what was going on, there was Fat with a half-dozen of the fellows having the time of their lives playing sailors. Fat was standing in the bow of the casco, which was reeling and tossing like it was drunk, and was yelling through his hands at the others, who didn't seem to be doing much of anything except see how reckless they could get climbing over the boat.

"One feller was playing look-out at the stern, and he'd holler:

" 'Breakers ahead, sir!'

" 'Where away?' Fat'd ask.

" 'Three sheets in the wind,' says the look-out.

" 'Luff, you lubber, luff!' bawls Fat, dancing about on the edge of the bow until I expect him to go heels over tea-kettle into the lake. Then he'd sing:

" 'A sailor's life is the life for me!'

"Down in the hold some one was bellering:

" 'Oh, Capting Fat of the Hoss Marines
Fed his soldiers on pork and beans!'

A stranger would've thought he was in the tack-house for sure.

"The storm kept up 'most all day, and nary a sign of our

tow did we see. Fat decided that we'd be pirates and prey
upon the vessels that come across our path—only none come.
We made Private Barnes come through with a white under-
shirt, the only one in the troop, which he wore because he
said the blue shirts scratched him, and we h'isted it for a
flag, after tearing out a square in the centre to represent
black.

"We had an election of officers, and Fat was made captain
and me first mate. Fat called himself Bloody Biscuit, the
Loose Character of the Laguna, and I was Jiggering Jasper,
the Pie-eyed Pirate of the Peskyhanna. We had Renegade
Rube and Three-fingered Jack and Desperate Dave and
Gory John; we had Stephen Stubbs, the Squint-eyed Scout,
and all the other names you ever read in the yellow-backs.
Fat had a christening of the boat. Someone had a bottle of
pickles in his haversack, so we busted that over the bow—
inside the boat, so the pickles wouldn't escape—and Fat
says:

" 'I christen thee the Bum Steer.'

"We ran everything shipshape, too. We'd talk about
'shivering our timbers' and 'dashing our toplights,' and we'd
jerk our forelocks and say, 'Aye, aye,' to each other. If we'd
only had some stray vessels to board, it'd been great.

"We figured some on making Barnes walk the plank
because he kicked about tearing his shirt, but we finally
compromised on making him sit in the bow for two hours
to represent the figurehead.

"Along towards night the storm goes down, but still we
couldn't see our tow. We drifted all day, and was in sight
of land and going in nearer to it all the time. We had plenty
of grub and tobacco to last us a few days, and so we wasn't
afraid of being lost. When night comes on, we could see the
lights of the houses on shore, and Fat decides that we needs
some lights 'aloft.'

" 'So's our tow can run into us,' he says.

"Well, we didn't have nothing but candles, and they don't stay lit without covers. Fat has a great idea.

" 'Go down and get them pumpkins and we'll make jack-o'-lanterns,' he says.

"We did. Everyone that had a candle gets a pumpkin and carves a scary-looking devil-head out of it. We h'isted them lanterns on sticks or hung them over the sides, and I'll bet no such looking craft was ever seen around that whole archipelago.

"Fat was as pleased as a kid with a new toy. 'That's real piratical now,' he says, and I don't doubt it was.

"We was drifting along slowly about a mile from the shore. Little towns fringed that lake clear around, and we could sometimes hear voices. Every one of the towns was an insurgent stronghold, and some were supposed to be well fortified, which was why they was sending a strong force to take 'em.

"After supper we was all on top of the casco, and Fat started us into practising them football yells again. No one thought about the noise. We gave them much better than the night before, and when sixty huskies are yelling all together out on the water on a still night it makes some disturbance, I'm telling you.

"We was having all kinds of fun when someone noticed the lights going out alongshore and mentioned it to Fat.

" 'Holy smoke!' he says. 'I forgot all about tipping our hand to the gugus. They'll commence shooting in a minute.'

"But they didn't. It was quiet as the grave, and all we could hear in towards shore was the lapping of the water.

" 'Oh, they're just going to bed,' says Fat, and we started in yelling again. We kept it up until midnight, with a few songs thrown in for good measure. Fat taught us to sing:

FAT FALLON

" 'Fifteen men on a dead man's chest
Yo-ho-ho, and a bottle of rum!'

and that made a big hit with everyone. We sung all the old songs we knew, and they listened mighty good to us, too.

"Well, we finally got tired and went to sleep, leaving a couple of guards posted. Fat had all the jack-o'-lanterns thrown overboard, as the candles had burnt out, and there didn't seem no chance of that tow picking us up that night.

"At daybreak next morning we was grounded on shore, having drifted too close in. We was near a good-sized town, but they didn't seem to be no signs of life in it. Fat had a couple of men slip over and take a look at the town, but they said they couldn't see a soul. They didn't go in very far, for fear of a trap.

"We was eating breakfast when the old side-wheeler we'd lost hove in sight, looking pretty battered about the edges, but still afloat. She came in close to us, and the naval lieutenant in command of her bawls out:

" 'Where you fellers been?'

" 'Looking for you,' says Fat.

" 'Well, we been a-looking for you, and so's a whole brigade of soldiers—looking for your bodies. We was just going to fire guns over the water to raise you,' says the naval man.

" 'Where's the brigade?' asks Fat.

" 'Right outside that town, and the old man's sore as a boil,' the lieutenant says. 'You'd better go over there and report.'

" 'Any gugus in town?' asks Fat.

" 'Gugus? I should say not,' says the naval man. 'That's what the old man's sore at. They ain't a single enemy nowhere.'

" 'By the way,' this lieutenant bawls, as Fat gives us orders

37

to unload, 'you didn't notice anything funny around the lake last night did you?'

" 'Nope,' says Fat; 'what do you mean?'

" 'Oh, nothing,' says the navy; 'only my sailors are a little superstitious, and they've got an idea they saw a new kind of Flying Dutchman last night.'

" 'Must have been smoking hop,' says Fat, and the side-wheeler backs off.

"We falls in on the shore and marches through the town, which was as deserted as if no one ever did live there. They was a lot of swell trenches where they ought to be some enemy, but they was no enemy to be seen.

"About a mile outside of town they was a most inspiring sight. A whole brigade of soldiers was camped out, infantry and field guns and everything else—just laying there doing nothing.

"They created some excitement when we marches up, and old General Hill comes a-tearing across the camp with a bunch of staff officers.

" 'Glad to see you, lieutenant,' he bawls at Fat.

" 'Feared you were lost in the storm. Had a terrible time, I guess?'

" 'Awful,' says Fat, not batting an eye. 'Where's the enemy, sir?'

"The old man looked mad a minute.

" 'You tell us,' he says. 'Here I bring a whole brigade to take towns that your troop alone could invest without any trouble. Not a single insurgent or anyone else in sight. Not any of them. All the natives, peaceful and otherwise, have taken to the hills. I guess they got scared of us, but it's the most remarkable thing I ever heard of. Men, women, and children—all gone. I was sure I had reliable information that this country was alive with insurgents, but they've gone, bag and baggage, leaving only their trenches. We've beaten this whole side of the lake and cannot find anyone in the towns. We caught some women who didn't seem able to keep up with the general scramble, but they're half crazy with fear. All the interpreters can get out of them is some nonsense about a spirit ship that cruised along-shore last night with a lot of screaming devils on board. They say that's what caused the people to hide out, but of course that's silly.'

" 'Well, what do you think of that?' says Fat to us, after the general had gone."

3. TWO MEN NAMED COLLINS

I KNOW some things all right if I could only think of them. These guys say I'm crazy—crazy in the head like a sheep; but I'm as happy as if I had good sense.

I hear 'em talking in the barracks when they think I'm not around, and I know what they say. I'll make some of 'em hard to catch, one of these days. They're afraid of me because I killed a man once. Well, I evened that up, but they don't know it.

When I get out of the army I'm going back to driving hack in Denver like it was before I enlisted. It ain't my fault I'm here. It's the old booze. I gets drunk one day and went out to Petersburg. I met a guy there who belonged to the army, and before I knew what I was about I had on one of these uniforms. I only got six months more, and you bet they won't get me again.

Before I go I'll get good and even with some of these guys. Ever I catch any of them fresh officers down around Arapahoe Street after dark I'll fix 'em.

I've heard 'em say I'm the orneriest white man in the army. I don't know why. I'm big and strong, but that ain't nothing. I can take this Krag and bend it double like it was made of tin; I did it once when I got mad at a sentry because he wouldn't let me be.

I can lift any man in this company waist high with one hand. I can tear open a can of tomatoes with my teeth. But them things don't make a guy ornery, do they?

I used to get drunk whenever I could, and it made me **mean**. They threw it into me, too. Guardhouse all the time, and hard work. Then one day I heard a non-com tell another they was laying for me with a general guard to give me a bobtail and a dash at Alcatraz next time I come up; so I quit. I haven't touched a drop in over a year.

They's something funny about me, though, and I don't know what it is. Whenever I walk post in front of the officers' quarters them fresh guys and their women get out on the porch and watch me. They talk just like I couldn't hear, too. I heard a woman say one day when I was stepping off the post—it's an even hundred of my steps from one end to the other—that I reminded her of a caged lion.

"More like a big bull behind a pasture gate," says an officer.

"Or a battery horse with the weaves," another sticks in.

Stuff like that, you know. Can you blame me for being sore?

About that man I killed. I didn't mean to do it. His name was just the same as mine, Charles Collins, only they called him Pretty Collins. He *was* pretty, too. He had a load of education, and he got into the army accidentally, same as me.

I've seen lots of his kind. They're mostly to be found around Torts or at Brown in evening clothes after a show, and they've paid me good money for hauling 'em around in my little old hack.

I used to feel like jumping up and saying, "Cab, sir," every time he came past me on the parade ground. He was a private like anyone else, but I've seen sentries half bringing their guns down to salute when they went by. It was the way he wore his clothes maybe.

I've heard some of these guys say he spent a barrel of money going the route, and broke his old lady's heart. His old man give him the run, or something, so he breaks into the army. The officers pitied him a lot, and he used to be something of a pet with them. They didn't holler and growl at him same as they do at me and the rest. I heard the top say once that they offered to get him discharged, but he wouldn't stand for it. Anyway, they used to treat him mighty white.

I had it in for him strong.

I didn't like him from the start because they used to kid us both, changing our names around and calling him Crummy and me Pretty. I know I ain't pretty, and I knew how they meant it.

The top, when he called the roll, used to put it Collins No. 1, which was him, and Collins No. 2, which was me. They ain't anything unusual about that, I've seen companies where they'd have four or five Johnsons, or Browns, or Smiths.

I got so I hated the sight of Collins. I hated his pink and white face, and I hated him because he wasn't supposed to be no better than me, but *was*, somehow.

He didn't know how much I had it in for him, but he did know I didn't like him, because one day he starts to joshing me with the rest, and I took him to the mat. I had my fingers on his throat and his white flesh came out between them like I had grabbed a lump of dough.

They broke me loose, but I told him then that if ever he tried to hand me anything again I'd bust his crust. He looked whiter then ever, but he bowed polite and says:

"All right, Collins; I beg your pardon. It won't happen again."

He offered me his hand, but I spit at it. He never spoke to me again. And I hated him more than ever for it.

They used to rawhide me something fierce in the company. I mean the non-coms did. I got all the extra duty there was doing. I knew I was getting the dirty end, but I couldn't holler. It wouldn't done me any good.

TWO MEN NAMED COLLINS

I've seen Pretty Collins come into quarters after taps just spifflicated, and nothing was ever done to him. Do you wonder I was sore on him?

Well, I just laid low and waited. I figured to get to him some day some way, so I laid low.

Finally we goes to Manila and gets sent out on the north line, where they was fighting about every day. That's when I gets next to Pretty Collins.

He was about my height and heft, so was in the same set of fours as me. When we fanned out in open order, that brought him next to me, on my right. The first scrap we went into I watched Pretty, and I was hep in a minute.

His face turned whiter than the time I grabbed him, and his hands trembled so he could hardly hold his gun. I sensed him, all right, all right. He was a coward.

When the bullets commenced to whistle I thought he was going to drop in his tracks. I'm no coward, whatever I am, and you bet I took a lot of satisfaction watching that guy suffer; because they do suffer—all the tortures of hell, I've heard.

I don't think anyone else noticed him, btu Pretty knew that I knew—he looked at me once and saw me grinning.

I used to own a pit dog—Sunday Morning. He was beat by Mitchell's Money on the Overland race track one Christmas day. He was nearly all out when I picked him up for his last scratch, and he looked at me out of his eyes like he was trying to tell me not to send him in again. Pretty reminded me of Sunday Morning when he looked at me across that rice paddy.

It wasn't much of a fight, but when it was over Pretty was as limp as a rag. The rest thought it was too much sun, but I knew—and Pretty knew I knew—and that was more satisfaction to me than if the whole brigade knew. He never said anything to me; just looked at me out of his eyes like Sunday Morning looked.

It wasn't long after that he was laying in front of a line of trenches which were across a river from us. The general commanding the brigade and his staff was with our outfit. The gugus was slapping a kind of blanket of bullets over our heads, and we was hugging the ground pretty close. The general sings out to our captain:

"Send a man down to Colonel Kelley on the left of the line and tell him to advance at once."

You know what that meant?

A man had to chase across that open field for a quarter of a mile with the gugus pecking at him. It was a two-ace bet that he would get his before he got half way. Cap looks down the line and says:

"Collins!"

He was looking right at Pretty, over my head, and he meant Pretty. Man! That fellow's face was already white, but it seemed to go dead all at once. I'll bet anything he couldn't have moved if he'd tried, his muscles being sort o' paralysed.

Cap kept looking at him—over my head. It wasn't three seconds, but it seemed three hours. When I first heard Cap call I felt glad, because it meant all day with Pretty. Then when I looked at Pretty's face I felt sorry, and there's where I made a sucker of myself. I jumped up and started on a run down the line. Cap didn't say anything. It looked like I had made a mistake and thought he meant me, but Cap knew better—and he knew I knew better—and Pretty knew better.

They shot at me considerable and winged me a little once, but I delivered the order and got back in time to go into the charge with my outfit.

I could've gone into the hospital if I'd wanted to, but I

wasn't hurt very bad. That night I was sleeping near Cap and the two lieutenants, and I heard Cap say:

"The old man is going to recommend Crummy Collins for a stiffycate of merit. He wanted to make him a lieutenant, but I showed him the"—something—"of such a course.

"I meant Pretty Collins all the time, because I knew it was a chance to take him out of the ranks. He could have won his shoulder straps right there, but——"

"Do you think he's——" something I didn't get again, one of the loots asked.

"I fear he is," says Cap, and I went to sleep.

Well, we put in nearly two years on the islands, but Pretty got transferred to special duty, and I didn't see no more of him until we sailed for home. He looked kind of bad in the face, like he'd been going too strong, but he was just as popular as ever in the company. No one knew what Cap and me knew, and I didn't tell, but Pretty kept away from me.

By this time the gang had commenced to treat me a little better, because I'd showed 'em I was a good game guy, but I didn't have no bunkies.

I'd almost forgotten Pretty while he was away, but when he comes back again he made me just as sore as ever at him—just by being around, you know.

He didn't get so much petting from the officers as he used to, but he was still the whole thing with the bucks.

We went to Fort D. A. Russell, just out of Cheyenne, from 'Frisco, and I gets my stiffycate of merit there. It's a big sheet of paper, something like an officer's commission, all engraved, with my name and outfit and telling what I'd done when I carried that order across the firing line. Best of all, it gives me a couple of bucks extra pay every month. I stuck it away in my chest and didn't show it to any of the guys, although they knew I got it. You're supposed to send them things home to the people, so they can frame 'em and hang 'em up in the parlour, but I didn't have no people or parlour either.

We hadn't been in Russell more'n a month when Pretty shows up one morning missing. They calls his name for ten mornings at roll-call, and then they posts him as a deserter. It like to broke these guys that'd been so friendly to him all up, and you bet I was glad.

They caught him in a couple of weeks up in Rock Springs on a drunk, and they brings him back to Russell and slaps him in the general prison. He's good for about eighteen months at the lowest, because the officers that had been so friendly to him shook him right away.

I was doing guard duty one day over a bunch of prisoners cleaning up quarters, and Pretty was one of 'em. I wasn't paying much attention to any but him, watching him moving around in that brown suit with the big white P on his back, when all of a sudden he makes a break.

He must a-gone nutty. He didn't have a chance in the world to get away. They told me he said before he cashed in that he got wild having my eyes follow him around, but that's rot. All I did, so help me, was just watch him, and I leave it to any one if that should make him go bugs.

I hollered at him to halt three times. Then I aimed at him, meaning to hit him in the leg. His head kept bobbing in front of my sights, and he was getting further away all the time, so I had to let go. He dropped and laid there kicking around.

The whole barracks come running up, and I don't remember much else, except that they relieved me and sent me to quarters.

None of the fellows would talk to me or tell me what was doing, but I heard someone say he was dead. I stayed in quarters all the next day, and no one come near me. If I'd walk up to some of the fellows they'd get up and move off, like they was afraid of me. The Cap come in towards evening and talked kind to me. He said I'd only done my duty, but that it would be best for me to be transferred, and they was going to send me to Plattsburg to join another regiment. That was all right with me. He told me to get my junk together and get ready to go right away.

It didn't take me no time to pack. While I was throwing my stuff into my chest I came across that stiffycate of merit and shoved it in the inside pocket of my blouse.

I heard some of the fellows talking that night, and they spoke about "him", so I knew they meant Pretty.

"His father and mother are coming in a special train from the East," one of them said. "The top and four non-coms are going to take him to Denver and turn him over to them."

No one even looked at me all this time.

Cap give me my transfer papers and transportation that night, and next morning I went to Cheyenne and got a train for Denver. Only the Cap said good-bye to me.

At Denver I missed the first I was to take east, and hung around the depot all day. Along towards evening a train of just a baggage car and a Pullman pulled in while I was looking through the fence outside the depot. The Pullman blinds were down, and it looked so mournful and still that I had a hunch right away that it was Pretty's folks. I was right, too. A grey-haired man, who moves around brisk and talks rough to the porters, gets off and helps a little old lady, all dressed in black, to the platform. You couldn't see much of her face on account of a heavy veil, but you could tell by her eyes that she had been crying a lot.

They hadn't more'n got on the platform when the regular Cheyenne train pulls in and the top sergeant and a squad of non-coms from my old company hops off. The old man leads the little old lady up to them, and they shook hands all around and stood talking awhile.

Then they went to the baggage car, and the squad hauls out a long wooden box with a flag across it. Somehow it made me sort o' sick to look at it, because I knew Pretty was inside.

The non-coms put the box on a truck and pushes it over to the special train and shoves the box in the Pullman—not in the baggage car.

The old lady follows it in, and the man stood at the end of the Pullman talking to the top. I couldn't stand it no longer. I wanted to hear what they said, so I sneaks through the gate and around behind a train on the track next to the Pullman.

The old man was saying:

"I'm mighty glad the boy died like a gentleman, anyway. He was always a little wild, but I never believed he was a coward. I was rather pleased when he joined the army, because I felt it would make a man of him."

"Yes, sir," the top says, "he was a man all right. He gave that prisoner a hard fight before he went under, and would have won out if the prisoner hadn't been stronger."

I see the drift all right. They was making this old man believe Pretty had been killed in the performance of his duty; see? I listens to a little more, and I makes out that the top has told him Pretty was guarding prisoners, when one of 'em turns on him and shoots him with his own gun. He was giving Pretty a great send-off.

Maybe you think I wasn't dead sore!

What right had they to tell all them lies? If it'd been me in the box they'd probably have said I was the worst black-guard in the army and got all that was coming to me.

The top and the other non-coms shake hands all around with the old man again, and then they hikes off. The old man goes into the Pullman, and the engine crew get ready to pull out. I make up my mind in about two seconds, Mex., to go in there and tell them folks all about Pretty and why I had to kill him. I see my chance to get good and even with him more than ever.

I climbed on the rear platform and opens the door. The box was in the aisle, and the old lady was setting in a seat beside it. The old man was with her, holding her hands, and she was crying, soft and easy like. He isn't crying, but he looks old and tired.

They both raise their heads when I come in and looked at me like they was waiting for me to say something.

"I soldiered with him," I says, pointing to the box.

The old lady looked at me out of Pretty's eyes, just as Pretty looked at me that day across the rice paddy. She almost smiled.

"He was all I had," she said. "He was his mother's boy."

The old man didn't say anything—just looked me over.

I don't know what got the matter with me. I couldn't say a thing—just stand there looking at them two like a sad-eyed dub. The words I wanted to tell 'em wouldn't come.

"He was a good soldier?" the old man finally asks.

It wasn't what I meant to say, but I just had to tell him yes.

"He was all we had," the old man said. "It is a hard blow, but it is softened by knowing that he served his country well and died in the line of duty."

I tried to shake myself together and tell them that their boy had been a coward and a deserter, and if he'd lived would have put in a year or so in prison, with a yellow bob-tail discharge at the end, but I couldn't do it—that's all.

The train commenced to back up, getting ready to start out.

"Do you know of any of his companions who have any

reminder of my darling boy?" the old lady asked. "They didn't bring anything—but his body."

I felt something crackle in my inside breast-pocket. Ain't I a sucker, though? I stuck my hand in and hauls out that stiffycate of merit.

"Here," I says, handing it to her. "They sent this to you by me."

And then I hikes out of that car, for fear I might get dingey and bust out crying myself.

I know some things, all right, all right.

4. AS BETWEEN FRIENDS

I

ABIMILECH FETCHER sat upon the front stoop of the Parkins County court-house, smoking a fretful pipe and paying no heed to the snow-lined breezes that searched his meagre apparel. He gazed with eyes of gloom upon the frame houses and store buildings, standing like serrated teeth; his gaze travelled moodily on to the vast expanse of flat country which aproned the small but enthusiastic town of Advance, and against the far horizon he could see the windmills, flogged by a relentless eastern Colorado wind, waving wildly. Abimilech Fetcher, Sheriff of the County of Parkins aforesaid, was a study of Gloom, done in heavy corpulent lines.

A tall, thin ragged young man, with a self-confident air and a lean, alert face, suddenly sketched himself into the picture and stood looking at Abimilech Fetcher, who returned the gaze morosely.

"Well," said the young man finally, "I may be wrong, but if I was guessin' and had just one guess, it'd be that there sits 'Chicago Fat,' lookin' as sad and forlorn as a millionaire in gaol."

The dull eye of Abimilech Fetcher slowly brightened.

"It's me," he said. "And you might be 'Kid' Switch."

He arose and extended a cheerless fat hand. "Set down, Kid, set down, and tell me how come you to git shoved offen the main line."

"You tell me what *you're* doin' here," said Kid Switch. "I

heard you'd quit hoboin' some years back and had settled down somewheres, but this can't be the where?"

"Yes," replied Abimilech drearily, "this is it. I'm the Sheriff. Also I'm a married man, with two children and a mortgage on my house, and I'm starvin' to death right now, Kid."

Kid Switch laughed uproariously.

"That's it—laugh!" said Abimilech bitterly. "I've gotta notion to vag you. You're the first feller that even looks like a possible prisoner I've seen in a year. Whatta you doin' here, anyway, Kid?"

"On my way to San Francisco," said Switch. "I didn't know this was a branch line until I got here. I snared a freight train at the junction, havin' been chased offen a varnished rattler, and I didn't know I wasn't pursuin' the main haulage-way until I peeked out and saw this wide place in the road. And to think I've scairt you up—Chicago Fat—who usta be one of the grandest hoboes in the world!"

"It's me, Kid," said Abimilech. "And I thank you for them words. Sometimes I wisht I'd stuck to the road, but I got remorse and fat and et cetery and here I be, starvin' to death. I was a good hobo—I was a good hobo when you was just a gay cat, and I might be a good one yet, barrin' the fat."

"Tell me what's the trouble," urged Switch, as he contemplated the stout figure and suppressed further hilarity.

"It's the cussed fee system," said Abimilech. "The Sheriff has to make his livin' offen fees. If he's on the main line, like ole Tobias over here in the next county, he can arrest enough of you hoboes in the winter time to make money. We git paid a dollar a day for feedin' prisoners and we kin feed 'em for ten cents a day, if we use judgment—that's ninety cents profit. If you've got enough prisoners you kin git fat. If you ain't got no prisoners, you starve, or go to work. I been Sheriff two years, come next month, and I ain't seen enough mallyfacters to keep me in kerosene and other delicacies."

"If you had, say twelve prisoners for, say, ten days each, would that help you any?" asked Kid Switch.

"Help?" said Abimilech. "Help? Say, Kid, it'd set me in swell! I'd perk up and take a reg'lar interest in life. But what's the use o' talkin'? How kin I git twelve prisoners? How kin I git any prisoners, when folks don't violate the law, or if they do they're friends o' yourn and you dassen't stick 'em?"

"I met 'Cleveland' George yesterday and he tells me a bunch of the fellers are layin' out the cold spell with your neighbour, Tobias," said Switch.

"He's a mean guy, is Tobias," interrupted Abimilech. "Bein' prosperous, he's natchally mean."

"Well, he's all right to the tourists," said Kid Switch. "And a dozen or more of them are hangin' up with him for a coupla weeks. They're nearly all ole time pals o' yourn and mine and'd be glad to help you out if it was put to 'em right. We'll call my end just half, if that's satisfactory to you."

"Talk sense, Kid," urged the bewildered Abimilech. "I don't git you. How'm I goin' to git them fellers? Tobias ain't goin' to lend me any. He's too blame stingy."

"Listen," said the Kid mysteriously. "But let's find some place where it ain't so crimpy around the edges."

2

Sheriff John Tobias, of Queever County, had at least a nodding acquaintance with all the gentry of the break-beams who travelled from East to West a few years ago. The county seat of Queever County is a division point on a transcontinental railroad and during the year hundreds of nomadic individuals pass that way.

The Queever County gaol is a rickety, but fairly comfortable structure and during bad weather it was the custom for the human birds of passage to lodge with Sheriff John Tobias and thus insure him, in return for good food and treatment, a prosperous business under the fee system.

He had a sort of gentleman's agreement with the veterans of the rail that they might plead guilty to a charge of vagrancy before the only justice of the peace in the town and ten days was the limit of their sentences. Novices, who were sensitive in the matter of being called vagrants, but who desired shelter over a stretch of untravellable weather, could plead to a charge of carrying concealed weapons—a razor being a weapon in those parts, and Sheriff John Tobias was obliging to the extent of furnishing the razor.

No one really had to remain in the Queever County gaol; it was of such a frail texture that even a sparrow might have escaped without great difficulty. Half a dozen tunnels beneath the floor, leading to sunshine and liberty, told of the passing, in days gone by, of many an itinerant from the hands of less obliging officers than Sheriff John Tobias. In his regime, if a prisoner happened to be in a hurry, Tobias would permit him to go before the expiration of his term, via the front door, and would speed him on his way with words of cheer.

Through the years of his long tenure of office this arrangement endured, an indictment against the fee system, perhaps, but a source of comfort to those who travelled the Western trails in that day. The town of Queever understood the situation, but when the gaol was filled, plenty of supplies had to be purchased of the local merchants, for Tobias was content with small profits and treated his patrons liberally; the local merchants consequently favoured the full county gaol, particularly as the burden of taxation fell upon the balance of the county, which probably, did not fully understand.

Sheriff John Tobias was viewing the snowstorm from the window of the gaol office with deep satisfaction; snow meant that his gaol population would rest contented against the coming of warmer weather. The darkened skies, pinned down all around the horizon, foretold a long continued storm.

The office bell jangled shrilly and Sheriff Tobias opened the door to look upon the damp figure of Kid Switch, who had found a ten-mile tramp across the snow a bit more of a hardship than he had figured on. Only freight trains ran to Advance and they were few and far between.

"Well! Well!" said Sheriff Tobias, heartily. "Come right in, Switch! I haven't seen you in over a year. Come in, boy, you'll find a lot of friends present, if you're plannin' to stay, and they'll be mighty glad to see you."

"I hope so," said the Kid. "Stake me to some dry clothes, Sheriff; I'm as wet as a fish. I'm goin' to hang up with you until it clears a little."

"Yes, sir!" said the Sheriff, with the unction of a hotel clerk greeting a wealthy guest and leading the way to a big steel door, from behind which came a subdued murmur of voices. "You'll find 'Red,' and Gordon, and Kline, and Kilgallon, and the 'Philadelphia Shine' and a lot of friends inside, Kid. Cleveland George left here yesterday. It's a good Winter for me, son."

Kid Switch was familiar with the personnel of Tobias' guests, having been enlightened by Cleveland George. He was prepared for the roar of greeting which arose when he stepped into the "bull-pen" of the none too commodious gaol. After having changed his wet clothing for capacious garments loaned by the Sheriff, Switch took a careful inventory of those present and found that, besides nine whom he knew personally, there were three subdued-looking individuals. He diagnosed them as "natives."

"They're holdovers to the next term of the district court," explained Kilgallon contemptuously. "Plain yaps charged with stealin' cattle or somethin'. They ain't even got sense enough to git out o' this pokey and we use 'em to do the cleanin' up. I thought you was on your way to the Coast, Kid?"

"I was," replied Switch. "But I've stopped over to do a friend a turn. Bring all the fellers except them rubes around me and I'll let you in on the play."

"You all know the old Chicago Fat?" was his introductory remark as he squatted upon the floor and nine choice gentlemen who had carved their initials on every water-tank between the coasts gathered about him. Most of them nodded, Kilgallon with emphasis.

"Ain't he the guy that got up the hoboes' convention?" he demanded. "Well, he done me dirt——"

"Never mind!" interrupted the Kid. "That's past and gone. He's in hard lines now."

With vivid eloquence he painted a verbal picture of Abimilech Fetcher, once Chicago Fat, starving at his own hearth-side, as it were; he etched in pathetic touches here and there which caused the inky face of Philadelphia Shine to wrinkle lugubriously.

"Fat was a good guy," said Kid Switch. "He was always helpin' someone else and now he's in distress it seems to me we oughta remember them ole ties—ties of brotherhood and such, I mean—and go over there and give him a play for ten days so he can make his fees offen us. We can step out through one of the ole tunnels to-night and hike over there in no time."

"No, sah!" dissented the Shine. "Ah ain't makin' no

premedjutated changes. Dis hive suits me an' Ah ain' movin' till mah rent comes due!"

"Shut up!" said Kid Switch savagely. "You'll go if the rest do."

"It ain't a bad idea," said Kline, a pallid young man who was known to the police between the two coasts as a hotel sneak-thief, but who was, withal, romantic-looking and interesting. "We've been pretty good to ole Tobias. And after we stay at Fat's for a week or so, if the weather is still bad, we can come back here and finish out with Tobe."

Kilgallon, Jack Gordon, the "Cincinnati Skin," "Red," Henry Hennessey, "One-Thumb" Cafferty, George, "the Greek" and Heine Barr nodded grave approval.

"We'd better take them felons, too," said Gordon. "They'll help swell the count."

"Them's vallyble felons and Tobias thinks as much of them as he does of his right arm," demurred Hennessey. "Supposin' they'd beat it?"

"They've got a fat chance!" said Kid Switch. "We'll take 'em right along and return 'em to Tobe when we git through. Set 'em to work cleanin' out one of them tunnels now."

3

Abimilech Fetcher doubted that Kid Switch would be able to carry out this plan successfully; long continued adversity had made Abimilech pessimistic, but he waited, nevertheless, in the rarely occupied bastille of Parkins County and amused himself playing solitaire as the night wore on. His teeth chattered as occasional wisps of wind sneaked through the chinks in the building and he shook his head dolefully as he looked about the bare quarters the thrifty commonwealth had designed for criminal habitation.

THE FIRST STORIES

As compared to the county gaol of Queever County, the Parkins place of incarceration was a shanty against a country villa. Queever County had at least provided heat and electric lights. Parkins County simply purchased a tier of steel cells, set them down upon the ground and walled them in with loosely laid brick. Lanterns were the source of whatever illumination was required.

"I never seen a worse one myelf," mused Abimilech. "And I've seen some bad ones. I never thought it looked so fierce before until it comes to offerin' it to my friends."

A shout aroused him from his shivering reverie and he opened the door to admit a terrific gust of wind and an assemblage of chilled and profane men.

"We're here," said Kid Switch, shaking a blanket of snow from his shoulders. "Maybe you think it ain't some job herdin' three felons through ten miles of snow, specially when they know the country and have a yen to go home. And that coon there——" He turned a baleful eye upon Philadelphia Shine who snuffled damply in a corner.

"He bus' me in the nose," whined the Shine dolorously.

Abimilech Fetcher was engaged in shaking hands with friends of another day. A pang of remorse bit at his vitals as he found himself surrounded by faces he had been more than glad to see in times gone by, and Kilgallon almost forgot the discomfort of that long march over the snow as he held a passage in rough repartee with Abimilech.

"I suttinly appreciates your kindness, fellers," said the Sheriff. "I suttinly do. Now if you'll step into them cells two in each, I'll bed you down for the night."

"Ah doan lak dis place," sniffled the Shine. "Ah reckon Ah'll go back to Mista Tobe's."

"Second the motion!" said One-Thumb Cafferty, who had been investigating the tiny cells.

At that moment the front door again opened and admitted

two stalwart individuals whose coats bulged ominously and who wore gleaming stars upon their bosoms. Abimilech was relieved. He had become slightly alarmed over the tardiness of these efficient farm-hands whom he had impressed as deputies that afternoon and whom he had instructed to hasten to the gaol upon the arrival of any strangers. His manner changed. He looked as stern as it is possible for a fat man to look.

"Silence!" he roared. "Gaol rules prohibit talkin'. Officers, put 'em in their cells!" he added, turning to the newcomers.

Kid Switch looked at Abimilech, startled.

"You ain't goin' to double-cross me?" he whispered.

"Ah-h-h," said Abimilech. "Of course not."

He personally escorted Switch into a small cell near the door and locked him up by himself.

"You're a swell actor, 'bo," he whispered. "They ain't on."

As the locks clicked behind the prisoners, Gordon shouted, "Turn on some heat, will you?"

"Heat!" bellowed Abimilech. "They ain't no heat! Lessee, you're Gordon, ain't you? I know a man what looks like you who would interest some people in Oskaloosa."

Gordon subsided immediately.

"Hey, you!" bawled Red Hennessey bitterly. "What about that church door welcome mat that got lost in Sacramento when you was there last?"

Abimilech went close to the door of the cell and hissed, "Statoot of limentations, Red: statoot of limentations. But maybe I kin dig up some place where the statoot ain't run gain Henry Hennessey."

Whereupon Red became strangely silent.

"If these guys git to chewin' the rag with you, just git

some pails o' cold water and throw it in on them," instructed Abimilech to his deputies, as he took his departure.

Then the night wore on in cold silence, broken only by the intermittent comment of the guards upon the weather and the prospective crops. The prisoners sat hunched up in their chilly cells whispering schemes of vengeance not only upon Abimilech Fetcher, but upon that incarnation of misguided philanthropy, Kid Switch, who slept the sleep of the just and innocent beneath a large country quilt which Abimilech had thoughtfully left in his cell.

Morning brought a succession of incidents, including some underdone beans and an apology for coffee. Abimilech also arrived accompanied by an aged bewhiskered individual who wore an air of vast solemnity and carried an enormous book.

Abimilech called him "Judge." A table was placed in the narrow corridor before the cells and Abimilech seated the tottering Judge thereat with much ceremony. Then the Judge opened his book, scanned the pages through gigantic horn spectacles and read:

"John Doe, *alias* George Kilgallon."

"That's this wicked-lookin' murderer here," said Abimilech, indicating the peaceful Kilgallon. "Stand up, you Doe, *alias* Kilgallon! This is your trial!"

"Who'd I resist and who'd I assault?" roared Kilgallon.

The Judge was evidently deaf, as Abimilech bawled in his ear:

"He says he's guilty and that you're a —— ole fool."

"Hey!" howled Kilgallon, in wild remonstrance.

"Six months!" piped the Judge, making an entry in his book.

"Richard Roe, *alias* the Philadelphia Shine," he read next. "Assault with a deadly weapon and attempt to commit arson."

"Ah wants a mouthpiece! Ah wants a lie-er!" yelled the Shine in a great dismay.

"He says he's guilty," bellowed Abimilech into the whiskers of the Court.

"Ninety days," said the Judge.

Hennessey got three months on a charge of stealing chickens; One-Thumb Cafferty got sixty days on a charge of disturbance; the three felons were given twenty days each for vagrancy and all the others received varying sentences on various charges without having the opportunity of saying a word. Some turmoil arose, as they endeavoured to voice their protests, but the deputies secured buckets of water and quelled the incipient disturbance by a dumb show of throwing it over the already half-frozen prisoners.

"Kid Switch," said the Judge finally. "You are charged with carrying concealed weapons!"

"Not guilty!" shouted the Kid from the depths of his cell, where he was still buried beneath the quilt.

"This man's a dangerous character," yelled Abimilech. "You'd better get rid of him."

"Two hours to leave town," squeaked the old man and then the procession filed out, while the prisoners babbled wildly. Abimilech stopped long enough to unlock Kid Switch's cell.

"You don't want to let dark ketch you here," he warned.

"You don't want to let me ketch you anywhere!" howled Gordon from his cell, regardless of the deputies, and there was a hoarse growling from the other prisoners.

Outside the gaol door, Abimilech handed Kid Switch a package of yellow bills.

"That represents every cent I could borry," he said. "It means a second mortgage on my house and everything else. I didn't like to hand it to the gang so hard, but I can't let this good thing get away from me. It'll never happen again.

I wouldn't want to be in your shoes when them parties gits out."

"Don't worry," said the Kid lightly. "I can square it with them."

"Square it!" said Abimilech. "What a chance! You better beat it out o' town now, before some of the citizens take a shot at you on general principles. Square it! What a nerve!"

"Good-bye," said Kid Switch blithely. "You won't hear from me for quite a while."

And then he set off, kicking the snow before him in little flurries and Sheriff Abimilech Fetcher looked at the gaol with a complacent grin.

"Here's where I either git rich or bankrupt the county," he said. "I may have give it to 'em a little strong, but a feller has got to snatch his opportunities nowadays. I suppose I will have to give 'em *some* heat."

4

When Sheriff John Tobias found his gaol depopulated he did not immediately notify the citizens. He sat down to think the matter over. By creating tumult, the people might beome cognizant of a laxity of vigilance around the bastille which would hardly redound to the credit of the Sheriff. Besides, Tobias felt that the strange exodus was no common gaol break.

Fresh snow had fallen during the night and the ground gave no clue. No train had passed through since the preceding day, owing to blockades, and it was quite cold. Tobias was satisfied that his guests would not have undertaken travel in such weather simply because of a sudden desire for freedom.

"Them boys wouldn't a-took my felons," he argued. "They wouldn't let no ornery cattle thieves go with them."

AS BETWEEN FRIENDS

So the old Sheriff sat quiet and pondered the matter throughout the day. The light of information broke upon him along in the evening and the people were aroused by the clamour of a huge bell in the tower of the court-house, used to apprise the public of trouble and festivity. The citizens hurried to the court-house, carrying lanterns, guns and pitchforks, to find Sheriff John Tobias waiting on the steps of the building.

As soon as he could secure order, the Sheriff made public an address.

"My friends," he said, "they's been a gaol burglary. My prisoners, including felons what stole cattle on the Piedras, was stole out of my gaol by Abimilech Fetcher, Sheriff of Parkins County, who now holds them without warrant o' law in his gaol. He larcenied my prisoners, bag and baggage, including them felons, well knowin' the same to be then and there my pussonel property and the goods and chattels o' Queever County. He figgers to collect fees offen his illgotten gains from the County o' Parkins, which never has no prisoners, because no prisoner would ever become such thereabouts if he had any sense. Shell this town stand for such injestice, my friends? I don't think it shell. Shell it allow my gaol to be burglarized and my prisoners stolen away to fatten the fee account o' Abimilech Fetcher? I don't think it shell."

The crowd yelled "No, no!"

"Then, my friends," said Sheriff John Tobias, "I want volunteers to go with me and rescue them poor prisoners from the clutches of the rapscallion Fetcher."

Forty or fifty men stepped forward with alacrity.

"Come on!" shouted Tobias.

In twenty minutes a weird procession of horse-men, light buggies and footmen was streaming across the snow towards Advance, clamouring for the blood of Abimilech Fetcher.

Arriving at the county seat of Parkins County and finding the town asleep, the citizens of Queever lost no time in assailing the gaol. The prisoners, who had put in a wretched day, were vastly alarmed, fearing that they were to be the victims of mob violence, but when they saw Sheriff Tobias leading a charge through the shattered door, they set up a cheer of welcome. Abimilech's deputies disappeared with amazing rapidity.

A general reunion was in progress inside and outside the gaol, the three felons being the only persons present not transported with joy at the turn of events, when Abimilech Fetcher, in a state of great dishevelment, rushed upon the scene.

"Hey! Whatta you doin' with my prisoners?" he roared at Sheriff Tobias. "It's agin the law!"

"Your prisoners! I like your nerve!" said Tobias. "Whose prisoners be you gents?" he asked of the assembled gaolbirds.

"Yours!" they cried in chorus.

"Come on, then, let's go home," said Tobias.

The prisoners assembled with alacrity, Abimilech viewed the proceedings with a feeling of dismay. Then a thought occurred to him.

"Lemme ask you one thing, Tobias," he said. "How'd you find out where them people was?"

"Why," said Tobias, "Kid Switch, he told me. I give him fifty dollars for the information. He wouldn't let it out until I paid him the money, either. What's the matter, 'Bimilech!"

5. THE INFORMAL EXECUTION
OF SOUPBONE PEW

What is it the Good Book says? I read it last night—it said:
That he who sheddeth another man's blood by man shall his
    blood be shed!
That's as fair as a man could ask it, who lives by the gun
    and knife—
But the Law don't give him an even break when it's taking
    away his life.
Ho, the Law's unfair when it uses a chair, and a jolt from an
    unseen Death;
Or it makes him flop to a six-foot drop and a rope shuts off
    his breath;
If he's got to die let him die by the Book, with a Death
    that he can see,
By a gun or knife, as he went through life, and both legs
    kicking free!

—Songs of the "Shut-Ins"

THE condemned man in the cell next to us laughed
incessantly. He had been sentenced that morning, and
they told us he had started laughing as soon as the words,
"May the Lord have mercy on your soul," were pronounced.
He was to be taken to the penitentiary next day to await
execution.

Chicago Red had manifested a lively interest in the case.
The man had killed a railroad brakeman, so one of the
guards told us; had killed him coldly, and without provoca-
tion. The trial had commenced since our arrival at the

C

county gaol and had lasted three days, during which time Red talked of little else.

From the barred windows of the gaol corridor, when we were exercising, we could see the dingy old criminal court across the yard and Red watched the grim procession to and from the gaol each day. He speculated on the progress of the trial; he knew when the case went to the jury, and when he saw the twelve men, headed by the two old bailiffs returning after lunch the third day, he announced:

"They've got the verdict, and it's first degree murder. They ain't talking and not a one has ever grinned."

Then when the unfortunate was brought back, laughing that dismal laugh, Red said:

"He's nutty. He was nutty to go. It ain't exactly right to swing that guy."

Red and I were held as suspects in connection with an affair which had been committed a full forty-eight hours before we landed in town. We had no particular fear of being implicated in the matter, and the officers had no idea that we had anything to do with it, but they were holding us as evidence to the public that they were working on the case. We had been "vagged" for ten days each.

It was no new experience for us in any respect—not even the condemned man, for we had frequently been under the same roof with men sentenced to die. The only unusual feature was Red's interest in the laughing man.

"Red," I asked, as we sat playing cards, "did you ever kill a man?"

He dropped a card calmly, taking the trick, and as he contemplated his hand, considering his next lead, he answered:

"For why do you ask me that?"

"Oh, I don't know; I just wondered," I said. "You've seen and done so many things that I thought you might accidentally have met with something of the sort."

"It isn't exactly a polite question," he replied. "I've seen some murders. I've seen quite a few, in fact. I've seen some pulled off in a chief's private office, when they was sweating some poor stiff, and I've seen some, other places."

"Did you ever kill a man?" I insisted.

He studied my lead carefully.

"I never did," he finally answered. "That is to say, I never bumped no guy off personal. I never had nothing to do with no job from which come ghosts to wake me up at night and bawl me out. They say a guy that kills a man never closes his eyes again, even when he really sleeps. I go to the hay, and my eyes are shut tight, so I know I ain't to be held now or hereafter for nothing like that."

We finished the game in silence, and Red seemed very thoughtful. He laid the cards aside, rolled a cigarette, and said:

"Listen! I never killed no guy personal, like I say; I mean for nothing he done to me. I've been a gun and crook for many years, like you know, but I'm always mighty careful about hurting anyone permanent. I'm careful about them pete jobs, so's not to blow up no harmless persons, and I always tell my outside men that, when they have to do shooting, not to try to hit anyone. If they did, accidental, that ain't my fault. One reason I took to inside work was to keep from having to kill anyone. I've been so close to being taken that I could hear the gates of the Big House slam, and one little shot would have saved me a lot of trouble, but I always did my best to keep from letting that shot go. I never wanted to kill no man. I've been in jams where guys were after me good and strong, and I always tried to get by without no killings.

"I said I never killed a guy. I helped once, but it wasn't murder. It's never worried me a —— bit since, and I sleep good."

He walked to the window and peered out into the yard where a bunch of sparrows were fluttering about. Finally he turned and said:

"I hadn't thought of that for quite a while, and I never do until I see some poor stiff that's been tagged to go away. Some of them make me nervous—especially this tee-hee guy next to us. I'll tell you about Soupbone Pew—some day you can write it, if you want to."

Soupbone Pew was a rat who trained years ago with Billy Coulon, the Honey Grove Kid, and a bunch of other old-timers that you've never seen. It was before my time, too, but I've heard them talk about him. He was in the Sioux City bank tear-off, when they all got grabbed and were sent to the Big House for fifteen years each. In them days Soupbone was a pretty good guy. He had nerve, and was smart, and stood well with everybody, but a little stretch in the big stir got to him. He broke bad. Honey Grove laid a plan for a big spring—a get-away—while they were up yonder. It looked like it would go through, too, but just as they were about ready, Soupbone got cold feet and gave up his insides.

For that he got a pardon, and quit the road right off. He became a railroad brakeman, and showed up as a shack running between Dodge City and La Junta. And he became the orneriest white man that God ever let live, too.

To hoboes and guns he was like a reformed soak towards a drunk. He treated them something fierce. He was a big, powerful stiff, who could kill a man with a wallop of his hands, if he hit him right, and his temper soured on the world. Most likely it was because he was afraid that every guy on the road was out to get him because of what he'd done, or maybe it was because he knew that they knew he was yellow. Anyway, they never tried to do him, that job belonging to Coulon, Honey Grove and the others.

THE INFORMAL EXECUTION OF SOUPBONE PEW

Soupbone cracked that no 'bo could ride his division, and he made it good, too. He beat them up when they tried it, and he made it so strong that the old heads wouldn't go against a try when he was the run. Once in a while some kid took a stab at it, but if he got caught by Soupbone he regretted it the rest of his life. I've heard of that little road into Hot Springs, where they say a reward used to be offered to any 'bo that rode it, and how a guy beat it by getting in the water-tank; and I've personally met that Wyoming gent on the Union Pacific, and all them other guys they say is so tough, but them stories is only fairy-tales for children beside what could be told about Pew. He went an awful route.

I've known of him catching guys in the pilot and throwing scalding water in on them; I've heard tell of him shovelling hot cinders into empties on poor bums laying there asleep. That trick of dropping a coupling-pin on the end of a wire down alongside a moving train, so that it would swing up underneath and knock a stiff off the rods, was about the mildest thing he did.

He was simply a devil. The other railroad men on the division wouldn't hardly speak to him. They couldn't stand his gaff, but they couldn't very well roar at him keeping 'boes off his trains because that was what he was there for.

His longest suit was beating guys up. He just loved to catch some poor old broken-down bum on his train and pound the everlasting stuffing out of him. He's sent many a guy to the hospital, and maybe he killed a few before my acquaintance with him, for all I know.

Once in a while he ran against some live one—some real gun, and not a bum—who'd give him a battle, but he was there forty ways with a sap and gat, and he'd shoot as quick as he'd slug. He didn't go so strong on the real guns, if he knew who they was, and I guess he was always afraid they might be friends of Honey Grove or Coulon.

He was on the run when I first heard of him, and some of the kids of my day would try to pot him from the road, when his train went by, but they never even come close. I've heard them talk of pulling a rail on him and letting his train go into the ditch, but that would have killed the other trainmen, and they was some good guys on that same run then. The best way to do was to fight shy of Soupbone, and keep him on ice for Honey Grove and Coulon.

Training with our mob in them days was a young kid called Manchester Slim—a real kid, not over eighteen, and as nice and quiet a youngster as I ever see. He wasn't cut out for the road. It seems he'd had some trouble at home and run away. Old man Muller, that Dutch prowler, used to have him on his staff, but he never let this kid in on any work for some reason. He was always trying to get Slim to go home.

"Der road is hell for der kits," he used to say. "Let der ole stiffs vork out dere string, und don't make no new vuns."

The Slim paid no attention to him. Still he had no great love for the life, and probably would have quit long before if he hadn't been afraid some one would think he was scared off.

They was a pete job on at La Junta, which me and 'Frisco Shine and Muller had laid out. We had jungled up—camped —in a little cottonwood grove a few miles out of town, and was boiling out soup—nitro-glycerine—from dynamite, you know—and Muller sent the Slim into town to look around a bit. It was Winter and pretty cold. We had all come in from the West and was headed East. We was all broke bad, too, and needed dough the worst way.

Slim come back from town much excited. He was carrying a Denver newspaper in his hand.

"I've got to go home, Mull," he said, running up to the old man and holding out the paper. "Look at this ad."

Muller read it and called to me. He showed me a little want ad. reading that Gordon Keleher, who disappeared from his home in Boston two years before, was wanted at home because his mother was dying. It was signed Pelias Keleher, and I knew who he was, all right—president of the National Bankers' Association.

"Well, you go," I said, right off the reel, and I could see that was the word he was waiting for.

"For certainly he goes," said Muller. "Nail der next rattler."

"All the passengers are late, but there's a freight due out of here to-night; I asked," said Slim.

"How much dough iss dere in dis mob?" demanded Muller, frisking himself. We all shook ourselves down, but the most we could scare up was three or four dollars.

"If you could wait until after to-night," I says, thinking of the job, but Muller broke me off with:

"Ve don't vant him to vait. Somedings might happens."

"I'd wire home for money, but I want to get to Kansas City first," said Slim. "That paper is a couple of days old, and there's no telling how long it may have been running that ad. I can stop over in K.C. long enough to get plenty of dough from some people I know there. I'm going to grab that freight."

"Soupbone on dat freight," said the 'Frisco Shine, a silent, wicked black.

"Ve'll see Soub," said Muller quietly. "I guess maybe he von't inderfere mit dis case."

We decided to abandon the job for the night, and all went uptown. The Slim was apparently very much worried, and he kept telling us that if he didn't get home in time he'd never forgive himself, so we all got dead-set on seeing him started.

We looked up the conductor of the freight due out that night and explained things to him. None of us knew him, but he was a nice fellow.

"I tell you, boys," he said. "I'd let the young fellow ride, but you'd better see my head brakeman, Soupbone Pew. He's a tough customer, but in a case like this he ought to be all right. I'll speak to him myself."

Muller went after Pew. He found him in a saloon, drinking all by his lonesome, although there was a crowd of other railroad men in there at the time. Muller knew Pew in the old days, but there was no sign of recognition between them. The old Dutchman explained to Pew very briefly, winding with:

"It vould pe a gread personal favour mit me, Soub; maype somedimes I return it."

"He can't ride my train!" said Pew shortly. "That's flat. No argument goes."

The Dutchman looked at him long and earnestly, murder showing in his eyes, and Pew slunk back close to the bar, and his hand dropped to his hip.

"Soub, der poy rides!" said Muller, his voice low but shaking with anger. "He rides your rattler. Und if anyding happens by dot poy, de Honey Grove Kit von't get no chance at you! Dot all, Soub!"

But when he returned to us, he was plainly afraid for the Slim.

"You don't bedder go to-nid," he said. "Dot Soub is a defil, und he'll do you."

"I'm not afraid," said Slim. "He can't find me, anyhow."

The old man tried to talk him out of the idea, but Slim was determined, and finally Muller, in admiration of his spirit, said:

THE INFORMAL EXECUTION OF SOUPBONE PEW

"Vell, if you vill go, you vill. Vun man can hide besser as two, but der Shine must go mit you as far as Dodge."

That was the only arrangement he would consent to, and while the Slim didn't want the Shine, and I myself couldn't see what good he could do, Muller insisted so strong that we all gave in.

We went down to the yards that night to see them off, and the old man had a private confab with the Shine. The only time I ever saw Muller show any feeling was when he told the boy good-bye. I guess he really liked him.

The two hid back of a pile of ties, a place where the trains slowed down, and me and Muller got off a distance and watched them. We could see Soupbone standing on top of a box-car as the train went by, and he looked like a tall devil. He was trying to watch both sides of the train at the same time, but I didn't think he saw either Slim or the Shine as they shot underneath the cars, one after the other, and nailed the rods. Then the train went off into the darkness, Soupbone standing up straight and stiff.

We went back to our camp to sleep, and the next morning before we were awake, the Shine came limping in, covered with blood and one arm hanging at his side.

I didn't have to hear his story to guess what had happened. Soupbone made them at the first stop. He hadn't expected two, but he did look for the kid. Instead of warning him off, he told him to get on top where he'd be safe. That was one of his old tricks. He didn't get to the Shine, who dodged off into the darkness, as soon as he found they were grabbed, and then caught the train after it started again. He crawled up between the cars to the deck, to tip the Slim off to watch out for Soupbone. Slim didn't suspect anything, and was thanking Soupbone, and explaining about his mother.

The moment the train got under way good, Soupbone says:

"Now my pretty boy, you're such a —— good traveller, let's see you jump off this train!"

The kid thought he was joshing, but there wasn't no josh about it. Soup pulled a gun. The Shine, with his own gun in hand, crawled clear on top and lay flat on the cars, trying to steady his aim on Soupbone. The kid was pleading and almost crying, when Soupbone suddenly jumped at him, smashed him in the jaw with the gun-barrel, and knocked him off the train. The Shine shot Soupbone in the back, and he dropped on top of the train, but didn't roll off. As the Shine was going down between the cars again, Soupbone shot at him and broke his arm. He got off all right, and went back down the road to find the kid dead—his neck broke.

Old man Muller, the mildest man in the world generally, almost went bug-house when he heard that spiel. He raved and tore around like a sure enough nut. I've known him to go backing out of a town with every man in his mob down on the ground, dead or dying, and not show half as much feeling afterward. You'd 'a' thought the kid was his own. He swore he'd do nothing else as long as he lived until he'd cut Soupbone's heart out.

The Shine had to get out of sight, because Soupbone would undoubtedly have some wild-eyed story to tell about being attacked by hoboes and being shot by one. We had no hope but what the Shine had killed him.

Old man Muller went into town and found out that was just what had happened, and he was in the hospital only hurt a little. He also found they'd brought Slim's body to town, and that most people suspected the real truth, too. He told them just how it was, especially the railroad men, and said the Shine had got out of the country. He also wired Slim's people, and we heard afterwards they sent a special train after the remains.

Muller was told, too, that the train conductor had notified Pew to let Slim ride, and that the rest of the train-crew had served notice on Pew that if he threw the boy off he'd settle with them for it. And that was just what made Soupbone anxious to get the kid. It ended his railroad career there, as we found out afterwards, because he disappeared as soon as he got out of the hospital.

Meantime me and Muller and the Shine went ahead with that job, and it failed. Muller and the nigger got grabbed, and I had a tough time getting away. Just before we broke camp the night before, however, Muller, who seemed to have a hunch that something was going to happen, called me and the Shine to him, and said, his voice solemn:

"I vant you poys to bromise me vun ting," he said. "If I don't get der chance myself, bromise me dot venefer you find Soupbone Bew, you vill kill him deat."

And we promised, because we didn't think we would ever be called on to make good.

Muller got a long jolt for the job; the Shine got a shorter one and escaped a little bit later on, while I left that part of the country.

A couple of years later, on a bitter cold night, in a certain town that I won't name, there was five of us in the sneezer, held as suspects on a house prowl job that only one of us had anything to do with—I ain't mentioning the name of the one, either. They was me, Kid Mole, the old prize-fighter, a hophead named Squirt McCue, that you don't know, Jew Friend, a dip, and that same 'Frisco Shine. We were all in the bull-pen with a mixed assortment of drunks and vags. All kinds of prisoners was put in there over night. This pokey is downstairs under the police station, not a million miles from the Missouri River, so if you think hard you can guess the place. We were walking around kidding the drunks, when a screw shoved in a long, tall guy who acted like he was drunk or nutty, and was hardly able to stand.

I took one flash at his map, and I knew him. It was Pew.

He flopped down in a corner as soon as the screw let go his arm. The Shine rapped to him as quick as I did, and officed Mole and the rest. They all knew of him, especially the Honey Grove business, as well as about the Manchester Slim, for word had gone over the country at the time.

As soon as the screw went upstairs I walked over to the big stiff, laying all huddled up, and poked him with my foot.

"What's the matter with you, you big cheese?" I said. He only mumbled.

"Stand up!" I tells him, but he didn't stir. The Shine and Mole got hold of him on either side and lifted him to his feet. He was as limber as a wet bar-towel. Just then we heard the screw coming downstairs and we got away from Pew. The screw brought in a jag—a laughing jag—a guy with his snoot full of booze and who laughed like he'd just found a lot of money. He was a little, thin fellow, two pounds lighter than a straw hat. He laughed high and shrill, more like a scream than a real laugh, and the moment the screw opened the door and tossed him in, something struck me that the laugh was phoney. It didn't sound on the level.

There wasn't no glad in it. The little guy laid on the floor and kicked his feet and kept on laughing. Soupbone Pew let out a yell at the sight of him.

"Don't let him touch me!" he bawled, rolling over against the wall. "Don't let him near me!"

"Why, you big stiff, you could eat him alive!" I says.

The jag kept on tee-heeing, not looking at us, or at Pew either for that matter.

THE INFORMAL EXECUTION OF SOUPBONE PEW

"He's nuts," said Jew Friend.

"Shut him off," I told the Shine.

He stepped over and picked the jag up with one hand, held him out at arm's length, and walloped him on the jaw with his other hand. The jag went to sleep with a laugh sticking in his throat. Soupbone still lay against the wall moaning, but he saw that business all right, and it seemed to help him. The Shine tossed the jag into a cell. Right after that the screw came down with another drunk, and I asked him about Pew.

"Who's this boob?" I said. "Is he sick?"

"Him? Oh, he's a good one," said screw. "He only killed his poor wife—beat her to death with his two fists, because she didn't have supper ready on time, or something important. That ain't his blood on him; that's hers. He's pretty weak, now, hey? Well, he wasn't so weak a couple of hours ago, the rat! It's the wickedest murder ever done in this town, and he'll hang sure, if he ain't lynched beforehand!"

He gave Soupbone a kick as he went out, and Soupbone groaned.

Said I: "It's got to be done, gents; swing or no swing, this guy has got to go. Who is it—me?"

"Me!" said the Shine, stepping forward.

"Me!" said the Jew.

"Me!" chimed in Mole.

"All of us!" said the hophead.

"Stand him up!" I ordered.

The lights had been turned down low, and it was dark and shadowy in the gaol. The only sound was the soft pad-pad of people passing through the snow on the sidewalks above our heads, the low sizzling of the water-spout at the sink, and the snores of the drunks, who were all asleep.

Us five was the only ones awake. The Shine and Mole lifted Soupbone up, and this time he was not so limp. He

77

seemed to know that something was doing. His eyes was wide open and staring at us.

"Pew," I said in a whisper, "do you remember the kid you threw off your rattler three years ago?"

"And shot me in the arm?" asked Shine.

Pew couldn't turn any whiter, but his eyes rolled back into his head.

"Don't!" he whispered. "Don't say that. It made me crazy! I'm crazy now! I was crazy when I killed that little girl to-night. It was all on account of thinking about him. He comes to see me often."

"Well, Pew," I said, "a long time back you were elected to die. I was there when the sentence was passed, and it'd been carried out a long time ago if you hadn't got away. I guess we'll have to kill you to-night."

"Don't, boys!" he whined. "I ain't fit to die! Don't hurt me!"

"Why, you'll swing anyway!" said Friend.

"No! My God, no!" he said. "I was crazy; I'm crazy now, and they don't hang crazy people!"

I was standing square in front of him. His head had raised a little as he talked and his jaw was sticking out. I suddenly made a move with my left hand, as though to slap him, and he showed that his mind was active enough by dodging, so that it brought his jaw out further, and he said, "Don't." Then I pulled my right clear from my knee and took him on the point of the jaw. The Shine and Mole jumped back. Soupbone didn't fall; he just slid down in a heap, like his body had melted into his shoes.

We all jumped for him at the same time, but an idea popped into my head, and I stopped them. Soupbone was knocked out, but he was coming back fast. You can't kill a guy like that by hitting him. The gaol was lighted by a few incandescent lights, and one of them was hung on a wire that reached down from the ceiling over the sink, and had a couple of feet of it coiled up in the middle. Uncoiled, the light would reach clear to the floor. I pointed to it, but the bunch didn't get my idea right away. The switch for the lights was inside the bull-pen, and I turned them off. I had to work fast for fear the screw upstairs would notice the lights was out and come down to see what the trouble was. A big arc outside threw a little glim through the sidewalk grating, so I could see what I was doing.

I uncoiled the wire and sawed it against the edge of the sink, close to the lamp, until it came in two. Then I bared the wire back for a foot. The gang tumbled, and carried Pew over to where the wire would reach him. I unfastened his collar, looped the naked end of the wire around his neck and secured it. By this time he was about come to, but he didn't seem to realize what was going on.

All but me got into their cells and I stepped over and turned the switch-button just as Pew was struggling to his feet. The voltage hit him when he was on all fours. He stood straight up, stiff, like a soldier at salute. There was a strange look on his face—a surprised look. Then, as though someone had hit him from behind, his feet left the floor and he swung straight out to the length of the wire and it broke against his weight, just as I snapped off the current. Pew dropped to the floor and curled up like a big singed spider, and a smell like frying bacon filled the room.

I went over and felt of his heart. It was still beating, but very light.

"They ain't enough current," whispered Mole. "We got to do it some other way."

"Hang him wid de wire," said the Shine.

"Aw—nix!" spoke up the Jew. "I tell you that makes me sick—bumping a guy off that way. Hanging and electricity see? That's combining them too much. Let's use the boot."

79

"It ain't fair, kind-a, that's a fact," whispered McCue. "It's a little too legal. The boot! Give him the boot!"

The voice of the screw came singing down the stairs:

"Is that big guy awake?"

"Yes," I shouted back, "we're all awake; he won't let us sleep."

"Tell him he'd better say his prayers!" yelled the screw. "I just got word a mob is forming to come and get him!"

"Let him alone," I whispered to the gang. Mole was making a noose of the wire, and the Shine had hunted up a bucket to stand Pew on. They drew back and Soupbone lay stretched out on the floor.

I went over and felt of his heart again. I don't remember whether I felt any beat or not. I couldn't have said I did, at the moment, and I couldn't say I didn't. I didn't have time to make sure, because suddenly there run across the floor something that looked to me like a shadow, or a big rat. Then the shrill laugh of that jag rattled through the bull-pen. He slid along half-stooped, as quick as a streak of light, and before we knew what was doing he had pounced on Soupbone and had fastened his hands tight around the neck of the big stiff. He was laughing that crazy laugh all the time.

"I'll finish him for you!" he squeaked. He fastened his hands around Soupbone's neck. I kicked the jag in the side of the head as hard as I could, but it didn't faze him. The bunch laid hold of him and pulled, but they only dragged Soupbone all over the place. Finally the jag let go and stood up, and we could see he wasn't no more drunk than we was. He let loose that laugh once more, and just as the Shine started the bucket swinging for his head, he said: "I'm her brother!" Then he went down kicking.

We went into our cells and crawled into our bunks. Soupbone lay outside. The Shine pulled the jag into a corner. I tell you true, I went to sleep right away. I thought the screw would find out when he brought the next drunk down, but it so happened that there wasn't no more drunks and I was woke up by a big noise on the stairs. The door flew open with a bang, and a gang of guys came down, wild-eyed and yelling. The screw was with them and they had tight hold of him.

"Keep in, you men!" he bawled to us.

"That's your meat!" he said to the gang, pointing at what had been Soupbone. The men pounced on him like a lot of hounds on to a rabbit, and before you could bat an eye they had a rope around Soupbone's neck and was tearing up the stairs again, dragging him along.

They must have thought he was asleep; they never noticed that he didn't move a muscle himself, and they took the person of Soupbone Pew, or anyways what had been him, outside and hung it over a telegraph wire.

We saw it there when we was sprung next morning. When the screw noticed the blood around the bull-pen, he said:

"Holy smoke, they handled him rough!" And he never knew no different.

If the mob hadn't come—but the mob did come, and so did the laughing jag. I left him that morning watching the remains of Soupbone Pew.

"She was my sister," he said to me.

I don't know for certain whether we killed Soupbone, whether the jag did it, or whether the mob finished him; but he was dead, and he ought to have died. Sometimes I wonder a bit about it, but no ghosts come to me, like I say, so I can't tell.

They's an unmarked grave in the potter's field of this town I speak of, and once in a while I go there when I'm passing through and meditate on the sins of Soupbone Pew.

But I sleep well of nights. I done what had to be done, and I close my eyes and I don't never see Soupbone Pew.

He turned once more to gazing out of the window.

"Well, what is there about condemned men to make you to nervous?" I demanded.

'I said some condemned men," he replied, still gazing. "Like this guy next door."

A loud, shrill laugh rang through the corridors.

"He's that same laughing jag," said Chicago Red.

6. MY FATHER

M Y father is a Pioneer.
Of such an institution, Mr. N. Webster, who was himself something of a pioneer, says:

"Pioneer. One who goes before, as into the wilderness, preparing the way for others to follow."

I do not know that this description covers my father's case accurately—it sounds more like a word picture of a Frémont or a Pike, or an irrigation promoter, with little bearing upon a man who was the playmate of the untamed William Hickok, Mr. B. Masterson, and such; nevertheless, I have my father's word for it that he is a Pioneer.

His high-heeled boots have left their imprint upon the old cattle trails down Abilene and Dodge City way. I can picture in my mind's eye his small but hardy frame encased in the fringes fashionable at that day, cleaving a path towards the setting sun as he hotly pursued the elusive maverick and furrowed the pine bars of the Red Light and the Pink Dog Cafés of that interesting period with his hard-earned dollars.

I have a deep reverence for my father as a Pioneer, which is not shared by my wife Ellen.

She sees only, in that weatherbeaten little figure, an old gentleman with a tremendous capacity for indenting the cushions in the Brown Palace Hotel, where he foregathers at night with his ancient friends and talks in a loud and querulous tone of voice.

THE FIRST STORIES

My wife was born in the West at a time when department stores and nickelodeon theatres had crowded out the picturesque landscape to make room for a ragged skyline. Her father is not a Pioneer. He is merely the general superintendent of a railroad and travels in a private car. Her mother is not a Pioneer, either. She is a society leader.

Ellen, therefore, is inured to an atmosphere of labour difficulties and bargain sales, and could hardly be expected to sense the romance of the sunset trail as personified in a mild-looking little man with a stringy goatee, who declines to shake up the furnace on cold days. My father stands in proper awe of Ellen, and while he may raise his voice in a loud "I—remember—when" down at the Brown Palace, his tone is low and well modulated around my house, where he resides.

Understand, Ellen is not a shrew—far from it. Neither is she inclined to be peckish. She simply came into the world at a time when pioneerism had become a sort of misdemeanour, so far as six-pistols and wild Indians are concerned, and society felt it best to preserve a respectable silence regarding certain early days.

Also, my wife—but this does not go if she hears it—is very obtuse when it comes to an appreciation of the historical value of the notches in my father's gun. I myself know, from rumour and otherwise, that in his day my father was a man of parts, and his aim was esteemed along the border.

The Society of Pioneers decided to hold a reunion one summer, and for the purposes of that gathering they picked the old city of Trinity. There was method in this selection. The average Pioneer, like my father, has daughters-in-law and other womenfolk holding receptions and functions about his family fireside, at which no account is taken of those hoary harbingers of civilization. Trinity is well

84

removed from the social trail and is without reserve regarding the old days.

When my father announced his intention of attending the reunion, my wife offered no objection.

"Just so you ridiculous old men do your pioneering outside the city limits, I'll be satisfied," she remarked.

So my father, with patient resignation, packed his suitcase full of buckskin clothing and other odds and ends, and betook himself to Trinity, in company with a large number of other old gentlemen whose voices began to touch the highest pitch in the vocal scale as soon as the train moved them beyond the zone of home hostility.

When I returned that evening, I found Ellen in quite a state of mind.

"The Daughters of the Revolution have appointed me a member of a committee to go to Trinity and assist in dedicating a museum to the Spanish explorers," she announced. "I am to make a speech."

Personally, I have always felt that the son of a man who fought at 'Dobe Walls was as good as the great-great-granddaughter of a family who pitchforked Britons in the Lexington road, but I do not say so. I never shall, openly.

"Trinity? That's where father has gone," I said.

"Well," Ellen replied tartly, "those foolish old men haven't anything to do with this museum. This is being done by the Daughters, and as other members of the committee are taking their husbands, you can go with me."

"It will be quite a surprise to father to see us," I suggested.

I do not feel called upon to explain that the dedication of the museum might have been arranged to coincide with the Pioneer reunion because of the connecting historical relation of the two events. I, a scoin of the 'Dobe Walls, will never gratuitously offend any Daughter of the Revolution.

I did not see my father, but I heard of him as soon as I registered our names at the best hotel in Trinity, and urged the grizzled man doing duty as clerk to give us good rooms.

"Kivingson, hey?" he remarked, scrutinizing the register. "Any relation to Bill Kivingson?"

"My father's name is William Kivingson," I replied coldly. My wife sniffed one of the most disdainful sniffs.

"The son of ole Bill Kivingson can have anything I've got," replied the old man. "Me'n' Bill are pards; we useter raise hell together around Lamar. . . ."

"Jonas, let us go to our rooms," interrupted Ellen scornfully.

"Yore old man's around town sum'eres," called the clerk, as we mounted the stairs.

Trinity is a small but enthusiastic town on the old Santa Fe trail, which preserves many of its old-time traditions and all of its saloons. It was humming with activity. The business houses and the streets were hung with bunting and beaming with hospitality, while grizzled men dotted the landscape freely. It appeared that there were really two celebrations—the Pioneers' reunion and the dedication of the museum, the latter designed by the women as a sort of antidote for the masculine gathering.

I soon discovered that, as the son of Bill Kivingson, I was a man of honour in those parts at that particular time. The clerk at the hotel took care to point me out in my capacity of Bill Kivingson's offspring; and my hand was cordially shaken by ageing men with a violence that threatened my physical well-being.

Ellen was busied with the other members of the committee of the Daughters, arranging the programme for the dedication, and I wandered about the town. My search was not an exhaustive one, as I did not care to encroach upon my father's vacation, and, in addition to my natural feelings, there *are* some places where a bank attaché cannot follow even a Pioneer parent.

As I went about, mingling with the queer crowds, I heard strange and disquieting rumours dealing with the personality and actions of one whom they called "Still Bill," who appeared to be a character of some vehemence.

"Still Bill's broke the faro bank over to the Blue Moose," announced an ancient exfrontiersman as he approached a group of bronzed old men at the hotel office that evening.

"Made 'em turn the box after he took out twenty-six hundred dollars!"

"That Bill's a grey wolf," replied a tall man with long straight hair. There was admiration in his tone. "If Still Bill gets to going good, there will be some fun in this burg!"

"He's eyes-going fair enough right now," replied the bearer of the news. "I mind the time at Trail City when he cleaned out the whole blame town. It was bustin' the bank started him that time, too."

"Yes," put in another, "I rec'leck how he stood off the marshal and the en-tire pop'lation of Dodge City for two days an' nights."

"Well," said the messenger, "he's got that ol' cap'n'ball pistol—that ole forty-five howitzer—an' he was tunin' up some when I left. He useter be able to singe your eyelashes with that weapon at fifty yards."

At this point a fat, breathless gentleman who added locomotion with a manzanita cane, hobbled excitedly into the office.

"He's loose!" panted this latest courier, in a quavering voice. "Ole Still Bill has done ontied himself! He's raisin' hell and puttin' a plug under ear over at the Moose! Like as not he'll come a'-bulgin' down this street pretty quick. I'm goin' home!'

"He useter be a long-winded cuss, too," said someone. "I don't reckon at his age, he can hold out more'n two days, but I seen the time when a week wasn't no limit!"

"They's been a-many a-ring-tailed, red-eyed son o' trouble turned loose in these here parts," quavered the courier. "I seen 'em come and I seen 'em go, but they's never been no white man could claw within a foot 'o the neck o' old Bill Kivingson!"

Kivingson! Bill Kivingson! *My Father!*

I approached the group. "Gentlemen," said I, "you surely do not mean Mr. William Kivingson—a smallish man with a goatee and...?"

"Still Bill! That's *him!*" came in full chorus.

"Why," said I, "it—it isn't possible that he should be performing actions such as you speak of! He is a harmless old man!"

"Harmless-*hell!*" snorted the fat old Pioneer. "Harmless like a mess o' rattlesnakes!"

"But I'm his son!" I argued.

"I don't give a hoo-raw who you are! I'm his pal and I *know* Still Bill Kivingson—knowed him before you was born. It's good night, all, fer me!"

Now of course my natural thought was to go and get my father and make him retire for the night; but the hotel clerk laid a kind restraining hand upon my arm.

"Lay off o' him, son," he said. "When Still Bill gits a-goin', you jest got to give him a clean track and keep well under kivver. I ain't seen him speed none in twenty years, but I know what he *could* do. Jest you go to bed and lay off o' him.

"He won't hurt nobody," he continued. "All the old-timers'll keep out of his way, and he never did kill no bartenders, or such, in his life, because he needs 'em. Don't you worry about him. It's just them animile sperrits which has been plugged up fer a long time, coming out an' sniffin' around. O' course, if he should happen to think o' somebody he don't like, he might bother 'em some; but they ain't no one about Trinity he ain't made up with long ago."

I debated the matter in my mind and came to the conclusion that I had better follow the clerk's advice. Who was I, that I should obstruct the course of a hero of the 'Dobe Walls, equipped with a cap and ball?

I lay awake for several hours, the tumult of the street pouring in at my window. Occasionally I heard above the hum of voices a pistol shot, which never failed to produce deep silence—after a great shuffling of feet. The pedestrians seemed to be seeking shelter. In the hush which followed these explosions there would come a voice, uplifted in war-like declamation. I could not make out the words, but there seemed to be a familiar ring to the belligerent chant.

When I went down the stairs the next morning, leaving Ellen at her toilet, a strange sight presented itself. It was nine o'clock. Outside, the sun was shining from a turquoise sky, and the air was soft as down, yet the lobby of the hotel was packed with men and women who stood gazing through the windows upon that scene of peace and quiet as if a terrible storm raged without.

Across the street, I could see, the stores were filled with similar crowds. The streets were deserted. An old man disengaged himself from the throng and sidled over to me. It was the hotel clerk.

"Son," said he, "I don't like fer to tell you-all, but yore old man, Still Bill, he's a-goin' good and strong this mornin'. He's plum' busted this celebration, which it can't go on with him a-streamin' up and down the streets like a pestilence. He's a-holdin' forth down yonder at the Moose, an' every now an' then he comes a-boilin' up this way to see if they's any defenceless folks he can devastate. Son, yore dad is a wolf—a curly wolf, that's all—and time don't change him none."

"He certainly is a long-winded ole body," declared another. "I reckon it's his superflus energy o' twenty year a-bubbin' out all to onct. He allows he has decided to postpone the parade an' celebration until to-morrow and that he ain't goin' to permit no moosee dedication a-a-a-tall. He ain't decided yet whether he'll move this town plum' away or not."

At that moment a high treble yell smote the air, and the crowd stayed back from the windows. I peered outside to see, far down the street, a small figure rocketing along at amazing speed. Clad in buckskins, feathered at the hems, a wide hat, it gave him the appearance of an animated mushroom, and waving a long-barrelled revolver, my father surged along in a billow of sound. While I watched, shame-faced, some of his expressions came to my ears.

"I'm a howlin' wolf from ole Mizzou, an' I'm a-huntin' gore!" he bawled. "I picks my teeth with bowie-knives, an' the bark o' six-guns is music to my ears! Yee-owo-wow! I'm a snake in the grass, an' I hiss when you pass, an' I'm searchin' for folks to eat! Wow!"

He had a clear path, and he swirled along the street for a block or two, then doubled back and disappeared in a vocal storm.

"Ain't he a bear?" inquired the hotel clerk; and I could see that among these Pioneers my father's exhibitions, however much it shamed me, had aroused considerable admiration.

"Has he hurt anybody?" I inquired nervously.

"*Hurt* 'em, son?" said the hotel clerk. "*Hurt* 'em? Boy, they ain't anybody get near enough to old Hell-on-Wheels out there to let him *hurt* 'em. He never *hurts* no one if he gits 'em. He jest KILLS 'em. An' he ain't bin able for to ketch no one here."

"Has he been going all night long?"

"All night," replied the clerk. "He ain't paused for drink for man or beast to date. An' bimeby we're goin' to set a bear trap out there in the street so business can proceed. Sim Leggins has gone after the trap now. Sim is the authorities, an' a pussonal friend o' yer dad's, but he's decided Still Bill has got his twenty years' worth."

Beyond the shadow of a doubt I should shortly have nerved myself to going after my father—there is no question in my mind but that I should have done it; but while I was steeling myself, my wife appeared—my wife, the immaculate Ellen, appeared in the crowded lobby, clad in a Japanese kimono, her hair in curl-papers.

"What is this I hear?" she demanded. "The members of my committee tell me that our dedication is being postponed by some beast of a man—what does this mean?"

I had not the heart to tell her that it was my father. I could never have found the heart to do so. But at that moment he disclosed his identity by reappearing in the street—gun in hand and a yell in his throat.

Again he careened past the hotel, the crowd falling back dismayed—and as I stood there, the picture of embarrassment, if nothing more, my wife edged close to the window and stared.

"Come back, Ellen, dear," I said. "They say he's very dangerous to people he does not like."

That was an unfortunate slip. I had never before suggested that my father did not like my wife—certainly he had never intimated such a thing.

"Yee-ow-wow!" yelled my father, as he swung back towards his Blue Moose retreat and disappeared.

My wife hurriedly left the hotel in a flutter of Japanese colouring, and with a toss of bedroom headgear. The crowd gasped. She was heading straight for the door of the Blue Moose. I followed—I have never permitted my wife to go where I do not go myself—and the crowd trailed along, nervously.

At the door of the Blue Moose saloon I paused, my heart beating with grave concern.

Imagine my feelings! My beloved wife, unappreciative of the danger attached to an eruption of twenty years of repressed pioneerial fervour, mindful only of the jeopardy of social standing, had flung herself headlong into the arms of Peril.

And my beloved father was Peril!

About me pressed the faces of the people, grey with apprehension, each head bent towards the door of the Blue Moose in a listening attitude.

Shortly I should have plunged through those doors regardless of consequences; shortly I should have rushed to my obvious duty.

From the interior of the Blue Moose arose a voice—a woman's voice—the voice of Ellen, my wife.

The door suddenly flew open with a bang, scattering the crowd like frightened sheep. My wife appeared. In one hand she held a long cap-and-ball revolver. In the other she clasped the left ear of a meek old gentleman, who was very white as to face, and who rubbed his hands together nervously.

"At your time of life, too!" my wife was saying. "You ought to be ashamed of yourself, you silly old man!"

The crowd collected itself again, amazed, startled.

"Now, Elly——" quavered my father.

"Hush!" she ordered, in tones such as I never wish to hear again. "Not another word, you ridiculous old man!"

MY FATHER

And up the street, now teeming with an astounded multitude, she led the resentless howl wolf and snake in the grass, while I, who seemed destined always to be in the rear of the procession, followed, still harassed by emotion.

"I'm going to lock you up in a closet until the next train leaves," my wife was saying. "You——"

"Don't lose my gun, Elly," my father exhorted humbly. "It's the one with notches on it."

A little boy, perhaps ten years of age, was running along beside them, whooping shrilly.

"Here, boy!" said Ellen, pushing the famous revolver into the youngster's hands. "Here's a nice plaything for you!"

"And now, ladies and gentlemen," said my wife, in closing her brief remarks at the dedication of the museum, "it is with a feeling of deepest reverence towards the wonderful men of that early period, and to those equally wonderful men who came at a later day to develop and perpetuate the path of progress that we dedicate this small monument in the hope that it will ever keep green the memory of the Spanish explorers and the American Pioneer!"

I have a high regard for my father as a Pioneer, which is not shared by my wife, Ellen.

STORIES À LA CARTE

7. MONEY FROM HOME

IT comes on a pleasant morning in the city of Baltimore, Md., and a number of citizens are standing in front of the Cornflower Hotel in Calvert Street, speaking of this and that, and one thing and another, and especially of the horse races that are to take place in the afternoon at Pimlico, because these citizens are all deeply interested in horse races, and in fact they are not interested in much of anything else in this world.

Among these citizens is The Seldom Seen Kid, who is called The Seldom Seen because he is seldom seen after anything comes off that anybody may wish to see him about, as he has a most retiring disposition, although he can talk a blue streak whenever talking becomes really necessary. He is a young guy of maybe twenty-five years of age, and he always chucks a good front, and has a kind face that causes people to trust him implicitly.

Then there is Hot Horse Herbie, who is called Hot Horse Herbie because he generally knows about some horse that is supposed to be hotter than a base-burner, a hot horse being a horse that is all heated up to win a horse race, although sometimes Hot Horse Herbie's hot horses turn out to be as cold as a landlord's heart. And there is also Big Reds, who is known to one and all as an excellent handicapper if his figures are working right.

Now these are highly respected characters, and if you ask them what they do, they will tell you that they are turf advisers, a turf adviser being a party who advises the public about horse races, and their services are sometimes quite valuable, even if the coppers at the race-tracks do say that turf advisers are nothing but touts, and are always jerking them around, and sometimes going so far as to bar them off the tracks altogether, which is a grave injustice, as it deprives many worthy citizens of a chance to earn a livelihood.

In fact, the attitude of these coppers is so odious towards turf advisers that there is some talk of organizing a National Turf Advisers' Association, for mutual protection, and bringing the names of the coppers up at the meetings and booing them for ten minutes each.

There is another guy standing in front of the Cornflower Hotel with The Seldom Seen Kid and Hot Horse Herbie and Big Reds, and this guy is a little, dark complected, slippery-looking guy by the name of Philly the Weeper, and he is called by this name because he is always weeping about something, no matter what. In fact, Philly the Weeper is such a guy as will go around with a loaf of bread under his arm weeping because he is hungry.

He is generally regarded as a most unscrupulous sort of guy, and in fact some people claim Philly the Weeper is downright dishonest, and ordinarily The Seldom Seen Kid, and Hot Horse Herbie and Big Reds do not associate with parties of this calibre, but of course they cannot keep Philly the Weeper from standing around in front of the Cornflower Hotel with them, because he resides there the same as they do.

In fact, Philly the Weeper is responsible at this time for The Seldom Seen Kid, and Hot Horse Herbie and Big Reds being able to continue residing in the Cornflower, as conditions are very bad with them, what with so few of the public being willing to take their advice about the horse races, and the advice turning out the wrong way even when the public takes it, and they are all in the hotel stakes, and

the chances are the management will be putting hickeys in
their keyholes if it is not for Philly the Weeper okaying
them.

The reason Philly the Weeper is able to okay them is
because a musical show by the name of "P's and Q's" is
trying out in Baltimore, and Philly the Weeper's fiancée,
Miss Lola Ledare, is a prominent member of the chorus,
and the company is stopping at the Cornflower Hotel, and
Philly the Weeper lets on that he has something to do with
them being there, so he stands first-class with the hotel
management, which does not think to ask anybody connected with the "P's and Q's" company about the matter.

If the hotel management does ask, the chances are it will
find out that the company regard Philly the Weeper as a
wrong gee, the same as everybody else, although it thinks
well of his fiancée, Miss Lola Ledare, who is one of these
large, wholesome blondes, and by no means bad-looking,
if you like them blonde. She is Philly the Weeper's fiancée
for several years, but nobody holds this against her, as it is
well known to one and all that love is something that cannot
be explained, and, anyway, Miss Lola Ledare does not seem
to let it bother her very much.

She is such a doll as enjoys going around and about, being
young, and full of vitality, as well as blonde, and if Philly
the Weeper is too busy, or does not have enough dough to
take her around and about, Miss Lola Ledare always seems
able to find somebody else who has a little leisure time on
their hands for such a purpose, and if Philly the Weeper does
not like it, he can lump it, and usually he lumps it, for Miss
Lola Ledare can be very, very firm when it comes to going
around and about.

In fact, Philly the Weeper is telling The Seldom Seen Kid
and Hot Horse Herbie and Big Reds, the very morning in
question, about Miss Lola Ledare and nine other members of

the "P's and Q's" company being around and about the night before with an English guy who checks in at the Corn-flower early in the evening, and who is in action in the matter of going around and about before anybody can say Jack Robinson.

"He is a young guy," Philly the Weeper says, "and from what Lola tells me, he is a very fast guy with a dollar. His name is the Honourable Bertie Searles, and he has a valet, and enough luggage to sink a barge. Lola says he takes quite a fancy to her, but," Philly the Weeper says, "every guy Lola meets takes quite a fancy to her, to hear her tell it."

Well, nobody is much interested in the adventures of Miss Lola Ledare, or any of the other members of the "P's and Q's" company, but when Philly the Weeper mentions the name of the English guy, The Seldom Seen Kid, who is reading the sport page of the *News*, looks up and speaks as follows:

"Why," he says, "there is a story about the Honourable Searles right here in this paper. He is the greatest amateur steeplechase rider in England, and he is over here to ride his own horse, Trafalgar, in some of our steeplechase races, including the Gold Vase at Belmont next week. It says here they are giving a fox hunt and a big dinner in his honour to-day at the Oriole Hunts Club."

Then he hands the *News* to Philly the Weeper, and Philly the Weeper reads the story himself, and says like this:

"Well," he says, "from what Lola tells me of the guy's condition when they get him back to the hotel about six bells this a.m., they will have to take him to the Oriole Hunts Club unconscious. He may be a great hand at kicking them over the sticks, but I judge he is also quite a rum-pot."

"Anyway," Hot Horse Herbie says, "he is wasting his time

riding anything in the Gold Vase. Personally," he says, "I do not care for amateur steeplechase riders, because I meet up with several in my time who have more larceny in them than San Quentin. They call them gentleman riders, but many of them cannot even spell gentleman. I will take Follow You and that ziggaboo jock of his in the Gold Vase for mine against any horse and any amateur rider in the world, including Marsh Preston's Sweep Forward."

"Yes," Big Reds says, "if there is any jumper alive that can lick Follow You, with the coon up, I will stand on my head in front of Mindy's restaurant on Broadway for twenty-four hours hand running, and I do not like standing on my head. Any time they go to the post," Big Reds says, "they are just the same as money from home."

Well, of course it is well known to one and all that what Hot Horse Herbie and Big Reds say about Follow You in the Gold Vase is very true, because this Follow You is a Maryland horse that is a wonderful jumper, and furthermore he is a very popular horse because he is owned by a young Maryland doll by the name of Miss Phyllis Richie, who comes of an old family on the Eastern Shore.

It is such an old family as once has plenty of dough, and many great race horses, but by the time the family gets down to Miss Phyllis Richie, the dough is all gone, and about all that is left is a house with a leaky roof on the Tred Avon River, and this horse, Follow You, and a coon by the name of Roy Snakes, who always rides the horse, and everybody in Maryland knows that Follow You supports Miss Phyllis Richie and her mother and the house with the leaky roof by winning jumping races here and there.

In fact, all this is quite a famous story of the Maryland turf, and nobody is violating any secrets or poking their nose into private family affairs in speaking of it, and any time Follow You walks out on a race-track in Maryland with Roy Snakes on his back in the red and white colours of the Richie stable, the band always plays "My Maryland", and the whole State of Maryland gets up and yells.

Well, anyway, jumping races do not interest such characters as The Seldom Seen Kid and Hot Horse Herbie and Big Reds, or even Philly the Weeper, very much, so they get to talking about something else, when all of a sudden down the street comes a spectacle that is considered most surprising.

It consists of a young guy who is dressed up in a costume such as is worn by fox hunters when they are out chasing foxes, including a pink coat, and tight pants, and boots, and a peaked cap, and moreover, the guy is carrying a whip in one hand, and a horn in the other, and every now and then he puts this horn to his mouth and goes ta-ta-tee-ta-ta-tee-ta-dah.

But this is not as surprising as the fact that behind the guy are maybe a dozen dogs of one kind and another, such as a dachshund, a Boston bull terrier, a Scottie, a couple of fox hounds, and a lot of just plain every-day dogs, and they are yipping, and making quite a fuss about the guy in the costume, and the reason is that between ta-ta-dees he tucks his horn under one arm and reaches into a side pocket of his pink coat, and takes out some little brown crackers, which he chucks to the dogs.

Well, the first idea anybody is bound to have about a guy going around in such an outfit baiting dogs to follow him, is that he is slightly daffy, and this is the idea The Seldom Seen Kid, and Hot Horse Herbie, and Big Reds, and Philly the Weeper have as they watch the guy, until he turns around to chide a dog that is nibbling at the seat of his tight pants, and they see that the guy has a sign on his back that reads as follows:

MONEY FROM HOME

"Barker's Dog Crullers"

Then of course they know the guy is only up to an advertising dodge, and Hot Horse Herbie laughs right out loud, and says like this:

"Well," Herbie says, "I will certainly have to be in tough shape to take such a job as this, especially for a guy like old Barker. I know him well," Herbie says. "He has a factory down here on Lombard Street, and he likes to play the horses now and then, but he is the toughest, meanest old guy in Maryland, and will just as soon bat your brains out as not. In fact, he is thinking some of batting my brains out one day at Laurel last year when I lay him on the wrong horse. But," Herbie says, "they tell me he makes a wonderful dog cruller, at that, and he is certainly a great hand for advertising."

By this time, the young guy in the fox hunter's costume is in front of the hotel with his dogs, and nothing will do but The Seldom Seen Kid must stop him, and speak to him.

"Hello," The Seldom Seen Kid says, "where is your horse?"

Well, the young guy seems greatly surprised at being accosted in this manner by a stranger, and he looks at The Seldom Seen Kid for quite a spell, as if he is trying to figure out where he sees him before, and finally he says like this:

"Why," the young guy says, "it is very strange that you ask me such a question, as I not only do not have a horse, but I hate horses. I am afraid of horses since infancy. In fact," he says, "one reason I leave my home town is because my father wishes me to give up my musical career and drive the delivery waggon for his grocery-store, although he knows how I loathe and despise horses."

Now, of course, The Seldom Seen Kid is only joking when he asks the young guy about his horse, and does not expect to get all this information, but the young guy seems so friendly, and so innocent, that The Seldom Seen Kid keeps talking to him, although the dogs bother the young guy quite some, while he is standing there, by trying to climb up his legs, and he has to keep feeding them the little brown crackers out of his pocket, and it seems that these crackers are Barker's Dog Crullers, and Hot Horse Herbie personally tries several and pronounces them most nutritious.

The young guy says his name is Eddie Yokum, and he comes from a town in Delaware that is called Milburn, and another reason he comes to Baltimore besides wishing to avoid contact with horses is that he reads in a paper that the "P's and Q's" company is there, and he wishes to get a position with the show, because it seems that back in Milburn he is considered quite an excellent singer, and he takes a star part in the Elks' minstrel show in the winter of 1933, and even his mother says it will be a sin and a shame to waste such talent on a delivery waggon, especially by a guy who can scarcely bear the sight of a horse.

Well, Eddie Yokum then starts telling The Seldom Seen Kid all about the Elks' minstrel show, and how he gives imitations of Eddie Cantor and Al Jolson in black face; and in fact he gives these imitations for The Seldom Seen right then and there, and both are exactly alike, except of course Eddie Yokum is not in black face, and The Seldom Seen Kid confesses the imitations are really wonderful, and Eddie Yokum says he thinks so, too, especially when you consider he never even sees Eddie Cantor or Al Jolson.

He offers to render a song by the name of "Silver Threads Among the Gold," which it seems is the song he renders in the Elks' minstrels in Milburn, while imitating Eddie Cantor and Al Jolson, but Hot Horse Herbie and Big Reds tell The Seldom Seen Kid that this will be going too far, and he agrees with them, although Eddie Yokum seems greatly disappointed.

He is a very nice-looking young guy, with big round eyes, and a pleasant smile, but he is so innocent that it is really surprising to think he can walk around Baltimore, Md., safe and sound, even made up as a fox hunter.

Well, it seems that when Eddie Yokum arrives in Baltimore, Md., from Milburn, he goes around to the theatre where the "P's and Q's" company is playing to see about getting a position with the show, but nobody wishes to listen to him, and in fact the stage doorman finally speaks very crossly to Eddie, and tells him that if he does not desire a bust in the beezer, he will go away from there. So Eddie goes away, as he does not desire a bust in the beezer.

By and by he has a great wish to eat food, and as he is now all out of money, there is nothing for him to do but go to work, so he gets this job with Barker's Dog Crullers, and here he is.

"But," Eddie Yokum says, "I hesitate at taking it at first because I judge from the wardrobe that a horse goes with it, but Mr. Barker says if I think he is going to throw in a horse after spending a lot of money on this outfit, I am out of my head, and in fact Mr. Barker tells me not to walk fast, so as not to wear out these boots too soon. I am commencing to suspect that Mr. Barker is a trifle near."

By this time, no one except The Seldom Seen Kid is paying much attention to Eddie Yokum, as anybody can see that he is inclined to be somewhat gabby, and quite a bore, and anyway there cannot possibly be any percentage in talking to such a guy.

Hot Horse Herbie and Big Reds are chatting with each other, and Philly the Weeper is reading the paper, while Eddie Yokum goes right along doing a barber, and the dogs are still climbing up his legs after the Barker's Dog Crullers, when all of a sudden Philly the Weeper looks at the dogs, and speaks to Eddie Yokum in a most severe tone of voice as follows:

"See here, young fellow," Philly says, "where do you get the two fox hounds you have with you? I just notice them, and I will thank you to answer me promptly, and without quibbling."

Well, it seems from what Eddie Yokum says that he does not get the fox hounds anywhere in particular, but that they just up and follow him as he goes along the street. He explains that the Boston bull, the dachshund, and the Scottie are what you might call stooges, because they belong to Mr. Barker personally, and Eddie has to see that they get back to the factory with him every day, but all the other dogs are strays that join out with him here and there on account of the crullers, and he shoos them away when his day's work is done.

"To tell the truth," Eddie Yokum says, "I am always somewhat embarrassed to have so many dogs following me, but Mr. Barker sometimes trails me in person, and if I do not have a goodly throng of dogs in my wake eagerly partaking of Barker's Dog Crullers, he is apt to become very peevish. But," Eddie says, "I consider these fox hounds a great feather in my cap, because they are so appropriate to my costume, and I am sure that Mr. Barker will be much pleased when he sees them. In fact, he may raise my salary, which will be very pleasant, indeed."

"Well," Philly the Weeper says, "your story sounds very fishy to me. These fox hounds undoubtedly belong to my old friend, Mr. Prendergast, and how am I to know that you do not steal them from his country place? In fact, now that I look at you closely, I can see that you are such a guy as is apt to sneeze a dog any time, and for two cents I will call a cop and give you in charge."

He is gazing at Eddie Yokum most severely, and at this crack about his friend Mr. Prendergast, and a country place, The Seldom Seen Kid reaches over and takes the newspaper out of Philly the Weeper's hands, because he knows Philly has no friend by the name of Mr. Prendergast, and that even if he does have such a friend, Mr. Prendergast has no more country place than a jay-bird, but he can see that Philly has something on his mind, and right away The Seldom Seen Kid raps to what it is, because there in the paper in black type is an advertisement that reads as follows:

"LOST, STRAYED, OR STOLEN. TWO LIVER-AND-WHITE FOX HOUNDS ANSWERING TO THE NAMES OF NIP AND TUCK. $200 REWARD AND NO QUESTIONS ASKED IF RETURNED TO THE ORIOLE HUNTS CLUB."

Hot Horse Herbie and Big Reds read the advertisement over The Seldom Seen Kid's shoulder, and each makes a lunge at a fox hound, Hot Horse Herbie grabbing one around the neck, and Big Reds snaring the other by the hind legs; and this unexpected action causes some astonishment and alarm among the other dogs, and also frightens Eddie Yokum no little, especially as The Seldom Seen Kid joins Philly the Weeper in gazing at Eddie very severely, and The Seldom Seen Kid speaks as follows:

"Yes," he says, "this is a most suspicious case. There is only one thing to do with a party who stoops so low as to steal a dog, and especially two dogs, and that is to clap him in the clink."

Now of course The Seldom Seen Kid has no idea whatever of clapping anybody in the clink, because as a matter of fact he is greatly opposed to clinks, and if he has his way about it, they will all be torn down and thrown away, but he figures that it is just as well to toss a good scare into Eddie

Yokum and get rid of him before Eddie discovers what this interest in the fox hounds is all about, as The Seldom Seen Kid feels that if there is any reward money to be cut up, it is best not to spread it around any more than is necessary.

Well, by this time, Eddie Yokum has a very good scare in him, indeed, and he is backing away an inch or two at a time from The Seldom Seen Kid and Philly the Weeper, while Hot Horse Herbie and Big Reds are struggling with the fox hounds, and just about holding their own, when who comes walking up very briskly but a plain-clothes copper by the name of Detective Wilbert Schmalz, because it seems that the manager of the Cornflower Hotel gets sick and tired of the dogs out in front of his joint, and telephones to the nearest station-house and wishes to know if there is no justice.

So the station-house gets hold of Detective Wilbert Schmalz and tells him to see about this proposition; and here he is, and naturally Detective Schmalz can see by Eddie Yokum's costume and by the dogs around him that he is undoubtedly very unlawful, and as he comes walking up Detective Schmalz speaks to Eddie Yokum as follows:

"Come with me," he says. "You are under arrest."

Now what Eddie Yokum thinks he is under arrest for is stealing the fox hounds, and by the time Detective Schmalz gets close to him, Eddie Yokum is near one of the two entrances to the Cornflower Hotel that open on Calvert Street, and both of these entrances have revolving doors.

So all of a sudden, Eddie Yokum makes a jump into one of these entrances, and at the same time Detective Schmalz makes a grab for him, as Detective Schmalz can see by Eddie Yokum's attempt to escape that he is undoubtedly a very great malefactor, but all Detective Schmalz gets is the sign off Eddie's back that reads "Barker's Dog Crullers."

Then Detective Schmalz finds himself tangled up in the

revolving door with the dachshund, which is trying to follow Eddie Yokum, and crying in a way that will break your heart, while Eddie is dashing out the other entrance, and there is a great confusion all around and about, with Hot Horse Herbie and Big Reds using language to the fox hounds that is by no means fit for publication.

In fact, there is so much confusion that very few people notice that as Eddie Yokum pops out the other entrance and heads for the middle of the street where he will have plenty of racing room, a big, shiny town car with a chauffeur and a footman pulls up at the kerb in front of the hotel, and the footman leaps off the seat and yanks open the door of the car right under Eddie Yokum's nose, and the next thing anybody knows, Eddie is inside the town car, and the car is tearing down the street.

Afterwards Eddie Yokum remembers hearing the footman mumble something about being sorry, they are late, but Eddie is too bewildered by his strange experience, and too happy to escape the law, to think of much of anything else for a while, and it does not come to him that he must be mistaken for somebody else until the town car is rolling up the driveway of the Oriole Hunts Club, a few miles out of Baltimore, and he sees a raft of guys and dolls strolling around and about, with the guys dressed up as fox hunters, just the same way he is.

Now, of course the guy Eddie Yokum is mistaken for is nobody but the Honourable Bertie Searles, who at this time is pounding his ear back in the Cornflower Hotel, and the chances are glad of it, but nobody can scarcely blame the chauffeur and the footman for the mistake when they see a guy dressed up as a fox hunter come bouncing out of a hotel, where they are sent to pick up an English gentleman rider, because anybody is apt to look like an Englishman, and a gentleman, too, if they are dressed up as a fox hunter.

Naturally, Eddie Yokum knows that a mistake is going on the minute he gets out of the car and finds himself surrounded by guys and dolls all calling him the Honourable Bertie Searles, and he realizes that there is nothing for him to do but to explain and apologize, and get away from there as quick as he can, and the chances are he will do this at once, as Eddie Yokum is really an honest, upright young guy, but before he can say a word, what does he see on the clubhouse veranda in riding clothes but the most beautiful doll he ever claps eyes on in his whole life.

In fact, this doll is so beautiful that Eddie Yokum is practically tongue-tied at once, and when she is introduced to him as Miss Phyllis Richie, he does not care what happens if he can only hang around here a little while, for this is undoubtedly love at first sight as far as Eddie Yokum is concerned, and Miss Phyllis Richie is by no means displeased with him, either, although she remarks that he is the first Englishman she ever sees who does not have an English accent.

So Eddie Yokum says to himself he will just keep his trap closed until the real Honourable Bertie Searles bobs up, or somebody who knows the real Honourable Bertie Searles comes around, and enjoy the sunshine of Miss Phyllis Richie's smile as long as possible; and to show you what a break he gets, it seems that nobody in the club ever sees the Honourable Bertie Searles in person, and they are all too busy getting the fox hunt in his honour going to bother to ask Eddie any questions that he cannot answer yes or no.

Anyway, Eddie Yokum keeps so close to Miss Phyllis Richie that nobody has much chance to talk to her, although a tall young guy with a little moustache and a mean look keeps trying, and Miss Phyllis Richie explains that this guy is nobody but Mr. Marshall Preston, who is as great an amateur rider in America as the Honourable Bertie Searle himself is in England.

Furthermore, she explains that Mr. Marshall Preston is the owner of a horse by the name of Sweet Forward, that is the only horse in this country that figures a chance to beat her horse, Follow You, in the Gold Vase, unless maybe the Honourable Bertie Searles' horse, Trafalgar, is an extra-good horse.

Then she commences asking Eddie Yokum about his horse, Trafalgar, and of course Eddie not only does not know he has such a horse, but he hates just even talking about horses, and he has quite a time switching the conversation, because Miss Phyllis Richie seems bound and determined to talk about horses, and especially her horse.

"I am only sorry," Miss Phyllis Richie says, "that it is not possible to let you ride Follow You over a course, just so you can see what a wonderful horse he is, but," she says, "it is a well-known peculiarity of his that he will not permit any one to ride him except a coloured boy, not even myself. In fact, several times we try to put white riders on Follow You, and he half kills them. It is most unfortunate, because you will really appreciate him."

Well, naturally Eddie Yokum does not consider this unfortunate by any means, as the last thing in the world he wishes to do is to ride a horse, but of course he does not mention the matter to Miss Phyllis Richie, as he can see that a guy who does not wish to ride horses is not apt to get to first base with her.

What bothers Eddie Yokum more than somewhat, however, is the way this Mr. Marshall Preston keeps scowling at him, and finally he asks Miss Phyllis Richie if she can figure out what is eating the guy, and Miss Phyllis Richie laughs heartily, and says like this:

"Oh," she says, "Mr. Marshall Preston seems to have an

idea that he loves me, and wishes to marry me. He hates anybody that comes near me. He hates my poor horse, Follow You, because he thinks if it is not for Follow You coming along and winning enough money to support us, I will have to marry him out of sheer poverty.

"But," Miss Phyllis Richie says, "I do not love Mr. Marshall Preston, and I will never marry except for love, and while things are not so good with us right now, everything will be all right after Follow You wins the Gold Vase, because it is a $25,000 stake. But no matter what happens, I do not think I will ever marry Mr. Marshall Preston, as he is very wild in his ways, and is unkind to horses."

Well, this last is really a boost for Mr. Marshall Preston with Eddie Yokum, but naturally he does not so state to Miss Phyllis Richie, and in fact he says that now he takes a second peek at Mr. Marshall Preston he can see that he may be a wrong gee in more ways than one, and that Miss Phyllis Richie is quite right in playing the chill for such a guy.

Now there is a great commotion about the premises, with guys coming up leading horses, and a big pack of fox hounds yapping around, and it seems that the fox hunt in honour of the Honourable Bertie Searles is ready to start, and Eddie Yokum is greatly horrified when he realizes that he is expected to take part in the fox hunt, and ride a horse, and in fact Miss Phyllis Richie tells him they pick out the very finest horse in the club stables for him to ride, although she says she is afraid it will not compare to the horses he is accustomed to riding in England.

Well, at this, Eddie Yokum is greatly nonplussed, and he figures that here is the blow-off sure enough, especially as a guy who seems to be a groom comes up leading a tall, fierce-looking horse, and hands Eddie the bridle-reins. But Eddie cannot think of words in which to put his confession, so when nobody seems to be noticing him, he walks off by himself towards the club stables, and naturally the horse follows him, because Eddie has hold of the reins.

Now the presence of this horse at his heels is very disquieting to Eddie Yokum, so when he gets behind the stables which shut him off from the sight of the crowd, Eddie looks around for something to tie the horse to, and finally drops the reins over the handle of a motor-cycle that is leaning up against a wall, this motor-cycle being there for the grooms to run errands on to and from the city.

Well, it seems that in the excitement over getting the fox hunt started, nobody missed Eddie Yokum at first, and away goes the crowd on their horses with the hounds yapping quite some, while Eddie is standing there behind the stables thinking of how to break the news about himself to one and all, and especially to Miss Phyllis Richie.

Then Eddie Yokum happens to look up, and who does he see coming up the driveway in such a direction that they cannot miss seeing him if he remains where he is, but Philly the Weeper and Hot Horse Herbie, leading a pair of hounds, which are undoubtedly the fox hounds they get from Eddie Yokum, and which they are now delivering to claim the reward.

Naturally, the sight of these parties is most distasteful to Eddie Yokum, because all he can think of is that in addition to everything else, he will now be denounced as a dog thief, and Eddie can scarcely bear to have Miss Phyllis Richie see him in such a light, so he grabs up the motor-cycle, and starts it going, and leaps in the saddle, and away he sprints down a country lane in the opposite direction from the driveway, for if there is one thing Eddie Yokum can do, it is ride a motor-cycle.

He forgets about the horse being hooked to the motor-cycle, and of course the poor horse has to follow him, and every time Eddie Yokum looks around, there is the horse, and Eddie gets the idea that maybe the horse is chasing him, so he gives the motor-cycle plenty of gas, and makes it zing. But it is very bumpy going along the country lane, and Eddie cannot lose the horse, and, besides, Eddie is personally becoming very tired, so finally he pulls up to take a rest.

By this time, the horse has enough lather on him to shave the House of David, and seems about ready to drop dead, and Eddie Yokum will not care a cuss if he does, as Eddie is sick and tired of the horse, although the horse is really not to blame for anything whatever.

Anyway, Eddie Yokum is lying stretched out on the ground taking a rest, when he hears the fox hounds barking away off, but coming closer right along, and he figures the fox hunters will also be moving in his direction, and as he does not wish to ever again be seen by Miss Phyllis Richie after ducking the hunt, he unhooks the horse from the motor-cycle, and gives it a good kick in the vestibule, and tells it to go on about its business, and then he crawls in under a big brush-heap beside the lane, dragging the motor-cycle in after him.

Well, what is under the brush-heap but a little bitsy fox, all tuckered out, and very much alarmed, and this little bitsy fox seems glad to see such a kind and sympathetic face as Eddie Yokum possesses, and it crawls into Eddie Yokum's lap, and roosts there shivering and shaking, and the next thing Eddie knows the brush-heap is surrounded by fox hounds, who are very anxious to get at the little bitsy fox, and maybe at Eddie Yokum, too, but Eddie remembers that he has some of Barker's Dog Crullers still left in his pocket, and he cools the hounds out no little by feeding them these appetizers.

MONEY FROM HOME

By and by the fox hunters come up, following the hounds, and they are greatly surprised when Eddie Yokum comes crawling out from under the brush-heap with the little bitsy fox in his arms, especially as they meet up with Eddie's horse all covered with perspiration, and figure he must just finish a terrible run, because of course they do not know about the motor-cycle hidden under the brush-heap.

They are all the more surprised when Eddie Yokum tell them that he does not believe in killing foxes, and that he always personally catches them with his bare hands after the dogs locate them, but Eddie feels rewarded when Miss Phyllis Richie smiles at him, and says he is the most humane guy she ever meets, especially when Eddie says his horse is too tired for him to ride him home, and insists on walking, carrying the little bitsy fox.

Well, Eddie is commencing to wonder again how he can confess what an impostor he is, and get away from this company, but the more he looks at Miss Phyllis Richie, the more he hates to do it, especially as she is talking about what a wonderful time they will have at the dinner in his honour later on in the evening, as it seems that this is to be a very fine affair, indeed, and Harry Richman and several other stars of the "P's and Q's" company are expected to be present to entertain, and Eddie Yokum can see where he may be missing a great opportunity to come in contact with such parties.

But by the time he gets back to the clubhouse, Eddie's mind is pretty well made up to get himself out of this predicament, no matter what, especially as the clubhouse doorman calls him aside, and says to him like this:

"Mr. Searles," the doorman says, "a most obnoxious character is here just a little while ago claiming he is you. Yes, sir," the doorman says, "he has the gall to claim he is the Honourable Bertie Searles, and he is slightly under the influence, and has several dolls with him, including a very savage blonde. Of course we know he is not you, and so we throw him out.

"He is very cheerful about it, at that, Mr. Searles," the doorman says. "He says it does not strike him as a very lively place, anyway, and that he is having more fun where he is. But the savage blonde is inclined to make much of the matter. In fact, she tries to bite me. It is a very strange world, Mr. Searles."

Well, Eddie Yokum figures right away that this must be the guy they mistake him for, and he also figures that the guy is a sure thing to be coming back sooner or later, and as it is now coming on dusk, Eddie starts easing himself down the driveway, although they tell him there is a nice room ready for him at the club where he can clean up and take a rest before dinner; but he does not get very far down the driveway, when who steps out of some bushes but Philly the Weeper, who speaks as follows:

"Well, well, well," Philly the Weeper says. "I know my eyes do not deceive me when I see you springing away on a motor-cycle, but," he says, "imagine my astonishment when I describe you to the doorman, and he tells me you are the Honourable Bertie Searles. Why, you can knock me over with the eighth pole, I am so surprised, because of course I know you are nothing but a dog thief, and I am waiting around here for hours to get an explanation from you for such goings on."

Naturally, Philly the Weeper does not mention that he already has Hot Horse Herbie collect two C's from the club secretary for returning the hounds, and that he sends Herbie on back to Baltimore, for Philly the Weeper has a nose like a beagle, and he smells something here the minute he sees Eddie Yokum going away on the motor-cycle, and he keeps himself in the background, while Hot Horse Herbie is collecting the dough, although Philly does not neglect to take the two C's off of Herbie afterwards, for safe-keeping.

Of course, Philly the Weeper has no idea Eddie Yokum is trying to run away entirely on the motor-cycle, or he will not be hanging around waiting for him to come back, but there Eddie is, and Philly the Weeper gets the whole story out of him in no time, because Eddie figures the best thing for him to do is to throw himself on the mercy of Philly the Weeper as far as the stolen dogs are concerned.

Well, Philly the Weeper is greatly interested and amused at Eddie's story of how he is mistaken for the Honourable Bertie Searles, and has to go fox hunting, and of his sudden and great love for Miss Phyllis Richie; but when Eddie gets down to telling him about how he is now trying to slip away from the scene, Philly the Weeper becomes very severe again, and speaks as follows:

"No, no," Philly says, "you are not to go away, at all. You are to remain here at the club for the dinner in your honour to-night, and, moreover, you are to take me into the club with you as your valet, because," Philly says, "I wish to play a joke on certain members of this organization, including my old friend, Mr. Prendergast, who will undoubtedly be present. If you will do this for me, I will forget about you stealing Mr. Prendergast's fox hounds, although he is inclined to be very drastic about the matter."

Now, of course, if Eddie Yokum is such a guy as does a little serious thinking now and then, the chances are he will see that there is something unusual about all this, but Eddie is not only very innocent, but by this time he is greatly confused, and all he can think of to say to Philly the Weeper is that he is afraid the real Honourable Bertie Searles will come back and expose him.

"You need not worry about this," Philly the Weeper says. "I am present in ambush when the Honourable Bertie Searles and his party, including my fiancée, Miss Lola Ledare, are given the bum's rush out of here a short time ago, and as they depart I hear him promising to give Lola and her friends a big party downtown to-night after the show to reimburse them for the churlish treatment they received here. Remember," Philly says, "you will not only be rounding yourself up for stealing Mr. Prendergast's dogs, but you will be able to be with the doll you love so dearly all evening."

So the upshot of it all is, Eddie Yokum goes back to the club, taking Philly the Weeper with him and explaining that Philly is his valet; and one thing about it, Philly makes Eddie more important than somewhat, at that, which is a good thing, as some of the members are commencing to wonder about Eddie, especially Mr. Marshall Preston, who is all burned up at the way Eddie is pitching to Miss Phyllis Richie.

Now, the reason Philly the Weeper wishes to get inside the clubhouse is not to play any jokes on anybody, as he says, especially on his friend Mr. Prendergast, because in the first place he has no friend named Mr. Prendergast, and in the second place, Philly the Weeper has no friends by any names whatever. The reason he wishes to get inside the clubhouse is to collect any little odds and ends of jewellery that he may find lying about the premises later on, for collecting articles of this kind is really one of Philly the Weeper's regular occupations, though naturally he does not mention it to Eddie Yokum.

As a matter of fact, he is of quite some service to Eddie Yokum when they go to the room that is assigned to Eddie, as he coaches Eddie in the way a guy shall act at dinner, and in talking to such a doll as Miss Phyllis Richie, and he also fixes Eddie's clothes up for him a little, as the dinner is to be in fox hunting costume, which is a good thing for Eddie, as he does not have any other costume.

The only argument they have is about the little bitsy fox, which Eddie Yokum is still carrying around with him, and which he wishes to keep with him at all times, as he is now very fond of the little creature, but Philly the Weeper convinces him that it is better to turn it loose, and let it return to its native haunts, and when Eddie does same the little bitsy fox creates a riot in the club kennels when it goes streaking past them headed for the woods.

Well, Eddie Yokum is a very hospitable soul, and he wishes Philly the Weeper to attend the dinner with him, but Philly says no, a valet is supposed to be a sort of hired hand, and does not go in for social functions with his boss, so Eddie goes down to dinner alone, leaving Philly the Weeper in the room, and Eddie is greatly delighted to find Miss Phyllis Richie is waiting for him to escort her in, and for the next couple of hours he is in a sort of trance, and cannot remember that he is not the Honourable Bertie Searles, but only Eddie Yokum, of Milburn, Del.

All he can remember is that he hauls off and tells Miss Phyllis Richie that he is in love with her, and she says she loves him right back, and the only trouble with this conversation is that Mr. Marshall Preston accidentally overhears it, and is so unhappy he can scarcely think, because it is only a couple of hours before that Mr. Marshall Preston asks Miss Phyllis Richie to please marry him.

Mr. Marshall Preston is so unhappy that he goes out to the bar before dinner is over and has a few drinks, and then goes upstairs to a room he is occupying for the evening, just in time to catch Philly the Weeper collecting a job lot of trinkets in the room to add to a bundle he already collects from other rooms.

Naturally, this unexpected intrusion is most embarrassing to Philly the Weeper, especially as Mr. Marshall Preston recognizes him as the Honourable Bertie Searles' valet, and it is perhaps just as well for Mr. Marshall Preston that Philly the Weeper is not rodded up at this time, as Philly never cares to be embarrassed. But Mr. Marshall Preston turns out to be very broad-minded, and instead of making a scene over finding Philly the Weeper at his collecting, he speaks to Philly as follows:

"Sit down," he says. "Sit down, and let us talk this over. What is there about this party who calls himself the Honourable Bertie Searles that causes me to wonder, and what is your real connection with him, and why does your face seem so familiar to me? Tell me your tale, and tell me true," Mr. Marshall Preston says, "or shall I call the gendarmes?"

Well, Philly the Weeper can see that Mr. Marshall Preston is no sucker, so he tells him that the Honourable Bertie Searles at the club is 100 per cent phoney, because he is nobody but Eddie Yokum, and he explains how he gets there, and that the real Honourable Bertie Searles is downtown enjoying himself with members of the "P's and Q's" company.

"And," Philly says, "the reason my face seems familiar to you may be because I am around the race-tracks quite often, although I never have much truck with the steeple-chasers."

Now, Mr. Marshall Preston listens to all this with great interest, and when Philly the Weeper gets through, Mr. Marshall Preston sits there quiet for awhile, as if he is studying something out, and finally he says like this:

"I will call up the Honourable Bertie Searles, and we will have him come here and expose this impostor," he says. "It will be a good lesson to Miss Phyllis Richie for taking up with such a character without first finding out something about him. But in the meantime," he says, "let us continue talking while I make up my mind about handing you over to the cops."

MONEY FROM HOME

They continue talking until Mr. Marshall Preston forgets about calling the Honourable Bertie Searles until an hour later, and then he may just as well save himself the trouble, for at the moment he is telephoning, the Honourable Bertie Searles is on his way to the Oriole Hunts Club with Miss Lola Ledare, and a taxi-load of other blondes, and a few brunettes, because right in the middle of a nice party, some of the blondes remember they are due at the club to help Harry Richman put on a number, and the Honourable Bertie Searles says he will go along and demand an explanation from the club for his treatment earlier in the day, although the Honourable Bertie Searles says he does not really care a whoop, as he is treated worse in better clubs.

Well, while all this is happening, the dinner is going along very nicely, and it is a gala scene, to be sure, what with the decorations, and music, and all, and Eddie Yokum is in more of a trance than ever over Miss Phyllis Richie, when all of a sudden an old phflug by the name of Mrs. Abernathy comes running into the dining-hall letting out a squawk that she is robbed. It seems that she leaves a purse containing some dough, and other valuables, with her wraps in the dolls' dressing-room upstairs, and when she goes up there to powder her nose, or some such, she finds somebody knocks off her poke.

Now, this causes other dolls to remember leaving their leathers laying around upstairs, and some of them investigate at once, and find they are clipped, too, and presently guys who occupy rooms in the club are also letting out bleats and it becomes apparent that some thievery is going on around and about, and the club manager telephones for the police, because the beefs are commencing to be most upsetting.

Well, naturally Eddie Yokum is paying little attention to this commotion, because he is too greatly interested in Miss

Phyllis Richie, but all of a sudden a bunch of coppers walk into the room, and who is among them but Detective Wilbert Schmalz, and the minute Eddie sees him, he becomes alarmed, as he is afraid Detective Schmalz may recognize him and put the arm on him for stealing the fox hounds, even though this matter is now supposed to be rounded up with Philly the Weeper.

So Eddie Yokum excuses himself to Miss Phyllis Richie and steps in back of a stand of potted plants, where he will not be conspicuous, and about this time he hears a familiar voice asking what is the trouble here, and why are all the coppers present, and somebody speaks up and says:

"Why, we are robbed."

Then Eddie Yokum hears the familiar voice again, which he recognizes as the voice of Mr. Barker, who makes the dog crullers, and it is quite a loud voice, at that, and very unpleasant, and in fact it is such a loud voice that it causes Eddie Yokum to tremble in his top-boots, for Mr. Barker states as follows:

"You are robbed?" he says. "Well, think of me, and how I am robbed, too. I am robbed of my hunting clothes, and I have to appear here at a hunts dinner for the first time in all the years I am a member of this club, the way you see me. If they do not happen to have sense enough to find their way home, I will also be robbed of Adolph, my dachshund, and Boggie, my Boston, and McTavish, my Scottie. But," Mr. Barker says, "if it takes me the rest of my life, I will find the young squirt who runs off with my hunting clothes and choke the tongue out of his head."

Well, at this, Eddie Yokum peeks around the potted plants, and he sees Mr. Barker standing nearby in a dinner jacket, and apparently very angry, indeed, and this is quite a situation for Eddie Yokum, because he is between Detective Schmalz, who may wish to put the arm on him, and Mr. Barker, who wishes to choke the tongue out of his head, and as if this is not enough, there is now a great commotion at the front door, with dolls squealing, and guys yelling, and Eddie Yokum hears somebody say that a guy is out there claiming he is the Honourable Bertie Searles, and trying to fight his way in.

The racket is so great it attracts everybody's attention, and Eddie Yokum sees his chance and slips away quietly, popping into the first door he comes to, and this door leads down a stairway into the furnace-room, so Eddie hides himself behind a furnace for awhile.

In the meantime, there is much excitement upstairs, as it seems that the Honourable Bertie Searles finally battles his way inside against great odds, and is identified by all the members of the "P's and Q's" company who are with him, including Harry Richman and the other stars, as the guy he claims he is, and he is demanding apologies from everybody connected with the club, while a search is going on for the phoney Honourable Bertie Searles.

Finally, Detective Schmalz, who joins the search, frisks the room that Eddie occupies, and finds a couple of missing purses, now empty, and everybody is saying that there is no doubt Eddie is not only an impostor, but that he and his valet are thieves; although Mr. Marshall Preston puts in here, and says he does not think the valet is a party to the crime, as he personally sees the valet leaving the premises some time before the robbery can possibly take place.

So then everybody agrees that Eddie must be a lone hand criminal, and Miss Phyllis Richie is so mortified she gets her wraps and goes out on the veranda, especially after somebody describes Eddie Yokum, and Mr. Barker says he is surely the guy who cops his hunting costume, and Detective Schmalz, who listens in on the description, states that he is positive the guy is a much wanted dog snatcher.

Mr. Marshall Preston goes out on the veranda and tries to console Miss Phyllis Richie, and in fact he tells her that it is now time for her to make up her mind to marry him and find safety from adventurers such as Eddie Yokum, but Miss Phyllis Richie gives him a very short answer, and there are undoubtedly large tears in her eyes as she speaks, and anybody can see that she is feeling very downhearted, so Mr. Marshall Preston leaves her to her sorrow.

Well, pretty soon the entertainment goes into action, and the real Honourable Bertie Searles becomes the guest of honour in place of Eddie Yokum, and everybody forgets the unpleasant incidents of the evening, because the Honourable Bertie Searles is full of life and spirits and does not centre his attention on any one doll, as Eddie does when he is guest of honour, but scatters his shots around and about, although it is plain to be seen that the Honourable Bertie Searles cares for Miss Lola Ledare more than somewhat, even if she does keep wishing to go back and fight the doorman all over again.

Meantime, Eddie Yokum is down in the furnace-room, and how to get out and away from the club without being observed becomes something of a problem, as Eddie is still in the fox hunting costume, and such a costume is bound to attract attention at all times, and, furthermore, the only entrance to the furnace-room seems to be the room through which Eddie comes in the first place.

Well, Eddie sits there behind the furnace thinking things over, and he can hear the music and the laughter upstairs, and he is wishing he is back in Milburn, Del., where he has a home, and friends, and thinking of Milburn, Del., reminds Eddie of the time he blacks up his face and gives imitations of Al Jolson and Eddie Cantor; and thinking of this gives him a brand-new idea.

This idea is to black up his face right there and walk out

to safety, because Eddie figures that anybody who sees him is bound to take him as an employee of the furnace-room, so he peeks into the furnace, and finds a lot of soot, and he makes his face blacker than a yard up a chimney.

Moreover, Eddie gets another break when he finds a suit of blue overalls left by some guy who works in the furnace-room, and also an old cap, and when he sneaks out the door a little later, he is nothing but a boogie, as far as anybody can see, and not a very clean boogie, at that, and the chances are he will be out of the club and gone in two minutes, if he does not happen to run into the Honourable Bertie Searles, who is teetering around looking for Miss Lola Ledare, who is absent from the scene longer than the Honourable Bertie Searles thinks is necessary.

As a matter of fact, Miss Lola Ledare is at this time off in a corner with Mr. Barker, giving Mr. Barker quite a canvass one way and another, for Miss Lola Ledare is a doll who believes in scattering her play, but of course this has nothing to do with the story.

Well, when he runs into Eddie Yokum, naturally the Honourable Bertie Searles thinks Eddie is really a coloured guy, and right away the Honourable Bertie Searles get a big idea, as guys who are rummed up a little always do. The Honourable Bertie Searles says that so far the entertainment in his honour lacks the old Southern touch he is led to believe he will find in such spots as Baltimore, Md., especially by coloured parties, and he considers Eddie a great capture, and insists on leading him out on the floor where the entertainment is going on, and presenting him to the crowd as a bit of real Southern atmosphere.

Naturally, Eddie Yokum is somewhat embarrassed, and alarmed, because he is afraid he will be recognized by somebody, but no one gives him a tumble for who he is, and everybody laughs heartily at what they consider the Honourable Bertie Searles' humour. Then the Honourable Bertie Searles says his protégé will now sing, and there is nothing for Eddie Yokum to do but sing, so he goes into "Silver Threads Among the Gold," and the orchestra picks him up nicely, and accompanies his singing.

Ordinarily, Eddie will be very glad to sing before such an audience, and even now he has a notion to give them Al Jolson and Eddie Cantor, then he commences thinking of what will happen to him if he is recognized, and he gets so alarmed he sings a little flat.

As he is singing, Eddie Yokum makes sure of the direction of the front entrance to the club, and he keeps edging in this direction as his song comes to a close, so it seems very natural when he finishes to bow himself off in an aisle leading to the entrance; only Eddie keeps right on going out the entrance, and he is on the veranda, and flying, when who does he run into but Miss Phyllis Richie.

Well, at the sight of Miss Phyllis Richie, Eddie Yokum forgets he is all sooted up, and looks like a smudge, and in fact all he can think of is how much he loves Miss Phyllis Richie, and he rushes up to her and speaks as follows:

"Darling," Eddie Yokum says, "I am in a bit of a hurry right now, and do not have time to explain matters, but do not believe anything you hear about me, because it is by no means true; and, anyway," Eddie says, "I adore you."

Naturally, Miss Phyllis Richie thinks at first that Eddie is a real jig, and she is somewhat startled for a moment, but then she recognizes his voice, and she becomes very indignant, indeed.

"Why," Miss Phyllis Richie says, "you impostor! You cad! You liar! Why," she says, "you dog stealer! You common burglar! If you do not get away from here at once, I will call Mr. Marshall Preston and he will thrash you within an inch of your life, and turn you over to the police!"

And with this, she hauls off and biffs Eddie Yokum a hard slap in the kisser, and then she bursts out crying, and there is nothing for Eddie Yokum to do but to continue on his way, because he hears the Honourable Bertie Searles yelling for him, and he does not desire any further complications at this time.

All Eddie Yokum wishes to do is to go away somewhere and sit down and rest, and get his nerves composed again, as he is feeling greatly fatigued; and the first thing he does is to go to his rooming-house and wash himself up, and put on his best suit of clothes, which he brings with him from Milburn, Del., and then he starts thinking things over, and what he especially thinks over is why Miss Phyllis Richie calls him a common burglar, for of course Eddie Yokum does not know he is suspected of prowling the Oriole Hunt Club, although he knows it the next morning when he reads all about the robbery in the paper, and also about how the coppers are looking for a guy who impersonates the Honourable Bertie Searles to get into the club for the purpose of committing the crime.

Well, this is a very great shock to Eddie Yokum, and he can see at once why he stands like a broken leg with Miss Phyllis Richie. Moreover, he can see that there is just one guy who can state that he does not get into the club to commit any crimes, and this guy is nobody but Philly the Weeper, so Eddie figures the thing for him to do is to find Philly the Weeper, and get him to straighten this matter out, although of course if Eddie is well acquainted with Philly the Weeper he will know that getting Philly to straighten anything out is just the same thing as asking a gimlet to straighten out.

But Eddie Yokum has great faith in human nature and

honesty, so the next morning he goes around in front of the Cornflower Hotel looking for Philly the Weeper; but Philly is by no means there, although The Seldom Seen Kid and Hot Horse Herbie and Big Reds are present; and at first none of them recognize Eddie without his fox hunter's costume until he asks The Seldom Seen Kid where Philly is, and The Seldom Seen Kid says like this:

"Well," he says, "if you can tell us, we will be greatly obliged, for we are seeking him ourselves to cut his ears off unless he kicks in with our share of a small score we make on some dogs. Yes," The Seldom Seen Kid says, "we will just love to see Philly the Weeper, but the 'P's and Q's' company goes to New York this morning, and the chances are he goes there, too, because he never gets far away from his fiancée, Miss Lola Ledare, for fear he will starve to death. But we will catch up with him sooner or later."

Then The Seldom Seen Kid seems to remember Eddie Yokum's face, and he starts to laugh, because the last time he sees Eddie Yokum it is a very humorous spectacle, to be sure; but Eddie Yokum does not see anything to laugh about, and he starts in telling The Seldom Seen Kid and Hot Horse Herbie and Big Reds how Philly the Weeper makes him take him into the club as his valet, and what happens, and how he wishes to find Philly to prove his innocence; and Hot Horse Herbie is especially horrified, and states as follows:

"Why," he says, "I ought to know this fink has something on his mind that spells larceny when he tells me he is going to stick around out there at the club awhile and sends me back to town. But," Herbie says, "it does not occur to me it is anything more serious than maybe stealing a couple of dogs over again to collect another reward. There is no doubt but what he prowls the joint and leaves this poor guy to take the fall."

"Philly the Weeper is a wrong gee," The Seldom Seen Kid says. "I know he is a wrong gee because he means to defraud us of our end of the two C's he gets yesterday, but I never figure he is wrong enough to do such a trick as he does to this guy here. It is really most preposterous. Well," The Seldom Seen Kid says, "the races are over here to-morrow and the best thing for you to do is to go with us and see if we can find Philly the Weeper. Anyway," he says, "if you stick around here you will be picked up and placed in the sneezer, and it is very, very difficult to get out of a Baltimore sneezer, once you are in."

So this is how Eddie Yokum comes to be in New York and around Mindy's restaurant on Broadway the next week with The Seldom Seen Kid, and Hot Horse Herbie, and Big Reds, and also with other prominent turf advisers, and followers of the sport of kings, for Mindy's restaurant is a great resort for such characters.

But although he looks high and low, Eddie Yokum do not see hide or hair of Philly the Weeper, and neither does The Seldom Seen Kid and Hot Horse Herbie and Big Reds, although his fiancée, Miss Lola Ledare, is around in different spots nearly every night with the Honourable Bertie Searles, and the price against the Honourable Bertie Searles' horse, Trafalgar, in the Gold Vase Steeplechase goes up by the minute, and some bookmakers will give you as good as 10 to 1 that the Honourable Bertie cannot even sit on a horse Saturday, let alone ride one.

Most of the conversation around Mindy's at this time is about the Gold Vase Steeplechase, but it is conceded by one and all that it is a set-up for Miss Phyllis Richie's Follow You, and every time Eddie Yokum hears her name he has a pain in his heart, because he even forgets to think of Philly the Weeper when he is thinking of Miss Phyllis Richie.

What with being around with parties interested in horse

racing, Eddie Yokum takes to reading the sport pages quite some, and when it comes to the day before the Gold Vase, he reads about Miss Phyllis Richie arriving at the Savoy-Plaza with a party of friends from all over Maryland to see the race, and he hangs around in front of the hotel for three hours just to get a peek at her, although he is somewhat discouraged when he sees Miss Phyllis Richie with Mr. Marshall Preston.

In the evening, he hears the citizens around Mindy's speaking of Mr. Marshall Preston's horse, Sweep Forward, and of other horses, but the conversation makes no impression on Eddie Yokum, because he does not know anything about racing, and in fact he never sees a race, because he hates horses so much, but there is so much excitement over the Gold Vase that finally he feels a desire to see this race, and he asks The Seldom Seen Kid and Hot Horse Herbie and Big Reds if they will take him with them the next day.

Well, they say they will, although they will much rather take somebody that has something, because the truth of the matter is, they are getting a little tired of Eddie Yokum, as he is strictly a non-producer at this time, and they have to sustain him as he goes along, and the only reason they do this is they feel sorry for him, and The Seldom Seen Kid and Hot Horse Herbie and Big Reds are noted for their kind hearts.

The Seldom Seen Kid is especially sorry for Eddie Yokum, because he knows of Eddie's love for Miss Phyllis Richie, as Eddie confides same to The Seldom Seen Kid one evening, and as The Seldom Seen often carries the old torch himself, he knows how it feels.

But he is wishing Eddie Yokum will get a job and forget Miss Phyllis Richie, as The Seldom Seen Kid regards it as a hopeless passion, especially as he reads in a paper that Miss

Phyllis Richie is planning to go abroad with a party that will include Mr. Marshall Preston immediately after the race for the Gold Vase, although The Seldom Seen Kid does not show this item to Eddie Yokum.

Well, the day of the Gold Vase Steeplechase is always a great day at Belmont Park, as it brings together all the greatest steeplechasers in the country, and the best riders, including gentleman jocks and professionals, and the finest society crowd, and Eddie Yokum is quite bewildered by what he sees and hears as he wanders around and about, although he cannot help a feeling of loathing that all this is over horses.

He looks around for Miss Phyllis Richie, and asks The Seldom Seen Kid where she is apt to be at such a place as a race-track, and The Seldom Seen says the chances are she will be out under the trees behind the grandstand where the horses are walked around and saddled not long before the big race, to take a peek at her horse, and furthermore The Seldom Seen Kid says:

"I only wish you are on speaking terms with her, at that," he says. "There is a rumour that Miss Phyllis Richie's nigger jockey, Roy Snakes, is off on a bender, or something to this effect. Anyway, they say he is missing, and if they cannot find him, or get another jig jock, they will have to scratch Follow You, because no white guy alive can ride Follow You in a race.

"Now," The Seldom Seen Kid goes on, "I hear there is not another coon steeplechaser in these parts just now, and if you can find out if Roy Snakes is really absent, I can get a fair price on Sweep Forward. With Follow You out, he is a triple-plated pipe. It will really be quite a favour to me, and some of my customers if you can secure this information for me before the rush sets in."

Well, Eddie Yokum does not understand what this is all

about, but he does get the idea that Miss Phyllis Richie may be in some sort of predicament, so he goes out under the trees behind the grandstand, and waits around there awhile, and sure enough he finally sees Miss Phyllis Richie standing under a tree around which an old guy by the name of Ike is leading a big chestnut horse, and there is a large ring of guys and dolls around the tree looking at the horse, and furthermore he sees that Miss Phyllis Richie's eyes are all red and swollen as if she is weeping.

Now at this spectacle, Eddie Yokum's heart goes out to Miss Phyllis Richie, and he will walk right up to her as bold as a lion if he is not afraid of the horse, so he waits awhile longer, and pretty soon Miss Phyllis Richie leaves the group and goes across the grass to the jockey-house, and what Miss Phyllis Richie is going to the jockey-house for is to ask if Roy Snakes shows up, or if they find another darky jockey for her.

But it seems the answer is no both ways, and Miss Phyllis Richie is turning away looking most despondent when Eddie Yokum steps up to her and speaks to her as follows:

"Miss Richie," Eddie says, "if there is anything I can do to help you out in this situation, kindly so state. I know you despise me," he says, "but I will gladly lay down my life for you."

Well, at this, Miss Phyllis Richie stops and gazes at him awhile, and there is great sarcasm in her voice when she finally says:

"Why, the last time I see you, you are coloured. It is a pity you are not the same way now, or you might take Roy Snakes' place in this race. Good-day to you, Mr. Burglar, or I will call a Pinkerton."

She turns away, and goes back to where the old guy is walking the horse around, and Eddie Yokum follows her at a distance, but gets up in time to hear her telling Ike it is no use waiting on Roy Snakes, or anybody else, and to go ahead and declare Follow You out of the Gold Vase Steeple-chase.

Then she disappears in the crowd, but Eddie Yokum can see that she is very sad, and he is sad himself, and he gets to talking to Ike, and he asks him what about a guy blacking himself up and fooling Follow You into thinking he is a smoke, and Ike says it is undoubtedly a great idea.

"In fact," Ike says, "if I am younger, I will do it myself, just to save Miss Phyllis Richie, because I hear if she does not win this stake, she is going to marry Mr. Marshall Preston, and this is a sad fate for a young doll, to be sure. Between you and me, Mr. Marshall Preston is far from being all right."

Well, at this news, Eddie Yokum becomes greatly agitated, and he tells Ike to get him some cork, and he will ride Follow You, and old Ike is so delighted that he does not bother to ask Eddie Yokum if he is a good rider. He leaves Follow You in charge of a stable boy, and takes Eddie Yokum over to the secretary's office and announces him as a gentleman jockey from Delaware, who is willing to help Miss Phyllis Richie out of her predicament about a jockey, and when they suggest that Eddie Yokum seems to be as white as any of the other white guys who try to ride Follow You and fail, and Ike says Eddie is going to ride blackface, there is quite a looking up of the rules.

But there is nothing in the rules against such a thing, although an old guy in the office with a big white mouser says it seems quite irregular, and that he does not recall a similar case in fifty years of experience. However, he says the office is willing to establish a precedent in the case of such a great horse as Follow You, though he cannot figure what on earth becomes of Roy Snakes, or why the only other two coloured steeplechase jockeys in the East,

Washington and Lincoln, find it necessary to go to Aiken two days before this race.

He is still muttering about the matter when Ike takes Eddie Yokum to the jockey-house, and then Ike sends in to Frank Stevens' bar in the clubhouse and buys several bottles of liquor to get corks for Eddie to burn and black up with, although Ike personally drinks all the liquor himself.

Well, all the time Eddie Yokum is blacking up, he is saying every prayer he knows that Roy Snakes, or one of the other dinge jockeys appears to ride Follow You, but no such thing happens, and by and by Eddie is out in the Richie colours, and is as black as anything, and maybe blacker, and while Follow You gives him quite a snuffing over when Eddie approaches him, the horse seems satisfied he is dealing with a smoke, and afterwards some people claim this is a knock to the way Eddie smells.

No one will ever know what Eddie Yokum suffers when he is hoisted up on Follow You, and there is considerable criticism of his riding technique, as he does not seem to be sure which is the front end and which is the back end of a horse.

But by this time, Eddie is determined to go through with this proposition if he gets killed, and it looks as if he will, at that, although it does not look as if he will get killed any sooner than the Honourable Bertie Searles, who arrives at the course slightly mulled, and who insists on practising a few tricks he once observes at a rodeo in England, when the horses are going to the post, because the Honourable Bertie Searles thinks Miss Lola Ledare is in the grandstand watching him, and he warns her to be sure and take note of his fancy riding.

Now, the Honourable Bertie Searles is riding along next to Eddie Yokum, and he seems such a good-natured sort of guy that Eddie figures it may not be a bad idea to get a little advice from him, so he asks the Honourable Bertie Searles what are the rules of such a race, and what is the best thing for a guy who does not know much about it to do; and while the Honourable Bertie Searles is somewhat surprised at the question, especially from a smudge rider, he answers as follows:

"Why," he says, "all you do is to try and keep going. If you fall off your horse, do not worry, but just get back on again, and take the jump all over and keep going, unless your neck is broken. Personally, I generally let my horse, Trafalgar, do the thinking for me in a race, because Trafalgar is quite a thinker, and maybe your horse is a thinker, too. But," he says, "keep going."

The most astonished guy around at seeing Eddie Yokum on Follow You is undoubtedly Mr. Marshall Preston, who is riding his horse Sweep Forward, but he is no more astonished than Miss Phyllis Richie, who is sitting in a box in the grandstand with a party of friends from Baltimore, Md., and who is still weeping, thinking her horse is out of the race.

She stops weeping when she sees her colours on the track, and looks at the jockey-board to see who is riding her horse, but the name E. Yokum on the board means nothing to her, as she never hears Eddie's real name before, and she does not recognize him at first, and figures he is some new coloured jockey old Ike digs up at the last minute.

The horse players on the lawn and the bookies under the stand are also somewhat astonished, because there nobody ever hears of E. Yokum before, either, except maybe The Seldom Seen Kid, and Hot Horse Herbie, and Big Reds, and even they do not know Eddie in his make-up until they run down to the rail to watch the post parade, and Eddie Yokum tips them a large wink, although the reason Eddie tips them this wink is to squeeze a large tear out of his eye, because Eddie is so alarmed he is half crying, and only love sustains him in the saddle.

Well, when The Seldom Seen Kid and Hot Horse Herbie and Big Reds see who is on Follow You, and see Eddie's wink, they figure that there must be something very special doing in this race, and they start running around everywhere, hoping they may be able to raise a few bobs to bet on Follow You, but of course nobody is going to let them have a few bobs for any purpose, and they are greatly discouraged about the matter, when who do they run into but Miss Lola Ledare, who is not in the grandstand at all, as the Honourable Bertie Searles thinks, but is standing on the edge of the betting ring with some large coarse banknotes in her hand.

Naturally, when they see Miss Lola Ledare in possession of funds, they are greatly interested, and they surround her and ask her what seems to be troubling her, and Miss Lola Ledare speaks freely to them, as she is not aware of any coolness between them and her fiancée, Philly the Weeper, and what she speaks is as follows:

"Why," she says, "they do not allow ladies in the betting ring, and I am waiting here for some one to come along and bet this money for me on Sweep Forward, so your arrival is most timely. The bet is for Philly. He raises this money on some old family heirlooms that I never know he possesses, and he requests me to place it for him. Personally," she says, "I think the Honourable Bertie Searles will win this race on Trafalgar, because he tells me so himself, and I have half a notion to bet some of the money on him, only I am afraid of what Philly will say if Trafalgar does not come in."

Well, The Seldom Seen Kid takes the dough out of Miss Lola Ledare's hand, and says to her like this:

"Lola," he says, "it will be a privilege and a pleasure for me to do Philly the service of betting this money for him—and by the way, where is Philly?"

"Why," Lola says, "he asks me not to mention to anybody that he is present, but I know he will not mind you knowing. He is sitting away up in one corner of the grandstand all by himself. To tell the truth, Philly has become somewhat solitary of late, and I am commencing to get somewhat displeased with him, because I like sociable guys, like the Honourable Bertie Searles."

Well, The Seldom Seen Kid is somewhat surprised to find that he takes ten large C's off of Miss Lola Ledare, because he does not know there is this much money in the world, and he hurries into the ring and bets it all on Follow You and gets 6 to 5 for the money, as Follow You is favourite, even with somebody by the name of E. Yokum up, which shows what the public thinks of the horse, although with Roy Snakes riding, the price will be 7 to 10.

There is a ton of money for Sweep Forward at the last minute, and some very, very smart guys are betting on him, and furthermore there is a rumour that Sweep Forward has help in the race, which is a way of saying that some of the others will be trying to assist Sweep Forward to win, and there is also a rumour that Follow You is a stiff in the race, and this is why Roy Snakes is not riding; but one thing about a race-track, you can always hear anything, and the public sticks to Follow You, no matter what.

There are ten other horses in the Gold Vase, and there is money for all of them, including Trafalgar, although Trafalgar is 15 to 1, as nobody seems to care for the way the Honourable Bertie Searles is riding the horse going to the post, what with the Honourable Bertie Searles doing handstands in the saddle, and otherwise carrying on.

Now the Gold Vase Steeplechase is a race of about three miles, or about two and a half times around the course, and the horses have to make about nineteen jumps over hedges and a water jump, and everybody that knows about these matters will tell you that this is the toughest race in this country, especially with a big field of starters, and many things can happen in the race, including death. In fact, a steeplechaser rider is regarded as a very poor risk, indeed, by all insurance companies, although it is perhaps just as well that Eddie Yokum does not know this as he goes to the post.

But Eddie is smart enough to remember what the Honourable Bertie Searles tells him about letting the horse do the thinking, and it happens that Follow You is quite a thinker, indeed, and very experienced, so when the starter tells them to come on, Eddie just hangs on to Follow You's mane and lets him do as he feels best, and Follow You feels that it is best to go right to the front.

At least Eddie Yokum hangs on to Follow You's mane until the horse hits the first jump, when Mr. Marshall Preston, on Sweep Forward, comes out of the pack with a rush, and yells look out, and Eddie is looking out as Follow You jumps with Sweep Forward, and Eddie lets go the mane so he can look out better, and the next thing Eddie knows he is on the grass, and the rest of the field is going past him, and Follow You is standing there looking greatly surprised.

Well, there is a groan from the grandstand, for here is the public choice apparently out of the race before it really starts, but Eddie suddenly remembers what the Honourable Bertie Searles tells him about keeping going, and taking all the jumps, so he gets on his feet, and backs Follow You up against the fence and climbs on him and sends him at the jump again, and this time Eddie does not forget to hang on to the horse's mane.

But all this takes up some time, and the rest of the field is anyway half a mile ahead, but three horses go down at the second jump, and two more at the third, and at both these jumps, Eddie Yokum falls off Follow You as the horse is jumping, and the public is commencing to marvel about Follow You making every jump twice, and wondering if it is a handicap he is giving the others, or what.

Sweep Forward is out in front going easy, and fencing like a bird, with Mr. Marshall Preston looking very graceful in the saddle, and who is laying right close to him all the time but the Honourable Bertie Searles, on Trafalgar. The rest are strung out all along the course, and it looks like a parade more than anything else.

Well, the real tough jump on the course is the water jump in front of the grandstand, and they take this jump twice during the race, and the first time Eddie Yokum falls off Follow You into the water he is so long coming up that many customers think maybe he is drowned, and most of them hope he is, at that.

But one thing about Follow You, he never runs away when he loses his rider, but stands perfectly still until Eddie is on his back again, although Follow You is commencing to look very pained, especially when it appears to be a sure thing that he will be lapped by Sweep Forward and Trafalgar, anyway, before the race is over.

However, other horses keep going down at the various jumps, and at the end of the second mile, only Sweep Forward and Trafalgar, and a horse that is called Great Shakes, with a professional jockey by the name of Smithers up, and Follow You are left in the race, although of course you cannot say Follow You is really in the race because he is now almost a full mile to the rear, and Miss Phyllis Richie faints three different times in the grandstand, once out of dismay, and twice out of vexation.

It seems that Miss Phyllis Richie does not recognize Eddie Yokum even yet, but she can see that the guy on her horse does not have any great knack for riding, and she is annoyed no little, especially as everybody on the premises is now uniting in a Bronx cheer for Follow You and his jockey.

The way Eddie Yokum is riding Follow You when he is not falling off is really something remarkable, as he is all over the horse, and sometimes halfway under him, and when the Honourable Bertie Searles sees this exhibition, he gets sored up, because he figures Eddie is trying to show him up as a trick rider, although of course Eddie has no such idea whatever.

Now Trafalgar is never more than two lengths off Sweep Forward at any stage of the race, and anybody can see that the Honourable Bertie Searles has a great horse under him, and in fact it looks as if he can go to the front whenever he is ready, and when Great Shakes falls with Smithers at about the fourteenth jump, it is strictly a two-horse race, because by this time Eddie Yokum is in the water jump again, and, anyway, Follow You is getting pretty much fagged out, because the way the race figures, Follow You does twice as much work as any of the other horses, and he is carrying top weight of 175 pounds, at that, counting Eddie's 150 and the lead in his saddle slots.

In fact, Follow You is so fagged out that he is just able to jog along, and the jumps in the last mile are as tough for him as they are for Eddie, and in fact once when Eddie is stretched out on the grass after a jump, it looks as if Follow You wishes to lay down beside him.

Well, in the meantime, Mr. Marshall Preston on Sweep Forward and the Honourable Bertie Searles on Trafalgar, are tearing for the last jump neck and neck, because the Honourable Bertie Searles now makes his serious challenge, and the crowd is up and yelling and nobody even thinks of Eddie Yokum and Follow You plugging along away back yonder, except maybe Miss Phyllis Richie.

Sweep Forward and Trafalgar take off for the final jump

just like a team, and as Trafalgar jumps, Mr. Marshall Preston gives him a smack across the nose with his riding bat, which upsets Trafalgar no little, and in fact causes him to stumble and fall as he clears the jump, but not before the Honourable Bertie Searles can reach out almost in mid-air and tweak Mr. Marshall Preston's saddle pad in such a way that Sweep Forward falls, too, because naturally the Honourable Bertie Searles is slightly irked by Mr. Marshall Preston playing such a dirty trick on Trafalgar.

Well, Mr. Marshall Preston lets out a loud cry as Sweep Forward falls, because Mr. Marshall Preston finds himself pinned down under the horse with a broken leg, and he is in great pain at once, and while the Honourable Bertie Searles is not hurt, Trafalgar gets up and runs off so fast there is no chance that the Honourable Bertie Searles can catch him, and by and by along the course comes Eddie Yokum on Follow You, the only horse left in the race, with one jump to go.

Well, the Honourable Bertie Searles runs up the course, somewhat excited, and begins coaching Eddie Yokum, telling him to take it easy, and to bear a little to the left going over the jump to keep from landing on Mr. Marshall Preston and Sweep Forward, and Eddie tries to do as he is told, but Follow You is now a mighty weary horse, and for the first time in years he falls taking a hurdle, and Eddie finds himself on the turf alongside Mr. Marshall Preston, who stops groaning long enough to look at Eddie Yokum in great surprise, and to speak to him as follows:

"I am dying," Mr. Marshall Preston says. "Tell Miss Phyllis Richie that with my last breath I ask her forgiveness for getting Philly the Weeper to slug her jockey, Roy Snakes, and put him out of business. She will find him in Harlem. Tell her I am also sorry I put Washington and Lincoln, the only other jig jocks around, under contract and

141

send them away, but it is necessary for me to win this stake and enough in bets to pay my wife in South Dakota some back alimony I owe her."

And with this, Mr. Marshall Preston closes his eyes and starts groaning again, and Eddie Yokum remembers about the race, especially as the Honourable Bertie Searles is calling on him to get up, and be a man, and keep going, so Eddie gets up and starts looking around for Follow You, but Follow You is now standing with his head hanging down, and when Eddie climbs on him again, Follow You does not seem inclined for any further action, especially in the way of making another jump.

Well, here is a predicament, to be sure, and as Eddie has no previous experience with balky horses, he scarcely knows what to do, especially as Follow You will not respond to kind words, or to kicks in the stomach, which are advised by the Honourable Bertie Searles, and in fact what does Follow You do but sit down there in the middle of the course, and Eddie slides right off his tail.

Then Eddie runs around in front of Follow You to argue with him face to face, and maybe give him a good yanking by the head, and for the first time since the race starts, Follow You gets a good look at who is riding him, and it seems that between the perspiration that is running down Eddie's face from his efforts, and falling into the water jump a couple of times, he is now no longer a boogie, but mostly white, and Follow You is not only startled but greatly insulted.

He starts scrambling to his feet at once, and Eddie Yokum is just barely able to climb back on the horse by his mane before Follow You starts running, taking the last jump again in wonderful shape, and then tearing on down the home stretch to finish inside the time limit as the winner of the race, and all that keeps Follow You from continuing on around the course again is the fact that Eddie falls off of him plumb exhausted.

Well, the excitement over this is very great, as Follow You's victory saves the public's money, and they take Follow You to the judge's stand, and put a blanket of roses on him, and Eddie Yokum is also there, holding himself up by leaning against old Ike, when Miss Phyllis Richie comes running up and starts kissing the rest of the burnt cork off of Eddie's face right in front of everybody, and speaking to him as follows:

"Oh," she says, "I recognize you when you come out of the water jump the last time, and I say to myself, then and there, I know he will win, because I remember your wonderful ride at the fox hunt. I love you," she says.

Naturally, Eddie Yokum tells Miss Phyllis Richie that her love is reciprocated, and he does not mention to her that the ride she speaks of at the fox hunt is negotiated on a motorcycle, because at this time there is further excitement, as it seems The Seldom Seen Kid and Hot Horse Herbie and Big Reds find Philly the Weeper up in the grandstand, and take him out back and give him quite a going over for beating them out of their end of the reward money he collects for the fox hounds, and also remove from his person a batch of pawn-tickets for the jewellery and other valuables he collects at the Oriole Hunts Club and converts into cash to bet on Sweep Forward.

Philly the Weeper says Mr. Marshall Preston permits him to keep the jewellery on condition he leaves a few articles in Eddie Yokum's room, after making a business deal with Philly the Weeper to take care of Roy Snakes in return for Mr. Marshall Preston's kindness in not turning him over to the police when he finds him collecting the knick-knacks.

"Mr. Marshall Preston is a hard guy," Philly the Weeper says. "He tells me he starts out making love to Miss Phyllis

Richie only with the idea of conning her into withdrawing Follow You from this race, so he can put over a big betting coup. But her having to have a ziggaboo jock makes it easier for him. But only a very hard guy will attempt to use love for such a base purpose," Philly the Weeper says. "Can you imagine me trifling with the love of Miss Lola Ledare in such a fashion?"

But Miss Lola Ledare says she is not going to give such a scalawag as Philly the Weeper a chance to trifle with her love any more, anyway, as she is much fonder of the Honourable Bertie Searles; and The Seldom Seen Kid turns the pawn-tickets he takes off Philly the Weeper over to Eddie Yokum, along with ten C's to remove the articles from hock, although he does not mention the sum of money he wins on Follow You with the ten C's.

It comes out that Mr. Marshall Preston is not too badly hurt, after all, so everybody is happy all the way around; but naturally Eddie Yokum is happiest of all, and he is standing around after the races mentioning his happiness to Miss Phyllis Richie, when all of a sudden he is seen to turn quite pale, and out of a clear sky, and as tired as he is, he starts running, and a large guy is observed running after him.

It is some hours before Miss Phyllis Richie sees Eddie Yokum to kiss him again, and to inquire why he seems to be trying to avoid one of her oldest and dearest Baltimore friends, Mr. Barker.

8. A STORY GOES WITH IT

ONE night I am in a gambling joint in Miami watching the crap game and thinking what a nice thing it is, indeed, to be able to shoot craps without having to worry about losing your potatoes.

Many of the high shots from New York and Detroit and St. Louis and other cities are around the table, and there is quite some action in spite of the hard times. In fact, there is so much action that a guy with only a few bobs on him, such as me, will be considered very impolite to be pushing into this game, because they are packed in very tight around the table.

I am maybe three guys back from the table, and I am watching the game by standing on tiptoe peeking over their shoulders, and all I can hear is Goldie, the stick man, hollering money-money-money every time some guy makes a number, so I can see the dice are very warm indeed, and that the right betters are doing first-rate.

By and by a guy by the name of Guinea Joe, out of Trenton, picks up the dice and starts making numbers right and left, and I know enough about this Guinea Joe to know that when he starts making numbers anybody will be very foolish indeed not to follow his hand, although personally I am generally a wrong better against the dice, if I bet at all.

Now all I have in my pocket is a sawbuck, and the hotel stakes are coming up on me the next day, and I need this saw, but with Guinea Joe hotter than a forty-five it will be overlooking a big opportunity not to go along with him, so when he comes out on an eight, which is a very easy number for Joe to make when he is hot, I dig up my sawbuck, and slide it past the three guys in front of me to the table, and I say to Lefty Park, who is laying against the dice, as follows:

"I will take the odds, Lefty."

Well, Lefty looks at my sawbuck and nods his head, for Lefty is not such a guy as will refuse any bet, even though it is as modest as mine, and right away Goldie yells money-money-money, so there I am with twenty-two dollars.

Next Guinea Joe comes out on a nine, and naturally I take thirty to twenty for my sugar, because nine is nothing for Joe to make when he is hot. He makes the nine just as I figure, and I take two to one for my half a yard when he starts looking for a ten, and when he makes the ten I am right up against the table, because I am now a guy with means.

Well, the upshot of the whole business is that I finally find myself with three hundred bucks, and when it looks as if the dice are cooling off, I take out and back off from the table, and while I am backing off I am trying to look like a guy who loses all his potatoes, because there are always many wolves waiting around crap games and one thing and another in Miami this season, and what they are waiting for is to put the bite on anybody who happens to make a little scratch.

In fact, nobody can remember when the bite is as painful as it is in Miami this season, what with the unemployment situation among many citizens who come to Miami expecting to find work in the gambling joints, or around the race track. But almost as soon as these citizens arrive, the gambling joints are all turned off, except in spots, and the bookmakers are chased off the track and the mutuels put in, and the consequences are the suffering is most intense. It is not only intense among the visiting citizens, but it is quite intense among the Miami landlords, because naturally if a citizen is not working, nobody can expect him to pay any room rent, but the Miami landlords do not seem to understand this situation, and are very unreasonable about their room rent.

Anyway, I back through quite a crowd without anybody biting me, and I am commencing to figure I may escape altogether and get to my hotel and hide my dough before the news gets around that I win about five G's, which is what my winning is sure to amount to by the time the rumour reaches all quarters of the city.

Then, just as I am thinking I am safe, I find I am looking a guy by the name of Hot Horse Herbie in the face, and I can tell from Hot Horse Herbie's expression that he is standing there watching me for some time, so there is no use in telling him I am washed out in the game. In fact, I cannot think of much of anything to tell Hot Horse Herbie that may keep him from putting the bite on me for at least a few bobs, and I am greatly astonished when he does not offer to bite me at all, but says to me like this:

"Well," he says, "I am certainly glad to see you make such a nice score. I will be looking for you to-morrow at the track, and will have some big news for you."

Then he walks away from me and I stand there with my mouth open looking at him, as it is certainly a most unusual way for Herbie to act. It is the first time I ever knew Herbie to walk away from a chance to bite somebody, and I can scarcely understand such actions, for Herbie is such a guy as will not miss a bite, even if he does not need it.

He is a tall, thin guy, with a sad face and a long chin, and he is called Hot Horse Herbie because he nearly always has a very hot horse to tell you about. He nearly always has a horse that is so hot it is fairly smoking, a hot horse being a horse that cannot possibly lose a race unless it falls down dead, and while Herbie's hot horses often lose without falling down dead, this does not keep Herbie from coming up with others just as hot.

In fact, Hot Horse Herbie is what is called a hustler around the race tracks, and his business is to learn about these hot horses, or even just suspect about them, and then get somebody to bet on them, which is a very legitimate business indeed, as Herbie only collects a commission if the hot horses win, and if they do not win Herbie just keeps out of sight awhile from whoever he gets to bet on the hot horses. There are very few guys in this world who can keep out of sight better than Hot Horse Herbie, and especially from old Cap Duhaine, of the Pinkertons, who is always around pouring cold water on hot horses.

In fact, Cap Duhaine, of the Pinkertons, claims that guys such as Hot Horse Herbie are nothing but touts, and sometimes he heaves them off the race track altogether, but of course Cap Duhaine is a very unsentimental old guy and cannot see how such characters as Hot Horse Herbie add to the romance of the turf.

Anyway, I escape from the gambling joint with all my scratch on me, and hurry to my room and lock myself in for the night, and I do not show up in public until along about noon the next day, when it is time to go over to the coffee shop for my java. And of course by this time the news of my score is all over town, and many guys are taking dead aim at me.

But naturally I am now able to explain to them that I have to wire most of the three yards I win to Nebraska to save my father's farm from being seized by the sheriff, and while everybody knows I do not have a father, and that if I do have a father I will not be sending him money for such a thing as saving his farm, with times what they are in Miami, nobody is impolite enough to doubt my word except a guy by the name of Pottsville Legs, who wishes to see my receipts from the telegraph office when I explain to him why I cannot stake him to a double sawbuck.

I do not see Hot Horse Herbie until I get to the track, and he is waiting for me right inside the grand-stand gate, and as soon as I show up he motions me off to one side and says to me like this:

"Now," Herbie says, "I am very smart indeed about a certain race to-day. In fact," he says, "if any guy knowing what I know does not bet all he can rake and scrape together on a certain horse, such a guy ought to cut his own throat and get himself out of the way forever. What I know," Herbie says, "is enough to shake the foundations of this country if it gets out. Do not ask any questions," he says, "but get ready to bet all the sugar you win last night on this horse I am going to mention to you, and all I ask you in return is to bet fifty on me. And," Herbie says, "kindly do not tell me you leave your money in your other pants, because I know you do not have any other pants."

"Now, Herbie," I say, "I do not doubt your information, because I know you will not give out information unless it is well founded. But," I say, "I seldom stand for a tip, and as for betting fifty for you, you know I will not bet fifty even for myself if somebody guarantees me a winner. So I thank you, Herbie, just the same," I say, "but I must do without your tip," and with this I start walking away.

"Now," Herbie says, "wait a minute. A story goes with it," he says.

Well, of course this is a different matter entirely. I am such a guy as will always listen to a tip on a horse if a story goes with the tip. In fact, I will not give you a nickel for a tip without a story, but it must be a first-class story, and most horse players are the same way. In fact, there are very few horse players who will not listen to a tip if a story goes with it, for this is the way human nature is. So I turn and walk back to Hot Horse Herbie, and say to him like this:

"Well," I say, "let me hear the story, Herbie."

"Now," Herbie says, dropping his voice away down low, in case old Cap Duhaine may be around somewhere listening, "it is the third race, and the horse is a horse by the name of Never Despair. It is a boat race," Herbie says. "They are going to shoo in Never Despair. Everything else in the race is a cooler," he says.

"Well," I say, "this is just an idea, Herbie, and not a story."

"Wait a minute," Herbie says. "The story that goes with it is a very strange story indeed. In fact," he says, "it is such a story as I can scarcely believe myself, and I will generally believe almost any story, including," he says, "the ones I make up out of my own head. Anyway, the story is as follows:

"Never Despair is owned by an old guy by the name of Seed Mercer," Herbie says. "Maybe you remember seeing him around. He always wears a black slouch hat and grey whiskers," Herbie says, "and he is maybe a hundred years old, and his horses are very terrible horses indeed. In caft," Herbie says, "I do not remember seeing any more terrible horses in all the years I am around the track, and," Herbie says, "I wish to say I see some very terrible horses indeed.

"Now," Herbie says, "old Mercer has a grand-daughter who is maybe sixteen years old, come next grass, by the name of Lame Louise, and she is called Lame Louise because she is all crippled up from childhood by infantile what-is-this, and can scarcely navigate, and," Herbie says, "her being crippled up in such a way makes old Mercer feel very sad, for she is all he has in the world, except these terrible horses."

"It is a very long story, Herbie," I say, "and I wish to see Moe Shapoff about a very good thing in the first race."

"Never mind Moe Shapoff," Herbie says. "He will only tell you about a bum by the name of Zachary in the first race, and Zachary has no chance whatever. I make Your John a stand-out in the first," he says.

"Well," I say, "let us forget the first and get on with your story, although it is commencing to sound all mixed up to me."

"Now," Herbie says, "it not only makes old man Mercer very sad because Lame Louise is all crippled up, but," he says, "it makes many of the jockeys and other guys around the race track very sad, because," he says, "they know Lame Louise since she is so high, and she always has a smile for them, and especially for Jockey Scroon. In fact," Herbie says, "Jockey Scroon is even more sad about Lame Louise than old man Mercer, because Jockey Scroon loves Lame Louise."

"Why," I say, very indignant, "Jockey Scroon is nothing but a little burglar. Why," I say, "I see Jockey Scroon do things to horses I bet on that he will have to answer for on the Judgment Day, if there is any justice at such a time. Why," I say, "Jockey Scroon is nothing but a Gerald Chapman in his heart, and so are all other jockeys."

"Yes," Hot Horse Herbie says, "what you say is very, very true, and I am personally in favour of the electric chair for all jockeys, but," he says, "Jockey Scroon loves Lame Louise just the same, and is figuring on making her his ever-loving wife when he gets a few bobs together, which," Herbie says, "makes Louise eight to five in my line to be an old maid. Jockey Scroon rooms with me downtown," Herbie says, "and he speaks freely to me about his love for Louise. Furthermore," Herbie says, "Jockie Scroon is personally not a bad little guy, at that, although of course being a jockey he is sometimes greatly misunderstood by the public.

"Anyway," Hot Horse Herbie says, "I happen to go home early last night before I see you at the gambling joint, and I hear voices coming out of my room, and naturally I pause outside the door to listen, because for all I know it may be the landlord speaking about the room rent, although," Herbie says, "I do not figure my landlord to be much worried at this time because I see him sneak into my room a few days before and take a lift at my trunk to make sure I have belongings in the same, and it happens I nail the trunk to the floor beforehand, so not being able to lift it, the landlord is bound to figure me a guy with property.

"These voices," Herbie says, "are mainly soprano voices, and at first I think Jockey Scroon is in there with some dolls, which is by no means permissible in my hotel, but, after listening awhile, I discover they are the voices of young boys, and I make out that these boys are nothing but jockeys, and they are the six jockeys who are riding in the third race, and they are fixing up this race to be a boat race, and to shoo in Never Despair, which Jockey Scroon is riding.

"And," Hot Horse Herbie says, "the reason they are fixing up this boat race is the strangest part of the story. It seems," he says, "that Jockey Scroon hears old man Mercer talking about a great surgeon from Europe who is a shark on patching up cripples such as Lame Louise, and who just arrives at Palm Beach to spend the winter, and old man Mercer is saying how he wishes he has dough enough to take Lame Louise to this guy so he can operate on her, and maybe make her walk good again.

"But of course," Herbie says, "it is well known to one and all that old man Mercer does not have a quarter, and that he has no way of getting a quarter unless one of his terrible horses accidentally wins a purse. So," Herbie says, "it seems these jockeys get to talking it over among themselves, and they figure it will be a nice thing to let old man Mercer win a purse such as the thousand bucks that goes with the third race to-day, so he can take Lame Louise to Palm Beach, and now you have a rough idea of what is coming off.

"Furthermore," Herbie says, "these jockeys wind up their meeting by taking a big oath among themselves that they will not tell a living soul what is doing so nobody will bet on Never Despair, because," he says, "these little guys are smart enough to see if there is any betting on such a horse there may be a very large squawk afterwards. And," he says, "I judge they keep their oath because Never Despair is twenty to one in the morning line, and I do not hear a whisper about him, and you have the tip all to yourself."

"Well," I say, "so what?" For this story is now commencing to make me a little tired, especially as I hear the bell for the first race, and I must see Moe Shapoff.

"Why," Hot Horse Herbie says, "so you bet every nickel you can rake and scrape together on Never Despair, including the twenty you are to bet for me for giving you this tip and the story that goes with it."

"Herbie," I say, "it is a very interesting story indeed, and also very sad, but," I say, "I am sorry it is about a horse Jockey Scroon is to ride, because I do not think I will ever bet on anything Jockey Scroon rides if they pay off in advance. And," I say, "I am certainly not going to bet twenty for you or anybody else."

"Well," Hot Horse Herbie says, "I will compromise with you for a pound note, because I must have something going for me on this boat race."

So I give Herbie a fiver, and the chances are this is about as strong as he figures from the start, and I forget all about his tip and the story that goes with it, because while I enjoy a story with a tip, I feel that Herbie overdoes this one.

Anyway, no handicapper alive can make Never Despair win the third race off the form, because this race is at six furlongs, and there is a barrel of speed in it, and anybody can see that old man Mercer's horse is away over his head. In fact, The Dancer tells me that any one of the other five horses in this race can beat Never Despair doing anything from playing hockey to putting the shot, and everybody else must think the same thing because Never Despair goes to forty to one.

Personally, I like a horse by the name of Loose Living, which is a horse owned by a guy by the name of Bill Howard, and I hear Bill Howard is betting plenty away on his horse, and any time Bill Howard is betting away on his horse a guy will be out of his mind not to bet on this horse, too, as Bill Howard is very smart indeed. Loose Living is two to one in the first line, but by and by I judge the money Bill Howard bets away commences to come back to the track, and Loose Living winds up seven to ten, and while I am generally not a seven-to-ten guy, I can see that here is a proposition I cannot overlook.

So, naturally, I step up to the mutuel window and invest in Loose Living. In fact, I invest everything I have on me in the way of scratch, amounting to a hundred and ten bucks, which is all I have left after taking myself out of the hotel stakes and giving Hot Horse Herbie the finnif, and listening to what Moe Shapoff has to say about the first race, and also getting beat a snoot in the second.

When I first step up to the window, I have no idea of betting all my scratch on Loose Living, but while waiting in line there I get to thinking what a cinch Loose Living is, and how seldom such an opportunity comes into a guy's life, so I just naturally set it all in.

A STORY GOES WITH IT

Well, this is a race which will be remembered by one and all to their dying day, as Loose Living beats the barrier a step, and is two lengths in front before you can say Jack Robinson, with a third by the name of Callipers second by maybe half a length, and with the others bunched except Never Despair, and where is Never Despair but last, where he figures.

Now any time Loose Living busts on top there is no need worrying any more about him, and I am thinking I better get in line at the pay-off window right away, so I will not have to wait long to collect my sugar. But I figure I may as well stay and watch the race, although personally I am never much interested in watching races. I am interested only in how a race comes out.

As the horses hit the turn into the stretch, Loose Living is just breezing, and anybody can see that he is going to laugh his way home from there. Callipers is still second, and a thing called Goose Pimples is third, and I am surprised to see that Never Despair now struggles up to fourth with Jockey Scroon belting away at him with his bat quite earnestly. Furthermore, Never Despair seems to be running very fast, though afterwards I figure this may be because the others are commencing to run very slow.

Anyway, a very strange spectacle now takes place in the stretch, as all of a sudden Loose Living seems to be stopping, as if he is waiting for a street cab, and what is all the more remarkable Callipers and Goose Pimples also seem to be hanging back, and the next thing anybody knows, here comes Jockey Scroon on Never Despair sneaking through on the rail, and personally it looks to me as if the jock on Callipers moves over to give Jockey Scroon plenty of elbow room, but of course the jock on Callipers may figure Jockey Scroon has diphtheria, and does not wish to catch it.

Loose Living is out in the middle of the track, anyway, so

he does not have to move over. All Loose Living has to do is to keep on running backwards as he seems to be doing from the top of the stretch, to let Jockey Scroon go past on Never Despair to win the heat by a length.

Well, the race is practically supernatural in many respects, and the judges are all upset over it, and they haul all the jocks up in the stand and ask them many questions, and not being altogether satisfied with the answers, they ask these questions over several times. But all the jocks will say is that Never Despair sneaks past them very unexpectedly indeed, while Jockey Scroon, who is a pretty fresh duck at that, wishes to know if he is supposed to blow a horn when he is slipping through a lot of guys sound asleep.

But the judges are still not satisfied, so they go prowling around investigating the betting, because naturally when a boat race comes up there is apt to be some reason for it, such as the betting, but it seems that all the judges find is that one five-dollar win ticket is sold on Never Despair in the mutuels, and they cannot learn of a dime being bet away on the horse. So there is nothing much the judges can do about the proposition, except give the jocks many hard looks, and the jocks are accustomed to hard looks from the judges, anyway.

Personally, I am greatly upset by this business, especially when I see that Never Despair pays $86.34, and for two cents I will go right up in the stand and start hollering copper on these little Jesse Jameses for putting on such a boat race and taking all my hard-earned potatoes away from me, but before I have time to do this, I run into The Dancer, and he tells me that Dedicate in the next race is the surest thing that ever goes to the post, and at five to one, at that. So I have to forget everything while I bustle about to dig up a few bobs to bet on Dedicate, and when Dedicate is beat a whisker, I have to do some more bustling to dig up a few bobs to bet on Vesta in the fifth, and by this time the third race is such ancient history that nobody cares what happens in it.

It is nearly a week before I see Hot Horse Herbie again, and I figure he is hiding out on everybody because he has this dough he wins off the fiver I give him, and personally I consider him a guy with no manners not to be kicking back the fin, at least. But before I can mention the fin, Herbie gives me a big hello, and says to me like this:

"Well," he says, "I just see Jockey Scroon, and Jockey Scroon just comes back from Palm Beach, and the operation is a big success, and Lame Louise will walk as good as anybody again, and old Mercer is tickled silly. But," Herbie says, "do not say anything out loud, because the judges may still be trying to find out what comes off in the race."

"Herbie," I say, very serious, "do you mean to say the story you tell me about Lame Louise, and all this and that, the other day is on the level?"

"Why," Herbie says, "certainly it is on the level, and I am sorry to hear you do not take advantage of my information. But," he says, "I do not blame you for not believing my story, because it is a very long story for anybody to believe. It is not such a story," Herbie says, "as I will tell to anyone if I expect them to believe it. In fact," he says, "it is so long a story that I do not have the heart to tell it to anybody else but you, or maybe I will have something running for me on the race.

"But," Herbie says, "never mind all this. I will be plenty smart about a race to-morrow. Yes," Herbie says, "I will be wiser than a treeful of owls, so be sure and see me if you happen to have any coconuts."

"There is no danger of me seeing you," I say, very sad, because I am all sorrowed up to think that the story he tells me is really true. "Things are very terrible with me at this time," I say, "and I am thinking maybe you can hand me back my finnif, because you must do all right for yourself with the fiver you have on Never Despair at such a price."

Now a very strange look comes over Hot Horse Herbie's face, and he raises his right hand, and says to me like this:

"I hope and trust I drop down dead right here in front of you," Herbie says, "if I bet a quarter on the horse. It is true," he says, "I am up at the window to buy a ticket on Never Despair, but the guy who is selling the tickets is a friend of mine by the name of Heeby Rosenbloom, and Heeby whispers to me that Big Joe Gompers, the guy who owns Callipers, just bets half a hundred on his horse, and," Herbie says, "I know Joe Gompers is such a guy as will not bet half a hundred on anything he does not get a Federal Reserve guarantee with it.

"Anyway," Herbie says, "I get to thinking about what a bad jockey this Jockey Scroon is, which is very bad indeed, and," he says, "I figure that even if it is a boat race it is no even-money race they can shoo him in, so I buy a ticket on Callipers."

"Well," I say, "somebody buys one five-dollar ticket on Never Despair, and I figure it can be nobody but you."

"Why," Hot Horse Herbie says, "do you not hear about this? Why," he says, "Cap Duhaine, of the Pinkertons, traces this ticket and finds it is bought by a guy by the name of Steve Harter, and the way this guy Harter comes to buy it is very astonishing. It seems," Herbie says, "that this Harter is a tourist out of Indiana who comes to Miami for the sunshine, and who loses all his dough but six bucks against the faro bank at Hollywood.

"At the same time," Herbie says, "the poor guy gets a telegram from his ever-loving doll back in Indiana saying she no longer wishes any part of him.

"Well," Herbie says, "between losing his dough and his

158

doll, the poor guy is practically out of his mind, and he figures there is nothing left for him to do but knock himself off.

"So," Herbie says, "this Harter spends one of his six bucks to get to the track, figuring to throw himself under the feet of the horses in the first race and let them kick him to a jelly. But he does not get there until just as the third race is coming up and," Herbie says, "he sees this name 'Never Despair', and he figures it may be a hunch, so he buys himself a ticket with his last fiver. Well, naturally," Herbie says, "when Never Despair pops down, the guy forgets about letting the horses kick him to a jelly, and he keeps sending his dough along until he runs nothing but a nubbin into six G's on the day.

"Then," Herbie says, "Cap Duhaine finds out that the guy, still thinking of Never Despair, calls his ever-loving doll on the phone, and finds she is very sorry she sends him the wire and that she really loves him more than somewhat, especially," Herbie says, "when she finds out about the six G's. And the last anybody hears of the matter, this Harter is on his way home to get married, so Never Despair does quite some good in this wicked old world, after all.

"But," Herbie says, "let us forget all this, because to-morrow is another day. To-morrow," he says, "I will tell you about a thing that goes in the fourth which is just the same as wheat in the bin. In fact," Hot Horse Herbie says, "if it does not win, you can never speak to me again."

"Well," I say, as I start to walk away, "I am not interested in any tip at this time."

"Now," Herbie says, "wait a minute. A story goes with it."

"Well," I say, coming back to him, "let me hear the story."

9. BROADWAY COMPLEX

IT is along towards four o'clock one morning, and I am
sitting in Mindy's restaurant on Broadway with Ambrose
Hammer, the newspaper scribe, enjoying a sturgeon sandwich, which is wonderful brain food, and listening to Ambrose tell me what is wrong with the world, and I am somewhat discouraged by what he tells me, for Ambrose is such
a guy as is always very pessimistic about everything.

He is especially very pessimistic about the show business,
as Ambrose is what is called a dramatic critic, and he has to
go around nearly every night and look at the new plays
that people are always putting in the theatres, and I judge
from what Ambrose says that this is a very great hardship,
and that he seldom gets much pleasure out of life.

Furthermore, I judge from what Ambrose tells me that
there is no little danger in being a dramatic critic, because it
seems that only a short time before this he goes to a play
that is called Never-Never, and Ambrose says it is a very
bad play, indeed, and he so states in his newspaper, and in
fact Ambrose states in his newspaper that the play smells in
nine different keys, and that so does the acting of the leading
man, a guy by the name of Fergus Appleton.

Well, the next day Ambrose runs into this Fergus
Appleton in front of the Hotel Astor, and what does Fergus
Appleton do but haul off and belt Ambrose over the noggin
with a cane, and ruin a nice new fall derby for Ambrose, and
when Ambrose puts in an expense account to his newspaper
for this kady they refuse to pay it, so Ambrose is out four
bobs.

BROADWAY COMPLEX

And anyway, Ambrose says, the theatregoing public never appreciates what a dramatic critic does for it, because it seems that even though he tips the public off that Never-Never is strictly a turkey, it is a great success, and, moreover, Fergus Appleton is now going around with a doll who is nobody but Miss Florentine Fayette, the daughter of old Hannibal Fayette.

And anybody will tell you that old Hannibal Fayette is very, very, very rich, and has a piece of many different propositions, including the newspaper that Ambrose Hammer works for, although of course at the time Ambrose speaks of Fergus Appleton's acting, he has no idea Fergus is going to wind up going around with Miss Florentine Fayette.

So Ambrose says the chances are his newspaper will give him the heave-o as soon as Fergus Appleton gets the opportunity to drop the zing in on him, but Ambrose says he does not care a cuss as he is writing a play himself that will show the theatre-going public what a real play is.

Well, Ambrose is writing this play ever since I know him, which is a matter of several years, and he tells me about it so often that I can play any part in it myself with a little practice, and he is just getting around to going over his first act with me again when in comes a guy by the name of Cecil Earl, who is what is called a master of ceremonies at the Golden Slipper night club.

Personally, I never see Cecil Earl but once or twice before in my life, and he always strikes me as a very quiet and modest young guy, for a master of ceremonies, and I am greatly surprised at the way he comes in, as he is acting very bold and aggressive towards one and all, and is speaking out loud in a harsh, disagreeable tone of voice, and in general is acting like a guy who is looking for trouble, which is certainly no way for a master of ceremonies to act.

But of course if a guy is looking for trouble on Broadway along towards four o'clock in the morning, anybody will tell you that the right address is nowhere else but Mindy's, because at such an hour many citizens are gathered there, and are commencing to get a little cross wondering where they are going to make a scratch for the morrow's operations, such as playing the horses.

It is a sure thing that any citizen who makes his scratch before four o'clock in the morning is at home getting his rest, so he will arise fully refreshed for whatever the day may bring forth, and also to avoid the bite he is apt to encounter in Mindy's from citizens who do not make a scratch.

However, the citizens who are present the morning I am speaking of do not pay much attention to Cecil Earl when he comes in, as he is nothing but a tall, skinny young guy, with slick black hair, such as you are apt to see anywhere along Broadway at any time, especially standing in front of theatrical booking offices. In fact, to look at Cecil you will bet he is maybe a saxophone player, as there is something about him that makes you think of a saxophone player right away and, to tell the truth, Cecil can tootle a pretty fair sax, at that, if the play happens to come up.

Well, Cecil sits down at a table where several influential citizens are sitting, including Nathan Detroit, who runs the crap game, and Big Nig, the crap shooter, and Regret, the horse player, and Upstate Red, who is one of the best faro bank players in the world whenever he can find a faro bank and something to play it with, and these citizens are discussing some very serious matters, when out of a clear sky Cecil ups and speaks to them as follows:

"Listen," Cecil says, "if youse guys do not stop making so much noise, I may cool you all off."

Well, naturally, this is most repulsive language to use to

such influential citizens, and furthermore it is very illiterate to say youse, so without changing the subject Nathan Detroit reaches out and picks up an order for ham and eggs, Southern style, that Charley, the waiter, just puts in front of Upstate Red, and taps Cecil on the onion with same.

It is unfortunate for Cecil that Nathan Detroit does not remove the ham and eggs, Southern style, from the platter before tapping Cecil with the order, because it is a very hard platter, and Cecil is knocked as stiff as a plank, and maybe stiffer, and it becomes necessary to summon old Doctor Moggs to bring him back to life.

Well, of course none of us know that Cecil is at the moment Jack Legs Diamond, or Mad Dog Coll, or some other very tough gorill, and in fact this does not come out until Ambrose Hammer later starts in investigating the strange actions of Cecil Earl, and then Nathan Detroit apologizes to Cecil, and also to the chef in Mindy's for treating an order of ham and eggs, Southern style, so disrespectfully.

It comes out that Cecil is subject to spells of being somebody else besides Cecil Earl, and Ambrose Hammer gives us a very long explanation of this situation, only Ambrose finally becomes so scientific that nobody can keep cases on him. But we gather in a general way from what Ambrose says that Cecil Earl is very susceptible to suggestion from anything he reads, or is told.

In fact, Ambrose says he is the most susceptible guy of this kind he ever meets up with in his life, and it seems that when he is going to Harvard College, which is before he starts in being a dramatic critic, Ambrose makes quite a study of these matters.

Personally, I always claim that Cecil Earl is a little screwy, or if he is not screwy that he will do very well as a pinch-hitter until a screwy guy comes to bat, but Ambrose Hammer says no. Ambrose says it is true that Cecil may be bobbing a trifle, but that he is by no means entirely off his nut. Ambrose says that Cecil only has delusions of grandeur, and complexes, and I do not know what all else, but Ambrose says it is 9 to 10 and take your pick whether Cecil is a genius or a daffydill.

Ambrose says that Cecil is like an actor playing a different part every now and then, only Cecil tries to live every part he plays, and Ambrose claims that if we have actors with as much sense as Cecil in playing parts, the show business will be a lot better off. But of course Ambrose cares very little for actors since Fergus Appleton ruins his kady.

Well, the next time I see Cecil he comes in Mindy's again, and this time it seems he is Jack Dempsey, and while ordinarily nobody will mind him being Jack Dempsey, or even Gene Tunney, although he is not the type for Gene Tunney, Cecil takes to throwing left hooks at citizens' chins, so finally Sam the Singer gets up and lets a right hand go inside a left hook, and once more Cecil folds up like an old accordion.

When I speak of this to Ambrose Hammer, he says that being Jack Dempsey is entirely a false complex for Cecil, brought on mainly by Cecil taking a few belts at the Golden Slipper liquor during the evening. In fact, Ambrose says this particular complex does not count. But I notice that after this Cecil is never anybody very brash when he is around Mindy's.

Sometimes he is somebody else besides Cecil Earl for as long as a week at a stretch, and in fact once he is Napoleon for two whole weeks, but Ambrose Hammer says this is nothing. Ambrose says he personally knows guys who are Napoleon all their lives. But of course Ambrose means that these guys are only Napoleons in their own minds. He says that the only difference between Cecil and them is that

BROADWAY COMPLEX

Cecil's complex breaks out on him in public, while the other guys are Napoleons only in their own bedrooms.

Personally, I think such guys are entitled to be locked up in spots with high walls around and about, but Ambrose seems to make nothing much of it, and anyway this Cecil Earl is as harmless as a bag of marshmallows, no matter who he is being.

One thing I must say for Cecil Earl, he is nearly always an interesting guy to talk to, because he nearly always has a different personality, and in fact the only time he is uninteresting is when he is being nobody but Cecil Earl. Then he is a very quiet guy with a sad face and he is so bashful and retiring that you will scarcely believe he is the same guy who goes around all one week being Mussolini in his own mind.

Now I wish to say that Cecil Earl does not often go around making any public display of these spells of his, except when the character calls for a display, such as the time he is George Bernard Shaw, and in fact unless you know him personally you may sometimes figure him just a guy sitting back in a corner somewhere with nothing whatever on his mind, and you will never even suspect that you are in the presence of J. Pierpont Morgan studying out a way to make us all rich.

It gets so that nobody resents Cecil being anything he pleases, except once when he is Senator Huey Long, and once when he is Hitler, and makes the mistake of wandering down on the lower East Side and saying so. In fact, it gets so everybody along Broadway puts in with him and helps him be whoever he is, as much as possible, although I always claim he has a bad influence on some citizens, for instance Regret, the horse player.

It seems that Regret catches a complex off of Cecil Earl one day, and for twenty-four hours he is Pittsburgh Phil, the race track plunger, and goes overboard with every bookie down at Belmont Park and has to hide out for some time before he can get himself straightened out.

Now Cecil Earl is a good master of ceremonies in a night club, if you care for masters of ceremonies, a master of ceremonies in a night club being a guy who is supposed to make cute cracks, and to introduce any celebrities who happen to be sitting around the joint, such as actors and prominent merchants, so the other customers can give them a big hand, and this is by no means an easy job, as sometimes a master of ceremonies may overlook a celebrity, and the celebrity becomes terribly insulted.

But it seems that Cecil Earl is smart enough to introduce all the people in the Golden Slipper every night and call for a big hand for them, no matter who they are, so nobody can get insulted, although one night he introduces a new head waiter, thinking he is nothing but a customer, and the head waiter is somewhat insulted, at that, and threatens to quit, because he claims being introduced in a night club is no boost for him.

Anyway, Cecil gets a nice piece of money for being master of ceremonies at the Golden Slipper, and when he is working there his complexes do not seem to bother him very much, and he is never anybody more serious than Harry Richman or Mort Downey. And it is at the Golden Slipper that he meets this guy, Fergus Appleton, and Miss Florentine Fayette.

Now Miss Florentine Fayette is a tall, slim, black-haired doll, and so beautiful she is practically untrue, but she has a kisser that never seems to relax, and furthermore she never seems much interested in anything whatever. In fact, if Miss Florentine Fayette's papa does not have so many cucumbers, I will say she is slightly dumb, but for all I know it may be against the law to say a doll whose papa has all these cucumbers is dumb. So I will only say that she does not strike me as right bright.

She is a great hand for going around night clubs and sitting there practically unconscious for hours at a time, and always this Fergus Appleton is with her, and before long it gets around that Fergus Appleton wishes to make Miss Florentine Fayette his ever-loving wife, and everybody admits that it will be a very nice score, indeed, for an actor.

Personally, I see nothing wrong with this situation because, to tell you the truth, I will just naturally love to make Miss Florentine Fayette my own ever-loving wife if her papa's cucumbers go with it, but of course Ambrose Hammer does not approve of the idea of her becoming Fergus Appleton's wife, because Ambrose can see how it may work out to his disadvantage.

This Fergus Appleton is a fine-looking guy of maybe forty, with iron-grey hair that makes him appear very romantic, and he is always well dressed in spats and one thing and another, and he smokes cigarettes in a holder nearly a foot long, and wears a watch on one wrist and a slave bracelet on the other, and a big ring on each hand, and sometimes a monocle in one eye, although Ambrose Hammer claims that this is strictly the old ackamarackuss.

There is no doubt that Fergus Appleton is a very chesty guy, and likes to pose around in public places, but I see maybe a million guys like him in my time on Broadway, and not all of them are actors, so I do not hate him for his posing, or for his slave bracelet, or the monocle either, although naturally I consider him out of line in busting my friend Ambrose Hammer's new derby, and I promise Ambrose that the first time Fergus Appleton shows up in a new derby, or even an old one, I will see that somebody busts it, if I have to do it myself.

The only thing wrong I see about Fergus Appleton is that

he is a smart-Alecky guy, and when he first finds out about Cecil Earl's complexes he starts working on them to amuse the guys and dolls who hang out around the Golden Slipper with him and Miss Florentine Fayette.

Moreover, it seems that somehow Cecil Earl is very susceptible, indeed, to Fergus Appleton's suggestions, and for a while Fergus Appleton makes quite a sucker of Cecil Earl.

Then all of a sudden Fergus Appleton stops making a sucker of Cecil, and the next thing anybody knows Fergus Appleton is becoming quite pally with Cecil, and I see them around Mindy's, and other late spots after the Golden Slipper closes, and sometimes Miss Florentine Fayette is with them, although Cecil Earl is such a guy as does not care much for the society of dolls, and in fact is very much embarrassed when they are around, which is most surprising conduct for a master of ceremonies in a night club, as such characters are usually pretty fresh with dolls.

But of course even the freshest master of ceremonies is apt to be a little bashful when such a doll as Miss Florentine Fayette is around, on account of her papa having so many cucumbers, and when she is present Cecil Earl seldoms opens his trap, but just sits looking at her and letting Fergus Appleton do all the gabbing, which suits Fergus Appleton fine, as he does not mind hearing himself gab, and in fact loves it.

Sometimes I run into just Cecil Earl and Fergus Appleton, and generally they have their heads close together, and are talking low and serious, like two business guys with a large deal coming up between them.

Furthermore I can see that Cecil Earl is looking very mysterious and solemn himself, so I figure that maybe they are doping out a new play together and that Cecil is acting one of the parts, and whatever it is they are doing I consider it quite big-hearted of Fergus Appleton to take such a friendly interest in Cecil.

But somehow Ambrose Hammer does not like it. In fact, Ambrose Hammer speaks of the matter at some length to me, and says to me like this:

"It is unnatural," he says. "It is unnatural for a guy like Fergus Appleton, who is such a guy as never has a thought in the world for anybody but himself, to be playing the warm for a guy like Cecil Earl. There is something wrong in this business, and," Ambrose says, "I am going to find out what it is."

Well, personally I do not see where it is any of Ambrose Hammer's put-in even if there is something wrong, but Ambrose is always poking his beezer into other people's business, and he starts watching Cecil and Fergus Appleton with great interest whenever he happens to run into them.

Finally it comes an early Sunday morning, and Ambrose Hammer and I are in Mindy's as usual, when in comes Cecil Earl all alone, with a book under one arm. He sits down at a table in a corner booth all by himself and orders a western sandwich and starts in to read his book, and nothing will do Ambrose Hammer but for us to go over and talk to Cecil.

When he sees us coming, he closes his book, and drops it in his lap and gives us a very weak hello. It is the first time we see him alone in quite a spell, and finally, Ambrose Hammer asks where is Fergus Appleton, although Ambrose really does not care where he is, unless it happens to turn out that he is in a pesthouse suffering from smallpox.

Cecil says Fergus Appleton has to go over to Philadelphia on business over the week-end, and then Ambrose asks Cecil where Miss Florentine Fayette is, and Cecil says he does not know but supposes she is home.

"Well," Ambrose Hammer says, "Miss Florentine Fayette is certainly a beautiful doll, even if she does look a little bit colder than I like them, but," he says, "what she sees in such a pish-tush as Fergus Appleton I do not know."

Now at this Cecil Earl busts right out crying, and naturally Ambrose Hammer and I are greatly astonished at such an exhibition, because we do not see any occasion for tears, and personally I am figuring on taking it on the Dan O'Leary away from there before somebody gets to thinking we do Cecil some great wrong, when Cecil speaks as follows:

"I love her," Cecil says. "I love her with all my heart and soul. But she belongs to my best friend. For two cents I will take this dagger that Fergus gives me and end it all, because life is not worth living without Miss Florentine Fayette."

And with this Cecil Earl outs with a big long stabber, which is a spectacle that is most disquieting to me as I know such articles are against the law in this man's town. So I make Cecil put it right back in his pocket and while I am doing this Ambrose Hammer reaches down beside Cecil and grabs the book Cecil is reading, and while Cecil is still sobbing Ambrose looks this volume over.

It turns out to be a book called The Hundred-Per-Cent-Perfect Crime, but what interests Ambrose Hammer more than anything else is a lead-pencil drawing on one of the blank pages in the front part of the book. Afterwards Ambrose sketches this drawing out for me as near as he can remember it on the back of one of Mindy's menu cards, and it looks to me like the drawing of the ground floor of a small house, with a line on one side on which is written the word Menahan, and Ambrose says he figures this means a street.

But in the meantime Ambrose tries to soothe Cecil Earl and to get him to stop crying, and when Cecil finally does dry up he sees Ambrose has his book, and he makes a grab for it and creates quite a scene until he gets it back.

Personally, I cannot make head or tail of the sketch that

Ambrose draws for me, and I cannot see that there is anything to it anyway, but Ambrose seems to regard it as of some importance.

Well, I do not see Ambrose Hammer for several days, but I am hearing strange stories of him being seen with Cecil Earl in the afternoons when Fergus Appleton is playing matinees in Never-Never, and early in the evenings when Fergus Appleton is doing his night performances, and I also hear that Ambrose always seems to be talking very earnestly to Cecil Earl, and sometimes throwing his arms about in a most excited manner.

Then one morning Ambrose Hammer looks me up again in Mindy's, and he is smiling a very large smile, as if he is greatly pleased with something, which is quite surprising as Ambrose Hammer is seldom pleased with anything. Finally he says to me like this:

"Well," Ambrose says, "I learn the meaning of the drawing in Cecil Earl's book. It is the plan of a house on Menahan street, away over in Brooklyn. And the way I learn this is very, very clever, indeed," Ambrose says. "I stake a chambermaid to let me into Fergus Appleton's joint in the Dazzy apartments, and what do I find there just as I expect but a letter from a certain number on this street?"

"Why," I say to Ambrose Hammer, "I am greatly horrified by your statement. You are nothing but a burglar, and if Fergus Appleton finds this out he will turn you over to the officers of the law, and you will lose your job and everything else."

"No," Ambrose says, "I will not lose my job, because old Hannibal Fayette is around the office yesterday raising an awful row about his daughter wishing to marry an actor, and saying he will give he does not know what if anybody can bust this romance up. The chances are," Ambrose says, "he will make me editor in chief of the paper, and then I will can a lot of guys I do not like. Fergus Appleton is to meet Cecil Earl here this morning, and in the meantime I will relate the story to you."

But before Ambrose can tell me the story, in comes Fergus Appleton, and Miss Florentine Fayette is with him, and they sit down at a table not far from us, and Fergus Appleton looks around and sees Ambrose and gives him a terrible scowl. Furthermore, he says something to Miss Florentine Fayette, and she looks at Ambrose, too, but she does not scowl or anything else, but only looks very dead-pan.

Fergus Appleton is in evening clothes and has on his monocle, and Miss Florentine Fayette is wearing such a gown that anybody can see how beautiful she is, no matter if her face does not have much expression. They are sitting there without much conversation passing between them, when all of a sudden in walks Cecil Earl, full of speed and much excited.

He comes in with such a rush that he almost flattens Regret, the horse player, who is on his way out, and Regret is about to call him a dirty name when he sees a spectacle that will always be remembered in Mindy's, for Cecil Earl walks right over to Miss Florentine Fayette as she is sitting there beside Fergus Appleton, and without saying as much as boo to Fergus Appleton, Cecil grabs Miss Florentine Fayette up in his arms with surprising strength and gives her a big sizzling kiss, and says to her like this:

"Florentine," he says, "I love you."

Then he squeezes her to his bosom so tight that it looks as if he is about to squeeze her right out through the top of her gown like squeezing toothpaste out of a tube, and says to her again, as follows:

"I love you. Oh, how I love you."

Well, at first Fergus Appleton is so astonished at this proposition that he can scarcely stir, and the chances are he cannot believe his eyes. Furthermore, many other citizens who are present partaking of their Bismarck herring, and one thing and another, are also astonished, and they are commencing to think that maybe Cecil Earl is having a complex about being King Kong, when Fergus Appleton finally gets to his feet and speaks in a loud tone of voice as follows:

"Why," Fergus Appleton says, "you are nothing but a scurvy fellow, and unless you unhand my fiancée, the chances are I will annihilate you."

Naturally, Fergus Appleton is somewhat excited, and in fact he is so excited that he drops his monocle to the floor, and it breaks into several pieces. At first he seems to have some idea of dropping a big right hand on Cecil Earl somewhere, but Cecil is pretty well covered by Miss Florentine Fayette, so Fergus Appleton can see that if he lets a right hand go he is bound to strike Miss Florentine Fayette right where she lives.

So he only grabs hold of Miss Florentine Fayette, and tries to pull her loose from Cecil Earl, and Cecil Earl not only holds her tighter, but Miss Florentine Fayette seems to be doing some holding to Cecil herself, so Fergus Appleton cannot peel her off, although he gets one stocking and a piece of elastic strap from somewhere. Then one and all are greatly surprised to hear Miss Florentine Fayette speak to Fergus Appleton like this:

"Go away, you old porous plaster," Miss Florentine Fayette says. "I love only my Cecil. Hold me tighter, Cecil, you great big bear," Miss Florentine Fayette says, although of course Cecil looks about as much like a bear as Ambrose Hammer looks like a porcupine.

Well, of course there is great commotion in Mindy's, because Cecil Earl is putting on a love scene such as makes many citizens very homesick, and Fergus Appleton does not seem to know what to do, when Ambrose Hammer gets to him and whispers a few words in his ear, and all of a sudden Fergus Appleton turns and walks out of Mindy's and disappears, and furthermore nobody ever sees him in these parts again.

By and by Mindy himself comes up and tells Cecil Earl and Miss Florentine Fayette that the chef is complaining because he cannot seem to make ice in his refrigerator while they are in the joint, and will they please go away. So Cecil Earl and Miss Florentine Fayette go, and then Ambrose Hammer comes back to me and finishes his story.

"Well," Ambrose says, "I go over to the certain number on Menahan Street, and what do I find there but a crippled-up, middle-aged doll who is nobody but Fergus Appleton's ever-loving wife, and furthermore she is such for over twenty years. She tells me that Fergus is the meanest guy that ever breathes the breath of life, and that he is persecuting her for a long time in every way he can think of because she will not give him a divorce.

"And," Ambrose says, "the reason she will not give him a divorce is because he knocks her downstairs a long time ago, and makes her a cripple for life, and leaves her to the care of her own people. But of course I do not tell her," Ambrose says, "that she narrowly escapes being murdered through him, for the meaning of the floor plan of the house in Cecil's book, and the meaning of the book itself, and of the dagger, is that Fergus Appleton is working on Cecil Earl until he has him believing that he can be the super-murderer of the age."

"Why," I say to Ambrose Hammer, "I am greatly shocked by these revelations. Why, Fergus Appleton is nothing but a fellow."

"Well," Ambrose says, "he is pretty cute, at that. He has Cecil thinking that it will be a wonderful thing to be the guy who commits the hundred-per-cent-perfect crime, and furthermore Fergus promises to make Cecil rich after he marries Miss Florentine Fayette."

"But," I say, "what I do not understand is what makes Cecil become such a violent lover all of a sudden."

"Why," Ambrose Hammer says, "when Cecil lets it out that he loves Miss Florentine Fayette, it gives me a nice clue to the whole situation. I take Cecil in hand and give him a little coaching and, furthermore, I make him a present of a book myself. He finds it more interesting than anything Fergus Appleton gives him. In fact," Ambrose says, "I recommend it to you. When Cecil comes in here this morning, he is not Cecil Earl, the potential Perfect Murderer. He is nobody but the world's champion heavy lover, old Don Juan."

Well, Ambrose does not get to be editor in chief of his newspaper. In fact, he just misses getting the outdoors, because Cecil Earl and Miss Florentine Fayette elope, and get married, and go out to Hollywood on a honeymoon, and never return, and old Hannibal Fayette claims it is just as bad for his daughter to marry a movie actor as a guy on the stage, even though Cecil turns out to be the greatest drawing card on the screen because he can heat up love scenes so good.

But I always say that Cecil Earl is quite an ingrate, because he refuses a part in Ambrose Hammer's play when Ambrose finally gets it written, and makes his biggest hit in a screen version of Never-Never.

10. SO YOU WON'T TALK!

·····

I<small>T</small> is along about two o'clock of a nippy Tuesday morning, and I am sitting in Mindy's restaurant on Broadway with Regret, the horse player, speaking of this and that, when who comes in but Ambrose Hammer, the newspaper scribe, and what is he carrying in one hand but a big bird cage, and what is in this bird cage but a green parrot.

Well, if anybody sits around Mindy's restaurant long enough, they are bound to see some interesting and unusual scenes, but this is undoubtedly the first time that anybody cold sober ever witnesses a green parrot in there, and Mindy himself is by no means enthusiastic about this spectacle.

In fact, as Ambrose Hammer places the cage on our table and then sits down beside me, Mindy approaches us, and says to Ambrose:

"Horse players, yes," Mindy says. "Wrong bettors, yes. Dogs and song writers and actors, yes. But parrots," Mindy says, "no. Take it away," he says.

But Ambrose Hammer pays no attention to Mindy and starts ordering a few delicacies of the season from Schmalz, the waiter, and Mindy finally sticks his finger in the cage to scratch the parrot's head, and goes cootch-cootch-cootch, and the next thing anybody knows, Mindy is sucking his finger and yelling bloody murder, as it seems the parrot starts munching on the finger as if it is a pretzel.

Mindy is quite vexed indeed, and he says he will go out and borrow a Betsy off of Officer Gloon and blow the parrot's brains out, and he also says that if anybody will make it worth his while, he may blow Ambrose Hammer's brains out, too.

"If you commit such a deed," Ambrose says, "you will be arrested. I mean, blowing this parrot's brains out. This parrot is a material witness in a murder case."

Well, this statement puts a different phase on the matter, and Mindy goes away speaking to himself, but it is plain to be seen, that his feelings are hurt as well as his finger, and personally, if I am Ambrose Hammer, I will not eat anything in Mindy's again unless I have somebody taste it first.

Naturally, I am very curious to know where Ambrose Hammer gets the parrot, as he is not such a character as makes a practice of associating with the birds and beasts of the forest, but of course I do not ask any questions, as the best you can get from asking questions along Broadway is a reputation for asking questions.

And of course I am wondering what Ambrose Hammer means by saying this parrot is a material witness in a murder case, although I know that Ambrose is always mixing himself up in murder cases, even when they are really none of his put-in. In fact, Ambrose's hobby is murder cases.

He is a short, pudgy character, of maybe thirty, with a round face and googly eyes, and he is what is called a dramatic critic on one of the morning blatters, and his dodge is to observe new plays such as people are always putting on in the theatres and to tell his readers what he thinks of these plays, although generally what Ambrose Hammer really thinks of them is unfit for publication.

In fact, Ambrose claims the new plays are what drive him to an interest in murder for relief. So he is always looking into crimes of this nature, especially if they are mysterious cases, and trying to solve these mysteries, and between doing this and telling what he thinks of the new plays, Ambrose finds his time occupied no little, and quite some.

He is a well-known character along Broadway, because he is always in and out, and up and down, and around and about, but to tell the truth, Ambrose is not so popular with the citizens around Mindy's, because they figure that a character who likes to solve murder mysteries must have a slight touch of copper in him which will cause him to start investigating other mysteries at any minute.

Furthermore, there is a strong knockout on Ambrose in many quarters because he is in love with Miss Dawn Astra, a very beautiful young Judy who is playing the part of a strip dancer in a musical show at the Summer Garden, and it is well known to one and all that Miss Dawn Astra is the sweet pea of a character by the name of Julius Smung, until Ambrose comes into her life, and that Julius' heart is slowly breaking over her.

This Julius Smung is a sterling young character of maybe twenty-two, who is in the taxicab business as a driver. He is the son of the late Wingy Smung, who has his taxi stand in front of Mindy's from 1922 down to the night in 1936 that he is checking up the pockets of a sailor in Central Park to see if the sailor has the right change for his taxi fare, and the sailor wakes up and strikes Wingy on the head with Wingy's own jack handle, producing concussion of the brain.

Well, when Wingy passes away, leaving behind him many sorrowing friends, his son Julius takes his old stand, and naturally all who know Wingy in life are anxious to see his son carry on his name, so they throw all the taxicab business they can to him, and Julius gets along very nicely.

He is a good-looking young character and quite energetic, and he is most courteous to one and all, except maybe sailors, consequently public sentiment is on his side when Ambrose Hammer moves in on him with Miss Dawn Astra, especially as Miss Dawn Astra is Julius Smung's sweet pea since they are children together over on Tenth Avenue.

Their romance is regarded as one of the most beautiful little romances ever seen in this town. In fact there is some talk that Julius Smung and Miss Dawn Astra will one day get married, although it is agreed along Broadway that this may be carrying romance a little too far.

Then Ambrose Hammer observes Miss Dawn Astra playing the part of a strip dancer, and it is undoubtedly love at first sight on Ambrose's part, and he expresses his love by giving Miss Dawn Astra better write-ups in the blatter he works for than he ever gives Miss Katharine Cornell, or even Mr. Noel Coward. In fact, to read what Ambrose Hammer says about Miss Dawn Astra, you will think that she is a wonderful artist indeed, and maybe she is, at that.

Naturally, Miss Dawn Astra reciprocates Ambrose Hammer's love, because all the time she is Julius Smung's sweet pea, the best she ever gets is a free taxi ride now and then, and Julius seldom speaks of her as an artist. To tell the truth, Julius is always beefing about her playing the part of a strip dancer, as he claims it takes her too long to get her clothes back on when he is waiting outside the Summer Garden for her, and the chances are Ambrose Hammer is a pleasant change to Miss Dawn Astra as Ambrose does not care if she never gets her clothes on.

Anyway, Miss Dawn Astra starts going around and about with Ambrose Hammer, and Julius Smung is so downcast over this matter that he scarcely knows what he is doing. In fact, inside of three weeks, he runs through traffic lights twice on Fifth Avenue, and once he almost drives his taxi off the Queensboro Bridge with three passengers in it, although it comes out afterwards that Julius thinks the passengers may be newspaper scribes, and nobody has the heart to blame him for this incident.

There is much severe criticism of Ambrose Hammer among the citizens around Mindy's restaurant, as they feel he is away out of line in moving in on Julius Smung's sweet pea, when any one of a hundred other Judys in this town will do him just as well and cause no suffering to anybody, but Ambrose pays no attention to this criticism.

Ambrose says he is very much in love with Miss Dawn Astra, and he says that, besides, taxi-cab drivers get enough of the best of it in this town as it is, although it is no secret that Ambrose never gets into a taxi after he moves in on Julius Smung without first taking a good look at the driver to make sure that he is not Julius.

Well, by the time it takes me to explain all this, Miss Dawn Astra comes into Mindy's, and I can see at once that Ambrose Hammer is not to blame for being in love with her, and neither is Julius Smung, for she is undoubtedly very choice indeed. She is one of these tall, limber Judys, with a nice expression in her eyes and a figure such as is bound to make anybody dearly love to see Miss Dawn Astra play the part of a strip dancer.

Naturally, the first thing that attracts Miss Dawn Astra's attention when she sits down at the table with us is the parrot in the cage, and she says to Ambrose:

"Why, Ambrose," she says, "where does the parrot come from?"

"This parrot is a material witness," Ambrose says. "Through this parrot I will solve the mystery of the murder of the late Mr. Grafton Wilton."

Well, at this, Miss Dawn Astra seems to turn a trifle pale around the gills, and she lets out a small gasp, and says:

"Grafton Wilton," she says, "Murdered?" she says. "When, and where, and how?"

"Just a few hours ago," Ambrose says. "In his apartment on Park Avenue. With a blunt instrument. This parrot is in the room at the time. I arrive ten minutes after the police. There is a small leopard there, too, also a raccoon and a couple of monkeys and several dogs.

"The officers leave one of their number to take care of these creatures," Ambrose says. "He is glad to let me remove the parrot, because he does not care for birds. He does not realize the importance of this parrot. In fact," Ambrose says, "this officer is in favour of me removing all the livestock except the monkeys, which he plans to take home to his children, but," Ambrose says, "this parrot is all I require."

Well, I am somewhat surprised to hear this statement, as I am acquainted with Grafton Wilton, and in fact, he is well known to one and all along Broadway as a young character who likes to go about spending the money his papa makes out of manufacturing soap back down the years.

This Grafton Wilton is by no means an odious character, but he is considered somewhat unusual in many respects, and in fact if his family does not happen to have about twenty million dollars, there is no doubt but what Grafton will be placed under observation long ago. But, of course, nobody in this town is going to place anybody with a piece of twenty million under observation.

This Grafton Wilton is quite a nature lover, and he is fond of walking into spots leading a wild animal of some description on a chain, or with a baboon sitting on his shoulder, and once he appears in the 9-9 Club carrying a young skunk in his arms, which creates some ado among the customers.

In fact, many citizens are inclined to censure Grafton for the skunk, but the way I look at it, a character who spends his money the way he does is entitled to come around with a boa-constrictor in his pockets if he feels like it.

I am really somewhat depressed to hear of Grafton Wilton being murdered, and I am sitting there wondering who will replace him in the community, when all of a sudden Miss Dawn Astra says:

"I hate parrots," she says.

"So do I," I say. "Ambrose," I say, "why do you not bring us the leopard? I am very fond of leopards."

"Anyway," Miss Dawn Astra says, "how can a parrot be a material witness to anything, especially such a thing as a murder?"

"Look," Ambrose says. "Whoever kills Grafton Wilton must be on very friendly terms with him, because every indication is that Grafton and the murderer sit around the apartment all evening, eating and drinking. And," Ambrose says, "anybody knows that Grafton is always a very solitary character, and he seldom has anybody around him under any circumstances. So it is a cinch he is not entertaining a stranger in his apartment for hours.

"Grafton has two servants," Ambrose says. "A butler, and his wife. He permits them to take the day off to go to Jersey to visit relatives. Grafton and his visitor wait on themselves. A private elevator that the passenger operates runs to Grafton's apartment. No one around the building sees the visitor arrive or depart.

"In the course of the evening," Ambrose says, "the visitor strikes Grafton down with a terrific blow from some blunt instrument, and leaves him on the floor, dead. The deceased has two black eyes and a badly lacerated nose. The servants find the body when they arrive home late to-night. The weapon is missing. There are no strange finger-prints anywhere around the apartment."

"It sounds like a very mysterious mystery, to be sure," I say. "Maybe it is a stick-up, and Grafton Wilton resists."

"No," Ambrose says, "there is no chance that robbery is

the motive. There is a large sum of money in Grafton's pockets, and thousands of dollars' worth of valuables scattered around, and nothing is touched."

"But where does the parrot come in?" Miss Dawn Astra says.

"Well," Ambrose says, "if the murderer is well known to Grafton Wilton, the chances are his name is frequently mentioned by Grafton during the evening, in the presence of this parrot. Maybe it is Sam. Maybe it is Bill or Frank or Joe. It is bound to be the name of some male character," Ambrose says, "because no female can possibly strike such a powerful blow as causes the death of Grafton Wilton.

"Now then," Ambrose says, "parrots pick up names very quickly and the chances are this parrot will speak the name he hears so often in the apartment, and then we will have a clue to the murderer. Maybe Grafton Wilton makes an outcry when he is struck down, such as 'Oh, Henry,' or 'Oh, George.' This is bound to impress the name on the parrot's mind," Ambrose says.

Naturally, after hearing Ambrose's statement, the parrot becomes of more interest to me, and I examine the bird in the cage closely, but as far as I can see, it is like any other green parrot in the world, except that it strikes me as rather stupid.

It just sits there on the perch in the cage, rolling its eyes this way and that and now and then going awk-awk-awk, as parrots will do, in a low tone of voice, and of course, nobody can make anything of these subdued remarks. Sometimes the parrot closes its eyes and seems to be sleeping, but it is only playing possum, and any time anybody gets close to the cage it opens its eyes, and makes ready for another finger, and it is plain to be seen that this is really a most sinister fowl.

"The poor thing is sleepy," Ambrose says. "I will now

take it home with me. I must never let it out of my sight or hearing," he says, "as it may utter the name at any moment out of a clear sky, and I must be present when this comes off."

"But you promised to take me to the Ossified Club," Miss Dawn Astra says.

"Tut-tut," Ambrose says. "Tut-tut-tut," he says. "My goodness, how can you think of frivolity when I have a big murder mystery to solve? Besides, I cannot go to the Ossified Club unless I take the parrot, and I am sure it will be greatly bored there. Come to think of it," Ambrose says, "I will be greatly bored myself. You run along home, and I will see you some other night."

Personally, I feel that Ambrose speaks rather crisply to Miss Dawn Astra, and I can see that she is somewhat offended as she departs, and I am by no means surprised the next day when Regret, the horse player, tells me that he sees somebody that looks very much like Miss Dawn Astra riding on the front seat of Julius Smung's taxicab as the sun is coming up over Fiftieth Street.

Naturally, all the blatters make quite a fuss over the murder of Grafton Wilton, because it is without doubt one of the best murders for them that takes place in this town in a long time, what with the animals in the apartment, and all this and that, and the police are also somewhat excited about the matter until they discover there is no clue, and as far as they can discover, no motive.

Then the police suggest that maybe Grafton Wilton cools himself off somehow in a fit of despondency, although nobody can see how such a thing is possible, and anyway, nobody will believe that a character with an interest in twenty million is ever despondent.

Well, the next night Ambrose Hammer has to go to a theatre to see the opening of another new play, and nothing will do but he must take the parrot in the cage to the theatre with him, and as nobody is expecting a dramatic critic to bring a parrot with him to an opening, Ambrose escapes notice going in.

It seems that it is such an opening as always draws the best people, and furthermore it is a very serious play, and Ambrose sets the cage with the parrot in it on the floor between his legs, and everything is all right until the acting begins on the stage. Then all of a sudden the parrot starts going awk-awk-awk in a very loud tone of voice indeed, and flapping its wings and attracting general attention to Ambrose Hammer.

Well, Ambrose tries to soothe the parrot by saying shush-shush to it, but the parrot will not shush, and in fact, it keeps on going awk-awk louder than ever, and presently there are slight complaints from the people around Ambrose, and finally the leading character in the play comes down off the stage and says he can see that Ambrose is trying to give him the bird in a subtle manner, and that he has a notion to punch Ambrose's nose for him.

The ushers request Ambrose to either check the parrot in the cloakroom or leave the theatre, and Ambrose says he will leave. Ambrose says he already sees enough of the play to convince him that it is unworthy of his further attention, and he claims afterwards that as he goes up the aisle with the birdcage in his hand he is stopped by ten different theatre-goers, male and female, who all whisper to him that they are sorry they do not bring parrots.

This incident attracts some little attention, and it seems that the editor of the blatter that Ambrose works for tells him that it is undignified for a dramatic critic to go to the theatre with a parrot, so Ambrose comes into Mindy's with the parrot again and informs me that I must take charge of the parrot on nights when he has to go to the theatre.

Ambrose says he will pay me well for this service, and as I am always willing to pick up a few dibbs, I do not object, although personally, I am by no means a parrot fan. Ambrose says I am to keep a notebook, so I can jot down anything the parrot says when it is with me, and when I ask Ambrose what it says to date, Ambrose admits that so far it does not say a thing but awk.

"In fact," Ambrose says, "I am commencing to wonder if the cat has got its tongue. It is the most noncommittal parrot I ever see in all my life."

So now I am the custodian of the parrot the next night Ambrose has to go to the theatre, and every time the parrot opens its trap, I out with my notebook and jot down its remarks, but I only wind up with four pages of awks, and when I suggest to Ambrose that maybe the murderer's name is something that begins with *awk*, such as 'Awkins, he claims that I am nothing but a fool.

I can see Ambrose is somewhat on edge to make a comment of this nature, and I forgive him because I figure it may be because he is not seeing as much of Miss Dawn Astra as formerly as it seems Miss Dawn Astra will not go around with the parrot, and Ambrose will not go around without it, so it is quite a situation.

I run into Miss Dawn Astra in the street a couple of times, and she always asks me if the parrot says anything as yet, and when I tell her nothing but awk, it seems to make her quite happy, so I judge she figures that Ambrose is bound to get tired of listening to nothing but awk and will return to her. I can see that Miss Dawn Astra is looking thin and worried, and thinks I, love is too sacred a proposition to let a parrot disturb it.

Well, the third night I am in charge of the parrot I leave it in my room in the hotel where I reside in West Forty-ninth Street, as I learn from Big Nig, the crap shooter, that a small game is in progress in a garage in Fifty-fourth Street, and the parrot does not act as if it is liable to say anything important in the next hour. But when I return to the room after winning a sawbuck in two passes in the game, I am horrified to find that the parrot is absent.

The cage is still there, but the gate is open, and so is a window in the room, and it is plain to be seen that the parrot manages to unhook the fastening of the gate and make its escape, and personally I will be very much pleased if I do not remember about Ambrose Hammer and think how bad he will feel over losing the parrot.

So I hasten at once to a little bird store over in Eighth Avenue, where they have parrots by the peck, and I am fortunate to find the proprietor just closing up for the night and willing to sell me a green parrot for twelve dollars, which takes in the tenner I win in the crap game and my night's salary from Ambrose Hammer for looking after his parrot.

Personally, I do not see much difference between the parrot I buy and the one that gets away, and the proprietor of the bird store tells me that the new parrot is a pretty good talker when it feels like it and that, to tell the truth, it generally feels like it.

Well, I carry the new parrot back to my room in a little wooden cage that the proprietor says goes with it and put it in the big cage, and then I meet Ambrose Hammer at Mindy's restaurant and tell him that the parrot says nothing at all worthy of note during the evening.

I am afraid Ambrose may notice that this is not the same old parrot, but he does not even glance at the bird, and I can see that Ambrose is lost in thought, and there is no doubt but what he is thinking of Miss Dawn Astra.

Up to this time the new parrot does not say as much as awk. It is sitting in the little swing in the cage rocking back and forth, and the chances are it is doing some thinking, too, because all of a sudden it lets out a yell and speaks as follows:

"Big heel! Big heel! Big heel!"

Well, at this, three characters at tables in different parts of the room approach Ambrose and wish to know what he means by letting his parrot insult them. and it takes Ambrose several minutes to chill these beefs.

In the meantime, he is trying to think which one of Grafton Wilton's acquaintances the parrot may have reference to, though he finally comes to the conclusion that there is no use trying to single out anyone, as Grafton Wilton has a great many acquaintances in his life.

But Ambrose is greatly pleased that the parrot at last displays a disposition to talk, and he says it will not be long now before the truth comes out, and that he is glad of it, because he wishes to renew his companionship with Miss Dawn Astra. He no sooner says this than the parrot lets go with a string of language that is by no means pure, and causes Ambrose Hammer himself to blush.

From now on, Ambrose is around and about with the parrot every night, and the parrot talks a blue streak at all times, though it never mentions any names, except bad names. In fact, it mentions so many bad names that the female characters who frequent the restaurants and night clubs where Ambrose takes the parrot commence complaining to the managements that they may as well stay home and listen to their husbands.

Of course I never tell Ambrose that the parrot he is taking around with him is not the parrot he thinks it is, because the way I look at it, he is getting more out of my parrot than he does out of the original, although I am willing to bet plenty that my parrot does not solve any murder mysteries. But I never consider Ambrose's theory sound from the beginning, anyway, and the chances are nobody else does, either. In fact, many citizens are commencing to speak of Ambrose Hammer as a cracky, and they do not like to see him come around with his parrot.

Now one night when Ambrose is to go to a theatre to witness another new play, and I am to have charge of the parrot for a while, he takes me to dinner with him at the 9-9 Club, which is a restaurant that is patronized by some of the highest-class parties, male and female, in this town.

As usual, Ambrose has the parrot with him in its cage, and although it is plain to be seen that the head waiter does not welcome the parrot, he does not care to offend Ambrose, so he gives us a nice table against the wall, and as we sit down, Ambrose seems to notice a strange-looking young Judy who is at the next table all by herself.

She is all in black, and she has cold looking black hair slicked down tight on her head and parted in the middle, and a cold eye, and a cold-looking, dead-white face, and Ambrose seems to think he knows her and half bows to her but she never gives him a blow.

So Ambrose puts the birdcage on the settee between him and the cold-looking Judy and orders our dinner, and we sit there speaking of this and that, but I observe that now and then Ambrose takes a sneak-peek at her as if he is trying to remember who she is.

She pays no attention to him, whatever, and she does not pay any attention to the parrot alongside her, either, although everybody else in the 9-9 Club is looking our way, and, the chances are, making remarks about the parrot.

Well, now what happens but the head waiter brings a messenger boy over to our table, and this messenger boy has a note which is addressed to Ambrose Hammer, and Ambrose opens this note and reads it and then lets out a low moan and hands the note to me, and I also read it, as follows:

Dear Ambrose: When you receive this Julius and I will be on our way to South America where we will be married and raise up a family. Ambrose I love Julius and will never be happy with anybody else. We are leaving so suddenly because we are afraid it may come out about Julius calling on Mr. Grafton the night of the murder to demand an apology from him for insulting me which I never tell you about Ambrose because I do not wish you to know about me often going to Mr. Grafton's place as you are funny that way.

They have a big fight, and Ambrose Julius is sorry he kills Mr. Wilton but it is really an accident as Julius does not know his own strength when he hits anybody.

Ambrose pardon me for taking your parrot but I tell Julius what you say about the parrot speaking the name of the murderer some day and it worries Julius. He says he hears parrots have long memories, and he is afraid it may remember his name although Julius only mentions it once when he is introducing himself to Mr. Wilton to demand the apology.

I tell him he is thinking of elephants but he says it is best to be on the safe side so I take the parrot out of the hotel and you will find your parrot in the bottom of the East River Ambrose and thanks for everything. Dawn.

P.S.—Ambrose kindly do not tell it around about Julius killing Mr. Wilton as we do not wish any publicity about this.—D.

Well, Ambrose is sitting there as if he is practically stunned, and shaking his head this way and that, and I am feeling very sorry for him indeed, because I can understand what a shock it is to anybody to lose somebody they dearly love without notice.

Furthermore, I can see that presently Ambrose will be seeking explanations about the parrot matter, but for maybe five minutes Ambrose does not say a word, and then he speaks as follows:

"What really hurts," Ambrose says, "is to see my theory go wrong. Here I am going around thinking it is somebody in Grafton Wilton's own circle that commits this crime, and the murderer turns out to be nothing but a taxicab driver. Furthermore, I make a laughing-stock of myself thinking a parrot will one day utter the name of the murderer. By the way," Ambrose says, "what does this note say about the parrot?"

Well, I can see that this is where it all comes out, but just as I am about to hand him the note and start my own story, all of a sudden the parrot in the cage begins speaking in a loud tone of voice as follows:

"Hello, Polly," the parrot says. "Hello, Pretty Polly."

Now I often hear the parrot make these remarks and I pay no attention to it, but Ambrose Hammer turns at once to the cold-looking Judy at the table next to him and bows to her most politely, and says to her like this:

"Of course," he says. "To be sure," he says. "Pretty Polly. Pretty Polly Oligant," he says. "I am not certain at first, but now I remember. Well, well, well," Ambrose says. "Two years in Auburn, if I recall, for trying to put the shake on Grafton Wilton on a phony breach-of-promise matter in 1932, when he is still under age. Strange I forget it for a while," Ambrose says. "Strange I do not connect you with this thing marked *P*, that I pick up in the apartment the night of the murder. I think maybe I am protecting some female character of good repute."

And with this, Ambrose pulls a small gold cigarette-case

out of his pocket that he never mentions to me before and shows it to her.

"He ruins my life," the cold-looking Judy says. "The breach-of-promise suit is on the level, no matter what the jury says. How can you beat millions of dollars? There is no justice in this world," she says.

Her voice is so low that no one around but Ambrose and me can hear her, and her cold eyes have a very strange expression to be sure as she says:

"I kill Grafton Wilton, all right," she says. "I am glad of it, too. I am just getting ready to go to the police and give myself up, anyway, so I may as well tell you. I am sick and tired of living with this thing hanging over me."

"I never figure a Judy," Ambrose says. "I do not see how a female can strike a blow hard enough to kill such a sturdy character as Grafton Wilton."

"Oh, that," she says. "I do not strike him a blow. I get into his apartment with a duplicate key that I have made from his lock, and I find him lying on the floor half conscious. I revive him, and he tells me a taxicab driver comes to his apartment and smashes him between the eyes with his fist when he opens the door, and Grafton claims he does not know why. Anyway," she says, "the blow does not do anything more serious to him than skin his nose a little and give him a couple of black eyes.

"Grafton is glad to see me," she says. "We sit around talking, and eating and listening to the radio all evening. In fact," she says, "we have such an enjoyable time that it is five hours later before I have the heart and the opportunity to slip a little cyanide in a glass of wine on him."

"Well," I say, "the first thing we must do is to look up Miss Dawn Astra's address and notify her that she is all wrong about Julius doing the job. Maybe," I say, "she will feel so relieved that she will return to you, Ambrose."

SO YOU WON'T TALK!

"No," Ambrose says, "I can see that Miss Dawn Astra is not the one for me. If there is anything I cannot stand it is a female character who does not state the truth at all times, and Miss Dawn Astra utters a prevarication in this note when she says my parrot is at the bottom of the East River, for here it is right here in this cage, and a wonderful bird it is, to be sure. Let us all now proceed to the police station, and I will then hasten to the office and write my story of this transaction, and never mind about the new play."

"Hello, Polly," the parrot says. "Pretty Polly."

11. DARK DOLORES

WALDO WINCHESTER, the newspaper scribe, is saying to me the other night up in the Hot Box that it is a very great shame that there are no dolls around such as in the old days to make good stories for the newspapers by knocking off guys right and left, because it seems that newspaper scribes consider a doll knocking off a guy very fine news indeed, especially if the doll or the guy belongs to the best people.

Then Waldo Winchester tells me about a doll by the name of Lorelei who hangs out in the Rhine River some time ago and stools sailors up to the rocks to get them wrecked, which I consider a dirty trick, although Waldo does not seem to make so much of it. Furthermore, he speaks of another doll by the name of Circe, who is quite a hand for luring guys to destruction, and by the time Waldo gets to Circe he is crying because there are no more dolls like her around to furnish news for the papers.

But of course the real reason Waldo is crying is not because he is so sorry about Circe. It is because he is full of the liquor they sell in the Hot Box, which is liquor that is apt to make anybody bust out crying on a very short notice. In fact, they sell the cryingest liquor in town up in the Hot Box.

Well, I get to thinking over these dolls Waldo Winchester speaks of, and, thinks I, the chances are Dolores Dark connects up with one of them away back yonder, and maybe with all of them for all I know, Dolores Dark being the name of a doll I meet when I am in Atlantic City with Dave the Dude the time of the big peace conference.

DARK DOLORES

Afterwards I hear she is called Dark Dolores in some spots on account of her complexion but her name is really the other way around. But first I will explain how it is I am in Atlantic City with Dave the Dude the time of the big peace conference as follows:

One afternoon I am walking along Broadway thinking of not much, when I come on Dave the Dude just getting in a taxicab with a suit-case in his duke, and the next thing I kow Dave is jerking me into the cab and telling the jockey to go to the Penn Station. This is how I come to be in Atlantic City the time of the big peace conference, although, of course, I have nothing to do with the peace conference, and am only with Dave the Dude to keep him company.

I am a guy who is never too busy to keep people company, and Dave the Dude is a guy who just naturally loves company. In fact, he hates to go anywhere, or be anywhere, by himself, and the reason is because when he is by himself Dave the Dude has nobody to nod him yes, and if there is one thing Dave is very, very fond of, it is to have somebody to nod him yes. Why it is that Dave the Dude does not have Big Nig with him I do not know, for Big Nig is Dave's regular nod-guy.

But I am better than a raw hand myself at nodding. In fact, I am probably as good a nod-guy as there is in this town, where there must be three million nod-guys, and why not, because the way I look at it, it is no bother whatever to nod a guy. In fact, it saves a lot of conversation.

Anyway, there I am in Atlantic City the time of the big peace conference, although I wish to say right now that if I know in advance who is going to be at this peace conference, or that there is going to be any peace conference, I will never be anywhere near Atlantic City, because the parties mixed up in it are no kind of associates for a nervous guy like me.

It seems this peace conference is between certain citizens of St. Louis, such as Black Mike Marrio, Benny the Blond Jew, and Scoodles Shea, who all have different mobs in St. Louis, and who are all ripping and tearing each other for a couple of years over such propositions as to who shall have what in the way of business privileges of one kind and another, including alky, and liquor, and gambling.

From what I hear there is plenty of shooting going on between these mobs, and guys getting topped right and left. Also there is much heaving of bombs, and all this and that, until finally the only people making any dough in the town are the undertakers, and it seems there is no chance of anybody cutting in on the undertakers, though Scoodles Shea tries.

Well, Scoodles, who is a pretty smart guy, and who is once in the war in France, finally remembers that when all the big nations get broke, and sick and tired of fighting, they hold a peace conference and straighten things out, so he sends word to Black Mike and Benny the Blond Jew that maybe it will be a good idea if they do the same thing, because half their guys are killed anyway, and trade is strictly on the bum.

It seems Black Mike and Benny think very well of this proposition, and are willing to meet Scoodles in a peace conference, but Scoodles, who is a very suspicious character, asks where they will hold this conference. He says he does not wish to hold any conference with Black Mike and Benny in St. Louis, except maybe in his own cellar, because he does not know of any other place in St. Louis where he will be safe from being guzzled by some of Black Mike's or Benny's guys, and he says he does not suppose Black Mike and Benny will care to go into his cellar with him.

So Scoodles Shea finally asks how about Atlantic City,

and it seems this is agreeable to Black Mike because he has a cousin in Atlantic City by the name of Pisano that he does not see since they leave the old country.

Benny the Blond Jew says any place is okay with him as long as it is not in the State of Missouri, because he says, he does not care to be seen anywhere in the State of Missouri with Black Mike and Scoodles, as it will be a knock to his reputation.

This seems to sound somewhat insulting, and almost busts up the peace conference before it starts, but finally Benny withdraws the bad crack, and says he does not mean the State of Missouri, but only St. Louis, so the negotiations proceed, and they settle on Atlantic City as the spot.

Then Black Mike says some outside guy must sit in with them as a sort of umpire, and help them iron out their arguments, and Benny says he will take President Hoover, Colonel Lindbergh, or Chief Justice Taft. Now of course this is great foolishness to think they can get any one of these parties, because the chances are President Hoover, Colonel Lindbergh and Chief Justice Taft are too busy with other things to bother about ironing out a mob war in St. Louis.

So finally Scoodles Shea suggests Dave the Dude. Both Black Mike and Benny say Dave is okay, though Benny holds out for some time for at least Chief Justice Taft. So Dave the Dude is asked to act as umpire for the St. Louis guys, and he is glad to do same, for Dave often steps into towns where guys are battling and straightens them out, and sometimes they do not start battling again for several weeks after he leaves town.

You see, Dave the Dude is friendly with everybody everywhere, and is known to one and all as a right guy, and one who always gives everybody a square rattle in propositions of this kind. Furthermore, it is a pleasure for Dave to straighten guys out in other towns, because the battling tangles up his own business interests in spots such as St. Louis.

Now it seems that on their way to the station to catch a train for Atlantic City, Scoodles Shea and Black Mike and Benny decide to call on a young guy by the name of Frankie Farrone, who bobs up all of a sudden in St. Louis with plenty of nerve, and who is causing them no little bother one way and another.

In fact, it seems that this Frankie Farrone is as good a reason as any other why Scoodles and Black Mike and Benny are willing to hold a peace conference, because Frankie Farrone is nobody's friend in particular and he is biting into all three wherever he can, showing no respect whatever to old-established guys.

It looks as if Frankie Farrone will sooner or later take the town away from them if they let him go far enough, and while each one of the three tries at different times to make a connection with him, it seems he is just naturally a lone wolf, and wishes no part of any of them. In fact, somebody hears Frankie Farrone say he expects to make Scoodles Shea and Black Mike and Benny jump out of a window before he is through with them, but whether he means one window or three different windows he does not say.

So there is really nothing to be done about Frankie Farrone but to call on him, especially as the three are now together, because the police pay no attention to his threats and make no move to protect Scoodles and Black Mike and Benny, the law being very careless in St. Louis at this time.

Of course, Frankie Farrone has no idea Scoodles and Black Mike and Benny are friendly with each other, and he is probably very much surprised when they drop in on him on their way to the station. In fact, I hear there is a surprised look still on his face when they pick him up later.

DARK DOLORES

He is sitting in a speak-easy reading about the Cardinals losing another game to the Giants when Scoodles Shea comes in the front door, and Black Mike comes in the back door, and Benny the Blond Jew slides in through a side entrance, it being claimed afterwards that they know the owner of the joint and get him to fix it for them so they will have no bother about dropping in on Frankie Farrone sort of unexpected like.

Well, anyway the next thing Frankie Farrone knows he has four slugs in him, one from Scoodles Shea, one from Benny, and two from Black Mike, who seems to be more liberal than the others. The chances are they will put more slugs in him, only they leave their taxi a block away with the engine running and they know the St. Louis taxi jockeys are terrible for jumping the meter on guys who keep them waiting.

So they go on to catch their train, and they are all at the Ritz Hotel in Atlantic City when Dave the Dude and I get there, and they have a nice lay-out of rooms looking out over the ocean, for these are high-class guys in every respect, and very good spenders.

They are sitting around a table with their coats off playing pinocle and drinking liquor when Dave and I show up, and right away Black Mike says: "Hello, Dave! Where do we find the tomatoes?"

I can see at once that this Black Mike is a guy who has little bringing up, or he will not speak of dolls as tomatoes, although, of course, different guys have different names for dolls, such as broads, and pancakes, and cookies, and tomatoes, which I claim are not respectful.

This Black Mike is a Guinea, and not a bad-looking Guinea at that, except for a big scar on one cheek.

Benny the Blond Jew is a tall, pale guy, with soft, light-coloured hair and blue eyes, and if I do not happen to know that he personally knocks off about nine guys I will consider him as harmless a looking guy as I ever see. Scoodles Shea is a big, red-headed muzzler with a lot of freckles and a big grin all over his kisser.

They are all maybe thirty-odd, and wear coloured silk shirts with soft collars fastened with gold pins, and Black Mike and Scoodles Shea are wearing diamond rings and wrist-watches. Unless you know who they are, you will never figure them to be gorills, even from St. Louis, although at the same time the chances are you will not figure them to be altar boys unless you are very simpleminded.

They seem to be getting along first-rate together, which is not surprising, because it will be considered very bad taste indeed for guys such as these from one town to go into another town and start up any heat. It will be regarded as showing no respect whatever for the local citizens.

Anyway, Atlantic City is never considered a spot for anything but pleasure, and even guys from Philly who may be mad at each other, and who meet up in Atlantic City, generally wait until they get outside the city limits before taking up any arguments.

Well, it seems that not only Black Mike wishes to meet up with some dolls, but Scoodles Shea and Benny are also thinking of such, because the first two things guys away from home think of are liquor and dolls, although personally I never give these matters much of a tumble.

Furthermore, I can see that Dave the Dude is not so anxious about them as you will expect, because Dave is now married to Miss Billy Perry, and if Miss Billy Perry hears that Dave is having any truck with liquor and dolls, especially dolls, it is apt to cause gossip around his house.

But Dave figures he is a sort of host in this territory,

DARK DOLORES

because the others are strangers to Atlantic City, and important people where they come from, so we go down to Joe Goss's joint, which is a big cabaret just off the Boardwalk, and in no time there are half a dozen dolls of different shapes and sizes from Joe Goss's chorus, and also several of Joe Goss's hostesses, for Joe Goss gets many tired business men from New York among his customers, and there is nothing a tired business man from New York appreciates more than a lively hostess. Furthermore, Joe Goss himself is sitting with us as a mark of respect to Dave the Dude.

Black Mike and Scoodles and Benny are talking with the dolls and dancing with them now and then, and a good time is being had by one and all, as far as I can see, including Dave the Dude after he gets a couple of slams of Joe Goss's liquor in him and commences to forget about Miss Billy Perry. In fact, Dave so far forgets about Miss Billy Perry that he gets out on the floor with one of the dolls, and dances some, which shows you what a couple of slams of Joe Goss's liquor will do to a guy.

Most of the dolls are just such dolls as you will find in a cabaret, but there is one among them who seems to be a hostess, and whose name seems to be Dolores, and who is a lily for looks. It is afterwards that I find out her other name is Dark, and it is Dave the Dude who afterwards finds out that she is called Dark Dolores in spots.

She is about as good a looker as a guy will wish to clap an eye on. She's tall and limber, like a buggy whip, and she has hair as black as the ace of spades, and maybe blacker, and all smooth and shiny. Her eyes are black and as big as doughnuts, and she has a look in them that somehow makes me think she may know more than she lets on, which I afterwards find out is very true indeed.

She does not have much to say, and I notice she does not drink, and does not seem to be so friendly with the other dolls, so I figure her a fresh-laid one around there, especially as Joe Goss himself does not act as familiar towards her as he does towards most of his dolls, although I can see him give her many a nasty look on account of her passing up drinks.

In fact, nobody gives her much of a tumble at all at first, because guys generally like gabby dolls in situations such as this. But finally I notice that Benny the Blond Jew is taking his peeks at her, and I figure it is because he has better judgment than the others, although I do not understand how Dave the Dude can overlook such a bet, because no better judge of dolls ever lives than Dave the Dude.

But even Benny does not talk to Dolores or offer to dance with her, and at one time when Joe Goss is in another part of the joint chilling a beef from some customer about a check, or maybe about the liquor, which calls for at least a mild beef, and the others are out on the floor dancing. Dolores and I are left alone at the table.

We sit there quite a spell with plenty of silence between us, because I am never much of a hand to chew the fat with dolls, but finally, not because I wish to know or care a whoop, but just to make small talk, I ask her how long she is in Atlantic City.

"I get here this afternoon, and go to work for Mr. Goss just this very night," she says. "I am from Detroit."

Now I do not ask her where she is from, and her sticking in this information makes me commence to think that maybe she is a gabby doll after all, but she dries up and does not say anything else until the others come back to the table.

Now Benny the Blond Jew moves into a chair alongside Dolores, and I hear him say:

"Are you ever in St. Louis? Your face is very familiar to me."

"No," she says. "I am from Cleveland. I am never in St. Louis in my life."

"Well," Benny says, "you look like somebody I see before in St. Louis. It is very strange, because I cannot believe it possible for there to be more than one wonderful beautiful doll like you."

I can see Benny is there with the old stuff when it comes to carrying on a social conversation, but I am wondering how it comes this Dolores is from Detroit with me and from Cleveland with him. Still, I know a thousand dolls who cannot remember off-hand where they are from if you ask them quick.

By and by Scoodles Shea and Black Mike notice Benny is all tangled in conversation with Dolores, which makes them take a second peek at her, and by this time they are peeking through plenty of Joe Goss's liquor, which probably makes her look ten times more beautiful than she really is. And I wish to say that any doll ten times more beautiful than Dolores is nothing but a dream.

Anyway, before long Dolores is getting much attention from Black Mike and Scoodles, as well as Benny, and the rest of the dolls finally take the wind, because nobody is giving them a tumble any more. And even Dave the Dude begins taking dead aim at Dolores until I remind him that he must call up Miss Billy Perry, so he spends the next half-hour in a phone booth explaining to Miss Billy Perry that he is in his hotel in the hay, and that he loves her very dearly.

Well, we are in Joe Goss's joint until five o'clock a.m., with Black Mike and Scoodles and Benny talking to Dolores and taking turns dancing with her, and Dave the Dude is plumb wore out, especially as Miss Billy Perry tells him she knows he is a liar and a bum, as she can hear an orchestra playing "I Get So Blue When It Rains," and for him to just wait until she sees him. Then we take Dolores and go to Childs's restaurant on the Boardwalk and have some coffee, and finally all hands escort her to a little flea-bag in North Caroline Avenue where she says she is stopping.

"What are you doing this afternoon, beautiful one?" asks Benny the Blond Jew as we are telling her good night, even though it is morning, and at this crack Black Mike and Scoodles Shea look at Benny, very, very cross.

"I am going bathing in front of the Ritz," she says. "Do some of you boys wish to come along with me?"

Well, it seems that Black Mike and Scoodles and Benny all think this is a wonderful idea, but it does not go so big with Dave the Dude or me. In fact, by this time, Dave the Dude and me are pretty sick of Dolores.

"Anyway," Dave says, "we must start our conference this afternoon and get through with it, because my ever-loving doll is already steaming, and I have plenty of business to look after in New York."

But the conference does not start this afternoon, or the next night, or the next day, or the next day following, because in the afternoons Black Mike and Scoodles and Benny are in the ocean with Dolores and at night they are in Joe Goss's joint, and in between they are taking her riding in rolling chairs on the Boardwalk, or feeding her around the different hotels.

No one guy is ever alone with her as far as I can see, except when she is dancing with one in Joe Goss's joint, and about the third night they are so jealous of each other they all try to dance with her at once.

Well, naturally even Joe Goss complains about this because it makes confusion on his dance floor, and looks unusual. So Dolores settles the proposition, by not dancing with anybody, and I figure this is a good break for her, as no doll's dogs can stand all the dancing Black Mike and Scoodles and Benny wish to do.

The biggest rolling chair on the Boardwalk only takes in three guys or two guys and one doll, or, what is much better, one guy and two dolls, so when Dolores is in a rolling chair with a guy sitting on each side of her the other walks alongside the chair, which is a peculiar sight, indeed.

How they decide the guy who walks I never know, but I suppose Dolores fixes it. When she is in bathing in the ocean Black Mike and Scoodles and Benny all stick so close to her that she is really quite crowded at times.

I doubt if even Waldo Winchester, the scribe, who hears of a lot of things, ever hears of such a situation as this with three guys all daffy over the same doll, and guys who do not think any too well of each other to begin with. I can see they are getting more and more hostile towards each other over her, but when they are not with Dolores they stick close to each other for fear one will cop a sneak, and get her to himself.

I am very puzzled, because Black Mike and Scoodles and Benny do not get their rods out and start a shooting match among themselves over her, but I find that Dave the Dude makes them turn in their rods to him the second day because he does not care to have them doing any target practice around Atlantic City.

So they cannot start a shooting match among themselves if they wish, and the reason they do not put the slug on each other is because Dolores tells them she hates tough guys who go around putting the slug on people. So they are gentlemen, bar a few bad cracks passing among them now and then.

Well, it comes on a Friday, and there we are in Atlantic City since a Monday and nothing stirring on the peace conference as yet, and Dave the Dude is very much disgusted indeed.

All night Friday and into Saturday morning we are in Joe Goss's, and personally I can think of many other places I will rather be. To begin with, I never care to be around gorills when they are drinking, and when you take gorills who are drinking and get them all crazy about the same doll, they are apt to turn out to be no gentlemen any minute.

I do not know who it is who suggests a daybreak swimming party, because I am half asleep, and so is Dave the Dude, but I hear afterwards it is Dolores. Anyway, the next thing anybody knows we are out on the beach, and Dolores and Black Mike and Scoodles Shea and Benny the Blond Jew are in their bathing suits and the dawn is touching up the old ocean very beautiful.

Of course, Dave the Dude and me are not in bathing suits, because in the first place neither of us is any hand for going in bathing, and in the second place, if we are going in bathing, we will not go in bathing at such an hour. Furthermore, as far as I am personally concerned, I hope I am never in a bathing suit if I will look no better in it than Black Mike, while Scoodles Shea is no Gene Tunney in regards to shape. Benny the Blond Jew is the only one who looks human, and I do not give him more than sixty-five points.

Dave the Dude and me stand around watching them, and mostly we are watching Dolores. She is in a red bathing suit with a red rubber cap over her black hair, and while most dolls in bathing suits hurt my eyes, she is still beautiful. I will always claim she is the most beautiful thing I ever see, bar Blue Larkspur, and of course Blue Larkspur is a racehorse and not a doll. I am very glad that Miss Billy Perry is not present to see the look in Dave the Dude's eyes as he watches Dolores in her bathing suit, for Miss Billy Perry is quick to take offence.

When she is in the water Dolores slides around like a big beautiful red fish. You can see she loves it. The chances are I can swim better on my back than Black Mike or Scoodles Shea can on their stomachs, and Benny the Blond Jew is no Gertrude Ederle, but of course, I am allowing for them being well loaded with Joe Goss's liquor, and a load of Joe Goss's liquor is not apt to float well anywhere.

Well, after they paddle around in the ocean a while, Dolores and her three Romeos lay out on the sand, and Dave the Dude and me are just figuring on going to bed, when all of a sudden we see Dolores jump up and start running for the ocean with Black Mike and Benny head-and-head just behind her, and Scoodles Shea half a length back.

She tears into the water, kicking it every which way until she gets to where it is deep, when she starts to swim, heading for the open sea. Black Mike and Scoodles Shea and Benny the Blond Jew are paddling after her like blazes. We can see it is some kind of a chase, and we stand watching it. We can see Dolores's little red cap bouncing along over the water like a rubber ball on a sidewalk, with Black Mike and Scoodles and Benny staggering along behind her, for Joe Goss's liquor will make a guy stagger on land or sea.

She is away ahead of them at first, but then she seems to pull up and let them get closer to her. When Black Mike, who is leading the other two, gets within maybe fifty yards of her, the red cap bounces away again, always going farther out. It strikes me that Dolores is sort of swimming in wide circles, now half turning as if coming back to the beach, and then taking a swing that carries her seaward again.

When I come to think it over afterwards, I can see that

when you are watching her it does not look as if she is swimming away from the beach, and yet all the time she is getting away from it.

One of her circles takes her almost back to Benny, who is a bad last to Black Mike and Scoodles Shea, and in fact she gets so close to Benny that he is lunging for her, when she slides away again, and is off faster than any fish I ever see afloat. Then she does the same to Black Mike and Scoodles. I figure they are playing tag in the water, or some such, and while this may be all right for guys who are full of liquor, and a light-headed doll, I do not consider it a proper amusement at such an hour for guys in their right senses, like Dave the Dude and me.

So I am pleased when he says we better go to bed because by this time Dolores and Black Mike and Scoodles Shea and Benny seem to be very far out in the water indeed. As we are strolling along the Boardwalk, I look back again and there they are, no bigger than pin points on the water, and it seems to me that I can see only three pin points, at that, but I figure Dolores is so far out I cannot see her through the haze.

"They will be good and tuckered out by the time they get back," I say to Dave the Dude.

"I hope they drown," Dave says, but a few days later he apologizes for this crack and explains he makes it only because he is tired and disgusted.

Well, I often think now that it is strange neither Dave the Dude or me see anything unnatural in the whole play, but we do not even mention Dolores or Black Mike or Scoodles Shea or Benny the Blond Jew until late in the afternoon when we are putting on the old grapefruit and ham and eggs in Dave's room and Dave is looking out over the ocean.

"Say," he says, as if he just happens to remember it, "do you know those guys are away out yonder the last we see of them? I wonder if they get back okay?"

And as if answering his question there is a knock on the door, and who walks in but Dolores. She looks all fagged out, but she is so beautiful I will say she seems to light up the room, only I do not wish anybody to think I am getting romantic. Anyway, she is beautiful, but her voice is very tired as she says to Dave the Dude:

"Your friends from St. Louis will not return, Mister Dave the Dude. They do not swim so well, but better than I thought. The one that is called Black Mike and Scoodles Shea turn back when we are about three miles out, but they never reach the shore. I see them both go down for the last time. I make sure of this, Mister Dave the Dude. The pale one, Benny, lasts a little farther, although he is the worst swimmer of them all, and he never turns back. He is still trying to follow me when a cramp gets him and he sinks. I guess he loves me the most at that as he always claims."

Well, naturally, I am greatly horrified by this news, especially as she tells it without batting one of her beautiful eyes.

"Do you mean to tell us you let these poor guys drown out there in all this salt water?" I say, very indignant. "Why, you are nothing but a cad."

But Dave the Dude makes a sign for me to shut up, and Dolores says:

"I come within a quarter of a mile of swimming the English Channel in 1927, as you will see by looking up the records," she says, "and I can swim the Mississippi one handed, but I cannot pack three big guys such as these on my back. Even," she says, "if I care to, which I do not. Benny is the only one who speak to me before he goes. The last time I circle back to him he waves his hand and says, I know all along I see you somewhere before. I remember now. You are Frankie Farrone's doll.' "

"And you are?" asks Dave the Dude.

"His widow," says Dolores. "I promise him as he lays in his coffin that these men will die, and they are dead. I spent my last dollar getting to this town by aeroplane, but I get there, and I get them. Only it is more the hand of Providence," she says. "Now I will not need this."

And she tosses out on the table among our breakfast dishes a little bottle that we find out afterwards is full of enough cyanide to kill forty mules, which always makes me think that this Dolores is a doll who means business.

"There is only one thing I wish to know," Dave the Dude says. "Only one thing. How do you coax these fatheads to follow you out in the water?"

"This is the easiest thing of all," Dolores says. "It is an inspiration to me as we lay out on the beach. I tell them I will marry the first one who reaches me in the water. I do not wish to seem hard-hearted, but it is a relief to me when I see Black Mike sink. Can you imagine being married to such a bum?"

It is not until we are going home that Dave the Dude has anything to say about the proposition, and then he speaks to me as follows:

"You know," Dave says, "I will always consider I get a very lucky break that Dolores does not include me in her offer, or the chances are I will be swimming yet."

12. DELEGATES AT LARGE

WHEN it comes on summer, and the nights get nice and warm, I love to sit on the steps in front of the bank at Forty-eighth Street and Seventh Avenue, where a guy can keep himself cool. Many other citizens are fond of sitting on the bank steps with me, and usually we sit with our coats off, speaking of this and that.

Sometimes you can see very prominent citizens sitting with me on the bank steps, including such as Regret, the horse player, and old Sorrowful, the bookie, and Doc Daro and Professor D. and Johnny Oakley and The Greek, and often strangers in the city, seeing us sitting there and looking so cool, stop and take off their coats and sit down with us, although personally if I am a stranger in the city I will be a little careful who I sit down with no matter how hot I am.

Well, one night I am sitting on the bank steps with Big Nig, the crap shooter, and a guy by the name of Skyrocket, who is nobody much, when all of a sudden I notice three guys standing on the sidewalk taking a very good long gander at me, and who are these guys but certain characters from Brooklyn by the name of Harry the Horse, and Spanish John and Little Isadore, and they are very hard characters indeed.

In fact, these characters are so hard that I am glad that none of the depositors of the bank can see them standing there, as such a scene is just naturally bound to make any depositor nervous. In fact, it makes me more nervous than somewhat, and I am by no means a depositor. But of course I do not let on to Harry the Horse and Spanish John and

Little Isadore that I am nervous, because they may get the idea that I am nervous about them and take offence.

Well finally I say hello to them, and they all say hello right back, and I can see that they are not inclined to take offence at me, but then they start looking at Big Nig and Skyrocket in such a way that I can see they are taking offence at Big Nig's face and at Skyrocket's too, and personally I do not blame them, at that, as these are faces such as may give offence to anybody.

Furthermore, Big Nig and Skyrocket can see that these Brooklyn characters are taking offence at their faces and in practically no time Big Nig and Skyrocket are walking briskly up Forty-eighth Street.

Then Harry the Horse and Spanish John and Little Isadore take off their coats and sit there with me quite a while, with nobody saying much of anything, and I am wondering what these characters are doing in this neighbourhood, because they know they are by no means welcome along Broadway or anywhere else in town for that matter, when finally Harry the Horse speaks as follows:

"Well," Harry says, "we are going out West to-morrow. Yes," he says, "we are going away out to Chicago, but," he says, "do not ask us to call on anybody in Chicago for you, as we will be very busy while we are there."

Now it happens I do not know anybody in Chicago for them to call on, and if I do know anybody there I will just as soon think of sending them a bottle of prussic acid as to ask Harry the Horse and Spanish John and Little Isadore to call on them, but naturally I do not mention such an idea out loud. And although I am dying to know why they are going to Chicago, of course I do not ask them, as such a question is bound to be regarded as inquisitive by these characters.

So I only say I hope and trust that they will have a very pleasant journey to Chicago and that they will return safe and sound, although I am secretly hoping they never return at all, because if there are any citizens this town can spare it is Harry the Horse and Spanish John and Little Isadore, and especially Harry the Horse.

In fact, the chances are that Brooklyn, where Harry resides, will be glad to pay him a bonus to move away from there, because he is always carrying on in such a way as to give Brooklyn a bad name, while Spanish John and Little Isadore are no boost to the borough, either. But Spanish John and Little Isadore only do what Harry tells them, and what Harry tells me is generally something that causes somebody plenty of bother.

There is no doubt that Harry the Horse has a wild streak in him and he is very mischievous, and is always putting Spanish John and Little Isadore up to such tricks as robbing their fellow citizens of Brooklyn and maybe taking shots at them, and sometimes Harry the Horse personally takes a shot or two himself. Naturally, this practice is most distasteful to the citizens of Brooklyn, who are very fond of peace and quiet.

Well, anyway, Harry the Horse and Spanish John and Little Isadore sit on the bank steps with me quite a while. Finally however, they get up and put on their coats and shake hands with me and say they hope to see me when they get back from Chicago, and then they go away, and I do not hear of them again for several weeks.

Now one hot night I am again sitting on the steps with a number of prominent citizens, when who comes along but Little Isadore, and he motions me to follow him up the street. It is the first time I ever see Little Isadore without either Harry the Horse or Spanish John and when I join him, naturally I ask him about the others, and Little Isadore speaks to me as follows:

"Harry is in a hospital in Chicago," Little Isadore says. "Spanish John is out there waiting for him to get well. I come back home," Little Isadore says," to raise some scratch to pay Harry's hospital fees.

"He is all bunged up. It comes of mixing in politics with a doll," he says. "Maybe you will like to hear the story."

Naturally I say I will be greatly pleased to hear it, so we walk around to Mindy's restaurant, and Little Isadore orders up a sirloin steak smothered in onions, and while he is eating this steak he begins to talk.

Well (Little Isadore says), we go to Chicago all right the day after we last see you, and we go to Chicago by special invitation of some very prominent parties out there. I will mention no names, but these parties are very prominent indeed, especially in beer, and they invite us out there to take care of a guy by the name of Donkey O'Neill, as it seems this Donkey O'Neill is also in beer in opposition to the prominent parties I speak of.

Naturally, these parties will not tolerate opposition, and there is nothing for them to do but to see that Donkey O'Neill is taken care of. But of course they do not wish him to be taken care of by local talent, as this is a very old-fashioned way of transacting such matters, and nowadays when anybody is to be taken care of in any town it is customary to invite outsiders in, as they are not apt to leave any familiar traces such as local talent is bound to do.

So the prominent parties in Chicago get in touch with Angie the Ox, in Brooklyn, and Angie speaks so highly of Harry the Horse and Spanish John and me that we get the invitation, which anybody will tell you is a great honour.

Furthermore, six G's and all expenses go with the invitation, and this is by no means alfalfa.

We go to Chicago by the Twentieth Century train, and it is a nice trip generally, except that while we are in the club car playing pinocle Harry the Horse gets to looking at a doll with more interest than somewhat. Now, it is by no means like Harry the Horse to look at a doll. In fact, in all the years I am associated with Harry the Horse, socially and in business, he never before looks at a doll more than once, or maybe twice, because he claims that all dolls are more or less daffy.

But I will say that the doll in the club car is worth looking at, and anybody can see that she has plenty of class, although personally I like them with legs that are not quite so spindly. She is by no means a real young doll, being maybe twenty-five or twenty-six, and anybody can see that she knows what time it is.

Furthermore, she is very stylish, and even if Harry the Horse is a guy who gives dolls a tumble this is about the last doll you will figure him to tumble, because she looks as if she may be such a doll as will holler for the gendarmes if anybody as much as says boo to her.

But Harry the Horse does not seem to be able to keep his eyes off her, and by and by he quits our pinocle game and takes a chair next to her and lets on he is reading a magazine. The next thing anybody knows, Harry is talking to the doll very friendly, which is a most astonishing sight to Spanish John and me, although Harry can talk first rate when he feels like it, and furthermore he is by no means as bad looking as the photos of him the cops send around make him out.

Well, the conversation between Harry the Horse and the doll is also most astonishing to Spanish John and me, because we hear her say to him like this:

"Yes," she says, "I am going to Chicago. I am going to

attend the convention," she says. "I am a member of the New York Delegation. Some great questions are to be decided in Chicago," she says. "I love politics, and I think it will be a good thing if all women take an interest in politics. Do you not think so?"

Well, Harry the Horse may not be the smartest guy in the country, but he is smart enough to say yes every now and then to the doll, because if a guy keeps yessing a doll long enough, she is bound to figure him a bright guy, and worth looking into.

By and by the doll mentions that her name is Miss Maribel Marlo and that she lives on Park Avenue in the winter and at Southampton in the summer, so it does not take a mind-reader to figure that she must have plenty of potatoes.

Finally she takes to asking Harry the Horse questions, and as Harry is about as good an off-hand liar as there is in the United States, his answers are very satisfactory indeed, although personally I figure he is stretching it a little bit when he tells her that we are also going to the convention in Chicago.

Well, Miss Maribel Marlo seems pleased to learn this news from Harry the Horse, and she says to him as follows: "Of course you are delegates?" she says.

"Yes," Harry says, "such is indeed the case."

"Why," Miss Maribel Marlo says, "we will all be in the convention together. How nice!" she says. "What district are you from?"

Well, naturally Harry does not wish to speak of Brooklyn, because it is never a good policy for a guy to mention his address when he is away from home, so he says we are from no district in particular, which does not sound to me like the right answer, but it seems to suit Miss Maribel Marlo.

"Oh," she says, "I understand. You are delegates at large."

Well, I am glad Harry the Horse lets it go at this and turns the conversation back to Miss Maribel Marlo, and anybody can see that Miss Maribel Marlo is such a doll as does not mind having the conversation about herself, although it makes me very nervous when I hear Harry the Horse speak to her as follows: "Lady," Harry says, "does anybody tell you how beautiful you are?"

Naturally, I expect to see Harry the Horse given plenty of wind at once for this crack, but it seems it proves interesting to Miss Maribel Marlo, and she is still listening to Harry when Spanish John and me go to bed.

Afterwards I learn Miss Maribel Marlo listens to Harry the Horse until midnight, which is most surprising because Harry is a guy whose grammar is by no means perfect, but it seems that no doll minds a guy's grammar as long as he is speaking well of her. And Harry the Horse tells me that he does not fail to give Miss Maribel Marlo plenty the best of it in all his remarks. Furthermore, Harry says, she is deserving of everything he says, which shows that Harry is impressed by Miss Maribel Marlo more than somewhat.

The next morning when our train pulls into Chicago we see her on the platform, but she is so surrounded by other dolls, and also by several guys who wear swell clothes and little moustaches, that she does not see us, and Harry the Horse is very thoughtful all the rest of the day.

Well, Chicago is a very large and busy city, with many citizens walking around and about, and among these citizens are many parties wearing large badges, and it seems that these parties are from different parts of the country and are delegates to the national convention that is going on in Chicago at this time.

Furthermore, it seems that this convention is a political proposition, and the idea is to nominate a candidate for

President, and also a candidate for Vice-President, if they can get anybody to take it. It is this convention that Miss Maribel Marlo is talking about on the train.

But of course Harry the Horse and Spanish John and me have no interest in a matter of this kind, because our business is to look up these prominent parties who invite us to Chicago, and find out just what is what. But Harry the Horse does not seem anxious to get down to business at once, and is wandering around looking as if he is slug-nutty, and I hear he goes over to the Blackstone on Michigan Boulevard where Miss Maribel Marlo is stopping, to see if he can get a peek at her.

Naturally, I am somewhat disgusted with Harry the Horse, and so is Spanish John to think that he becomes interested in a doll when we have important business to attend to, so I am very glad when a representative of the prominent parties who invite us to Chicago calls on us at our hotel to explain just what our hosts expect of us. This representative is a guy by the name of Snooksy, and he is very apologetic because he says it looks as if we may be delayed in town a few days.

"This Donkey O'Neill has plenty of political strength," Snooksy says. "In fact," he says, "he is a delegate to the big convention, and," he says, "we figure it may not be a good idea to take care of him when he is in such a prominent spot. It may cause gossip," Snooksy says. "The idea is to wait until after the convention, and in the meantime I will entertain you gentlemen the best I know how."

Well, this seems fair enough, and the news cheers up Harry the Horse, as he figures the delay will give him more chance to see Miss Maribel Marlo, although he admits to me that he cannot get near her at the Blackstone, what with her having so many friends around.

I ask Harry the Horse why he does not walk right in and

send his name up to her, but it seems he cannot remember the name he gives her on the train, and anyway, he does not wish her to find out that it is all the phonus bolonus about us being delegates to the convention.

Harry says there is no doubt in his mind that he must be in love with Miss Maribel Marlo, and he will not listen to my idea that maybe it is the change in climate that does not agree with him.

Well, I wish to say that this Snooksy is a splendid entertainer in every respect, and he takes us around and about the city of Chicago, and wherever we go he introduces us to many prominent characters, although I noticed that Snooksy never introduces us by the same names twice, and before the evening is over I am from four different cities, including San Francisco, Dallas, Texas, Shreveport, Louisiana, and Oskaloosa, Iowa.

But nobody ever asks any questions, as it seems the citizens of Chicago are very polite in this respect, so we all enjoy ourselves thoroughly, especially Spanish John, who claims the beer in Chicago is almost as good as the kind Angie the Ox sells in Brooklyn.

Well, for a couple of days and nights we are entertained by Snooksy, and even Harry the Horse cheers up, and I commence to think he forgets Miss Maribel Marlo, until early one a.m. we are in a joint where there is plenty of beer and other entertainment, including blondes, when a bunch of guys wearing badges happen in.

Anybody can see from the badges that these guys are delegates such as are walking around and about all over town, and, furthermore, that some of them are delegates from New Jersey, which is a spot well known to Harry the Horse and Spanish John and me, although one guy seems to be from Massachusetts and another from Texas. But they are all full of fun and beer, and one thing and another, and they take a table next to us, and the first thing anybody knows we are very neighbourly together.

Well, by and by I notice Harry the Horse examining the badge one of the New Jersey guys is wearing, and I also hear Harry asking questions about it, and it seems from what the guy says that anybody wearing such a badge and carrying a certain card can walk in and out of the convention, and no questions asked. Then I hear Harry the Horse speak to the guy as follows:

"Well," Harry says, "I am never in a convention in my life. I only wish I have such a badge," he says, "so I can see how a convention works."

"Why," the guy says, speaking out loud so the others hear him, "this is a terrible state of affairs. Here is a guy who is never in a convention," he says. "Why," he says, "you will have my seat at the morning session while I will be catching up on some sleep, although," the guy says, "the chances are you will find it all very tiresome."

With this the guy unpins the badge on his chest and pins it on Harry the Horse, and furthermore he takes a card out of his pocket and gives it to Harry, and then he calls for more beer, while the other boys commence asking Snooksy and Spanish John and me if we will care to see the convention, too.

Personally, I do not care a whoop about seeing any convention, but the guys are so cordial about the matter that I do not have the heart to say no, so pretty soon there I am wearing a New Jersey badge, while Spanish John has a Massachusetts badge and Snooksy the badge belonging to the guy from Texas.

Also, we have cards saying we are delegates, and are full of instructions how to act and what to answer in case anybody starts asking questions. And now you know how it comes that Snooksy and Harry the Horse and Spanish John and me are sitting in the convention next day, although Spanish John and Snooksy are not doing much sitting, but are wandering around, and afterwards I hear there is some complaint from delegates about losing their leathers containing their return tickets and funds.

Now of course I never have any idea of going to the convention when the guys pin the badges on us, and I have no idea Harry the Horse will even think of such a thing, but nothing will do him but we must go, and he will not listen to my argument that the other delegates from New Jersey will see that we are strictly counterfeit. So there we are, and as it turns out there is great confusion in the convention when we get in, and nobody pays any attention to anybody else, which is a break for us.

In fact, Harry the Horse and me become quite pally with some of the guys around us, especially as Harry remembers before we start for the convention about a case of good beer that Snooksy sends us, and figuring we may need a refreshing dram while sitting in the convention, he slips several of these bottles into his pockets and wraps up several more, and this beer goes very nice indeed when Harry starts passing it about.

Personally I am greatly disappointed in the convention, because it is nothing but a lot of guys and dolls in a large hall, with signs stuck up here and there on sticks, with the names of different states on the signs. A guy up on a big platform is hammering on a table and yelling very loud, and everybody else seems to be yelling, and it strikes me as most undignified, especially as some of the guys start marching up and down the aisles carrying on quite some.

Several of the signs with the names of states on them are being lugged up and down the aisles, and every now and

then a new sign bobs up in the procession, and then the
racket gets worse than ever. I am about to mention to Harry
the Horse that we will be better off in some more quiet spot
when I notice him looking towards a sign that says New
York on it, and who is sitting in a chair alongside this sign
but Miss Maribel Marlo, looking very beautiful indeed.

Well, I know enough to know that this sign means that
the New York delegates are somewhere around close, and I
am wondering if any of my friends from my old home town
are present among them, because by this time I am getting
more homesick than somewhat.

Then all of a sudden some of the New York bunch joins
the marchers, and a tall, skinny guy reaches for the New
York sign with the idea of carrying it on the march.

At this, Miss Maribel Marlo stands up on her chair and
grabs hold of the sign, and the skinny guy starts to pull and
haul with her, trying to get the sign away from her. Personally, I will not give you two cents for a roomful of such
signs, but afterwards somebody explains to me that the
marching up and down the aisles, and the hollering, is a
demonstration in favour of some proposition before the
convention, such as a candidate, or something else, and in
this case it turns out to be something else.

It seems that a state sign in such a procession means that
the delegates from this state like the proposition, but it also
seems that sometimes the delegates from a state are all split
up, and some are by no means in favour of the proposition,
and they do not like to see their sign lugged around and
about, as it gives a wrong impression.

Well, it all sounds like a lot of foolishness to me and most
unbecoming of grown guys and dolls, but there the skinny
guy is, tugging one way at the New York sign, and there
Miss Maribel Marlo is, tugging the other way and showing
a strength that is most surprising. In fact, she is even money

in my book to out-tug the skinny guy, when Harry the Horse arrives on the spot and lets go with a neat left hook which connects with the skinny guy's chin.

He drops to the floor all spraddled out, leaving Miss Maribel Marlo still standing on the chair with the sign, and anybody can see that she is greatly pleased with Harry the Horse's hook, as she gives him a large smile and speaks as follows:

"Oh," she says, "thank you so much! I am glad to see you are on our side."

Well, just then a short chunky guy makes a reach for the sign, and Harry the Horse lets go another hook, but this one lands on the guy's noggin and only staggers him. Now the marching seems to stop, and one and all commence surging towards Harry the Horse.

Nearly everybody present, including many dolls, seems to be trying to get a pop at Harry, and he is letting punches fly right and left, and doing very well with them indeed. In fact, he has quite a number of guys down when a guy who seems to be about seven feet high and very thick through the chest, comes pushing his way through the crowd.

The big guy is wearing an Illinois badge, and as he pushes through the crowd he speaks as follows: "Let me attend to this matter," he says. Then when he finally gets close enough to Harry, he hauls off and hits the back of Harry's neck and knocks him into the chair on which Miss Maribel Marlo is standing. Personally I consider the blow a rabbit punch, which is very illegal, but anybody can see that the big guy is such a guy as is not apt to pay any attention to the rules.

The chair on which Miss Maribel Marlo is standing goes down as Harry the Horse hits it, and Miss Maribel Marlo goes with it, still holding on to the sign, and as she gets down she lets out a loud scream. She is up at once, however, and she does not seem to be hurt, but she is very indignant, because she realizes the public must see what kind of underwear she has on when she goes down.

She is holding the sign in both hands as she arises, and at the same time Harry the Horse also comes up, but very weak and staggering, and it is nothing but instinct that causes Harry to reach for his hip pocket, because generally Harry has the old equalizer in his pocket.

But when we arrive in town one of the first things Snooksy tells us is that we must not go around rodded up except when he tells us, as it seems that being rodded up is against the law in Chicago, especially for strangers, so instead of the old equalizer what does Harry find in his hip pocket but a bottle of good beer.

And when Harry finds this bottle of good beer in his hip pocket, he also remembers about another bottle of good beer in the side pocket of his coat, so he outs with both these bottles of good beer, holding one in each hand by the nozzle, and starts waving them around to get a good wind-up on them before dropping them on some near-by noggins.

Well, personally I always consider this action most unfortunate, as it seems the bottles of good beer give Miss Maribel Marlo a wrong impression of Harry the Horse, especially as one of the bottles suddenly pops open with a bang, what with the good beer getting all churned up from the waving around, and the foam flies every which way, some of it flying over Miss Maribel Marlo, who speaks to Harry the Horse as follows:

"Oh," she says, "so you are one of the enemy, too, are you?"

And with this, Miss Maribel Marlo hauls off and whacks Harry over the noggin with the New York sign, busting the sign staff in two pieces, and knocking Harry out into the aisle, where the big guy with the Illinois badge walks across Harry's chest, with Colorado, Indiana, New Mexico, California and Georgia following him one after the other.

Personally, I consider Miss Maribel Marlo's action very unladylike, especially as it causes a great waste of good beer, but when I visit Harry the Horse in hospital the next day he does not seem as mad at her as he is sorrowful, because Harry says he learns she makes a mistake, and he says anybody is apt to make a mistake.

But, Harry says, it ends all his ideas of romance because he can see that such mistakes are bad for a guy's health, especially as this one mistake gives him five broken ribs, a broken collar bone, a cauliflower ear and internal injuries. Harry says his future will be devoted entirely to getting even with the big guy with the Illinois badge, although, he says, he will not take this matter up until after we dispose of the business for which we are invited to Chicago.

But Snooksy, who is present at this discussion, does not seem to think there will be any business for us. In fact, Snooksy states that our hosts are disappointed in the outcome of our visit.

"You see," Snooksy says, "the big guy who assaults Harry is nobody but Donkey O'Neill himself, in person, and," Snooksy says, "the chances are, if he ever sees Harry again he will break his legs as well as his ribs. So," Snooksy says, "my people think the best thing you can do is to go home as soon as you are able, although," he says, "they are greatly obliged to you, at that."

Now (Little Isadore says) you know the story of our trip to Chicago, and what happens out there.

"But," I says to Little Isadore, "what is this convention of which you speak, a Republican or a Democratic convention?"

"Well," Little Isadore says, "I never think to ask, and anyway, this is not worrying me one way or the other. What is worrying me," he says, "and what is also worrying Harry the Horse and Spanish John, is that Angie the Ox may hear the false rumour that is being circulated in Chicago that we try to break up a demonstration in the convention, in favour of beer because of Harry the Horse's love for Miss Maribel Marlo. You see," Little Isadore says, "it seems that Miss Maribel Marlo is one of the most notorious Drys in this country."

13. A LIGHT IN FRANCE

IN the summer of 1936, a personality by the name of Blond Maurice is found buried in a pit of quicklime up in Sullivan County, or, anyway, what is found is all that is left of Maury, consisting of a few odds and ends in the way of bones, and a pair of shoes which have Brown the shoemaker's name in them, and which Brown identifies as a pair of shoes he makes for Maury some months before, when Maury is in the money and is able to have his shoes made to order.

It is common gossip in all circles along Broadway that Maury is placed in this quicklime by certain parties who do not wish him well, and it is also the consensus of opinion that placing him there is by no means a bad idea, at that, as Maury is really quite a scamp and of no great credit to the community. In fact, when it comes out that there is nothing left of him but a pair of shoes, it is agreed by one and all that it is two shoes too many.

Well, knowing that Maury is quicklimed, it is naturally something of a surprise to me to come upon him in Mindy's restaurant one evening in the spring of 1943, partaking of cheese blintzes. At first I think I am seeing a ghost, but, of course, I know that ghosts never come in Mindy's, and if they do, they never eat cheese blintzes, so I realize that it is nobody but Maury himself.

Consequently I step over to his table and give him a medium hello, and he looks up and gives me a medium hello right back, for, to tell the truth, Maury and I are never bosom friends. In fact, I always give him plenty of the back of my neck because I learn long ago that it is best not to associate with such harum-scarum personalities unless, of course, you need them.

But naturally I am eager to hear of his experiences in the quicklime as I never before meet a guy who returns from being buried in this substance, so I draw up a chair and speak to him as follows:

"Well, Maury," I say, "where are you all this time that I do not see you around and about?"

"I am in a place called France," Maury says. "I leave there on account of the war. Perhaps you hear of the war?"

"Yes," I say, "I hear rumours of it from time to time."

"It is a great nuisance," Maury says.

"But, Maury," I say, "how do you come to go to a place where there is a war?"

"Oh," Maury says, "there is no war when I go there. The war is here in New York. This city is very unsettled at the time, what with the unpleasantness between my employer, the late Little Kishke, and Sammy Downtown developing cases for the medical examiner all over the layout. I am pleased to find on my return that law and order now prevail."

"But, Maury," I say, "how do you stand with reference to law and order?"

"I am in favour of both," Maury says.

"Oh, I am all right. Immediately upon my return, I call on the D.A. in Manhattan to see if he has anything he wishes me to plead guilty to, and he cannot find a thing, although he seems somewhat regretful, at that.

"Then," Maury says, "I go over to Brooklyn and call on the D.A. there, and he consults the books of Murder, Incorporated, and he states that all he can find entered under my name is that I am deceased, and that he hopes and trusts I will remain so. I am as clean as a whistle, and," Maury says, "maybe cleaner."

"Well," I say, "I am glad to hear this, Maury. I always know you are sound at bottom. By the way, do you run into Girondel on your travels? We hear that he is over there also. At least, he is absent quite a spell. Girondel is always a great one for going around and about in foreign lands."

"No," Maury says, "I do not see him there. But if you care to listen, I will now relate to you my adventures in France."

Well (Maury says), I go to France when things come up that convince me that I am not as popular as formerly with Sammy Downtown and his associates, and, furthermore, I am tired out and feel that I can use a little rest and peace.

And the reason I pick this France as a place to go to is because I take a fancy to the country when I am there once on a pleasure trip all over Europe as a guest of the late Drums Capello, who is in the importing business, and what he imports is such merchandise as morphine and heroin and sometimes a little opium.

But I wish to state that I have no part of Drums' play in this respect and no part of his fall when the Brush finally catches up with him. And, furthermore, I wish to state that I never approve of his enterprise in any way whatever, but I must say he is a fine host and takes me all over England and Germany, and introduces me to many of his friends and business associates, and you can have them.

Now, the exact spot in France to which I go is a sleepy little town on the seacoast, but I cannot reveal the name at this time as it is a military secret and, anyway, I am unable to pronounce it. The main drag of this town faces a small harbour, and you can stand in front of any place of business along the stem and almost flip a dime into the water—if you happen to have a dime to spare.

It is an old fishing spot, and when I first go there, it is infested by fishermen with hay on their chins, and while most of them inhabit dinky little houses in the town, others live on farms about the size of napkins just outside the burg, and they seem to divide their time between chasing fish and cows. But it is quiet and peaceful there, and very restful after you get used to not hearing the Broadway traffic.

I reside in a tiny gaff that is called a hotel on the main street, and this gaff is run by a French bim by the name of Marie. In fact, all bims in France seem to be named Marie when they are not named Yvonne. I occasionally notice an old sack in the background who may be Marie's mamma or her aunt or some such, but Marie is strictly the boss of the trap and operates it in first-class style. She is the chief clerk and the headwaiter and she is also the bartender in the little smoky bar-room that opens directly on the street, so, if the door is left open, you get herring with your cognac.

I know she makes the beds and dusts up the three tiny bedrooms in the joint, so you can see she is an all-around personality. She is maybe twenty years old, and I will not attempt to describe her except to say that if I am interested in the hugging and kissing department, I will most certainly take my business to Marie, especially as she speaks English, and you will not have to waste time with the sign language.

Well, it is very pleasant, to be sure, strolling around the little town talking to the fishermen or wandering out into the country and observing the agriculturists, who seem to be mostly female personalities who are all built in such a way that they will never be able to sit down in a washtub with comfort, and who really have very little glamour.

It is also very pleasant to nuzzle a dram or two in the cool of the evening at a little table in front of Marie's hotel and it is there I make the acquaintance of the only other roomer in the hotel. He is a fat old guy who is nobody but Thaddeus T. Blackman, a rich zillionaire from the city of New York and a lam-master from the Brush boys back home for over twenty years on an income-tax beef.

It seems that Thaddeus T. is mixed up in a large scandal about oil lands, and a grand jury hands out readers right and left among some of the best people in the U.S.A., although all they do is swindle the government, and it is a great shock to them to learn that this is against the law.

Anyway, Thaddeus T. starts running as soon as he gets wind of the beef and does not pause for breath until he arrives in this little town in France, and there he lives all these years. It seems the Brush cannot touch him there, and why this is I do not know, but I suppose it is because he is smart enough to take his zillions with him, and naturally this kind of moolouw is protection on land or sea.

He discusses his case with me once and gives me to understand that it is a bum beef as far as he is concerned and that he only takes the fall for others, but of course this is by no means an unfamiliar tale to me, and, as he never mentions why he does not try to chill the beef by paying the government the dough, I do not consider it tactful to bring the matter up.

He is up in the paint-cards in age when I meet him, being maybe close to seventy, and he is a fashion plate of the fashion of about 1922. Moreover, he seems to be a lonely old gee, though how anybody can be lonely with all his zillions is a great mystery to me. He always has a short briar pipe in his mouth and is generally lighting it with little wax matches, and, in fact, I never see a pipe man who is not generally lighting his pipe, and if ever I get time I will invent a pipe that stays lit and make a fortune.

Anyway, Thaddeus T. and I become good friends over

the little table in front of the hotel, and then one day who shows up but an old pal of mine out of the city of Boston, Mass, who is also an absentee from a small charge of homicide in his home town.

He is called by the name of Mike the Mugger because it seems his occupation is reaching out of doorways on dark nights and taking passers-by by the neck and pulling them in close to him with one hand and examining into their pockets with the other hand, the idea of the hand around the neck being to keep them from complaining aloud until he is through with them.

Personally, I do not consider this occupation at all essential or even strictly ethical, but I always say every guy to his own taste and naturally I have to respect Mike as the very top guy in his profession who never makes a mistake except the one time he clasps a customer too tight and too long and becomes involved in this difficulty I mention.

He is about thirty-odd and is a nifty drifty in his dress and very good company, except that he is seldom holding anything and is generally leaning on me. However, I am personally loaded at this time and I am not only pleased to okay Mike with Marie for the last of her three rooms, but I stake him to walk-about money, which is money for his pocket, and he is grateful to me in every respect.

Naturally, Mike joins out with Thaddeus T. and me in strolling here and there and in sitting at the little table in front of the hotel or in the bar-room, talking and playing cards, and what we generally talk about, of course, is the good old U.S.A., which is a subject of great interest to all three of us.

A few fishermen and small merchants of the town are also usually in the bar-room, and Marie is always behind the bar, and it is not long before I notice that both Thaddeus

T. and Mike the Mugger are paying considerable attention to her. In fact, Mike tells me he is in love with her and is surprised that I am not in the same condition.

"But," Mike says, "of course I will never mention my love to Marie because I am undoubtedly a low-class personality with a tough beef against me and am unfit to associate with a nice lady saloon-keeper."

As far as I can see, Thaddeus T.'s interest in Marie is more fatherly than anything else, which is very nice if you like an old wolf for a father. He tells me he wishes he has her for his daughter because, he says, the one of his own back in the U.S.A. is a dingbat and so is her mamma, and from the way he carries on about them, I can see that Thaddeus T.'s former home life is far from being a plug for matrimony.

Now it comes on 1939 and with it the war, and Thaddeus T., who can gabble the frog language quite fluently and is always around on the Ear-ie finding out what is going on, tells me that the people of the town are pretty much worked up and that some of the guys are going away to join the army, but it makes little difference in our lives, as we seem to be outside the active war zone, and all we know about any actual fighting is what we hear.

We still sit out in front of the hotel in the afternoon and in the bar-room at night, though I observe Marie now pays more attention to other customers than she does to us and is always chattering to them in a most excited manner, and Thaddeus T. says it is about the war. He says Marie is taking it to heart no little and quite some.

But it is not until the summer of 1940 that Thaddeus T. and me and even Mike really notice the war, because overnight the little town fills up with German soldiers and other German guys who are not soldiers but seem to be working gees, and it is plain to be seen that something big is doing.

Thaddeus T. says he hears they are making a submarine base of the harbour because it is a very handy spot for the subs to sneak out of and knock off the British ships, and in fact after a while we see many subs and other shipping along the quays.

Anyway, the Germans pay very little attention to us at first except to examine our papers, and the officers who come into Marie's bar for drinks are quite polite and nod to us and sometimes talk to Thaddeus T., who speaks German better than he does French. Presently we are practically ignoring the presence of the Germans in our midst, although naturally Marie has no fancy for them whatever and is always making faces at them behind their backs and spitting on the ground when they pass, until I tell her that this is unladylike.

Well, on coming home one night from a little stroll, I hear a commotion in the kitchen, which is just off the bar-room, and on entering I observe Marie wrestling with a big blubber in civilian clothes who is wearing a small scrubbly moustache and a derby hat and who has practically no neck whatever.

They are knocking kitchen utensils right and left, including a pot of spaghetti which I know Marie prepares for my dinner and which vexes me no little. Marie is sobbing and I can see that the blubber is outwrestling her and in fact has a strangle hold on her that figures to win him the fall very shortly. I am standing there, admiring his technique in spite of my vexation over the spaghetti, when Marie sees me and calls to me as follows:

"Please help me, Chauncey," which, as I forget to tell you before, is at this time my monicker, and I am then in possession of passports and other papers to prove same.

Naturally, I pay no attention to her, as I do not know on

what terms she is wrestling the blubber, but finally I see she is in some distress, so I step forward and tap the bloke on the shoulder and say to him like this:

"I beg your pardon," I say, "but the strangle hold is illegal. If you are going to wrestle, you must obey the rules."

At this, the guy lets go of Marie and steps back and I say to her in English, "Who is this plumber?"

"He is Herr Klauber," Marie says back to me in English. "He is the head of the Gestapo in this district."

Well, then I get a good glaum at the gee and I see that he is nobody but the same Klauber that Drums Capello does business with in Hamburg the time I am Drums' guest, only in those days he is not usually called by the name of Klauber. He is called the Vasserkopf, which is a way of saying "waterhead" in German, because he has an extra large sconce piece that is practically a deformity and as the Vasserkopf he is known far and wide on two continents, and especially here in New York where he once operates, as a very sure-footed merchant in morphine, heroin, opium and similar commodities.

Naturally, it is a great pleasure to me to behold a familiar puss in a strange place, even if it is only the Vasserkopf's puss, so I give him a sizeable hello and speak to him as follows:

"Well, Vasser," I say, "this is an unexpected privilege, to be sure. There you are and here I am, and much water runs over the dam since last we met, and how are you anyway?"

"Who are you?" the Vasserkopf says in English and in a most unfriendly manner.

"Come, come, Vasser," I say. "Let us not waste time in shadow-boxing. Do you know our old pal Drums finally takes a fall in Milwaukee, Wis., for a sixer?"

Then the Vasserkopf comes close to me and speaks to me in a low voice like this: "Listen," he says, "it is in my mind to throw you in the gaol house."

"Tut-tut, Vass," I say, "if you throw me in the gaol house, I will be compelled to let out a bleat. I will be compelled to remember the time you ship the cargo of Santa Clauses out of Nuremberg and each Santa contains enough of the white to junk up half of the good old U.S.A. I hear your Fuehrer is a strait-laced gee, and what will he say if he hears one of his big coppers peddles junk and maybe uses it?"

I can see the Vasserkopf turns a little pale around the guzzle at this statement and he says: "Come outside. We will talk."

So I go outside the gaff with him, and we stand in the street in the darkness and have quite a chat and the Vasserkopf becomes more friendly and tells me that he is now a real high-muck-a-muck with the Gestapo and the greatest spy catcher in the racket. Then he wishes to know what I am doing in these parts, and I tell him quite frankly that I am there for my health and explain my ailment to him. I also tell him why Thaddeus T. and Mike the Mugger are there because I know that, as a former underworld personality, the Vasserkopf is apt to be understanding and sympathetic in such situations, especially when he knows my hole card is my knowledge of his background in junk.

"Now, Vass," I say, "all we wish is to be let alone, and if you can assist us in any way, I will personally be much obliged. What is more," I say, "I will see that you are well rewarded, if a member of the Gestapo takes."

"Sure," the Vasserkopf says. "Only let us understand one thing right off the reel. The broad belongs to me. I am crazy about her. But there is talk to-day at headquarters of closing this place and putting her out of business because

236

of her attitude, and because one of our officers becomes ill after drinking cognac in here last night.

"I will tell the dumb military he probably has a touch of ptomaine," he continues. "I will tell them I need this hotel as a listening post to find out what is going on among the people around here. I will advise them not to molest you, as you are neutrals, and it may make trouble with your government, although," the Vasserkopf says, "I can see that the only trouble your government may make will be for you. But the Reich is not interested in American lammeroos, and neither am I as long as you remember the dame is mine and see that I collect a hundred a week in your money. I can scarcely sleep nights thinking of her."

Now this seems to me to be a very reasonable proposition all the way round, except for the hundred a week. The way I look at it, the Vasserkopf is at least entitled to Marie for his trouble because, to tell the truth, it will be most inconvenient for Thaddeus T. and Mike the Mugger and me to leave this spot at the moment, as there is no other place we can go and no way of getting there if there is such a place.

So I shave the Vasserkopf to half a C every week, and then I go back into the hotel to find Marie in the bar with Thaddeus T. and Mike, and I can see that she is quite agitated by her recent experience with the Vasserkopf. I also learn from her that it is not his first visit.

"He is here several times before," Marie says. "He comes to me first with news of my brother who is a prisoner in a camp near Hamburg. Herr Klauber tells me he can make things easier for Henri and perhaps get him released. He comes again and again on different excuses. I am frightened because I fear his motive." Then all of a sudden Marie puts her fingers to her lips and says, "Hark!"

We hark, and I hear away off somewhere a sound that I

know must come from a lot of planes, and as this sound grows louder and louder, and then dies away again, Marie says:

"English bombers," she says. "Every night they pass over here and go on up the coast to drop their bombs. They do not know what is going on here. Oh, if we can only show a light here to let them know this is a place to strike —this nest of snakes."

"A light?" I say. "Why, if you show a light around here, these squareheads will settle you in no time. Besides," I say, "it may get me and my friends in a jam, and we are Americans and very neutral. Let us not even think of showing a light and, Marie," I say, "kindly cease sizzling every time you serve a German, and, Mike, if you have any more Mickey Finns on your person, please take them yourself instead of dropping them in officers' drinks."

"Who? Me?" Mike the Mugger says.

Well, I see the Vasserkopf in the hotel almost every day after this talking to Marie, and he always gives me an E-flat hello and I give him the same, and, while I can see that Marie is afraid of him, she says he is now very polite to her and does not try to show her any more holds.

Of course, I do not tell Marie about my deal with the Vasserkopf and I do not tell Mike either, though I inform Thaddeus T., as I expect him to kick with some of the dough, and he says okay and that he is glad to learn that the Vasserkopf is on the take, only he thinks the half a C is enough without throwing in Marie. But he says a deal is a deal, and I can count on his co-operation.

From now on as far as we are concerned, everything seems to be almost the same as before there is any war whatever, except that we cannot go near the water front where the Germans are working and everything has to be blacked out good after dark, and you cannot as much as strike a

match in the street, which is a great nuisance to Thaddeus
T., as he is always striking matches. In fact, he almost gets
his toupee blown off by sentries before he can break himself of the habit of striking matches outdoors at night.

I can see that the Vasserkopf must be keeping his agreement to front for us at headquarters, all right, and I am
greasing him every week per our arrangement, but I find
myself bored by the place, and I have a feeling that it is
time for Mike the Mugger and maybe Thaddeus T., too, to
leave, especially as the Vasserkopf accidentally drops a hint
one day that he finds himself impeded in his progress with
Marie by our constant presence in the hotel and that he
thinks he is getting the short end of the deal. Finally, I have
a conference with Thaddeus T. and state my views to him.

"Yes," Thaddeus T. says, "you are a hundred per cent.
right. But," he says, "leaving here is not a simple matter
for us now. I am reliably informed that the military is
likely to oppose our departure for the present, because the
sub base here is a great secret and they do not care to run
the risk of having us noise it about.

"In fact," he says, "I am told that they are sorry they
do not chase us when they first come here, but now that
they make this mistake, they are not going to make another
by letting us depart, and other information that I hesitate
to credit is that they may wind up clapping us in a detention
camp somewhere."

"Thaddeus T.," I say, "I am an American and so is
Mike and so are you, and our country is not concerned in
this war. No one can hold us here against our wishes."

Well, at this, Thaddeus T. lets out a large laugh, and I
can see his point and laugh with him, and then he informs
me that for some days he is personally laying plans for our
departure and that he buys a slightly tubercular motor-boat
from a certain personality, and has it hidden at this very

moment in a little cove about a mile up the coast and that all he now needs is a little petrol, which is a way of saying gasoline, to run the boat with the three of us in it out to sea, where we will have the chance of being picked up.

Thaddeus T. explains to me that all the petrol in this vicinity is in the hands of the Germans, but he says that where there is a will, there is a way. Consequently, he makes arrangements with the same personality who sells him the boat for a supply of gasoline, and who is this personality but the Vasserkopf, and Thaddeus is paying him more per gill for the gas than the old Vass ever gets per ounce for his hop, and, as I am personally paying him regularly, I can see that he is getting his coming and going and, naturally, I have to admire his enterprise.

However, Thaddeus states that the Vasserkopf is really most co-operative in every respect, and that he is to deliver the gas at the hotel the following night, and moreover that he is going to escort us to the cove so we will not be molested by any sentries we may encounter in that vicinity, which I say is very nice of the Vasserkopf though I seem to remember that there are never any sentries in that vicinity anyway, as it is part of the coast that does not seem to interest the Germans in any manner.

Then I get to meditating more and more on the Vasserkopf and on what a big heart he has, to be sure, and as I am meditating I am also sauntering late the next evening in a roundabout way up the coast as I wish to confirm the presence of the boat in the cove because, of course, there is the possibility of it getting away after the Vasserkopf has it placed there.

My roundabout saunter carries me across the fields of the little farms beyond the town that in some places run almost down to the sea, and it is a route that the Germans are not apt to suspect as taking me on any considerable journey, even if they notice me sauntering, which I take care they do not.

Finally, I saunter through a field to a slight rise of ground that overlooks the little cove, and there is just enough daylight left by now for me to see a boat floating just offshore, and at this same moment, I am surprised to scent the odour of fresh-turned earth near at hand, and the reason I am surprised is because it is now winter and by no means ploughing time.

Consequently, I look around and I am further surprised to observe on this rise a newly made trench on the ground of a size and shape that brings back many memories to me. So I saunter back in a more roundabout way still meditating no little and quite some on the Vasserkopf.

But, sure enough, he shows up this very night around nine o'clock after Marie closes her place, and he brings with him two five-gallon cans of gasoline which he delivers to Thaddeus T. in the bar where Thaddeus and me and Mike the Mugger are waiting to receive the gas. Then, after handing over the cans, the Vass goes looking for Marie, saying he wishes to speak to her before escorting us to the boat.

As soon as he leaves the bar, Mike the Mugger outs with his pocketknife and stabs holes in two corners of the can and speaks as follows: "It smells like gasoline on the outside, but we smear the outside of cans with booze in the old bootleg days for the liquor smell when there is only water inside the cans. I hear the Vasserkopf is an old booter and he may remember the trick, and, besides, I do not trust him on general principles."

Now Mike lifts the can up as if it is no more than a demitasse and he holds it to his mouth so he can get a swig of the contents through one of the holes, when all of a sudden who comes into the bar all out of breath but Marie and who is right behind her but the Vasserkopf, and there is no doubt that Marie is greatly flustered, and the Vasserkopf is much perturbed.

"So," he says to me, "you are double-crossing me and are going to take this omelete with you, hey? Well, it is a good thing I walk in on her as she is packing a keister, and I am now arresting her as a dangerous spy."

Marie begins to weep and wail and to carry on as bims will do when they are flustered, and naturally Thaddeus T. and me and Mike the Mugger are quite perplexed by this situation and, in fact, Mike is so perplexed that he is still holding the can in his hands and his cheeks are bulged out on each side from the gasoline in his mouth as if he has the mumps.

I am about to say something to cool the Vasserkopf off, for, to tell the truth, up to this minute I have no idea Marie is going with us, though I can see from the way Thaddeus T. and Mike the Mugger look that it is undoubtedly their idea. And, before I can say anything, Mike steps up to the Vasserkopf and gives a huge ploo-oo-oo and spews his mouthful of gasoline right in the Vasserkopf's kisser and, as he gets his mouth clear, Mike says, "Why, you muzzler, it is somewhat watered, just as I suspect."

Well, naturally, the gasoline runs off the Vasserkopf's face and down over his clothes and he is standing there looking quite nonplussed, and, as Mike the Mugger sees me gazing at him disapprovingly, he becomes embarrassed and self-conscious and, maybe to cover his confusion, he lifts the can of gasoline and holds it over the Vasserkopf's head, and the gas pours out and splashes off the old Vass' derby hat and splatters over his shoulders while he just stands there nonplussed.

Thaddeus T. Blackman is leaning against the bar and, as usual, he is lighting his pipe with a little wax match and

watching the Vasserkopf, and Marie has stopped crying
and is laughing, and I am just standing there, when we
again hear the sound of the planes high overhead and
Thaddeus T. speaks as follows:

"A light you say, Marie?" he says. "A light for the
English?"

Then he flips the lighted match on the Vasserkopf, whose
clothes burst into flames at once and, almost as if they plan
it all out beforehand, Mike jumps to the front door and
opens it, and Thaddeus T. pushes the Vasserkopf, all
ablaze, out the door into the street and yells at him:

"Run for the water!" he yells. "Run, run, run!"

The Vasserkopf seems to see what he means and starts
galloping lickity-split towards the water front with Thaddeus T. puffing along behind him and giving him a shove
whenever he shows signs of lagging, and Mike the Mugger
runs up behind the Vasserkopf and keeps throwing little
spurts of gasoline on him by jerking the can at him and,
from the way it burns on the Vasserkopf, I think Mike's
statement of its dilution may be a slight exaggeration.

As he runs and burns, the Vasserkopf is letting out loud
cries which bring soldiers from every which way, and presently they start shooting off their rifles in different direc-
tions. He is really quite a bonfire there in the darkness, and
now I hear once more far overhead the drone of planes and
I figure the English bombers see the light and turn back
over the town.

All of a sudden there is a whistling sound and then a big
ker-bloom, and then more whistling and more *ker-blooms*,
and there is no doubt in my mind that it is Katie-bar-
the-door for the water front and the subs lying along the
quays.

I can see the Vasserkopf still blazing and I can hear
Thaddeus T. still urging him to run, and now the bombs

are shellacking the surrounding buildings, and presently I hear, in between the blasts of the bombs, some rifle shots, and I know the soldiers are firing at Thaddeus T. and Mike the Mugger and maybe at the Vasserkopf, too, for making the light.

In fact, by the glow shed by the Vasserkopf, I see old Thaddeus stumble and fall, and Mike the Mugger go down right afterwards with his can of gasoline blazing over him, but the Vasserkopf continues on still in flames until he falls off the quay into the water and, the chances are, goes out with a zizz.

Well, when I think of Marie, I turn from these unusual scenes to the little hotel, but it is no longer there, because a bomb flattens it, too, and it is now nothing but a pile of miscellany. I do not have much time to look for Marie, as the German soldiers are all over the layout, trying to learn what happens, but I finally locate her with a big beam across her chest, and I can see that there is nothing I can do for her except kiss her and say good-bye, and when I do this, she murmurs, "Thanks," but I am sure it is only for Thaddeus T. and Mike the Mugger and the light.

You will scarcely believe the difficulty I experience in getting away from this unpleasant situation and out of the country. In fact, I have only a vague recollection of my adventures now, but I will always remember very clearly how neatly I slip past four German soldiers sitting in the new-made trench on the rise of ground above the cove, with a machine gun covering the cove itself, and how I get in the boat and cut it loose and work it, with my hands for paddles, to open water, before they realize what is going on.

And I can never again have any respect for the memory of the Vasserkopf when I take to meditating on his unsportsmanlike conduct in trying to double-cinch a sure thing with a machine gun, although there are times before

I am picked up at sea by an English destroyer that I find myself wishing that Mike the Mugger does not waste all the gasoline on the Vass, even if it is watered.

And this is all there is to the story (Maury says).

"But, Maury," I say, "do you not know that some re-mainders found in a pit of quicklime up in Sullivan County are supposed to be yours? They have on your shoes, which are identified by Brown the shoemaker. Are you ever in a quicklime pit in Sullivan County and, if so, what is it like?"

"Oh," Maury says, "I am in Sullivan County, all right, but never in a quicklime pit. I go to Sullivan County at the invitation of Girondel, and the purpose of his invitation is to discuss ways and means of getting me straightened out with his chief, Sammy Downtown.

"But one day," Maury says, "Girondel invites me to a stroll in the woods with him and, while we are strolling, he is talking about the beauties of the landscape and calling my attention to the flowers and the birds, which is all very interesting, to be sure, but something tells me that Girondel is by no means the nature lover he seems.

"Finally," Maury says, "he strolls me to a spot in the deep, tangled wildwood, and all of a sudden I catch an odour of something I never scent but once before in my life but will never again forget, and that is the time we lay the late Bugs Wonder to rest in Greenvale Cemetery. It is the odour of the fresh-turned earth from Bugs' last resting place.

"And as I catch this again in the woods," Maury says, "I realize that somebody does some digging around there lately, so I quietly give Girondel a boff over his pimple with a blackjack and flatten him like a welcome mat. Then I examine my surroundings and, sure enough, there, hidden by the shrubbery, I find a deep fresh-made hole lined with quicklime, and I place Girondel in it and cover him up and leave him with my best wishes.

"But, first," Mary says, "I changes shoes with him because my own are badly worn and, besides, I know that if ever he is found the shoes will outlast the quicklime and be traced as mine, and I wish Girondel's connection to think I am no more. By the way," he says, "the odour I mention is the same I notice on the rise of ground at the cove in France which causes me to distrust the Vasserkopf. I guess I am just naturally allergic to the odour of new-made graves."

14. OLD EM'S KENTUCKY HOME

ALL this really begins the April day at the Jamaica race track when an assistant starter by the name of Plumbuff puts a twitch on Itchky Ironhat's fourteen-year-old race mare, Emaleen, who is known to one and all as Em for short.

A twitch is nothing but a rope loop that they wrap around a horse's upper lip and keep twisting with a stick to make the horse stand quiet at the starting gate and while I never have a twitch on my own lip and hope and trust that I never have same, I do not see anything wrong with putting twitches on horses' lips, especially the ones I am betting against as it generally keeps them so busy thinking of how it hurts that they sometimes forget about running.

However, it seems that Itchky Ironhat not only considers a twitch very painful to horses, but he also considers it undignified for such a horse as old Em, because while everybody else regards Em as strictly a porcupine, Itchky thinks she is the best horse in the world and loves her so dearly he cannot bear to see her in pain or made to look undignified. To tell the truth, it is common gossip that Itchky loves old Em more than he loves anything else whatever including his ever-loving wife, Mousie.

In fact, when Mousie tells him one day that the time comes for a show down and that it is either her or old Em and Itchky says well, he guesses it is old Em, and Mousie packs up on him at once and returns to her trade as an artists' model many citizens who remember Mousie's shape think Itchky makes a bad deal, although some claim that the real reason Itchky decides in favour of Em against Mousie is not so much love as it is that Em never wishes for any large thick sirloin steaks such as Mousie adores.

Anyway, it seems that Itchky always goes to the trouble of personally requesting the assistant starters not to place twitches on Em's lip, even though he knows very well that she is by no means a bargain at the post and that she greatly enjoys nibbling assistant starters' ears off and when Plumbuff ignores his request it vexes Itchky no little.

The night after the race he calls on Plumbuff at his home in Jackson Heights and chides him quite some and he also gives him such a going-over that Plumbuff is compelled to take to his bed slightly indisposed for several weeks.

When the racing officials learn of the incident they call Itchky before them and address him in very severe terms. They ask him if he thinks old Em is Mrs. Man o' War, or what, that he expects great courtesy for her from assistant starters and they say they have half a mind to rule Itchky off the turf for life and old Em along with him. But Itchky states that he only acts in self-defence and that he can produce twenty witnesses who will testify that Plumbuff pulls a blunt instrument on him first.

The chances are Itchky can produce these witnesses, at that, as all he will have to do is go down to Mindy's restaurant on Broadway and summon the first twenty horse players he sees. Horse players hate and despise assistant starters because they feel that the assistants are always giving the horses they bet on the worst of the starts and naturally these horse players will deem it a privilege and a pleasure to perjure themselves in a case of this nature, especially for Itchky Ironhat, who is a popular character.

His right name is something in twelve letters, but he is called Itchky Ironhat because he always wears a black derby hat and generally he has it pulled down on his head until the brim is resting on his ears and as Itchky is a short, roly-poly guy with a fat puss he really looks a great deal like a corked jug.

Finally the racing officials say they will not rule Itchky or old Em off this time but that he must remove Em from the New York tracks and run her elsewhere and this is wonderful news to the assistant starters, who are awaiting the decision with interest.

They feel that they are all sure to wind up daffy if they have to always be deciding on whether to cater to old Em at the post or take a going-over from Itchky Ironhat and in fact they say the only thing that keeps them from going daffy on account of old Em long before this is that she does not go to the post often.

She is entered in more races than any horse that ever lives, but just before a race comes up Itchky generally starts figuring that maybe the track will not suit her, or that the race is too long, or maybe too short, or that it is not the right time of day, or that old Em will not feel just like running that day, so he usually withdraws her at the last minute.

Sometimes the racing officials are a little tough with owners who wish to scratch horses from a race at the last minute, but they never argue a second with Itchky Iron hat. In fact, they often give three cheers when Em is taken out of a race, not only because she is so cross at the post but because she is so slow that she is always getting in the way of other horses and inconveniencing them more than somewhat.

It is the way Itchky thinks old Em feels that figures with him in taking her out of a race more than anything else, and to hear him talk you will think she comes right out and informs him how she feels every day. Indeed, Itchky converses with old Em as if she is a human being and he claims

she can understand everything he says, though personally I
do not believe any horse can understand a slightly Yiddish
dialect such as Itchky employs.

She is a big bay mare with a sway-back and of course she
is quite elderly for a horse, and especially a race horse,
but Itchky says she does not look her years. She is as fat
as a goose what with him feeding her candy, apples, cakes
and ice-cream, besides a little hay and grain, and she is
wind-broken and a bleeder and has knobs on her knees the
size of baseballs.

She has four bad ankles and in fact the only thing that
is not the matter with her is tuberculosis and maybe anæmia.
It makes some horse owners shudder just to look at her
but in Itchky Ironhat's eyes old Em is more beautiful than
Seabiscuit.

A guy by the name of Crowbar gives her to Itchky at the
Woodbine track in Canada when she is just a two-year-old,
rising three. This guy Crowbar buys her as a yearling out
of a sale at Saratoga for fifty fish but becomes discouraged
about her when he notices that she cannot keep up with a
lead pony even when the pony is just walking.

On top of this she bows a tendon, so Crowbar is taking
her out to shoot her to save the expense of shipping her
and he is pretty sore at having to waste a cartridge on her
when he meets up with Itchky Ironhat and Itchky asks what
is coming off. When Crowbar explains, Itchky takes a closer
look at Em and she gazes at him with such a sorrowful
expression that Itchky's heart is touched.

He asks Crowbar to give her to him, although at this
time Itchky is just doing the best he can around the tracks
and has about as much use for a racehorse as he has for a
hearse, and naturally Crowbar is pleased to make the
saving of a cartridge. So this is how Itchky becomes the
owner of old Em and from now on he practically lives

with her even after he marries Mousie, which is what starts Mousie to complaining, as it seems she does not care to be excluded from her home life by a horse.

It is no use trying to tell Itchky that Em is nothing but an old buzzard, because he keeps thinking of her as a stake horse and saying she is bound to win a large stake someday and he spends every dime he can get hold of in entering her in big races and on shipping her and feeding her and on jockey fees.

And all this is very surprising to be sure, as Itchky Ironhat is by no means a sucker when it comes to other horses and he makes a pretty good living hustling around the tracks. What is more, the way he can bring old Em back to the races every time she breaks down, which is about every other time she starts in a race, shows that Itchky is either a natural-born horse trainer or a horse hypnotist.

When he is very desperate for a little moolah, he will place Em in a cheap selling race and it is in spots such as this that she occasionally wins. But then Itchky always worries himself sick for fear somebody will claim her, the idea of a claiming race being that another owner can always claim a horse in such a race by putting up the price for which the horse is entered, which may be anywhere from a few hundred dollars on up, according to the conditions of the race and what the owner thinks his horse is worth.

Naturally, Itchky has to run old Em for as cheap a price as horses are ever run for her to win a race, but even then there is really no sense in him worrying about her being claimed as no owner with any brains wants such a lizard as old Em in his barn, and especially after what happens to a character by the name of One Thumb Haverstraw.

This One Thumb is considered quite a joker and one day in Maryland he claims old Em out of a race for eight

hundred boffoes just for a joke on Itchky, although personally I always figure the joke is on One Thumb when he
gets her for this price.

Itchky is really greatly dejected over losing old Em and
he goes to see One Thumb right after the race and tries to
buy her back for two hundred dollars over the claiming
price, but One Thumb is so pleased with his joke that he
refuses to sell and then the most surprising things begin to
occur to him.

A few nights later a ghost in a white sheet appears at his
barn and frightens away all the coloured parties who are
working for him as stable-hands and turns all of One
Thumb's horses out of their stalls except old Em and chases
them around the country until they are worn plumb out and
are no good for racing for some weeks to come.

What is more, every time One Thumb himself steps into
the open at night, a bullet whistles past him and finally one
breezes through the seat of his pants and at this he hunts
up Itchky Ironhat and returns old Em to him for four
hundred less than the claiming price and considers it a great
bargain, at that, and nobody ever plays any more jokes on
Itchky with old Em.

Now the night of the racing officials' decision, I am
sitting in Mindy's restaurant enjoying some choice pot
roast with potato pancakes when in comes Itchky Ironhat
looking somewhat depressed and, as he takes a seat at my
table, naturally I tell him I deeply regret hearing that he
will no longer be permitted to run old Em in New York,
and Itchky sighs and says:

"Well," he says, "it is a great loss to the racing public
of this state, but I always wish to do something nice for
old Em and this gives me the opportunity of doing it."

"What will be something nice for her, Itchky?" I say.

"Why," Itchky says, "I take her many places the past

dozen years, but there is one place I never take her and that is her old home. You see, Em comes from the Bluegrass country of Kentucky and I get to thinking that the nicest thing I can do for her is to take her there and let her see the place where she is born."

"Itchky," I say, "how is the bank roll?"

"It is thin," Itchky says. "In fact, if you are thinking of a touch, it is practically invisible."

"I am not thinking of such a thing," I say. "What I am thinking of is it will cost a gob to ship old Em to Kentucky."

"Oh," Itchky says, "I do not intend to ship her. I intend to take her there in person by motor truck and I am wondering if you will not like to go with us for company, Old Em loves company. After we let her see her old home we can drop her in a stake race at Churchill Downs and win a package."

Then Itchky explains to me that he acquires a truck that very afternoon from a vegetable pedlar for the sum of sixty dollars and that he also gets a couple of wide, strong planks which he figures he can let down from the rear end of the truck like a runway so old Em can walk on them getting on and off the truck and that by driving by day and resting by night he can take her to the Bluegrass of Kentucky this way very nicely.

Now it is coming on time for the Kentucky Derby and if there is one thing I wish to see it is this event, and furthermore I never get around the country much and I figure that such a journey will be most educational to me so I tell Itchky he has a customer. But if I see the truck first I will certainly never think of trying to get anywhere in it, not even to the Polo Grounds.

Of course when Itchky tells me the truck costs him only sixty dollars, I am not looking for a fancy truck, but I have no idea it is going to be older than Henry Ford, or anyway Edsel, and not much bigger than a pushcart and with no top whatever, even over the seat.

The body of the truck is not long enough for old Em to stand in it spraddled out, the way horses love to stand, or her hind legs will be hanging out the rear end, so what Itchky does is to push her front legs back and her hind legs forward, so that all four feet are close together under her like she is standing on a dime.

Personally, I consider this an uncomfortable position all the way around for a horse but when Itchky and I get on the seat and Em finds she can rest her head on Itchky's shoulder, she seems quite happy, especially as Itchky talks to her most of the time.

It is no time after we start that we find old Em makes the truck top-heavy and in fact she almost falls overboard every time we take a curve and Itchky has to choke down to about two miles per hour until all of a sudden Em learns how to lean her weight to one side of the truck or the other on the curves and then Itchky can hit it up to the full speed of the truck, which is about ten miles per hour. I will say one thing for old Em, I never see a brighter horse in my life.

The first time we stop to take her off for the night, we find that the plank runway is all right for loading her because she can run up the boards like a squirrel but they have too much of a pitch for her to walk down them, so finally we drop the tail gate and get hold of the front end of the truck and lift it gently and let her slide down to the ground like she was on a toboggan and I always claim that old Em likes this better than any other part of the trip.

It seems to be a most surprising spectacle to one and all along our route to see a truck going past with a horse leaning this way and that to keep balanced and with forty per cent. of her sticking out of one end of the truck, and twenty per cent. of her sticking out of the other end, and we often attract many spectators when we stop. This is whenever we have a blow-out, which is every now and then. Sometimes there is much comment among these spectators about old Em and as it is generally comment of an unfavourable nature, I am always having difficulty keeping Itchky from taking pops at spectators.

We sleep at night in the truck with old Em tied to the rear end and we use her spare blankets for covering as Em has more blankets than any other horse in the country and most of them are very fancy blankets, at that. It is not bad sleeping except when it rains and then Itchky takes all the blankets off us and puts them on Em and my overcoat too, and we have to sit up under the truck and the way Itchky worries about Em catching cold is most distressing.

Sometimes when we are rolling along the road and Em is dozing on Itchky's shoulder, he talks to me instead of her, and I ask him if he knows just where to find Em's old home in the Bluegrass country.

"No," he says, "I do not know just where, but the record book gives the breeder of Em as the Tucky Farms and it must be a well-known breeding establishment to produce such a horse as Em, so we will have no trouble finding it. By the way," Itchky says, "Em comes of a very high-class family. She is by an important stallion by the name of Christofer out of a mare called Love Always, but," he says, "the curious thing about it is I am never able to learn of another horse of this breeding in this country, though Christofer is once a good race horse in France."

Personally, I consider it a great thing for this country that there is only one horse bred like Em but naturally I do not mention such a thought to Itchky Ironhat, not only because I know it will displease him but because I am afraid old Em may overhear me and be greatly offended.

The road signs state that we are a few miles out of the city of Lexington, Ky., and we know we are now down in the Bluegrass country, when we come upon a tall old guy leaning against a fence in front of a cute little white house. This old guy looks as if he may be a native of these parts as he is wearing a wide-brimmed soft hat and is chewing on a straw, so Itchky stops the truck and puts on a Southern accent and speaks to him as follows:

"Suh," Itchky says, "can you all direct me to a place called the Tucky Farms, suh?"

The tall old guy gazes at Itchky and then he gazes at me and finally he gazes at old Em and he never stops chewing on the straw and after a while he smiles and points and says:

"It is about three miles up that road," he says. "It is a big red brick house with some burned-down barns in the background, but friend," he says, "let me give you a piece of good advice. I do not know what your business is, but keep away from that place with anything that looks like a horse. Although," he says, "I am not sure that the object you have on your truck answers such a description."

Of course Itchky can see from this crack that the old guy is making fun of Em and he starts to sizzle all over and forgets his Southern accent at once and says:

"You do not like my horse?"

"Oh, it is a horse, then?" the old guy says. "Well, the party who owns Tucky Farms is a trifle eccentric about horses. In fact, he is eccentric about everything, but horses most of all. He does not permit them on his premises. It is a sad case. You may meet a disagreeable reception if you go there with your so-called horse."

Then he turns and walks into the cute little white house and I have all I can do to keep Itchky from going after him and reprimanding him for speaking so disrespectfully of old

Em, especially as the old guy keeps looking around at us and we can see that he is smiling more than somewhat.

Itchky drives on up the road a little ways and, just as the old guy says, we come upon a big red brick house and there is no doubt that this is the Tucky Farms because there is a faded sign over an arched gateway that so states. The house is all shuttered up and is on a small hill pretty well back from the road and not far from the house are the remainders of some buildings that look as if they burned down a long time ago and are never fixed up again or cleared away.

In fact, the grounds and the house itself all look as if they can stand a little attention and there is not a soul in sight and it is rather a dismal scene in every respect. The gate is closed, so I get down off the truck and open it and Itchky drives the truck in and right up to the front door of the house under a sort of porch with white pillars.

Now the truck makes a terrible racket and this racket seems to stir up a number of coloured parties who appear from around in back of the house, along with a large white guy. This large guy is wearing corduroy pants and laced boots and a black moustache and he is also carrying a double-barrelled shotgun and he speaks to Itchky in a fierce tone of voice as follows:

"Pigface," he says, "get out of here. Get out of here before you are hurt. What do you mean by driving in here with a load of dog meat such as this, anyway?"

He points a finger at old Em who has her head up and is snuffling the air and gazing about her with great interest, and right away Itchky climbs down off the seat of the truck and removes his derby and places it on the ground and takes off his coat and starts rolling up his sleeves.

"It is the last straw," Itchky Ironhat says. "I will first make this big ash can eat that cannon he is lugging and

then I will beat his skull in. Nobody can refer to Emaleen
as dog meat and live."

Now the front door of the house opens and out comes a
thin character in a soiled white linen suit and at first he
seems to be quite an old character as he has long white
hair but when he gets closer I can see that he is not so very
old at that, but he is very seedy-looking and his eyes have a
loose expression. I can also see from the way the large guy
and the coloured parties step back that this is a character
who packs some weight around here. His voice is low and
hard as he speaks to Itchky Ironhat and says:

"What is this?" he says. "What name do I just hear
you pronounce?"

"Emaleen," Itchky says. "It is the name of my race
mare which you see before you. She is the greatest race
mare in the world. The turf records say she is bred right
here at this place and I bring her down here to see her old
home, and everybody insults her. So this is Southern
hospitality?" Itchky says.

The new character steps up to the truck and looks at old
Em for quite a spell and all the time he is shaking his head
and his lips are moving as if he is talking to himself, and
finally he says to the large guy:

"Unload her," he says. "Unload her and take good care
of her, Dobkins. I suppose you will have to send to one
of the neighbours for some feed. Come in, gentlemen," he
says to Itchky and me and he holds the front door of the
house open. "My name is Salsbury," he says. "I am the
owner of Tucky Farms and I apologize for my foreman's
behaviour but he is only following orders."

As we go into the house I can see that it is a very large
house and I can also see that it must once be a very grand
house because of the way it is furnished, but everything
seems to be as run-down inside as it does outside and I can

see that what this house needs is a good cleaning and straightening out.

In the meantime, Mr. Salsbury keeps asking Itchky Iron-hat questions about old Em and when he hears how long Itchky has her and what he thinks of her and all this and that, he starts wiping his eyes with a handkerchief as if the story makes him very sad, especially the part about why Itchky brings her to the Bluegrass.

Finally, Mr. Salsbury leads us into a large room that seems to be a library and at one end of this room there is a painting taller than I am of a very beautiful Judy in a white dress and this is the only thing in the house that seems to be kept dusted up a little and Mr. Salsbury points to the painting and says:

"My wife, Emaleen, gentlemen. I name the horse you bring here after her long ago, because it is the first foal of her favourite mare and the first foal of a stallion I import from France."

"By Christofer, out of Love Always," Itchky Ironhat says.

"Yes," Mr. Salsbury says. "In those days, Tucky Farm is one of the great breeding and racing establishments of the Bluegrass. In those days, too, my wife is known far and wide for her fondness for horses and her kindness to them. She is the head of the humane society in Kentucky and the Emaleen Salsbury annual award of a thousand dollars for the kindest deed towards a horse brought to the attention of the society each year is famous.

"One night," Mr. Salsbury continues, "there is a fire in the barns and my wife gets out of bed and before anyone can stop her she rushes into the flames trying to save her beautiful mare, Love Always. They both perish, and," he says, "with them perishes the greatest happiness ever given a mortal on this earth."

By this time, Itchky Ironhat and I are feeling very sad, indeed, and in fact all the creases in Itchky's face are full of tears as Mr. Salsbury goes on to state that the only horses on the place that are saved are a few yearlings running in the pastures. He sends them all with a shipment a neighbour is taking to Saratoga to be disposed of there for whatever they will bring.

"Your mare Emaleen is one of those," he says. "I forget all about her at the time. Indeed," he says, "I forget everything but my unhappiness. I feel I never wish to see or hear of a horse again as long as I live and I withdraw myself completely from the world and all my former activities. But," he says, "your bringing the mare here awakens old fond memories and your story of how you cherish her makes me realize that this is exactly what my wife Emaleen will wish me to do. I see where I sadly neglect my duty to her memory. Why," he says, "I never even keep up the Emaleen Salsbury award."

Now he insists that we must remain there a while as his guests and Itchky Ironhat agrees, although I point out that it will be more sensible for us to move on to Louisville and get into action as quickly as possible because we are now practically out of funds. But Itchky takes a look at old Em and he says she is enjoying herself so much running around her old home and devouring grass that it will be a sin and a shame to take her away before it is absolutely necessary.

After a couple of days, I tell Itchky that I think absolutely necessary arrives, but Itchky says Mr. Salsbury now wishes to give a dinner in honour of old Em and he will not think of denying her this pleasure. And for the next week the house is overrun with coloured parties, male and female, cleaning up the house and painting and cooking and dusting and I do not know what all else, and furthermore I hear there is a great to-do all through the Bluegrass country when the invitations to the dinner start going around, because this is the first time in over a dozen years that Mr. Salsbury has any truck whatever with his neighbours.

On the night of the dinner, one of the male coloured parties tells me that he never before sees such a gathering of the high-toned citizens of the Bluegrass as are assembled in a big dining hall at a horse-shoe shaped table with an orchestra going and with flowers and flags and racing colours all around and about. In fact, the coloured party says it is just like the old days at Tucky Farms when Mr. Salsbury's wife is alive, although he says he does not remember ever seeing such a character sitting alongside Mr. Salsbury at the table as Itchky Ironhat.

To tell the truth, Itchky Ironhat seems to puzzle all the guests no little and it is plain to be seen that they are wondering who he is and why he is present, though Itchky is sharpened up with a fresh shave and has on a clean shirt and of course he is not wearing his derby hat. Personally, I am rather proud of Itchky's appearance, but I can see that he seems to be overplaying his knife a little, especially against the mashed potatoes.

Mr. Salsbury is dressed in a white dinner jacket and his eyes are quiet and his hair is trimmed and his manner is most genteel in every way and when the guests are seated he gets to his feet and attracts their attention by tapping on a wineglass with a spoon. Then he speaks to them as follows:

"Friends and neighbours," he says. "I know you are all surprised at being invited here but you may be more surprised when you learn the reason. As most of you are aware, I am as one dead for years. Now I live again. I am going to restore Tucky Farms to all its old turf glory in breeding and racing, and," he says, "I am going to re-establish the Emaleen Salsbury award, with which you are familiar, and carry on again in every way as I am now certain my late beloved wife will wish."

Then he tells them the story of old Em and how Itchky Ironhat cares for her and loves her all these years and how he brings her to the Bluegrass just to see her old home, but of course he does not tell them that Itchky also plans to later drop her in a race at Churchill Downs, as it seems Itchky never mentions the matter to him.

Anyway, Mr. Salsbury says that the return of old Em awakens him as if from a bad dream and he can suddenly see how he is not doing right with respect to his wife's memory and while he is talking a tall old guy who is sitting next to me, and who turns out to be nobody but the guy who directs us to Tucky Farms, says to me like this:

"It is a miracle," he says. "I am his personal physician and I give him up long ago as a hopeless victim of melancholia. In fact, I am always expecting to hear of him dismissing himself from this world entirely. Well," the old guy says, "I always say medical science is not everything."

"My first step towards restoring Tucky Farms," Mr. Salsbury goes on, "is to purchase the old mare Emaleen from Mr. Itchky Ironhat here for the sum of three thousand dollars, which we agree upon this evening as a fair price. I will retire her of course for the rest of her days, which I hope will be many."

With this he whips out a cheque and hands it to Itchky and naturally I am somewhat surprised at the sum mentioned because I figure if old Em is worth three G's War Admiral must be worth a jillion. However, I am also greatly pleased because I can see where Itchky and I will have a nice taw for the races at Churchill Downs without having to bother about old Em winning one.

OLD EM'S KENTUCKY HOME

"Now," Mr. Salsbury says, "for our guest of honour."

Then two big doors at one end of the banquet hall open wide and there seems to be a little confusion outside and a snorting and a stamping as if a herd of wild horses is coming in and all of a sudden who appears in the doorway with her mane and tail braided with ribbons and her coat all slicked up but old Em and who is leading her in but the large guy who insults her and also Itchky on our arrival at Tucky Farms.

The guests begin applauding and the orchestra plays My Old Kentucky Home and it is a pleasant scene to be sure, but old Em seems quite unhappy about something as the large guy pulls her into the hollow of the horseshoe-shaped table, and the next thing anybody knows, Itchky Ironhat climbs over the table, knocking glasses and dishes every which way and flattens the large guy with a neat left hook in the presence of the best people of the Bluegrass country.

Naturally, this incident causes some comment and many of the guests are slightly shocked and there is considerable criticism of Itchky Ironhat for his lack of table manners. But then it is agreed by one and all present that Itchky is undoubtedly entitled to the Emaleen Salsbury kindness to horses award when I explain that what irks him is the fact that the large guy leads old Em in with a twitch on her lip.

Well, this is about all there is to the story, except that Itchky and I go over to the Louisville the next day and remain there awaiting the Kentucky Derby and we have a wonderful time, to be sure, except that we do not seem to be able to win any bets on the horse races at Churchill Downs.

In fact, the day before the Derby, Itchky remarks that the bank roll is now lower than a turtle's vest buttons and when I express surprise that we toss off four G's in such a short period, Itchky says to me like this:

"Oh," he says, "it is not four G's. I send the Emaleen

Salsbury kindness-to-horses award of one G to Mousie. I figure she is legally entitled to this for leaving me with Em. Otherwise, we will never get even the three and besides," Itchky says, "I love Mousie. In fact, I invite her to join me here and she agrees to come after I promise I will never as much as think of old Em again.

"By the way," Itchky says, "I call up Tucky Farms this morning and Mr. Salsbury brings old Em into his study and lets her hear my voice over the phone. Mr. Salsbury says she is greatly pleased. I give her your love, but of course not as much of yours as I give her of mine," he says.

"Thanks, Itchky," I say, and at this moment I am somewhat surprised to notice a metal ash tray removing Itchky's derby hat from his head and, gazing about, who do I observe standing in the doorway and now taking dead aim at Itchky with another tray but his ever-loving wife, Mousie.

15. JOHNNY ONE-EYE

TʜɪS cat I am going to tell you about is a very small cat, and in fact it is only a few weeks old, consequently it is really nothing but an infant cat. To tell the truth, it is just a kitten.

It is grey and white and very dirty and its fur is all frowzled up, so it is a very miserable-looking little kitten to be sure the day it crawls through a broken basement window into an old house in East Fifty-third Street over near Third Avenue in the city of New York and goes from room to room saying merouw, merouw in a low, weak voice until it comes to a room at the head of the stairs on the second story where a guy by the name of Rudolph is sitting on the floor thinking of not much.

One reason Rudolph is sitting on the floor is because there is nothing else to sit on as this is an empty house that is all boarded up for years and there is no furniture whatever in it, and another reason is that Rudolph has a .38 slug in his side and really does not feel like doing much of anything but sitting. He is wearing a derby hat and his overcoat as it is in the wintertime and very cold and he has an automatic Betsy on the floor beside him and naturally he is surprised quite some when the little kitten comes merouwing into the room and he picks up the Betsy and points it at the door in case anyone he does not wish to see is with the kitten. But when he observes that it is all alone, Rudolph puts the Betsy down again and speaks to the kitten as follows:

"Hello, cat," he says.

Of course the kitten does not say anything in reply except merouw but it walks right up to Rudolph and climbs on his lap, although the chances are if it knows who Rudolph is it will hightail it out of there quicker than anybody can say scat. There is enough daylight coming through the chinks in the boards over the windows for Rudolph to see that the kitten's right eye is in bad shape, and in fact it is bulged half out of its head in a most distressing manner and it is plain to be seen that the sight is gone from this eye. It is also plain to be seen that the injury happened recently and Rudolph gazes at the kitten a while and starts to laugh and says like this:

"Well, cat," he says, "you seem to be scuffed up almost as much as I am. We make a fine pair of invalids here together. What is your name, cat?"

Naturally the kitten does not state its name but only goes merouw and Rudolph says, "All right, I will call you Johnny. Yes," he says, "your tag is now Johnny One-Eye."

Then he puts the kitten in under his overcoat and pretty soon it gets warm and starts to purr and Rudolph says:

"Johnny," he says, "I will say one thing for you and that is you are plenty game to be able to sing when you are hurt as bad as you are. It is more than I can do."

But Johnny only goes merouw again and keeps on purring and by and by it falls sound asleep under Rudolph's coat and Rudolph is wishing the pain in his side will let up long enough for him to do the same.

Well, I suppose you are saying to yourself, what is this Rudolph doing in an old empty house with a slug in his side, so I will explain that the district attorney is responsible for this situation. It seems that the D.A. appears before the grand jury and tells it that Rudolph is an extortion guy and a killer and I do not know what all else, though some of these statements are without doubt a great injustice to Rudolph as, up to the time the D.A. makes them, Rudolph does not kill anybody of any consequence in years.

It is true that at one period of his life he is considered a little wild but this is in the 1920's when everybody else is, too, and for seven or eight years he is all settled down and is engaged in business organization work, which is very respectable work, indeed. He organizes quite a number of businesses on a large scale and is doing very good for himself. He is living quietly in a big hotel all alone, as Rudolph is by no means a family guy, and he is highly spoken of by one and all when the D.A. starts poking his nose into his affairs, claiming that Rudolph has no right to be making money out of the businesses, even though Rudolph gives these businesses plenty of first-class protection.

In fact, the D.A. claims that Rudolph is nothing but a racket guy and a great knock to the community, and all this upsets Rudolph no little when it comes to his ears in a roundabout way. So he calls up his lawbooks and requests legal advice on the subject and lawbooks says the best thing he can think of for Rudolph to do is to become as inconspicuous as possible right away but to please not mention to anyone that he gives this advice.

Lawbooks says he understands the D.A. is requesting indictments and is likely to get them and furthermore that he is rounding up certain parties that Rudolph is once associated with and trying to get them to remember incidents in Rudolph's early career that may not be entirely to his credit. Lawbooks says he hears that one of these parties is a guy by the name of Cute Freddy and that Freddy makes a deal with the D.A. to lay off of him if he tells everything he knows about Rudolph, so under the circumstances a long journey by Rudolph will be in the interest of everybody concerned.

So Rudolph decides to go on a journey but then he gets to thinking that maybe Freddy will remember a little matter that Rudolph long since dismisses from his mind and does not wish to have recalled again, which is the time he and Freddy do a job on a guy by the name of The Icelander in Troy years ago and he drops around to Freddy's house to remind him to be sure not to remember this.

But it seems that Freddy, who is an important guy in business organization work himself, though in a different part of the city than Rudolph, mistakes the purpose of Rudolph's visit and starts to out with his rooty-toot-toot and in order to protect himself it is necessary for Rudolph to take his Betsy and give Freddy a little tattooing. In fact, Rudolph practically crockets his monogram on Freddy's chest and leaves him exceptionally deceased.

But as Rudolph is departing from the neighbourhood, who bobs up but a young guy by the name of Buttsy Fagan, who works for Freddy as a chauffeur and one thing and another, and who is also said to be able to put a slug through a keyhole at forty paces without touching the sides though I suppose it will have to be a pretty good-sized keyhole. Anyway, he takes a long-distance crack at Rudolph as Rudolph is rounding a corner, but all Buttsy can see of Rudolph at the moment is a little piece of his left side and this is what Buttsy hits, although no one knows it at the time, except of course Rudolph, who just keeps on departing.

Now this incident causes quite a stir in police circles, and the D.A. is very indignant over losing a valuable witness and when they are unable to locate Rudolph at once, a reward of five thousand dollars is offered for information leading to his capture alive or dead and some think they really mean dead. Indeed, it is publicly stated that it is not a good idea for anyone to take any chances with Rudolph as he is known to be armed and is such a character as will be sure to resent being captured, but they do not explain that this is only because Rudolph knows the D.A. wishes to place him in the old rocking chair at Sing Sing and that Rudolph is quite allergic to the idea.

Anyway, the cops go looking for Rudolph in Hot Springs and Miami and every other place except where he is, which is right in New York wandering around town with the slug in his side, knocking at the doors of old friends requesting assistance. But all the old friends do for him is to slam the doors in his face and forget they ever see him, as the D.A. is very tough on parties who assist guys he is looking for, claiming that this is something most illegal called harbouring fugitives. Besides Rudolph is never any too popular at best with his old friends as he always plays pretty much of a lone duke and takes the big end of everything for his.

He cannot even consult a doctor about the slug in his side as he knows that nowadays the first thing a doctor will do about a guy with a gunshot wound is to report him to the cops, although Rudolph can remember when there is always a sure-footed doctor around who will consider it a privilege and a pleasure to treat him and keep his trap closed about it. But of course this is in the good old days and Rudolph can see they are gone forever. So he just does the best he can about the slug and goes on wandering here and there and around and about and the blats keep printing his picture and saying, where is Rudolph?

Where he is some of the time is in Central Park trying to get some sleep, but of course even the blats will consider it foolish to go looking for Rudolph there in such cold weather, as he is known as a guy who enjoys his comfort at all times. In fact, it is comfort that Rudolph misses more than anything as the slug is commencing to cause him great pain and naturally the pain turns Rudolph's thoughts to the author of same and he remembers that he once hears somebody say that Buttsy lives over in East Fifty-third Street.

So one night Rudolph decides to look Buttsy up and cause him a little pain in return and he is moseying through Fifty-third when he gets so weak he falls down on the sidewalk in front of the old house and rolls down a short flight of steps that lead from the street level to a little railed-in area-way and ground floor or basement door and before he stops rolling he brings up against the door itself and it creaks open inward as he bumps it. After he lays there awhile Rudolph can see that the house is empty and he crawls on inside.

Then when he feels stronger, Rudolph makes his way upstairs because the basement is damp and mice keep trotting back and forth over him and eventually he winds up in the room where Johnny One-Eye finds him the following afternoon and the reason Rudolph settles down in this room is because it commands the stairs. Naturally, this is important to a guy in Rudolph's situation, though after he is sitting there for about fourteen hours before Johnny comes along he can see that he is not going to be much disturbed by traffic. But he considers it a very fine place, indeed, to remain planted until he is able to resume his search for Buttsy.

Well, after a while Johnny One-Eye wakes up and comes from under the coat and looks at Rudolph out of his good eye and Rudolph waggles his fingers and Johnny plays with them, catching one finger in his front paws and biting it gently and this pleases Rudolph no little as he never before has any personal experience with a kitten. However, he remembers observing one when he is a boy down in Houston Street, so he takes a piece of paper out of his

pocket and makes a little ball of it and rolls it along the floor
and Johnny bounces after it very lively indeed. But Rudolph
can see that the bad eye is getting worse and finally he says
to Johnny like this:

"Johnny," he says, "I guess you must be suffering more
than I am. I remember there are some pet shops over on
Lexington Avenue not far from here and when it gets good
and dark I am going to take you out and see if we can find
a cat croaker to do something about your eye. Yes,
Johnny," Rudolph says, "I will also get you something to
eat. You must be starved."

Johnny One-Eye says merouw to this and keeps on playing with the paper ball but soon it comes on dark outside
and inside, too, and, in fact, it is so dark inside that Rudolph
cannot see his hand before him. Then he puts his Betsy in a
side pocket of his overcoat and picks up Johnny and goes
downstairs, feeling his way in the dark and easing along a
step at a time until he gets to the basement door. Naturally,
Rudolph does not wish to strike any matches because
he is afraid someone outside may see the light and get
nosey.

By moving very slowly, Rudolph finally gets to Lexington
Avenue and while he is going along he remembers the time
he walks from 125th Street in Harlem down to 110th with
six slugs in him and never feels as bad as he does now. He
gets to thinking that maybe he is not the guy he used to be,
which of course is very true as Rudolph is now forty-odd
years of age and is fat around the middle and getting bald,
and he also does some thinking about what a pleasure it
will be to him to find this Buttsy and cause him the pain he
is personally suffering.

There are not many people in the streets and those that
are go hurrying along because it is so cold and none of
them pay any attention to Rudolph or Johnny One-Eye

either, even though Rudolph staggers a little now and then like a guy who is rummed up, although of course it is only weakness. The chances are he is also getting a little feverish and lightheaded because finally he stops a cop who is going along swinging his arms to keep warm and asks him if he knows where there is a pet shop and it is really most indiscreet of such a guy as Rudolph to be interviewing cops. But the cop just points up the street and goes on without looking twice at Rudolph and Rudolph laughs and pokes Johnny with a finger and says:

"No, Johnny One-Eye," he says, "the cop is not a dope for not recognizing Rudolph. Who can figure the hottest guy in forty-eight states to be going along a street with a little cat in his arms? Can you, Johnny?"

Johnny says merouw and pretty soon Rudolph comes to the pet shop the cop points out. Rudolph goes inside and says to the guy like this:

"Are you a cat croaker?" Rudolph says. "Do you know what to do about a little cat that has a hurt eye?"

"I am a kind of a vet," the guy says.

"Then take a glaum at Johnny One-Eye here and see what you can do for him," Rudolph says.

Then he hands Johnny over to the guy and the guy looks at Johnny a while and says:

"Mister," he says, "the best thing I can do for this cat is to put it out of its misery. You better let me give it something right now. It will just go to sleep and never know what happens."

Well, at this, Rudolph grabs Johnny One-Eye out of the guy's hands and puts him under his coat and drops a duke on the Betsy in his pocket as if he is afraid the guy will take Johnny away from him again and he says to the guy like this:

"No, no, no," Rudolph says. "I cannot bear to think

of such a thing. What about some kind of an operation? I remember they take a bum lamp out of Joe the Goat at Bellevue one time and he is okay now."

"Nothing will do your cat any good," the guy says. "It is a goner. It will start having fits pretty soon and die sure. What is the idea of trying to save such a cat as this? It is no kind of a cat to begin with. It is just a cat. You can get a million like it for a nickel."

"No," Rudolph says, "this is not just a cat. This is Johnny One-Eye. He is my only friend in the world. He is the only living thing that ever comes pushing up against me warm and friendly and trust me in my whole life. I feel sorry for him."

"I feel sorry for him, too," the guy says. "I always feel sorry for animals that get hurt and for people."

"I do not feel sorry for people," Rudolph says. "I only feel sorry for Johnny One-Eye. Give me some kind of stuff that Johnny will eat."

"Your cat wants milk," the guy says. "You can get some at the delicatessen store down at the corner. Mister," he says, "you look sick yourself. Can I do anything for you?"

But Rudolph only shakes his head and goes on out and down to the delicatessen joint where he buys a bottle of milk and this transaction reminds him that he is very short in the moo department. In fact, he can find only a five-dollar note in his pockets and he remembers that he has no way of getting any more when this runs out, which is a very sad predicament indeed for a guy who is accustomed to plenty of moo at all times.

Then Rudolph returns to the old house and sits down on the floor again and gives Johnny One-Eye some of the milk in his derby hat as he neglects buying something for Johnny to drink out of. But Johnny offers no complaint. He laps up the milk and curls himself into a wad in Rudolph's lap and purrs.

Rudolph takes a swig of the milk himself but it makes him sick for by this time Rudolph is really far from being in the pink of condition. He not only has the pain in his side but he has a heavy cold which he probably catches from lying on the basement floor or maybe sleeping in the park and he is wheezing no little. He commences to worry that he may get too ill to continue looking for Buttsy, as he can see that if it is not for Buttsy he will not be in this situation, suffering the way he is, but on a long journey to some place.

He takes to going off into long stretches of a kind of stupor and every time he comes out of one of these stupors the first thing he does is to look around for Johnny One-Eye and Johnny is always right there either playing with the paper ball or purring in Rudolph's lap. He is a great comfort to Rudolph but after a while Rudolph notices that Johnny seems to be running out of zip and he also notices that he is running out of zip himself especially when he discovers that he is no longer able to get to his feet.

It is along in the late afternoon of the day following the night Rudolph goes out of the house that he hears someone coming up the stairs and naturally he picks up his Betsy and gets ready for action when he also hears a very small voice calling kitty, kitty, kitty, and he realizes that the party that is coming can be nobody but a child. In fact, a minute later a little pretty of maybe six years of age comes into the room all out of breath and says to Rudolph like this:

"How do you do?" she says. "Have you seen my kitty?"

Then she spots Johnny One-Eye in Rudolph's lap and runs over and sits down beside Rudolph and takes Johnny in her arms and at first Rudolph is inclined to resent this and has a notion to give her a good boffing but he is too weak to exert himself in such a manner.

"Who are you?" Rudolph says to the little pretty, "and," he says, "where do you live and how do you get in this house?"

"Why," she says, "I am Elsie, and I live down the street and I am looking everywhere for my kitty for three days and the door is open downstairs and I know kitty likes to go in doors that are open so I came to find her and here she is."

"I guess I forgot to close it last night," Rudolph says. "I seem to be very forgetful lately."

"What is your name?" Elsie asks, "and why are you sitting on the floor in the cold and where are all your chairs? Do you have any little girls like me and do you love them dearly?"

"No," Rudolph says. "By no means and not at all."

"Well," Elsie says, "I think you are a nice man for taking care of my kitty. Do you love kitty?"

"Look," Rudolph says, "his name is not kitty. His name is Johnny One-Eye, because he has only one eye."

"I call her kitty," Elsie says. "But," she says, "Johnny One-Eye is a nice name too and if you like it best I will call her Johnny and I will leave her here with you to take care of always and I will come to see her every day. You see," she says, "if I take Johnny home Buttsy will only kick her again."

"Buttsy?" Rudolph says. "Do I hear you say Buttsy? Is his other name Fagan?"

"Why, yes," Elsie says. "Do you know him?"

"No," Rudolph says, "but I hear of him. What is he to you?"

"He is my new daddy," Elsie says. "My other one and

my best one is dead and so my mamma makes Buttsy my new one. My mamma says Buttsy is her mistake. He is very mean. He kicks Johnny and hurts her eye and makes her run away. He kicks my mamma too. Buttsy kicks everybody and everything when he is mad and he is always mad."

"He is a louse to kick a little cat," Rudolph says.

"Yes," Elsie says, "that is what Mr. O'Toole says he is for kicking my mamma but my mamma says it is not a nice word and I am never to say it out loud."

"Who is Mr. O'Toole?" Rudolph says.

"He is the policeman," Elsie says. "He lives across the street from us and he is very nice to me. He says Buttsy is the word you say just now, not only for kicking my mamma but for taking her money when she brings it home from work and spending it so she cannot buy me nice things to wear. But do you know what?" Elsie says. "My mamma says some day Buttsy is going far away and then she will buy me lots of things and send me to school and make me a lady."

Then Elsie begins skipping around the room with Johnny One-Eye in her arms and singing I am going to be a lady, I am going to be a lady, until Rudolph has to tell her to pipe down because he is afraid somebody may hear her. And all the time Rudolph is thinking of Buttsy and regretting that he is unable to get on his pins and go out of the house.

"Now I must go home," Elsie says, "because this is a night Buttsy comes in for his supper and I have to be in bed before he gets there so I will not bother him. Buttsy does not like little girls. Buttsy does not like little kittens, Buttsy does not like little anythings. My mamma is afraid of Buttsy and so am I. But," she says, "I will leave Johnny here with you and come back to-morrow to see her."

"Listen, Elsie," Rudolph says, "does Mr. O'Toole come home to-night to his house for his supper, too?"

"Oh, yes," Elsie says. "He comes home every night. Sometimes when there is a night Buttsy is not coming in for his supper my mamma lets me go over to Mr. O'Toole's and I play with his dog Charley but you must never tell Buttsy this because he does not like O'Toole either. But this is a night Buttsy is coming and that is why my mamma tells me to get in early."

Now Rudolph takes an old letter out of his inside pocket and a pencil out of another pocket and he scribbles a few lines on the envelope and stretches himself out on the floor and begins groaning, oh, oh, oh, and then he says to Elsie like this:

"Look, Elsie," he says, "you are a smart little kid and you pay strict attention to what I am going to say to you. Do not go to bed to-night until Buttsy gets in. Then," Rudolph says, "you tell him you come in this old house looking for your cat and that you hear somebody groaning like I do just now in the room at the head of the stairs and that you find a guy who says his name is Rudolph lying on the floor so sick he cannot move. Tell him the front door of the basement is open. But," Rudolph says, "you must not tell him that Rudolph tells you to say these things. Do you understand?"

"Oh," Elsie says, "do you want him to come here? He will kick Johnny again if he does."

"He will come here, but he will not kick Johnny," Rudolph says. "He will come here, or I am the worst guesser in the world. Tell him what I look like, Elsie. Maybe he will ask you if you see a gun. Tell him you do not see one. You do not see a gun, do you, Elsie?"

"No," Elsie says, "only the one in your hand when I come in but you put it under your coat. Buttsy has a gun and Mr. O'Toole has a gun but Buttsy says I am never, never to tell anybody about this or he will kick me the way he does my mamma."

"Well," Rudolph says, "you must not remember seeing mine, either. It is a secret between you and me and Johnny One-Eye. Now," he says, "if Buttsy leaves the house to come and see me, as I am pretty sure he will, you run over to Mr. O'Toole's house and give him this note, but do not tell Buttsy or your mamma either about the note. If Buttsy does not leave, it is my hard luck, but you give the note to Mr. O'Toole anyway. Now tell me what you are to do, Elsie," Rudolph says, "so I can see if you have got everything correct."

"I am to go on home and wait for Buttsy," she says, "and I am to tell him Rudolph is lying on the floor of this dirty old house with a fat stomach and a big nose making noises and that he is very sick and the basement door is open and there is no gun if he asks me, and when Buttsy comes to see you I am to take this note to Mr. O'Toole but Buttsy and my mamma are not to know I have the note and if Buttsy does not leave I am to give it to Mr. O'Toole anyway and you are to stay here and take care of Johnny my kitten."

"That is swell," Rudolph says. "Now you run along."

So Elsie leaves and Rudolph sits up again against the wall because his side feels easier this way and Johnny One-Eye is in his lap purring very low and the dark comes on until it is blacker inside the room than in the middle of a tunnel and Rudolph feels that he is going into another stupor and he has a tough time fighting it off.

Afterwards some of the neighbours claim they remember hearing a shot inside the house and then two more in quick succession and then all is quiet until a little later when Officer O'Toole and half a dozen other cops and an ambu-

lance with a doctor come busting into the street and swarm
into the joint with their guns out and their flashlights going.
The first thing they find is Buttsy at the foot of the stairs
with two bullet wounds close together in his throat, and
naturally he is real dead.

Rudolph is still sitting against the wall with what seems
to be a small bundle of bloody fur in his lap but which turns
out to be what is left of this little cat I am telling you about,
although nobody pays any attention to it at first. They are
more interested in getting the come-alongs on Rudolph's
wrists but before they move him he pulls his clothes
aside and shows the doctor where the slug is in his side
and the doctor take one glaum and shakes his head and
says:

"Gangrene," he says. "I think you have pneumonia,
too, from the way you are blowing."

"I know," Rudolph says. "I know this morning. Not
much chance, hey, croaker?"

"Not much," the doctor says.

"Well, cops," Rudolph says, "load me in. I do not
suppose you want Johnny, seeing that he is dead."

"Johnny who?" one of the cops says.

"Johnny One-Eye," Rudolph says. "This little cat here
in my lap. Buttsy shoots Johnny's only good eye out and
takes most of his noodle with it. I never see a more wonderful shot. Well, Johnny is better off but I feel sorry about
him as he is my best friend down to the last."

Then he begins to laugh and the cop asks him what
tickles him so much and Rudolph says:

"Oh," he says, "I am thinking of the joke on Buttsy. I
am positive he will come looking for me, all right, not only
because of the little altercation between Cute Freddy and
me but because the chances are Buttsy is greatly embarrassed
by not tilting me over the first time, as of course he never

knows he wings me. Furthermore," Rudolph says, "and this is the best reason of all, Buttsy will realize that if I am in his neighbourhood it is by no means a good sign for him, even if he hears I am sick.

"Well," Rudolph says, "I figure that with any kind of a square rattle I will have a better chance of nailing him than he has of nailing me, but that even if he happens to nail me, O'Toole will get my note in time to arrive here and nab Buttsy on the spot with his gun on him. And," Rudolph says, "I know it will be a great pleasure to the D.A. to settle Buttsy for having a gun on him.

"But," Rudolph says, "as soon as I hear Buttsy coming on the sneaksby up the stairs, I can see I am taking all the worst of it because I am now wheezing like a busted valve and you can hear me a block away except when I hold my breath, which is very difficult indeed, considering the way I am already greatly tuckered out. No," Rudolph says, "it does not look any too good for me as Buttsy keeps coming up the stairs, as I can tell he is doing by a little faint creak in the boards now and then. I am in no shape to manœuvre around the room and pretty soon he will be on the landing and then all he will have to do is to wait there until he hears me which he is bound to do unless I stop breathing altogether. Naturally," Rudolph says, "I do not care to risk a blast in the dark without knowing where he is as something tells me Buttsy is not a guy you can miss in safety.

"Well," Rudolph says, "I notice several times before this that in the dark Johnny One-Eye's good glim shines like a big spark, so when I feel Buttsy is about to hit the landing, although of course I cannot see him, I flip Johnny's ball of paper across the room to the wall just opposite the door and tough as he must be feeling Johnny chases after it when he hears it light. I figure Buttsy will hear Johnny playing with the paper and see his eye shining and think it is me and take a pop at it and that his gun flash will give me a crack at him.

"It all works out just like I dope it," Rudolph says, "but," he says, "I never give Buttsy credit for being such a marksman as to be able to hit a cat's eye in the dark. If I know this, maybe I will never stick Johnny out in front the way I do. It is a good thing I never give Buttsy a second shot. He is a lily. Yes," Rudolph says, "I can remember when I can use a guy like him."

"Buttsy is no account," the cop says. "He is a good riddance. He is the makings of a worse guy than you."

"Well," Rudolph says, "it is a good lesson to him for kicking a little cat."

Then they take Rudolph to a hospital and this is where I see him and piece out this story of Johnny One-Eye, and Officer O'Toole is at Rudolph's bedside keeping guard over him, and I remember that not long before Rudolph chalks out he looks at O'Toole and says to him like this:

"Copper," he says, "there is no chance of them outjuggling the kid on the reward moo, is there?"

"No," O'Toole says, "no chance. I keep the note you send me by Elsie saying she will tell me where you are. It is information leading to your capture just as the reward offer states. Rudolph," he says, "it is a nice thing you do for Elsie and her mother, although," he says, "it is not nearly as nice as icing Buttsy for them."

"By the way, copper," Rudolph says, "there is the remainders of a pound note in my pants pocket when I am brought here. I want you to do me a favour. Get it from the desk and buy Elsie another cat and name it Johnny, will you?"

"Sure," O'Toole says. "Anything else?"

"Yes," Rudolph says, "be sure it has two good eyes."

16. BROADWAY INCIDENT

ONE night Ambrose Hammer, the newspaper scribe, comes looking for me on Broadway and he insists that I partake of dinner with him at the Canary Club, stating that he wishes to talk to me. Naturally, I know that Ambrose must be in love again, and when he is in love he always wishes to have somebody around to listen to him tell about how much he is in love and about the way he is suffering, because Ambrose is such a guy as must have his suffering with his love. I know him when he first shows up on Broadway, which is a matter of maybe eight or ten years ago, but in all this time I seldom see him when he is not in love and suffering and especially suffering, and the reason he suffers is because he generally falls in love with some beautiful who does not care two snaps of her fingers about him and sometimes not even one snap.

In fact, it is the consensus of opinion along Broadway that Ambrose is always very careful to pick a beautiful who does not care any snaps of her fingers whatever about him because if he finds one who does care these snaps there will be no reason for him to suffer. Personally, I consider Ambrose's love affairs a great bore but as the Canary Club is a very high-class gaff where the food department is really above par, I am pleased to go with him.

So there we are sitting on a leather settee against the wall in the Canary Club and I am juggling a big thick sirloin steak smothered in onions while Ambrose is telling me how much he loves a beautiful by the name of Hilda Hiffenbrower and how he is wishing he can marry her and live happily ever afterwards, but he is unable to complete this transaction because there is an ever-loving husband by the name of Herbert in the background from whom Hilda is separated but not divorced. And the way Ambrose tells it, Hilda cannot get a divorce because Herbert is just naturally a stinker and does not wish to see her happy with anybody else and will not let her have same.

Well, I happen to know Hilda better than Ambrose does. To tell the truth, I know her when her name is Mame something and she is dealing them off her arm in a little eating gaff on Seventh Avenue, which is before she goes in show business and changes her name to Hilda, and I also know that the real reason Herbert will not give her this divorce is because she wants eight gallons of his heart's blood and both his legs in the divorce settlement, but as Herbert has a good business head he is by no means agreeable to these terms, though I hear he is willing to compromise on one leg to get rid of Hilda.

Furthermore, I know that Hilda is never very sympathetic towards marriage in any manner, shape or form, as she has a few other husbands prior to this and dismisses them before they are in office very long, and I am willing to bet that she has an ice-cream cone where her heart is supposed to be. But of course I do not feel disposed to mention this matter to Ambrose Hammer, especially while I am enjoying his steak.

So I just go on eating and listening and Ambrose seems about ready to burst into tears as he tells me about his suffering because of his love for Hilda, when who comes into the Canary Club all dressed up in white tie and tails but a guy by the name of Brogan Wilmington, who is what is called a playwright by trade, a playwright being a guy who writes plays which are put on the stage for people to see.

As Ambrose is a dramatic critic, it is his duty to go and view these plays and to tell the readers of the blat for which he works what he thinks of them, and it seems that he tells them that the play written by this Brogan Wilmington is a twenty-two-carat smeller. In fact, it seems that Ambrose tells them it is without doubt the worst case of dramatic halitosis in the history of civilization and it is plain to be seen that Brogan Wilmington is somewhat vexed as he approaches our table and addresses Ambrose as follows:

"Ah," he says, "here you are."

"Yes," Ambrose says, "here I am, indeed."

"You do not care for my play?" Brogan Wilmington says.

"No," Ambrose says, "I loathe and despise it."

"Well," Brogan Wilmington says, "take this."

Then he lets go with his right and grazes Ambrose Hammer's chin but in doing so, Brogan Wilmington's coat-tails swing out behind him and across a portion of lobster Newburg that a beautiful at the next table is enjoying and in fact the swinging coat-tails wipe about half the portion off the plate on to the floor.

Before Brogan Wilmington can recover his balance, the beautiful picks up what is left of her lobster Newburg, plate and all, and clops Brogan on the pimple with it and knocks him plumb out on to the dance floor where many parties, male and female, are doing the rumba with great zest.

Naturally, Ambrose is slightly surprised at this incident, but as he is a gentleman at all times, even if he is a dramatic critic, he turns to the beautiful and says to her like this:

"Miss," Ambrose says, "or madam, I am obliged to you. Waiter," he says, "bring this lovely creature another dash of lobster Newburg and put it on my check."

Then he resumes his conversation with me and thinks

284

no more of the matter, because of course it is by no means a novelty for Ambrose Hammer to have playwrights throw punches at him, although generally it is actors and sometimes producers. In the meantime, the parties out on the dance floor find they cannot rumba with any convenience unless Brogan Wilmington is removed from their space, so a couple of waiters pick Brogan up and carry him away and Ambrose notices that the beautiful who slugs Brogan with the lobster Newburg now seems to be crying.

"Miss," Ambrose says, "or madam, dry your tears. Your fresh portion of lobster Newburg will be along presently."

"Oh," she says, "I am not crying about the loss of my lobster Newburg. I am crying because in my agitation I spill the little bottle of cyanide of potassium I bring in here with me and now I cannot commit suicide. Look at it all over my bag."

"Well," Ambrose says, "I am sorry, but I do not approve of anybody committing suicide in the Canary Club. It is owned by a friend of mine by the name of Joe Gloze and every Christmas he sends me a dozen expensive ties, besides permitting me to free-load here at will. A suicide in his club will be bad publicity for him. It may get around that death ensues because of the cooking. However, miss," Ambrose says, "or madam, if you are bound and determined to commit this suicide you may walk around the corner to a deadfall called El Parcheeso, which is Joe's rival, and I will follow you and observe your action in all its sad details and it will be a fine story for me."

Well, the beautiful seems to be thinking this proposition over and Ambrose is so occupied watching her think that he loses the thread of his story of his love for Hilda and seems to forget some of his suffering, too, and finally the beautiful turns to him and says:

"Sir, do you rumba?"

"Do I rumba?" Ambrose says. "Miss," he says, "or madam, you now behold the best rumba dancer in the Western Hemisphere, bar Havana. There is one guy there who can defeat me, although," Ambrose says, "it is a photo finish. Let us put it on."

So they get out on the floor and rumba quite a while and after that they samba some and then they conga and Ambrose can see that the beautiful has a very liberal education, indeed, along these lines. In fact, he can see that she rumbas and sambas and congas much better than any married beautiful should, because between a rumba and a samba she informs him that her name is Mrs. Brumby News and that she is the ever-loving wife of a doctor by the same name without the Mrs., who is much older than she is.

Finally they get all tuckered out from dancing and are sitting at the table talking of this and that and one thing and another, and I can tell from Mrs. News' conversation that she is far from being as intellectual as Professor Einstein and to tell the truth she does not seem right bright and Ambrose Hammer probably notices the same thing, but when it comes to beautifuls, Ambrose does not care if they are short fifteen letters reciting the alphabet. So he is really enjoying his chat with her and presently he asks her why she ever figures on knocking herself off and she relates a somewhat surprising story.

She states that her husband is always too busy trying to find out what is wrong with his patients to pay much attention to her and as she has no children but only a chow dog by the name of Pepe to occupy her time and as her maid can look after the dog better than she can, she takes to visiting this same Canary Club and similar traps seeking diversion.

She says that on one of these afternoons some months

back she meets a fat blonde by the name of Mrs. Bidkar and they become great friends as they both like to gab and sip cocktails and sometimes pick up rumbas with stray guys as beautifuls will do when they are running around loose, although it seems from what Mrs. News says that Mrs. Bidkar is by no means a beautiful but is really nothing but a bundle and a little smooth on the tooth in the matter of age. However, she is good company and Mrs. News says they find they have much in common including the cocktails and the rumbas.

It seems they both also like to play bridge and Mrs. Bidkar invites Mrs. News to her apartment, stating that she has several friends in every so often to play this bridge. So Mrs. News goes to the apartment, which is in East Fifty-seventh Street and very nice, at that, and she discovers that the friends are all young and married beautifuls like herself. There are three of them and one has the name of Mrs. Smythe and another the name of Mrs. Brown, but what the third one's name is Mrs. News says she does not remember as it is a long name, and anyway this one does not seem as well acquainted with Mrs. Bidkar as the others and does not have much to say.

Anyway, from now on they all play bridge in Mrs. Bidkar's apartment three or four afternoons a week and sip plenty of cocktails in between hands and a pleasant time is had by one and all, according to Mrs. News. Then one day after playing bridge they are sitting around working on the cocktails and talking of different matters, when it comes out that they are all unhappy in their married lives. In fact, it comes out that they all hate their husbands no little and wish to be shed of them and Mrs. News states that the one who wishes this the most is Mrs. Bidkar.

Mrs. News says that Mrs. Bidkar declares she wishes her Olaf is dead so she can collect his life insurance and lead her own life in her own way, and then she starts asking the others if their husbands carry such insurance and it seems they do and finally Mrs. Bidkar says as if in a joke that it will be a good idea if they dispose of their husbands and put the insurance moo in a common pool. She says one may put more in the jackpot than another, but since it will scarcely be possible for them to dispose of five different husbands all at once the pool will give each a drawing account after it starts until the whole deal is carried out.

Well, it seems from the way Mrs. News tells it that Mrs. Bidkar keeps making quite a joke about the idea and the others join in, especially as they keep pecking away at the cocktails, and after a while it is a big laugh all the way around. Then Mrs. Bidkar suggests that to make it more of a joke they deal out the cards to see which is to be the first to dispose of her husband and the one who draws the nine of diamonds is to be it, and Mrs. News gets the nine.

So the party breaks up with everybody still laughing and joking with Mrs. News over winning the prize and she is laughing, too, but as she is leaving Mrs. Bidkar calls her back and hands her a little vial which she states contains cyanide of potassium and whispers that after Mrs. News thinks it over she will see that many a true word is said in jest and that perhaps she will wish to use the cyanide where it will do the most good. Then Mrs. News says before she can say aye, yes, or no, Mrs. Bidkar pushes her out the door and closes it, still laughing.

"So," Mrs. News says, "I come here to the Canary Club and I get to thinking what a great sin I am guilty of in participating in such a joke, even though my husband is really nothing but an old curmudgeon and is related to Clarence Closeclutch when it comes to money, and I become so remorseful that I decide to take the cyanide myself when

BROADWAY INCIDENT

I am interrupted by the good-looking gentleman striking you. By the way," she says, "do you know if he rumbas?"

Now this story seems rather interesting to me and I am expecting Ambrose Hammer to become greatly excited by it, because it sounds like a crime mystery and next to love Ambrose Hammer's greatest hobby is crime mystery. He often vexes the cops quite some by poking his nose into their investigations and trying to figure out who does what. To tell the truth, Ambrose's interest is sometimes so divided between love and crime that it is hard to tell whether he wishes to be Clark Gable or Sherlock Holmes, though the chances are he wishes to be both. But I can see that Ambrose is half asleep and when Mrs. News concludes her tale he speaks to her quite severely as follows:

"Madam," he says, "of course you are a victim of a gag. However," he says, "you are such a swell rumba dancer I will overlook your wasting my time with such a dreary recital. Let us shake it up a little more on the dance floor and then I must return to my office and write a Sunday article advising the sanitation authorities to suppress Brogan Wilmington's play before it contaminates the entire community. He is the guy you flatten with your lobster Newburg. He is not good-looking, either, and he cannot rumba a lick. I forget to mention it before," Ambrose says, "but I am Ambrose Hammer."

Mrs. News does not seem to know the name and this really cuts Ambrose deeply, so he is not sorry to see her depart. Then he goes to his office and I go home to bed and the chances are neither of us will give the incident another thought if a guy by the name of Dr. Brumby News does not happen to drop dead in the Canary Club one night while in the act of committing the rumba with his wife.

Ambrose and I are sitting in Mindy's restaurant on Broadway when he reads an item in an early edition of a morning blat about this, and as Ambrose has a good memory for names he calls my attention to the item and states that the wife in question is undoubtedly the beautiful who tells us the unusual story.

"My goodness, Ambrose," I say, "do you suppose she gives the guy the business after all?"

"No," Ambrose says, "such an idea is foolish. It says here he undoubtedly dies of heart disease. He is sixty-three years old and at this age the price is logically thirty to one that a doctor will die of heart disease. Of course," Ambrose says, "if it is known that a doctor of sixty-three is engaging in the rumba, the price is one hundred to one."

"But Ambrose," I say, "maybe she knows the old guy's heart is weak and gets him to rumba figuring that it will belt him out quicker than cyanide."

"Well," Ambrose says, "it is a theory, of course, but I do not think there is anything in it. I think maybe she feels so sorry for her wicked thoughts about him that she tries to be nice to him and gets him to go out stepping with her, but with no sinister motives whatever. However, let us give this no further consideration. Doctors die of heart disease every day. Do I tell you that I see Hilda last night and that she believes she is nearer a settlement with Hiffenbrower? She is breakfasting with him at his hotel almost every morning and feels that he is softening up. Ah," Ambrose says, "how I long for the hour I can take her in my arms and call her my own dear little wife."

I am less interested in Hilda than ever at this moment, but I am compelled to listen for two hours to Ambrose tell about his love for her and about his suffering and I make up my mind to give him a miss until he gets over this one. Then about a week later he sends for me to come to his office saying he wishes me to go with him to see a new play, and while I am there waiting for Ambrose to finish some work, who comes in but Mrs. News. She is all in mourning and as soon as she sees Ambrose she begins to cry and she says to him like this:

"Oh, Mr. Hammer," she says, "I do not kill my husband."

"Why," Ambrose says, "certainly not. By no means and not at all. But," Ambrose says, "it is most injudicious of you to permit him to rumba at his age."

"It is his own desire," Mrs. News says. "It is his method of punishing me for being late for dinner a few times. He is the most frightful rumba dancer that ever lives and he knows it is torture to me to dance with a bad rumba dancer, so he takes me out and rumbas me into a state approaching nervous exhaustion before he keels over himself. Mr. Hammer, I do not like to speak ill of the dead but my late husband really has a mean disposition. But," she says, "I do not kill him."

"Nobody says you do," Ambrose says.

"Yes," Mrs. News says, "somebody does. Do you remember me telling you about drawing the cards at Mrs. Bidkar's apartment to see who is to dispose of her husband first?"

"Oh," Ambrose says, "you mean the little joke they play on you? Yes," he says, "I remember."

"Well," Mrs. News says, "Mrs. Bidkar now says it is never a joke at all. She says it is all in earnest and claims I know it is all the time. She is around to see me last night and says I undoubtedly give my husband poison and that I must turn his insurance money into the pool when I collect it. There is quite a lot of it. Over two hundred thousand dollars, Mr. Hammer."

"Look," Ambrose says, "this is just another of Mrs.

Bidkar's little jokes. She seems to have quite a sense of humour."

"No," Mrs. News says, "it is no joke She is very serious. She says unless I turn in the money she will expose me to the world and there will be a horrible scandal and I will go to gaol and not be able to collect a cent of the insurance money. She just laughs when I tell her I spill the cyanide she gives me and says if I do, I probably get more poison somewhere else and use it and that she and the others are entitled to their share of the money just the same because she furnishes the idea. Mr. Hammer, you must remember seeing me spill the cyanide."

"Mrs. N.," Ambrose says, "does anyone tell you yet that you make a lovely widow? But no matter," he says. "Yes I remember hearing you say you spill something but I do not look to see. Are you positive you do not do as Mrs. Bidkar suggests and get some other destructive substance and slip it to your husband by accident?"

Well, at this Mrs. News begins crying very loudly indeed, and Ambrose has to spend some time soothing her and I wish to state that when it comes to soothing a beautiful there are few better soothers than Ambrose Hammer on the island of Manhattan. Then when he gets her quieted down he says to her like this:

"Now," Ambrose says, "just leave everything to me. I am commencing to sniff something here. But," he says, "in the meantime remain friendly with Mrs. Bidkar. Let her think you are commencing to see things her own way. Maybe she will hold another drawing."

"Oh," Mrs. News says, "she has. She tells me the one whose name I cannot remember draws the nine of diamonds only the day before my husband departs this life. It is a long name with a kind of a foreign sound. Mrs. Bidkar says she has a lot of confidence in this one just on her looks although she does not know her intimately. I only wish I can think of the name. I have a dreadful time thinking of names. I remember yours when I happen to see it over an article in the paper the other day about Brogan Wilmington's play and then I remember, too, that you mention that he is the good-looking gentleman in the Canary Club the night we meet. Mr. Hammer," she says, "you say some very mean things about his play."

"Well," Ambrose says, "I do not know about the propriety of a beautiful in widow's weeds attending the theatre, but I happen to have a couple of skulls to Wilmington's play right here in my desk and I will give them to you and you can go and see for yourself that it really is most distressing. Probably you will see Wilmington himself standing in the lobby taking bows for no reason whatever, and I hope and trust you take another close glaum at him and you will see that he is not good looking. And," Ambrose says, "I tell you once more he is a total bust at the rumba."

"Why," Mrs. News says, "I will be delighted to see his play. It may help break the monotony of being a widow, which is quite monotonous to be sure, even after a very short time. I almost miss poor Brummy in spite of his narrow views on punctuality for dinner, but please do something about Mrs. Bidkar."

Then she leaves us, and Ambrose and I gaze at the new play which seems to me to be all right but which Ambrose says is a great insult to the theatre because Ambrose is very hard to please about plays, and it is some days before I see him again. Naturally, I ask him if he does anything about Mrs. News' case and Ambrose says:

"Yes," he says, "I prod around in it to some extent and I find it is an attempt at blackmail, just as I suspect. It is a most ingenious set-up, at that. I look up Mrs. Smythe and

Mrs. Brown and one is a chorus gorgeous by the name of Beerbaum and the other is a clerk in a Broadway lingerie shop by the name of Cooney. Neither of them is ever married as far as anybody knows. Mrs. Bidkar is originally out of Chicago and has a husband, but," Ambrose says, "nobody seems to know who he is or where he is."

"But Ambrose," I say, "how can Mrs. Smythe and Mrs. Brown enter into a deal to dispose of their husbands as Mrs. News states when they have no husbands? Is this entirely honest?"

"Why," Ambrose says, "they are stooges. You see," he says, "Mrs. Bidkar has a little moo and she rents this apartment and uses these two as trimming. Her idea is to pick up dumb beautifuls such as Mrs. News who are not too happy with their husbands and get them wedged in on such a situation as develops here, and the other two help out."

"Ambrose," I say, "do you mean to tell me this Mrs. Bidkar is so heartless as to plan to have these beautifuls she picks up chill their husbands?"

"No," Ambrose says. "This is not her plan at all. She has no idea they will actually do such a thing. But she does figure to manœuvre them into entering into the spirit of what she calls a joke just as she does Mrs. News, the cocktails helping out no little. It all sounds very harmless to the married beautiful until Mrs. Bidkar comes around afterwards and threatens to tell the husband that his wife is a party to a scheme of this nature. Naturally," Ambrose says, "such a wife is very eager to settle with Mrs. Bidkar for whatever she can dig up."

"Why, Ambrose," I say, "it is nothing but a shakedown, which is very old-fashioned stuff."

"Yes," Ambrose says, "it is a shake, all right. And," he says, "it makes me very sad to learn from Mrs. Smythe and Mrs. Brown, who work with Mrs. Bidkar in other cities, that many husbands must be willing to believe anything of their ever-lovings, even murder, and that the wives know it, because they always settle promptly with Mrs. Bidkar. She is a smart old broad. It is a pity she is so nefarious. Mrs. Smythe and Mrs. Brown are very grateful when they find I am not going to put them in gaol," Ambrose says. "I have their phone numbers."

"Well," I say, "now there is nothing left to be done but to clap this Mrs. Bidkar in the pokey and inform Mrs. News that she can quit worrying. Why, goodness gracious, Ambrose," I say, "Mrs. Bidkar is really a great menace to be at large in a community. She ought to be filed away for life."

"Yes," Ambrose says, "what you say is quite true, but if we put her in gaol it will all come out in the blats and Mrs. News cannot afford such notoriety. It may bother her in collecting her insurance. Let us go and see Mrs. Bidkar and explain to her that the best thing she can do is to hit the grit out of town."

So we get in a taxi-cab and go to an address in East Fifty-seventh Street that turns out to be a high-toned apartment house, and Ambrose stakes the elevator guy to a deuce and the guy takes us up to the sixth floor without going to the trouble of announcing us on the house phone first and points to a door. Then Ambrose pushes the buzzer and presently a female character appears and gazes at us in a most hospitable manner.

She is short and is wearing a negligée that permits her to widen out freely all the way around and she has straw-coloured hair and a large smile and while she is by no means a beautiful, still you cannot say she is a crow. In fact, I am somewhat surprised when Ambrose asks her if she is Mrs. Bidkar and she states that she is, as I am expecting a genuine old komoppo. We enter an elegantly furnished living-room and she asks our business, and Ambrose says:

"Well, Mrs. B.," he says, "you almost get a good break when old Doc News drops dead after you stake his wife to the poison because it looks as if you have her where she can never wiggle off no matter what she says. But," Ambrose says, "my friend Mrs. News is cute enough to seek my advice and counsel."

"Yes?" Mrs. Bidkar says. "And who are you?"

"Never mind," Ambrose says. "I am here to tell you that if you are present in these parts to-morrow morning you will find yourself in the canneroo."

At this, Mrs. Bidkar stops smiling and a very hard look indeed comes into her eyes and she says:

"Listen, guy, whoever you are," she says. "If you are a friend of Mrs. News you will tell her to get it on the line at once and save herself trouble. I may go to gaol," she says, "but so will she and I can stand it better than she can because I am there before, and anyway the charge against me will not be poisoning my husband."

"Mrs. Bidkar," Ambrose says, "you know Mrs. News does not poison her husband."

"No?" Mrs. Bidkar says. "Who does, then? They cannot pin it on me because Mrs. News herself claims she spills the stuff I give her and which she thinks is cyanide but which is really nothing but water, so she must get something else to do the job. Her own statement lets me out. But if you take her story that she does not poison him at all, you must be dumber than she is, although," Mrs. Bidkar says, "I will never believe such a thing is possible."

"Water, hey?" Ambrose says. "Well, Mrs. Bidkar," he says, "I can see that you really believe Mrs. News is guilty of this poisoning, so I will have to show you something I have here," he says, "a little document from the medical examiner stating that an autopsy on the remains of the late Dr. Brumby News discloses no sign of poison whatever. You can confirm this by calling up the district attorney, who has the autopsy performed and who is still very angry at me for putting him to a lot of bother for nothing," Ambrose says.

"An autopsy?" Mrs. Bidkar says, taking the paper and reading it. "I see. To-morrow morning, do you say? Well," she says, "you need not mind looking in again as I will be absent. Good day," she says.

Then Ambrose and I take our departure and when we are going along the street I suddenly think of something and I say to him like this:

"An autopsy, Ambrose?" I say. "Why, such an action indicates that you never entirely believe Mrs. News yourself, does it not?"

"Oh," Ambrose says, "I believe her, all right, but I always consider it a sound policy to look a little bit behind a beautiful's word on any proposition. Besides, cyanide has an odour and I do not remember noticing such an odour in the Canary Club and this makes me wonder somewhat about Mrs. News when I begin looking the situation over. But," Ambrose says, "of course Mrs. Bidkar clears this point up. Do you know what I am wondering right this minute? I am wondering what ever happens to Mrs. Bidkar's husband," he says.

Well, personally I do not consider this a matter worth thinking about, so I leave Ambrose at a corner and I do not see him again for weeks when we get together in the Canary Club for another dinner, and while we are sitting there who comes past our table without her mourning and looking very gorgeous indeed but Mrs. Brumby News.

When she sees Ambrose she stops and gives him a large good evening and Ambrose invites her to sit down and she does same but she states that she is on a meet with a friend and cannot remain with us long. She sits there chatting with Ambrose about this and that and he is so attentive that it reminds me of something and I say to him like this:

"Ambrose," I say, "I understand the course of your true love with Hilda may soon be smoothed out. I hear Hiffenbrower is in a hospital and may not be with us much longer. Well," I say, "let me be the first to congratulate you."

Now Mrs. News looks up and says:

"Hilda?" she says. "Hiffenbrower?" she says. "Why, this is the name of the other girl at Mrs. Bidkar's I am never able to remember. Yes, Hilda Hiffenbrower."

Naturally, I am greatly surprised and I gaze at Ambrose and he nods and says:

"Yes," he says, "I know it from the day I begin my investigation, but," he says, "I am too greatly shocked and pained to mention the matter. She becomes acquainted with Mrs. Bidkar the same way Mrs. News does. Hilda is always quick to learn and personally I feel that Hiffenbrower makes a mistake in not cancelling her out as the beneficiary of his insurance when they first separate. It is unfair to place great temptation before any beautiful and," Ambrose says, "especially Hilda.

"Well," he says, "Hiffenbrower is suffering from prolonged doses of powdered glass in his cereal but you are wrong about his condition. They are laying even money he beats it, although of course his digestion may be slightly impaired. I hear the cops trace Hilda to South America. Oh, well," Ambrose says, "I am through with the beautifuls for ever. Mrs. N., do you care to push a rumba around with me?"

"No," Mrs. News says, "here comes my friend. I think you meet him before. In fact," she says, "you are responsible for us getting together by sending me to the theatre on the free tickets that night."

And who is the friend but this Brogan Wilmington, the playwright, whose play is now running along quite successfully and making plenty of beesom in spite of what Ambrose states about it, and as Mrs. News gets up from the table to join him, Brogan Wilmington gazes at Ambrose and says to him like this:

"Bah," Brogan Wilmington says.

"Bah right back to you," Ambrose says, and then he begins going through his pockets looking for something.

"Now where do I put those phone numbers of Mrs. Smythe and Mrs. Brown?" Ambrose says.

17. THE IDYLL OF MISS SARAH BROWN

O F all the high players this country ever sees, there is
no doubt but that the guy they call The Sky is the
highest. In fact, the reason he is called The Sky is because
he goes so high when it comes to betting on any proposition
whatever. He will bet all he has, and nobody can bet any
more than this.

His right name is Obadiah Masterson, and he is originally
out of a little town in southern Colorado where he learns
to shoot craps, and play cards, and one thing and another,
and where his old man is a very well-known citizen, and
something of a sport himself. In fact, The Sky tells me
that when he finally cleans up all the loose scratch around
his home town and decides he needs more room, his old
man has a little private talk with him and says to him like
this:

"Son," the old guy says, "you are now going out into
the wide, wide world to make your own way, and it is a
very good thing to do, as there are no more opportunities
for you in this burg. I am only sorry," he says, "that I am
not able to bank-roll you to a very large start, but," he says,
"not having any potatoes to give you, I am now going to
stake you to some very valuable advice, which I personally
collect in my years of experience around and about, and I
hope and trust you will always bear this advice in mind.

"Son," the old guy says, "no matter how far you travel,
or how smart you get, always remember this: Some day,

somewhere," he says, "a guy is going to come to you and show you a nice brand-new deck of cards on which the seal is never broken, and this guy is going to offer to bet you that the jack of spades will jump out of this deck and squirt cider in your ear. But, son," the old guy says, "do not bet him, for as sure as you do you are going to get an ear full of cider."

Well, The Sky remembers what his old man says, and he is always very cautious about betting on such propositions as the jack of spades jumping out of a sealed deck of cards and squirting cider in his ear, and so he makes few mistakes as he goes along. In fact, the only real mistake The Sky makes is when he hits St. Louis after leaving his old home town, and loses all his potatoes betting a guy St. Louis is the biggest town in the world.

Now of course this is before The Sky ever sees any bigger towns, and he is never much of a hand for reading up on matters such as this. In fact, the only reading The Sky ever does as he goes along through life is in these Gideon Bibles such as he finds in the hotel rooms where he lives, for The Sky never lives anywhere else but in hotel rooms for years.

He tells me that he reads many items of great interest in these Gideon Bibles, and furthermore The Sky says that several times these Gideon Bibles keep him from getting out of line, such as the time he finds himself pretty much frozen-in over in Cincinnati, what with owing everybody in town except maybe the mayor from playing games of chance of one kind and another.

Well, The Sky says he sees no way of meeting these obligations and he is figuring the only thing he can do is to take a run-out powder, when he happens to read in one of these Gideon Bibles where it says like this:

"Better is it," the Gideon Bible says, "that thou shouldest not vow, than that thou shouldest vow and not pay."

Well, The Sky says he can see that there is no doubt whatever but that this means a guy shall not welsh, so he remains in Cincinnati until he manages to wiggle himself out of the situation, and from that day to this, The Sky never thinks of welshing.

He is maybe thirty years old, and is a tall guy with a round kisser, and big blue eyes, and he always looks as innocent as a little baby. But The Sky is by no means as innocent as he looks. In fact, The Sky is smarter than three Philadelphia lawyers, which makes him very smart, indeed, and he is well established as a high player in New Orleans, and Chicago, and Los Angeles, and wherever else there is any action in the way of card-playing, or crap-shooting, or horse-racing, or betting on the baseball games, for The Sky is always moving around the country following the action.

But while The Sky will bet on anything whatever, he is more of a short-card player and a crap-shooter than anything else, and furthermore he is a great hand for propositions, such as are always coming up among citizens who follow games of chance for a living. Many citizens prefer betting on propositions to anything you can think of, because they figure a proposition gives them a chance to out-smart somebody, and in fact I know citizens who will sit up all night making up propositions to offer other citizens the next day.

A proposition may be only a problem in cards, such as what is the price against a guy getting aces back-to-back, or how often a pair of deuces will win a hand in stud, and then again it may be some very daffy proposition, indeed, although the daffier any proposition seems to be, the more some citizens like it. And no one ever sees The Sky when he does not have some proposition of his own.

THE IDYLL OF MISS SARAH BROWN

The first time he ever shows up around this town, he goes to a baseball game at the Polo Grounds with several prominent citizens, and while he is at the ball game, he buys himself a sack of Harry Stevens' peanuts, which he dumps in a side pocket of his coat. He is eating these peanuts all through the game, and after the game is over and he is walking across the field with the citizens, he says to them like this:

"What price," The Sky says, "I cannot throw a peanut from second base to the home plate?"

Well, everybody knows that a peanut is too light for anybody to throw it this far, so Big Nig, the crap shooter, who always likes to have a little the best of it running for him, speaks as follows:

"You can have 3 to 1 from me, stranger," Big Nig says.

"Two C's against six," The Sky says, and then he stands on second base, and takes a peanut out of his pocket, and not only whips it to the home plate, but on into the lap of a fat guy who is still sitting in the grand stand putting the zing on Bill Terry for not taking Walker out of the box when Walker is getting a pasting from the other club.

Well, naturally, this is a most astonishing throw, indeed, but afterwards it comes out that The Sky throws a peanut loaded with lead, and of course it is not one of Harry Stevens' peanuts, either, as Harry is not selling peanuts full of lead at a dime a bag, with the price of lead what it is.

It is only a few nights after this that The Sky states another most unusual proposition to a group of citizens sitting in Mindy's restaurant when he offers to bet a C note that he can go down into Mindy's cellar and catch a live rat with his bare hands and everybody is greatly astonished when Mindy himself steps up and takes the bet, for ordinarily Mindy will not bet you a nickel he is alive.

But it seems that Mindy knows that The Sky plants a

tame rat in the cellar, and this rat knows The Sky and loves him dearly, and will let him catch it any time he wishes, and it also seems that Mindy knows that one of his dish washers happens upon this rat, and not knowing it is tame, knocks it flatter than a pancake. So when The Sky goes down into the cellar and starts trying to catch a rat with his bare hands he is greatly surprised how inhospitable the rat turns out to be, because it is one of Mindy's personal rats, and Mindy is around afterwards saying he will lay plenty of 7 to 5 against even Strangler Lewis being able to catch one of his rats with his bare hands, or with boxing gloves on.

I am only telling you all this to show you what a smart guy The Sky is, and I am only sorry I do not have time to tell you about many other very remarkable propositions that he thinks up outside of his regular business.

It is well-known to one and all that he is very honest in every respect, and that he hates and despises cheaters at cards, or dice, and furthermore The Sky never wishes to play with any the best of it himself, or anyway not much. He will never take the inside of any situation, as many gamblers love to do, such as owning a gambling house, and having the percentage run for him instead of against him, for always The Sky is strictly a player, because he says he will never care to settle down in one spot long enough to become the owner of anything.

In fact, in all the years The Sky is drifting around the country, nobody ever knows him to own anything except maybe a bank roll, and when he comes to Broadway the last time, which is the time I am now speaking of, he has a hundred G's in cash money, and an extra suit of clothes, and this is all he has in the world. He never owns such a thing as a house, or an automobile, or a piece of jewellery. He never owns a watch, because The Sky says time means nothing to him.

THE IDYLL OF MISS SARAH BROWN

Of course some guys will figure a hundred G's comes under the head of owning something, but as far as The Sky is concerned, money is nothing but just something for him to play with and the dollars may as well be doughnuts as far as value goes with him. The only time The Sky ever thinks of money as money is when he is broke, and the only way he can tell he is broke is when he reaches into his pocket and finds nothing there but his fingers.

Then it is necessary for The Sky to go out and dig up some fresh scratch somewhere, and when it comes to digging up scratch, The Sky is practically supernatural. He can get more potatoes on the strength of a telegram to some place or other than John D. Rockefeller can get on collateral, for everybody knows The Sky's word is as good as wheat in the bin.

Now one Sunday evening The Sky is walking along Broadway, and at the corner of Forty-ninth Street he comes upon a little bunch of mission workers who are holding a religious meeting, such as mission workers love to do of a Sunday evening, the idea being that they may round up a few sinners here and there, although personally I always claim the mission workers come out too early to catch any sinners on this part of Broadway. At such an hour the sinners are still in bed resting up from their sinning of the night before, so they will be in good shape for more sinning a little later on.

There are only four of these mission workers, and two of them are old guys, and one is an old doll, while the other is a young doll who is tootling on a cornet. And after a couple of ganders at this young doll, The Sky is a goner, for this is one of the most beautiful young dolls anybody ever sees on Broadway, and especially as a mission worker. Her name is Miss Sarah Brown.

She is tall, and thin, and has a first-class shape, and her

hair is a light brown, going on blonde, and her eyes are like I do not know what, except that they are one-hundred-per-cent eyes in every respect. Furthermore, she is not a bad cornet player, if you like cornet players, although at this spot on Broadway she has to play against a scat band in a chop-suey joint near by, and this is tough competition, although at that many citizens believe Miss Sarah Brown will win by a large score if she only gets a little more support from one of the old guys with her who has a big bass drum, but does not pound it hearty enough.

Well, The Sky stands there listening to Miss Sarah Brown tootling on the cornet for quite a spell, and then he hears her make a speech in which she puts the blast on sin very good, and boosts religion quite some, and says if there are any souls around that need saving the owners of same may step forward at once. But no one steps forward, so The Sky comes over to Mindy's restaurant where many citizens are congregated, and starts telling us about Miss Sarah Brown. But of course we already know about Miss Sarah Brown, because she is so beautiful, and so good.

Furthermore, everybody feels somewhat sorry for Miss Sarah Brown, for while she is always tootling the cornet, and making speeches, and looking to save any souls that need saving, she never seems to find any souls to save, or at least her bunch of mission workers never gets any bigger. In fact, it gets smaller, as she starts out with a guy who plays a very fair sort of trombone, but this guy takes it on the lam one night with the trombone, which one and all consider a dirty trick.

Now from this time on, The Sky does not take any interest in anything but Miss Sarah Brown, and any night she is out on the corner with the other mission workers, you will see The Sky standing around looking at her, and naturally after a few weeks of this, Miss Sarah Brown must know The Sky is looking at her, or she is dumber than seems possible. And nobody ever figures Miss Sarah Brown dumb, as she is always on her toes, and seems plenty able to take care of herself, even on Broadway.

Sometimes after the street meeting is over, The Sky follows the mission workers to their headquarters in an old storeroom around in Forty-eighth Street where they generally hold an indoor session, and I hear The Sky drops many a large coarse note in the collection box while looking at Miss Sarah Brown, and there is no doubt these notes come in handy around the mission, as I hear business is by no means so good there.

It is called the Save-a-Soul Mission, and it is run mainly by Miss Sarah Brown's grandfather, an old guy with whiskers, by the name of Arvide Abernathy, but Miss Sarah Brown seems to do most of the work, including tootling the cornet, and visiting the poor people around and about, and all this and that, and many citizens claim it is a great shame that such a beautiful doll is wasting her time being good.

How The Sky ever becomes acquainted with Miss Sarah Brown is a very great mystery, but the next thing anybody knows, he is saying hello to her, and she is smiling at him out of her one-hundred-per-cent eyes, and one evening when I happen to be with The Sky we run into her walking along Forty-ninth Street, and The Sky hauls off and stops her, and says it is a nice evening, which it is, at that. Then The Sky says to Miss Sarah Brown like this:

"Well," The Sky says, "how is the mission dodge going these days? Are you saving any souls?" he says.

Well, it seems from what Miss Sarah Brown says the soul-saving is very slow, indeed, these days.

"In fact," Miss Sarah Brown says, "I worry greatly

about how few souls we seem to save. Sometimes I wonder if we are lacking in grace."

She goes on up the street, and The Sky stands looking after her, and he says to me like this:

"I wish I can think of some way to help this little doll," he says, "especially," he says, "in saving a few souls to build up her mob at the mission. I must speak to her again, and see if I can figure something out."

But The Sky does not get to speak to Miss Sarah Brown again, because somebody weighs in the sacks on him by telling her he is nothing but a professional gambler, and that he is a very undesirable character, and that his only interest in hanging around the mission is because she is a good-looking doll. So all of a sudden Miss Sarah Brown plays a plenty of chill for The Sky. Furthermore, she sends him word that she does not care to accept any more of his potatoes in the collection box, because his potatoes are nothing but ill-gotten gains.

Well, naturally, this hurts The Sky's feelings no little, so he quits standing around looking at Miss Sarah Brown, and going to the mission, and takes to mingling again with the citizens in Mindy's, and showing some interest in the affairs of the community, especially the crap games.

Of course the crap games that are going on at this time are nothing much, because practically everybody in the world is broke, but there is a head-and-head game run by Nathan Detroit over a garage in Fifty-second Street where there is occasionally some action, and who shows up at this crap game early one evening but The Sky, although it seems he shows up there more to find company than anything else.

In fact, he only stands around watching the play, and talking with other guys who are also standing around and watching, and many of these guys are very high shots during the gold rush, although most of them are now as clean as a jaybird, and maybe cleaner. One of these guys is a guy by the name of Brandy Bottle Bates, who is known from coast to coast as a high player when he has anything to play with, and who is called Brandy Bottle Bates because it seems that years ago he is a great hand for belting a brandy bottle around.

This Brandy Bottle Bates is a big, black-looking guy, with a large beezer, and a head shaped like a pear, and he is considered a very immoral and wicked character, but he is a pretty slick gambler, and a fast man with a dollar when he is in the money.

Well, finally The Sky asks Brandy Bottle why he is not playing and Brandy laughs, and states as follows:

"Why," he says, "in the first place I have no potatoes, and in the second place I doubt if it will do me much good if I do have any potatoes the way I am going the past year. Why," Brandy Bottle says, "I cannot win a bet to save my soul."

Now this crack seems to give The Sky an idea, as he stands looking at Brandy Bottle very strangely, and while he is looking, Big Nig, the crap shooter, picks up the dice and hits three times hand-running, bing, bing, bing. Then Big Nig comes out on a six and Brandy Bottle Bates speaks as follows:

"You see how my luck is," he says. "Here is Big Nig hotter than a stove, and here I am without a bob to follow him with, especially," Brandy says, "when he is looking for nothing but a six. Why," he says, "Nig can make sixes all night when he is hot. If he does not make this six, the way he is, I will be willing to turn square and quit gambling forever."

"Well, Brandy," The Sky says, "I will make you a proposition. I will lay you a G note Big Nig does not get

his six. I will lay you a G note against nothing but your
soul," he says. "I mean if Big Nig does not get his six,
you are to turn square and join Miss Sarah Brown's mission
for six months."

"Bet!" Brandy Bottle Bates says right away, meaning
the proposition is on, although the chances are he does not
quite understand the proposition. All Brandy understands
is The Sky wishes to wager that Big Nig does not make his
six, and Brandy Bottle Bates will be willing to bet his soul a
couple of times over on Big Nig making his six, and figure
he is getting the best of it, at that, as Brandy has great confidence in Nig.

Well, sure enough, Big Nig makes the six, so The Sky
weeds Brandy Bottle Bates a G note, although everybody
around is saying The Sky makes a terrible over-lay of the
natural price in giving Brandy Bottle a G against his soul.
Furthermore, everybody around figures the chances are The
Sky only wishes to give Brandy an opportunity to get in
action, and nobody figures The Sky is on the level about
trying to win Brandy Bottle Bates' soul, especially as The
Sky does not seem to wish to go any further after paying
the bet.

He only stands there looking on and seeming somewhat
depressed as Brandy Bottle goes into action on his own
account with the G note, fading other guys around the
table with cash money. But Brandy Bottle Bates seems to
figure what is in The Sky's mind pretty well, because Brandy
Bottle is a crafty old guy.

It finally comes his turn to handle the dice, and he hits a
couple of times, and then he comes out on a four, and
anybody will tell you that a four is a very tough point to
make, even with a lead pencil. Then Brandy Bottle turns
to The Sky and speaks to him as follows:

"Well, Sky," he says, "I will take the odds off you on

this one. I know you do not want my dough," he says. "I know you only want my soul for Miss Sarah Brown, and," he says, "without wishing to be fresh about it, I know why you want it for her. I am young once myself," Brandy Bottle says. "And you know if I lose to you, I will be over there in Forty-eighth Street in an hour pounding on the door, for Brandy always settles.

"But, Sky," he says, "now I am in the money, and my price goes up. Will you lay me ten G's against my soul I do not make this four?"

"Bet!" The Sky says, and right away Brandy Bottle hits with a four.

Well, when word goes around that The Sky is up at Nathan Detroit's crap game trying to win Brandy Bottle Bates' soul for Miss Sarah Brown, the excitement is practically intense. Somebody telephones Mindy's, where a large number of citizens are sitting around arguing about this and that, and telling one another how much they will bet in support of their arguments, if only they have something to bet, and Mindy himself is almost killed in the rush for the door.

One of the first guys out of Mindy's and up to the crap game is Regret, the horse player, and as he comes in Brandy Bottle is looking for a nine, and The Sky is laying him twelve G's against his soul that he does not make this nine, for it seems Brandy Bottle's soul keeps getting more and more expensive.

Well, Regret wishes to bet his soul against a G that Brandy Bottle gets his nine, and is greatly insulted when The Sky cannot figure his price any better than a double saw, but finally Regret accepts this price, and Brandy Bottle hits again.

Now many other citizens request a little action from The Sky, and if there is one thing The Sky cannot deny a citizen it is action, so he says he will lay them according to how he figures their word to join Miss Sarah Brown's mission if Brandy Bottle misses out, but about this time The Sky finds he has no more potatoes on him, being now around thirty-five G's loser, and he wishes to give markers.

But Brandy Bottle says that while ordinarily he will be pleased to extend The Sky this accommodation, he does not care to accept markers against his soul, so then The Sky has to leave the joint and go over to his hotel two or three blocks away, and get the night clerk to open his damper so The Sky can get the rest of his bank roll. In the meantime the crap game continues at Nathan Detroit's among the small operators, while the other citizens stand around and say that while they hear of many a daffy proposition in their time, this is the daffiest that ever comes to their attention, although Big Nig claims he hears of a daffier one, but cannot think what it is.

Big Nig claims that all gamblers are daffy anyway, and in fact he says if they are not daffy they will not be gamblers, and while he is arguing this matter back comes The Sky with fresh scratch, and Brandy Bottle Bates takes up where he leaves off, although Brandy says he is accepting the worst of it, as the dice have a chance to cool off.

Now the upshot of the whole business is that Brandy Bottle hits thirteen licks in a row, and the last lick he makes is on a ten, and it is for twenty G's against his soul, with about a dozen other citizens getting anywhere from one to five C's against their souls, and complaining bitterly of the price.

And as Brandy Bottle makes his ten, I happen to look at The Sky and I see him watching Brandy with a very peculiar expression on his face, and furthermore I see The Sky's right hand creeping inside his coat where I know he always packs a Betsy in a shoulder holster, so I can see something is wrong somewhere.

But before I can figure out what it is, there is quite a fuss at the door, and loud talking, and a doll's voice, and all of a sudden in bobs nobody else but Miss Sarah Brown. It is plain to be seen that she is all steamed up about something.

She marches right up to the crap table where Brandy Bottle Bates and The Sky and the other citizens are standing, and one and all are feeling sorry for Dobber, the doorman, thinking of what Nathan Detroit is bound to say to him for letting her in. The dice are still lying on the table showing Brandy Bottles Bates' last throw, which cleans The Sky and gives many citizens the first means they enjoy in several months.

Well, Miss Sarah Brown looks at The Sky, and The Sky looks at Miss Sarah Brown, and Miss Sarah Brown looks at the citizens around and about, and one and all are somewhat dumbfounded, and nobody seems to be able to think of much to say, although The Sky finally speaks up as follows:

"Good evening," The Sky says. "It is a nice evening," he says. "I am trying to win a few souls for you around here, but," he says, "I seem to be about half out of luck."

"Well," Miss Sarah Brown says, looking at The Sky most severely out of her hundred-per-cent eyes, "you are taking too much upon yourself. I can win any souls I need myself. You better be thinking of your own soul. By the way," she says, "are you risking your own soul, or just your money?"

Well, of course up to this time The Sky is not risking anything but his potatoes, so he only shakes his head to Miss Sarah Brown's question, and looks somewhat disorganized.

"I know something about gambling," Miss Sarah Brown says, "especially about crap games. I ought to," she says. "It ruins my poor papa and my brother Joe. If you wish to gamble for souls, Mister Sky, gamble for your own soul."

Now Miss Sarah Brown opens a small black leather pocketbook she is carrying in one hand, and pulls out a two-dollar bill, and it is such a two-dollar bill as seems to have seen much service in its time, and holding up this deuce, Miss Sarah Brown speaks as follows:

"I will gamble with you, Mister Sky," she says. "I will gamble with you," she says, "on the same terms you gamble with these parties here. This two dollars against your soul, Mister Sky. It is all I have, but," she says, "it is more than your soul is worth."

Well, of course anybody can see that Miss Sarah Brown is doing this because she is very angry, and wishes to make The Sky look small, but right away The Sky's duke comes from inside his coat, and he picks up the dice and hands them to her and speaks as follows:

"Roll them," The Sky says, and Miss Sarah Brown snatches the dice out of his hand and gives them a quick sling on the table in such a way that anybody can see she is not a professional crap shooter, and not even an amateur crap shooter, for all amateur crap shooters first breathe on the dice, and rattle them good, and make remarks to them, such as "Come on, baby!"

In fact, there is some criticism of Miss Sarah Brown afterwards on account of her haste, as many citizens are eager to string with her to hit, while others are just as anxious to bet she misses, and she does not give them a chance to get down.

Well, Scranton Slim is the stick guy, and he takes a gander at the dice as they hit up against the side of the table and bounce back, and then Slim hollers, "Winner, winner, winner," as stick guys love to do, and what is showing on the dice as big as life, but a six and a five, which makes eleven, no matter how you figure, so The Sky's soul belongs to Miss Sarah Brown.

She turns at once and pushes through the citizens around the table without even waiting to pick up the deuce she lays down when she grabs the dice. Afterwards a most obnoxious character by the name of Red Nose Regan tries to claim the deuce as a sleeper and gets the heave-o from Nathan Detroit, who becomes very indignant about this, stating that Red Nose is trying to give his joint a wrong rap.

Naturally, The Sky follows Miss Brown, and Dobber, the doorman, tells me that as they are waiting for him to unlock the door and let them out, Miss Sarah Brown turns on The Sky and speaks to him as follows:

"You are a fool," Miss Sarah Brown says.

Well, at this Dobber figures The Sky is bound to let one go, as this seems to be most insulting language, but instead of letting one go, The Sky only smiles at Miss Sarah Brown and says to her like this:

"Why," The Sky says, "Paul says 'If any man among you seemeth to be wise in this world, let him become a fool, that he may be wise.' I love you, Miss Sarah Brown," The Sky says.

Well, now, Dobber has a pretty fair sort of memory, and he says that Miss Sarah Brown tells The Sky that since he seems to know so much about the Bible, maybe he remembers the second verse of the Song of Solomon, but the chances are Dobber muffs the number of the verse, because I look the matter up in one of these Gideon Bibles, and the verse seems a little too much for Miss Sarah Brown, although of course you never can tell.

Anyway, this is about all there is to the story, except that Brandy Bottle Bates slides out during the confusion so quietly even Dobber scarcely remembers letting him out, and he takes most of The Sky's potatoes with him, but he soon gets batted in against the faro bank out in Chicago, and the last anybody hears of him he gets religion all over again, and is preaching out in San Jose, so The Sky always claims he beats Brandy for his soul, at that.

I see The Sky the other night at Forty-ninth Street and Broadway, and he is with quite a raft of mission workers, including Mrs. Sky, for it seems that the soul-saving business picks up wonderfully, and The Sky is giving a big bass drum such a first-class whacking that the scat band in the chop-suey joint can scarcely be heard. Furthermore, The Sky is hollering between whacks, and I never see a guy look happier, especially when Mrs. Sky smiles at him out of her hundred-per-cent eyes. But I do not linger long, because The Sky gets a gander at me, and right away he begins hollering:

"I see before me a sinner of deepest dye," he hollers. "Oh, sinner, repent before it is too late. Join with us, sinner," he hollers, "and let us save your soul."

Naturally, this crack about me being a sinner embarrasses me no little, as it is by no means true, and it is a good thing for The Sky there is no copper in me, or I will go to Mrs. Sky, who is always bragging about how she wins The Sky's soul by outplaying him at his own game, and tell her the truth.

And the truth is that the dice with which she wins The Sky's soul, and which are the same dice with which Brandy Bottle Bates wins all his potatoes, are strictly phony, and that she gets into Nathan Detroit's just in time to keep The Sky from killing old Brandy Bottle.

18. THE MELANCHOLY DANE

I͏ᴛ is a matter of maybe two years back that I run into
Ambrose Hammer, the newspaper scribe, one evening
on Broadway and he requests me to attend the theatre with
him, as Ambrose is what is called a dramatic critic and his
racket is to witness all the new plays and write what he
thinks about them in a morning blat.

I often hear the actors and the guys who write the plays
talking about Ambrose in Mindy's restaurant when they
get the last edition and read what he has to say, and as
near as I can make out, they feel that he is nothing but a
low criminal type because it seems that Ambrose practically
murders one and all connected with any new play. So I
say to him like this:

"No, Ambrose," I say, "I may happen to know the guy
who writes the play you are going to see, or one of the
actors, and as I understand it is always about nine to five
that you will put the blister on a new play, I will be running
the risk of hurting myself socially along Broadway. Furthermore," I say, "where is Miss Channelle Cooper who
accompanies you to the new plays for the past six months
hand-running?"

"Oh," Ambrose says, "you need not worry about the
guy who writes this play, as his name is Shakespeare and he
is dead quite a spell. You need not worry about any of the
actors, either, as they are just a bunch of plumbers that no
one ever hears of before, except maybe the leading one
who has some slight notoriety. And, as for Miss Channelle
Cooper, I do not know where she is at this particular

moment and, not to give you a short answer, I do not give a D and an A and an M and an N."

"Why, Ambrose," I say, "the last time we meet, you tell me that you are on fire with love for Miss Channelle Cooper, although, of course," I say, "you are on fire with love for so many different broads since I know you that I am surprised you are not reduced to ashes long ago."

"Look," Ambrose says, "let us not discuss such a tender subject as Miss Cooper at this time or I am apt to break into tears and be in no mood to impartially perform my stern duty towards this play. All I know is she sends me a letter by messenger this morning, stating that she cannot see me to-night because her grandmother's diabetes is worse and she has to go to Yonkers to see her.

"And," Ambrose goes on, "I happen to know that in the first place her grandmother does not have diabetes but only a tumour, and in the second place she does not live in Yonkers but in Greenwich Village, and in the third place Miss Cooper is seen late this afternoon having tea at the Plaza with an eighteen-carat hambola by the name of Mansfield Sothern. I wonder," Ambrose says, "if the bim is ever born who can tell the truth?"

"No, Ambrose," I say, "or anyway not yet. But," I say, "I am surprised to hear Miss Cooper turns out unstable, as she always strikes me as the reliable sort and very true to you, or at least as true as you can expect these days. In fact," I say, "I have it on good authority that she turns down Lefty Lyons, the slot-machine king, who offers to take charge of her career and buy a night club for her. But of course Mansfield Sothern is something else again. I often enjoy his comedy on the stage."

"He is a hunk of Smithfield who steals the names of two great actors to make one for himself," Ambrose says. "I will admit that he is sometimes endurable in musical comedy, if you close your eyes when he is on the boards and make believe he is somebody else, but, like all actors, he is egotistical enough to think he can play Hamlet. In fact," Ambrose says, "he is going to do it to-night and I can scarcely wait."

Well, I finally go to the theatre with Ambrose and it is quite a high-toned occasion with nearly everybody in the old thirteen-and-odd because Mansfield Sothern has a big following in musical comedy and it seems that his determination to play Hamlet produces quite a sensation, though Ambrose claims that most of those present are members of Mansfield's personal clique from café society and he also claims that it is all nothing but a plot to make Mansfield seem important.

Personally, I am not a Shakespeare man, although I see several of his plays before and, to tell you the truth, I am never able to savvy them, though naturally I do not admit this in public as I do not wish to appear unintelligent. But I stick with Ambrose through the first act of this one and I observe that Mansfield Sothern is at least a right large Hamlet and has a voice that makes him sound as if he is talking from down in a coal mine, though what he is talking about is not clear to me and consequently does not arouse my interest.

So as Ambrose seems very thoughtful and paying no attention to me, I quietly take my departure and go to Mindy's where some hours later along in the early morning, I notice Miss Channelle Cooper and this gee Mansfield Sothern reading Ambrose's column, and Mansfield is shedding tears on the paper until the printer's ink runs down into his bacon and eggs. Naturally, I go out and buy a paper at once to see what causes his distress and I find that Ambrose writes about the play as follows:

'After Mansfield Sothern's performance of Hamlet at

the Todd Theatre last night, there need no longer be controversy as to the authorship of the immortal drama. All we need do is examine the graves of Shakespeare and Bacon, and the one that has turned over is it."

Now I do not clap eyes on Ambrose Hammer again until the other evening when he enters Mindy's at dinnertime, walking with a cane and limping slightly. Furthermore, he is no longer roly-poly, but quite thin and he gives me a huge hello and sits down at my table and speaks to me as follows:

"Well, well," Ambrose says, "this is indeed a coincidence. The last time we meet I take you to a theatre and now I am going to take you again on my first night back in harness. How is the *gedemte brust* and the *latkas* you are devouring?"

"The *latkas* are all right, Ambrose," I say, "but the *brust* is strictly second run. The war conditions are such that we must now take what we can get, even when it comes to *brust*. I do not see you for a spell, Ambrose. Are you absent from the city and why are you packing the stick?"

"Why," Ambrose says, "I am overseas and I am wounded in North Africa. Do you mean to tell me I am not missed in these parts?"

"Well, Ambrose," I say, "now that you mention it, I do remember hearing you are mixed up in the war business, but we are so busy missing other personalities that we do not get around to missing you as yet. And as for going to the theatre with you, I must pass, because the last time you steer me up against a most unenjoyable evening. By the way, Ambrose," I say, "I wonder what ever becomes of that bloke Mansfield Sothern and Miss Channelle Cooper. And what are you doing in North Africa, anyway?"

I am in North Africa (Ambrose says) risking my life for

my paper as a war correspondent because one day my editor calls me into his office and speaks to me as follows:

"Hammer," he says, "kindly go to the front and send us back human-interest stories about our soldiers. Our soldiers are what our readers are interested in. Please eat with them and sleep with them and tell us how they live and what they think about and how they talk and so forth and so on."

So I go to London, and from London, I go to North Africa on a transport, and on this voyage I endeavour to start following my instructions at once, but I find that eating with the soldiers has its disadvantages as they can eat much faster than I can because of their greater experience and I am always getting shut out on the choicer titbits.

And when I ask one of them if I can sleep with him, he gives me a strange look, and afterwards I have a feeling that I am the subject of gossip among these gees. Furthermore, when I try to listen in on their conversation to learn how they talk, some of them figure I am a stool pigeon for the officers and wish to dunk me in the ocean. It is by no means a soft touch to be a war correspondent who is supposed to find out how the soldiers live and how they talk and what they think about, and when I mention my difficulties to one of the officers, he says I may get closer to the boys if I enlist, but naturally I figure this will be carrying war correspondenting too far.

But I write these human-interest stories just the same and I think they are pretty good even if I do hear a guy in the censor's office call me the poor man's Quentin Reynolds, and I always mingle with the soldiers as much as possible to get their atmosphere and finally when they learn I am kindly disposed towards them and generally have plenty of cigarettes, they become quite friendly.

I am sorry I do not have time to tell you a great deal

about my terrible personal experiences at the front, but I am putting them all in the book I am writing, and you can buy a copy of it later. In fact, I have enough terrible experiences for three books, only my publisher states that he thinks one book per war correspondent is sufficient for the North African campaign. He says that the way correspondents are writing books on North Africa with Sicily and Italy coming up, he does not figure his paper supply to last the war out.

I first arrive at a place called Algiers in North Africa and I find it is largely infested by Arabs and naturally I feel at home at once, as in my younger days in show business when I am working for a booking office, I personally book a wonderful Arab acrobatic troop consisting of a real Arab by the name of Punchy, two guys by the name of O'Shea, and a waffle who is known as Little Oran, though her square monicker is really Magnolia Shapiro.

Consequently I have great sentiment for Arabs, and the sights and scenes and smells of Algiers keep me thinking constantly of the good old days, especially the smells. But I will not tax your patience with the details of my stay in Algiers because by the time I reach there the war moves away off to a place called Tunisia and I am willing to let it stay there without my presence. Then, after a week, my editor sends me a sharp message asking why I am not at the front getting human-interest stories instead of loitering in Algiers wasting my time on some tamale, although, as a matter of fact, I am not wasting my time. And how he learns about the tamale I have no idea, as she does not speak a word of English.

However, one way and another I proceed to a place called Bone and then I continue on from there one way and another, but mostly in a little consumptive car, in the general direction of Tunis, and as I go, I keep asking passing

THE MELANCHOLY DANE

British and American soldiers where is the front. And they say the front is up front, and I keep going and in my travels I get very sick and tired of the war because the enemy is always dropping hot apples all over the landscape out of planes, and sprinkling the roads with bullets or throwing big shells that make the most uncouth noises around very carelessly indeed.

Naturally, this impedes and delays my progress quite some because, from time to time, I am compelled to pause and dismount from my little bucket and seek refuge from these missiles in holes in the earth, and, when I cannot find a hole, I seek the refuge by falling on my face on the ground. In fact, I fall so often on my face that I am commencing to fear I will wind up with a pug nose.

Part of the time I am travelling with another newspaper scribe by the name of Herbert something, but he goes to Foldsville on me soon after we leave Bone, with a case of heartburn caused by eating Army rations, which reminds me that I must speak to the F.B.I. about these rations some day as it is my opinion that the books of the guy who invents them should be looked over to see which side he is betting on.

Well, all the time I keep asking where is the front, and all the time the soldiers say the front is up front. But I do not seem to ever find the front and, in fact, I later learn from an old soldier that nobody ever finds the front because by the time they get to where it ought to be, the front is apt to be the rear or the middle, and it is all very confusing to be sure.

Early one morning, I arrive at what seems to be the ruins of a little town, and at the same moment, an enemy battery on a hill a couple of miles away starts throwing big biscuits into the town, although I do not see hide or hair of anyone there, and whether it is because they think some of our troops are in the town or just have a personal grudge against me, I never learn.

Anyway, all of a sudden something nudges my little wagon from under me and knocks it into pieces the size of confetti and at the same moment I feel a distinct sensation of pain in my Francesca. It comes to my mind that I am wounded and I lie there with what I know is blood running down the inside of my pants leg which gives me a most untidy feeling, indeed, and what is more, I am mentally depressed quite some as I am already behind with my copy and I can see where this will delay me further and cause my editor to become most peevish.

But there is nothing I can do about it, only to keep on lying there and to try to stop the blood as best I can and wait for something to happen and also to hope that my mishap does not inconvenience my editor too greatly.

It is coming on noon, and all around and about it is very quiet, and nothing whatever seems to be stirring anywhere when who appears but a big guy in our uniform, and he seems more surprised than somewhat when he observes me, as he speaks to me as follows:

"Goodness me!" he says. "What is this?"

"I am wounded," I say.

"Where?" he says.

"In the vestibule," I say.

Then he drops on one knee beside me and outs with a knife and cuts open my pants and looks at the wound, and as he gets to his feet, he says to me like this:

"Does it hurt?" he says. "Are you suffering greatly?"

"Sure I am," I say. "I am dying."

Now the guy laughs ha-ha-ha-ha, as if he just hears a good joke and he says, "Look at me, Hammer," he says. "Do you not recognize me?"

Naturally I look and I can see that he is nobody but this

THE MELANCHOLY DANE

Mansfield Sothern, the actor, and of course I am greatly pleased at the sight of him.

"Mansfield," I say, "I am never so glad to see an old friend in my life."

"What do you mean by old friend?" Mansfield says. "I am not your old friend. I am not even your new friend. Hammer," he says, "are you really in great pain?"

"Awful," I say. "Please get me to a doctor."

Well, at this, he laughs ha-ha-ha-ha again and says, "Hammer, all my professional life, I am hoping to one day see a dramatic critic suffer, and you have no idea what pleasure you are now giving me, but I think it only fair for you to suffer out loud with groans and one thing and another. Hammer," Mansfield says, "I am enjoying a privilege that any actor will give a squillion dollars to experience."

"Look, Mansfield," I say, "kindly cease your clowning and take me somewhere. I am in great agony."

"Ha-ha-ha-ha," Mansfield Sothern ha-has. "Hammer, I cannot get you to a doctor because the Jeremiahs seem to be between us and our lines. I fear they nab the rest of my patrol. It is only by good luck that I elude them myself and then, lo and behold, I find you. I do not think there are any of the enemy right around this spot at the moment and I am going to lug you into yonder building, but it is not because I take pity on you. It is only because I wish to keep you near me so I can see you suffer."

Then he picks me up in his arms and carries me inside the walls of what seems to be an old inn, though it has no roof and no windows or doors, and even the walls are a little shaky from much shellfire, and he puts me down on the floor and washes my wound with water from his canteen and puts sulpha powder on my wound and gives me some to swallow, and all the time he is talking a blue streak.

"Hammer," he says, "do you remember the night I give my performance of Hamlet and you knock my brains out? Well, you are in no more agony now than I am then. I die ten thousand deaths when I read your criticism. Furthermore, you alienate the affections of Miss Channelle Cooper from me, because she thinks you are a great dramatic critic, and when you say I am a bad Hamlet, she believes you and cancels our engagement. She says she cannot bear the idea of being married to a bad Hamlet. Hammer," he says, "am I a bad Hamlet?"

"Mansfield," I say, "I now regret I cause you anguish."

"Mr. Sothern to you," Mansfield says. "Hammer," he says, "I hear you only see two acts of my Hamlet."

"That is true," I say. "I have to hasten back to my office to write my review."

"Why," he says, "how dare you pass on the merits of an artist on such brief observation? Does your mad jealousy of me over Miss Channelle Cooper cause you to forget you are a human being and make a hyena of you? Or are all dramatic critics just naturally hyenas, as I suspect?"

"Mansfield," I say, "while I admit to much admiration and, in fact, love for Miss Channelle Cooper, I never permit my emotions to bias my professional efforts. When I state you are a bad Hamlet, I state my honest conviction and while I now suffer the tortures of the damned, I still state it."

"Hammer," Mansfield Sothern says, "listen to me and observe me closely because I am now going to run through the grave-diggers' scene for you which you do not see me do, and you can tell me afterwards if Barrymore or Leslie Howard or Maurice Evans ever gives a finer performance."

And with this, what does he do but pick up a big stone from the floor and strike a pose and speak as follows:

"'Alas, poor Yorick! I knew him, Horatio; a fellow

of infinite jest, of most excellent fancy; he hath borne me on his back a thousand times; and now, how abhorred in my imagination it is! my gorge rises at it. Here hung those lips that I have kissed I know not how oft. Where be your gibes now? your gambols? your songs? your flashes of merriment, that were wont to set the tables on a roar? Not one, now, to mock your own grinning? quite chap-fallen? Now get you to my lady's chamber, and tell her, let her paint an inch thick, to this favour she must come; make her laugh at that. Pr'ythee, Horatio, tell me one thing' "

Now Mansfield stops and looks at me and says: "Come, come, Hammer, you're Horatio. Throw me the line."

So I try to remember what Horatio remarks at this point in Hamlet and finally I say, " 'How is that, my lord?' "

"No, no," Mansfield says. "Not 'How is that?' but 'What's that?' And you presume to criticize me!"

"All right, Mansfield," I say. " 'What's that, my lord?' "

And Mansfield says, " 'Dost thou think Alexander looked o' this fashion i' the earth?' "

I say, " 'E'en so.' "

" 'And smelt so?' pah!" Mansfield says, and with this, he throws the stone to the floor, and at the same moment I hear another noise and, on looking around, what do I see in the doorway but two German officers covered with dust, and one of them says in English like this:

"What is going on here?"

Naturally, I am somewhat nonplussed at the sight of these guys, but Mansfield Sothern does not seem to notice them and continues reciting in a loud voice.

"He is an actor in civil life," I say to the German. "He is now presenting his version of Hamlet to me."

" 'To what base uses we may return, Horatio!' " Mansfield Sothern says. " 'Why may not imagination trace the noble dust of Alexander——!' "

" 'Till he finds it stopping a bunghole?' " the German cuts in and then Mansfield looks at him and say:

" 'Find,' not 'finds,' " he says.

"Quite right," the German says. "Well, you are now prisoners. I will send some of my soldiers to pick you up immediately. Do not attempt to leave this place or you will be shot, as we have the town surrounded."

Then the two depart and Mansfield stops reciting at once and says, "Let us duffy out of here. It is growing dark outside, and I think we can make it. Are you still suffering first class, Hammer?"

"Yes," I say, "and I cannot walk an inch, either."

So Mansfield laughs ha-ha-ha and picks me up again as easy as if I am nothing but a bag of wind and carries me out through what seems to have been a back door to the joint, but before we go into the open, he throws himself face downward on the ground and tells me to pull myself on his back and hook my arms around his neck and hold on, and I do the same. Then he starts crawling along like he is a turtle and I am its shell. Naturally, our progress is very slow, especially as we hear guys everywhere around us in the dark talking in German.

Every few yards, Mansfield has to stop to rest, and I roll off his back until he is ready to start again and, during one of these halts, he whispers, "Hammer, are you still suffering?"

"Yes," I say.

"Good," Mansfield says, and then he goes on crawling.

I do not know how far he crawls with me aboard him because I am getting a little groggy, but I do remember him whispering very softly to himself like this:

THE MELANCHOLY DANE

" 'Imperious Cæsar, dead and turn'd to clay,
Might stop a hole to keep the wind away.' "

Well, Mansfield crawls and crawls and crawls until he crawls himself and me right into a bunch of our guys, and the next thing I know is I wake up in a hospital, and who is sitting there beside me but Mansfield Sothern and, when he sees I am awake, he says like this:

" 'O, I die, Horatio.' "

"Mansfield," I say, "kindly cheese it and permit me to thank you for saving my life."

"Hammer," he says, "the pleasure is all mine. I am sustained on my long crawl (which they tell me is a new world record for crawling with a guy on the deck of the crawler) by the thought that I have on my back a dramatic critic who is suffering keenly every inch of the way.

"I suppose," he says, "that you hear I am decorated for rescuing you, but kindly keep it quiet, as the Actors' Guild will never forgive me for rescuing a critic. Also, Hammer, I am being sent home to organize overseas entertainment for my comrades, and naturally it will be along Shakespearean lines. Tell me, Hammer, do you observe your nurse as yet?"

And, with this, Mansfield points to a doll in uniform standing not far away, and I can see that it is nobody but Miss Channelle Cooper, and I can also see that she is hoping she is looking like Miss Florence Nightingale. When she notices I am awake, she starts towards my cot, but at her approach, Mansfield Sothern gets up and departs quite hastily without as much as saying boo to her and and as she stands looking at him, tears come to her eyes and I can see that a coolness must still prevail between them.

Naturally, I am by no means displeased by this situation

because the sight of Miss Channelle Cooper even in a nurse's uniform brings back fond memories to me and, in fact, I feel all my old love for her coming up inside me like a lump, and, as she reaches my bedside, I can scarcely speak because of my emotion.

"You must be quiet, Ambrose," she says. "You know you are delirious for days and days, and in your delirium you say things about me that cause me much embarrassment. Does Mansfield happen to mention my name?"

"No," I say. "Forget him, Channelle. He is a cad as well as a bad Hamlet."

But the tears in her eyes increase, and suddenly she leaves me and I do not see her for some days afterward and, in fact, I do not even think of her because my editor is sending me messages wishing to know what I am doing in a hospital on his time and to get out of there at once, and what do I mean by putting a horse in my last expense account, which of course is an error in bookkeeping due to my haste in making out the account. What I intend putting in is a hearse, as I figure that my editor will be too confused by such an unexpected item to dispute it.

So here I am back in the good old U.S.A. (Ambrose says) and now as I previously state I am going to take you to the theatre again with me, and who are you going to see but our old friend Mansfield Sothern playing Hamlet once more!

Now this prospect by no means thrills me, but I am unable to think of a good out at once, so I accompany Ambrose, and when we arrive at the theatre, we find the manager, who is a guy by the name of James Burdekin, walking up and down in front of the joint and speaking in the most disparaging terms of actors, and customers are milling around the lobby and on the sidewalks outside.

They are going up to James Burdekin and saying,

"What is the matter, Burdekin?" and "When does the curtain go up?" and "Who do you think you are?" and all this and that, which only causes him to become very disrespectful indeed in his expressions about actors and, in fact, he is practically libellous, and it is several minutes before Ambrose and I can figure out the nature of his emotion.

Then we learn that what happens is that Mansfield Sothern collapses in his dressing-room a few minutes before the curtain is to rise, and, as the gaff is all sold out, it is naturally a terrible predicament for James Burdekin, as he may have to refund the money, and thinking of this has James on the verge of a collapse himself.

"Hammer," he says to Ambrose, "you will do me a favour if you will go backstage and see if you can find out what is eating this hamdonny. I am afraid to trust myself to even look at him at the moment."

So Ambrose and I go around to the stage entrance and up to Mansfield Sothern's dressing room, and there is Mansfield sprawled in a chair in his Hamlet make-up, while his dresser, an old stovelid by the name of Crichton, is swabbing Mansfield's brow with a towel and speaking soothing words to him in a Southern accent.

"Why, Mansfield," Ambrose says, "what seems to ail you that you keep an eager audience waiting and put James Burdekin in a condition bordering on hysteria?"

"I cannot go on," Mansfield says. "My heart is too heavy. I just learn of your return and, as I am sitting here thinking of how you must make plenty of hay-hay with Miss Channelle Cooper when you are lying there under her loving care in North Africa and telling her what a bad Hamlet I am, I am overcome with grief. Ambrose," he says, "is there any hope of you being crippled for life?"

"No." Ambrose says. "Come, come, Mansfield," he

says. "Pull yourself together. Think of your career and of poor James Burdekin and the box-office receipts. Remember the ancient tradition of the theatre: The show must go on—although, personally, I do not always see why."

"I cannot," Mansfield says. "Her face will rise before me, and my words will choke me as I think of her in another's arms. Ambrose, I am in bad shape, but I am man enough to congratulate you. I hope and trust you will always be happy with Miss Channelle Cooper, even if you are a dramatic critic. But I cannot go on in my present state of mind. I am too melancholy even for Hamlet."

"Oh," Ambrose says, "do not worry about Miss Channelle Cooper. She loves you dearly. The last time I see her, I request her to be my ever-loving wife when this cruel war is over, but she says it can never be, as she loves only you. I say all right; if she wishes to love a bad Hamlet instead of a good correspondent, to go ahead. And then," Ambrose says, "Miss Channelle Cooper speaks to me as follows:

" 'No, Ambrose,' she says. 'He is not a bad Hamlet. A better judge than you says he is a fine Hamlet. Professor Bierbauer, the great dramatic coach of Heidelberg, now a colonel in the German army, tells me he witnesses a performance by Mansfield in a ruined tavern in a town near the front, that, under the conditions, is the most magnificent effort of the kind he ever views.'

"It seems," Ambrose says, "that the professor is wounded and captured by our guys when they retake the town, and, at the moment Miss Channelle Cooper is addressing me, he is one of her patients in a near-by ward, where I have no doubt he gets quite an earful on your history and her love. Where are you going, Mansfield?"

"Why," Mansfield says, "I am going around the corner to send a cablegram to Miss Channelle Cooper, telling her I reciprocate her love and also requesting her to get Professor Bierbauer's opinion in writing for my scrapbook."

Well, I wait up in Mindy's restaurant with Mansfield to get the last editions containing the reviews of the critics and, naturally, the first review we turn to is Ambrose Hammer's, and at Mansfield's request I read it aloud as follows:

" 'Mansfield Sothern's inspired performance of Hamlet at the Todd Theatre last night leads up to the hope that in this sterling young actor we have a new dramatic force of the power of Shakespearean roles of all the mighty figures of another day, perhaps including even the immortal Edwin Booth."

"Well, Mansfield," I say, when I finish, "I think Ambrose now pays you off in full on your account with him, including saving his life, what with giving you Miss Channelle Cooper and this wonderful boost, which, undoubtedly, establishes your future in the theatre."

"Humph!" Mansfield says. "It seems a fair appraisal at that, and I will send a clipping to Miss Channelle Cooper at once, but," he says, "there is undoubtedly a streak of venom left in Ambrose Hammer. Else, why does he ring in Booth?"

19. BARBECUE

❖❖

O NE afternoon in an early November, I am sitting in
Chesty Charles' little Sharkskin Grill on Biscayne Boulevard in the city of Miami, Florida, chatting of this and that
with a guy by the name of High-C Homer, who is called by
this name because he loves to sing songs in a real high voice.

In fact, Homer tells me that when he is much younger
he wishes to become a singer by trade and tries out one
amateur night at the old Colonial Theatre in New York
but he says professional jealousy is very strong at the time
and somebody in the audience pegs a turnip at him while
he is singing Sweet Alice, Ben Bolt and hits him on the
Adam's apple and affects his vocal cords so his voice is
never again good enough for the stage, but all right for
back rooms.

Anyway, when he sees there is no hope for him in a
musical career, Homer has to find something else to do
and what he does is the best he can, which is one thing and
another, and he is explaining to me in the Sharkskin Grill
that even doing the best he can, he is not doing so good,
when in comes a fuzz by the name of Finnegan, a fuzz being
a way of saying a plain-clothes copper, who steps up to
Homer and speaks to him as follows:

"Homer, the chief of police will consider it a favour if
you will kindly bid us farewell."

"Why?" Homer says. "What is his idea?"

"Does the chief have to have one?" Finnegan asks.

"No," Homer says, "by no means and not at all. I am
just wondering."

BARBECUE

"Well," Finnegan says, "when he first mentions your name he requests me to bring you in because it seems a large touch comes off in West Palm Tuesday night and right away the chief thinks of you. But," Finnegan says, "I remember seeing you in the police station all night Tuesday night trying to square that traffic violation, so you cannot also be in West Palm and when I speak of this to the chief he says all right but to suggest your departure anyway. You may thank me if you wish."

"Thanks," Homer says. "Do you mind telling me the details of the touch to which you refer?"

"Oh," Finnegan says, "it is a pay-off swindle. They beat an old simkin from Iowa for fifty thousand tears of blood."

"A fifty-er?" Homer says. "My goodness, this is important moo. But, Finnegan," he says, "I am not in the pay-off world and I do not see how anybody can associate me with such incidents. I am an operator on the race courses and quite upright and legitimate."

"Well," Finnegan says, "if you call skinning marks on those phony tip sheets you peddle legitimate, maybe you are legit, but perhaps the chief looks through the files on you. I seem to be able to remember some things myself."

"Never mind," Homer says. "Tell the cheese of police good-bye for me, Finnegan, and the same to you."

Then Homer thinks a while and finally he guesses he will go over to Tampa and he invites me to accompany him and as it is quite a while before the races start in Miami and I have nothing on my mind at the moment and the fuzz also gives me some severe looks, I accept the invitation.

So Homer goes to a parking lot not far away where he keeps an old bucket parked and presently we are rolling along the Tamiami Trail headed west, and as we journey along Homer sings several songs to me that sound very soothing but all the time he seems to be in deep thought and finally he sighs and says to me like this:

"Well," Homer says, "fifty thou is undoubtedly a splendid tally but I am glad I am not in on it. Honesty is the best policy, to be sure. There are no handholds on a wrong dollar. The way of the transgressor is hard. But," he says, "if it is the guys I think it is, they at least owe me the courtesy of a refusal to participate because of past favours rendered. I never hear a word from them."

Then Homer begins singing again and I get to thinking that it is really most remarkable that there are still marks in this world for the pay-off, as the pay-off is really a very old-fashioned dodge in which the marks are convinced that they are being let in on crooked horse races and are permitted to win a while in an astonishing manner, but when they commence asking about being paid off they are told they must first prove they will be able to settle if they happen to lose.

So the marks generally send to their banks and get the cash money to prove this, as the pay-off guy never picks marks who do not have cash money in banks, and the next thing anybody knows the money disappears and so do the pay-off guys. Furthermore, the marks seldom squawk, as the pay-off guys are cute enough to pick marks who cannot afford to let it become noised about that they are trying to make a few dishonest dibs, though it is well known to one and all that when such a mark does squawk it is the loudest squawk ever heard on land or sea.

There is no doubt that the pay-off requires great perseverance and much preparation and expense, but personally I do not approve of this method of making a living, as it calls for much deceit.

Now the Tamiami Trail is a road that runs from Miami towards Tampa and vice versa through the Everglades, and

BARBECUE

the Everglades is a big stretch of flat country that makes you feel very lonesome indeed after the sun goes down. And soon after dusk it comes on to blow and after a while it is quite a high breeze and, in fact, the wind is picking up our old can in one place and setting it down in another yards away and this makes riding in it a trifle bumpy.

Furthermore, it begins raining more than somewhat and it is darker than a yard down a bear's throat except when it lightnings and I tell Homer it may be a good idea to pull up and wait until the storm blows over. Homer says he quite agrees with me and that in fact he is looking for a gaff he knows of which ought to be somewhere along about where we are at the moment, and I tell him he better find it very shortly as it does not look as if the old rattle-and-jar can hold the road much longer.

Finally we notice some streaks of light through the dark and the rain off to one side of the road and Homer says this must be the spot and he turns the car in that direction and we come on a long, low frame building which I can see seems to be some kind of a jook, which is a sort of a roadhouse where refreshments are sold and dancing goes on and I do not know what all else.

Homer runs his old pail as close as possible to the side of the building where the other cars are parked and we get out and he locates a door that figures to open outward and we pull on it together with the wind pushing against us for several minutes before we can pull it wide enough to ease inside. And there we are in a long, narrow room with a number of tables scattered around in it and a small bar and an old piano on one side and with big gas lamps swinging back and forth from the ceiling as the wind shakes the building.

There are maybe half a dozen guys in the joint sitting at the tables and behind the bar is a short, stocky-built female party of maybe half past thirty-eight, to give her a few hours the best of it. She is by no means fashionably dressed and, in fact, she has on a short-sleeved ragged sweater and her brown hair with streaks of grey in it is flying every which way about her head and she is far from beautiful. In fact, she is strictly a blouwzola, but when Homer sees her he seems greatly pleased and he walks up to the bar and speaks to her as follows:

"Hello, Barbecue," he says. "Big wind outside."

"Big wind inside now," she says. "Well, Homer," she says, "what line of larceny are you engaged in this season?"

"Look, Barbecue," Homer says, "why do you always speak of larceny to me when I come to pay you a social call? It hurts my feelings, especially," he says, "when I am now as honest as the day is long."

"The days are getting shorter," this Barbecue says. "Homer," she says, "I never ask you to pay me any social calls. In fact, it seems to me that when you are here a year ago I tell you to please remain away forever. It is the time you persuade me to bet forty dollars of my hard-earned funds on some catfish in a race at Hialeah stating you know something, and it is not in yet. It is also the time I miss a tenner from my damper after you go, Homer," she says. "I am always hearing strange things about you from the cops who come around asking questions whenever you are in this part of the country, and besides," she says, "you remind me of gloomy days. But," she says, "I will not turn a dog out on such a night. Sit down, Homer, and keep quiet and do not try to talk me into anything," she says.

So we go to a table and sit down and Homer seems very sad and finally I say to him:

"Homer," I say, "what is the idea of this old komoppo speaking to you in such a discourteous manner? Who is she and how well do you know her?"

BARBECUE

"I know her well," Homer says. "She is no komoppo. In fact, I think she is quite handsome if you look at her from a certain angle. She is once my wife. Her name is Sadie but everybody calls her Barbecue since she opens this drum because she specializes in barbecued spareribs, which is a very tasty morsel, indeed. She divorces me years ago because she claims my way of life is not substantial. But," Homer says, "I still love her. Every time I see her I love her more than ever. I hear she does very nicely here, too. I am always hoping to win her back again, but she seems somewhat hostile this evening. Can I always pick winners?" Homer says.

Naturally, I am somewhat surprised to learn that Homer High-C is ever married and I am more surprised that he seems to be carrying the torch for such a looking pancake as this Barbecue. Personally I will just as soon carry one for a crocodile, but, of course, I do not mention these sentiments to Homer. On the contrary I express my deepest sympathy for him and about now Homer notices two guys sitting at a table in a corner away back in the rear of the room and gives them a hello. It is not a large hello and, in fact, it is a very small hello and they hello him back just as small and maybe smaller and Homer lowers his voice to a whisper and says to me like this:

"The big guy is Dandy Jock McQueen out of St. Louis," he says. "The little guy is Johnny Aquitania. They are very rapid guys in every way, shape, manner and form."

"What is their business?" I say.

"They have a pay-off background," Homer says. "Now I can understand the touch Finnegan the fuzz speaks of because these parties are connected with a pay-off store which operates out of Tampa. Yes," Homer says, "it will be a privilege and a pleasure to me to get a glaum at the contents of the little brown suit-case under the table there.

I will almost guarantee it contains the beesom they take off the marks in West Palm and they are undoubtedly on their way back to Tampa with it."

I am looking the guys over when there is a noise at the front door and in comes a guy and a pretty thing and the guy is dragging what seems to be a big bull-fiddle in a zippered-up canvas case behind him, a bull-fiddle being a large musical instrument about six feet long which is some-times called a bass viol and which is played with great zest by musicians in orchestras. In fact, I recognize the guy as a party by the name of Juliano who has an orchestra of his own in a night trap in Miami where I go occasionally though I do not know him personally and I do not re-member him playing a bull-fiddle, either. What I remember him playing is a clarinet and very hot too.

He is a young guy and the pretty with him is also young and she is wearing a long raincoat and has a felt hat pulled down to her eyes but I can see enough of her face to judge that she is quite a lovely object to behold, if you like blondes, and I like blondes. They sit down at a table not far from Homer and me and Juliano lays the bull-fiddle case down on the floor beside him and they both glance around in a way that causes me to figure that they are somewhat agitated.

But naturally I also figure their agitation comes of their experience in the storm outside and I am thinking that they make a fine-looking young couple together when I happen to observe the bull-fiddle case more closely and I say to Homer like this:

"Homer," I say, "I think there is something in the bull-fiddle case that is not a bull-fiddle."

"Why?" Homer says.

"Because," I say, "it is something too limp for a bull-fiddle and I notice it pulls heavy for a bull-fiddle when the guy drags it in. Besides," I say, "you do not lay a bull-fiddle flat on the floor. What you do with a bull-fiddle is to stand it up against the wall."

Well, at this, Homer takes a good glaum himself at the bull-fiddle case and finally he says:

"No," he says, "it is not a bull-fiddle in the bull-fiddle case. It is a body. I see a finger sticking out of a place where the zipper comes open a little. But," he says, "I cannot tell from the finger whether it is a male or a female body."

"Homer," I say, "why do you suppose they are carrying a body around in a bull-fiddle case?"

"Oh," Homer says, "perhaps it is just a hobby. Any way," he says, "it is a live body because the finger just wiggles."

Well, I can see the finger for myself and sure enough, it is wiggling though not very much and I have a notion to go over and ask Juliano and the pretty what is the idea of a body in the bull-fiddle case, only I am afraid they may think I am inquisitive. Then Juliano seems to notice that Homer and I are glauming the bull-fiddle case though he does not seem to observe the finger himself and in fact by this time the finger disappears from view. But presently Juliano says something to the pretty and they get up and go out the front door again, this Juliano dragging the bull-fiddle case after him.

We can hear their car starting even above the wind but they are not gone more than five minutes before they are back again but without the bull-fiddle case and Juliano stops at the bar and remarks to Barbecue that the breeze is too strong for them to think of continuing their journey.

They sit down at their table again and Homer whispers to me that their going out is just a stall to plant the bull-fiddle case in their car because the chances are our gazing at it makes Juliano nervous and he also tells me not to stare at them any more as it is most impolite. So I pay no more attention to them and neither does Homer and they pay no more attention to us, which makes it even, but continue talking to each other very earnestly with their heads close together and finally Homer whispers to me like this:

"I am commencing to be a little curious about the bull-fiddle case," Homer says. "Follow me," he says, "but," he says, "make it nonchalant."

Then he gets up but instead of going towards the front he saunters in the direction of the back end of the room and as I tail him I can see that Homer is somewhat familiar with these premises. He leads the way into a kitchen where an old coloured guy with a bald head is cooking meat on a revolving spit over a charcoal brazier and producing very savoury odours, indeed, and then on into a small room opening off the kitchen which I can see is a sort of store-room. It is full of sacks and boxes and there are vegetables and other truck hanging from the rafters including a middling sized dressed pig and Homer points to this pig and says:

"Barbecue personally raises them and butchers them for her business," he says. "She is really a smart broad," he says. "Do you wonder I love her?"

Now Homer goes out-a-door of the storeroom into the wind and I go with him and he moves around the parked cars fumbling in each one in the dark until he finds what he is looking for, which is the bull-fiddle case. It is jammed in the back seat of a big limousine and Homer lifts it out and drags it into the storeroom where he unzippers the case from top to bottom and what falls out of it but a little tiny grey-haired guy with a little tiny grey moustache who is in dinner clothes and whose hands are tied in front of him with cords.

BARBECUE

His feet are also tied and he has a gag in his mouth, and naturally Homer and I are greatly surprised at this spectacle and Homer says to the guy like this:

"What is the idea of putting yourself in a bull-fiddle case?" he says.

But the guy just rolls his eyes and it is plain to be seen that he cannot speak with the gag in his mouth, so Homer out with his pocket knife and cuts all the cords and lifts the guy to his feet and says:

"Come, come," he says. "Please explain this hiding in a bull-fiddle case, will you? It is not dignified for a party of your years."

"They put me in it," the little guy finally says. "My wife Dimples and Juliano. She hits me over the head with a blunt instrument when I am not looking and when I regain consciousness I am tucked in this bull-fiddle case. I have a terrible headache. They think I am dead and are driving out into the Glades to cast my remains into a swamp. I hear them discussing the matter when I revive in the bull-fiddle case. My name is Greebins."

"Tut, tut," Homer says. "This sounds most unconstitutional. What is their idea?"

"Dimples is in love with Juliano," Greebins says. "She wishes to get rid of me so she can acquire my money and marry Juliano and live happily ever afterward. Well," he says, "I cannot blame her. I am nearly three times her age and by no means vivacious, and Dimples enjoys laughter and music and the rumba."

"Well," Homer says, "now you can step in and confront them and they will think they are seeing a ghost and after we scare them half to death we will turn them over to the law, although," he says, "personally I am opposed to doing the law any favours."

"No," Greebins says. "I will not confront them now. It

343

will be too great a shock to Dimples. She is a nervous little thing. Let us consider this situation."

Then he sits down on a box and I suggest to Homer that while we are doing this considering, Juliano may miss us from the scene inside and become uneasy and take it into his head to see if his bull-fiddle case is still where he places it and not finding it, he and the pretty may fan off and we will have nothing to consider and Homer says this is undoubtedly true and that we must not waste too much time.

At this moment, the old coloured guy comes into the storeroom and removes the dressed pig from its hook on the rafter, probably with the idea of lugging it into the kitchen and carving it up, but Homer stops him and takes the pig himself and puts it in the bull-fiddle case and zippers it up tight. Then Homer goes out into the wind again dragging the bull-fiddle case and when he returns he says:

"Now," he says, "we can consider at our leisure. I put the bull-fiddle case back in their car, pig and all, so if they investigate they will find everything in order."

"Why," Greebins says, "you are really a genius. You settle the whole problem. If I confront them now it will not only be a great shock to Dimples' nervous system but they will flee in dismay and I may never see her again. But if we let them go on their way and dispose of this bull-fiddle case in a swamp thinking I am still in it, they will not know I am still alive until Dimples tries to collect my money. Then," he says, "when she finds she is unable to do this while I am alive, she will return to me because Dimples cannot do without money and Juliano does not have a quarter. Of course," Greebins says, "it is somewhat humiliating to use a pig as a stand-in. I will prefer a lamb."

"Greebins," Homer says, "do you mean to state that you will take her back after all this? Why?"

"I love her," Greebins says.

BARBECUE

"Ah," Homer says. "I see your point. Well," he says, "you remain out of sight in the kitchen until the storm passes and they leave and we will drive you back to Miami where you can await developments. That is," Homer says, "if my car is not blown there already."

So Homer and I go back into the large room and nobody seems to notice our return any more than they do our departure and it may be because one and all now have something else to think about, which is the way the building is shaking in the wind. In fact, everyone is just sitting still looking somewhat perturbed and there is no conversation and finally Barbecue speaks up and says like this:

"Listen," Barbecue says, "is this a wake, or what? Homer," she says, "sing something, will you? I will play for you."

Then she goes over to the old piano and begins playing and what she plays is Sweet Alice, Ben Bolt, and Homer sings as follows:

> *"Oh, don't you remember,*
> *Sweet Alice, Ben Bolt,*
> *Dad-dah, de, dah-dah,*
> *Dad, de dah."*

"Homer," Barbecue says, "a little less of the dah-de-dah stuff and more words."

"I do not remember the words," Homer says. "I do not sing this song in years. Not since I used to sing it to you. Barbecue," he says, "you know I still love you. What about you and me trying it again?"

"Homer," she says, "you are not really a bad guy at heart and I like you, but," she says, "you are loaded with larceny and I fear you always will be. Come back a year from to-day and if you can tell me you live 100 per cent. on the square during this period, there is a chance for you."

Well, all of a sudden there is quite a crash and the roof over the rear of the room caves in, and it caves in over the spot where the piano is located, too, and Homer pulls Barbecue off the stool and out of the way just in time and all of us go to the front part of the joint where a piece of the roof still holds, including this Juliano and the pretty who is sobbing and carrying on in such a manner that I can see she is indeed high-strung. Personally, I flatten out on the floor and the others soon follow my example and now there is nothing else to do but to lie there and to hope and trust that the rest of the gaff does not go.

Finally when daylight comes on, the wind dies down and the sun shines and we can look around and see what happens and it is something of a mess, to be sure, though not as bad as you will expect. The parked cars outside the building seem to be pushed around no little, but I can see that at least one of them is not damaged, as I observe Juliano and the pretty departing lickity-split with the bull-fiddle case bouncing up and down in the back of the car, they are going so rapidly. And what becomes of them I do not know and, furthermore, I do not care, as I consider them most unworthy characters, indeed, though from what I see of the pretty I judge Greebins calls the turn in figuring her to come back to him when she discovers the true situation about his money.

Now I remember that the guys Homer High-C mentions as Dandy Jock McQueen and Johnny Aquitania never seem to be among us after the roof caves in, so I go to the spot where they are sitting the last time I see them and I behold them under a pile of rubbage, lying quite still, and I tell Homer that I fear these parties are no more.

"Yes," Homer says, "I know this several hours ago. You do not notice it, but during the confusion I crawl over there figuring to help them, only to find I am too late. It is very sad. I also secure the little brown suit-case while I am about it. Just as I suspect, it is full of the soft. It is all in neat stacks. I can tell by feeling around in it in the dark. I have a wonderful sense of feeling for banknotes. Yes," he says, "it contains plenty of moo. I am most fortunate."

"Why, Homer," I say, "you do not intend keeping it, do you? It seems to me," I say, "that there is a law requiring you to turn this property over to the heirs of the deceased."

"Can this be true?" Homer says. "Well," he says, "such a course will only lead to legal complications and take a lot of time. I am going to South America and establish a home and live there honestly on these funds for a year from date to keep my promise to Barbecue. Then I will return and we will resume our happiness where we leave off. Do I tell you she kisses me for yanking her away from the piano and saving her life? But, come," Homer says, "let us find our friend Greebins and return to Miami."

Well, as we are making ready to depart Barbecue comes up to Homer and puts her arms around him and gives him a large hug and says to him like this:

"Be strong, Homer," she says. "Think of me when you feel temptation and never do the least little thing out of line, because," she says, "it may come to my ears and cancel my promise. Return to me pure and we will finish our lives together in great happiness. I am going to trust you once more, Homer," she says.

"Barbecue," Homer says, "wild horses will not be able to drag me from the straight and narrow path from now on, and," he says, "this even goes for race horses, too."

Then he points the car for Miami and we are off, with Barbecue and the old coloured guy waving us farewell, and I observe that tears are running down Homer's cheeks and splashing on the little brown suit-case which is resting in his lap, so I can see that he is deeply touched.

So I suggest to Homer that we go to the Sharkskin Grill and have a few drinks and maybe they will cheer Greebins up too, and Homer thinks the drinks a good idea even if they do not cheer Greebins up, and presently we are lined up in front of the Sharkskin Grill bar having these drinks when who comes in but Finnegan, the fuzz, and he walks up to Homer and says:

"Hello," he says, "I am very glad to see you again, Homer, although it seems to me I tell you to take it on the lammeroo out of here just yesterday. Or am I mistaken?"

"No," Homer says, "you are not mistaken. I go, but I am driven back by the big storm."

"What big storm?" Finnegan says. "Do you mean the slight squall over the Glades? Look, Homer," he says, "you must not speak of such a minor disturbance as a big storm. The chamber of commerce will disapprove of your statement as a knock to our weather, which is wonderful at all times. Anyway," he says, "I repeat I am glad to see you because I now have a definite order for your arrest."

"Copper," Homer says, "I tell you again I am not in the pay-off department. I have nothing whatever to do with the West Palm matter. You may arrest me if you choose but I will immediately summon a lawbooks and sue you for false imprisonment."

"Well, I choose," Finnegan says. "Come with me."

Now all this time Homer is carrying the little brown suit-case and in fact he never loosens his clutch on it for a minute.

And at this point Greebins, who does not say much more than yes or no for several hours, steps up to Homer and taps him on the shoulder and speaks as follows:

"Brother," Greebins says, "I am trying to think of

BARBECUE

where I see you before ever since I stand out in the kitchen last night and hear you sing Sweet Alice, Ben Bolt. It just this very instant comes to me. It is years ago at the Colonial Theatre and you appear on the stage and sing the same song. You are really terrible both times, but," he says, "this is neither here nor there. I peg a vegetable at you from the Colonial audience and score a bull's-eye under your chin. It is the only unconventional conduct of which I am ever guilty and I wish now to make you a belated apology."

"Ah," Homer says. "So you are the one? Do you realize," he says, "that you ruin my whole life? If it is not for your destroying my musical career with your vegetable I will probably still be married to Barbecue and partaking of her profits and never come in contact with such scurvy characters as this copper."

I am greatly surprised to note that Homer High-C appears to be labouring under strong emotion because he is usually quite calm, no matter what. In fact, he appears to be losing control of himself for the moment. Suddenly he swings this little brown suit-case around his head like Hubbell taking a windup and belts Greebins over the pimple with it, almost knocking him loose from his little grey moustache. It is a blow of such great force that it not only flattens Greebins but it breaks open the suit-case and a number of fat packages of banknotes spill out over the floor and Finnegan picks up one of these packages and observes that the band around it has the name of a Des Moines bank on it.

"Well, well," Finnegan says. "Well, well, well, well. Des Moines, eh? Iowa, eh? The West Palm swag, eh? Homer," he says, "how fortunate for me you boff this little old gee with such a weapon as your suit-case, although, Homer," he says, "it strikes me as most unsportsmanlike considering the difference in your ages. But if I do not see

349

this money with my own eyes, I will never suspect you of being mixed up in the West Palm skulduggery, especially when I know you are right here in this city when it comes off. I will get promoted for this, I hope," he says.

"Wait a minute," Homer says. "What do you mean you will never suspect me? Do you not just put the arm on me for it? Do you not just state you have an order for my arrest?"

"Oh," Finnegan says, "the arrest order is for something entirely different, Homer. I am wondering why you keep beefing about the pay-off thing when I do not even dream of connecting you with it. The chief gets a call to-day from a biscuit by the name of Barbecue who runs an eating joint out on the Trail and who states that she can prove by the eye-witness testimony of a coloured party who works for her that you rob her of a pig. Come on, Homer."

20. LITTLE PINKS

ONE night in the Canary Club, Case Ables, the book-maker, slaps a redheaded chorus Judy who is called Your Highness across the mouth and knocks her down a flight of stairs and he uses only his bare hand, at that.

It is agreed by one and all that Case Ables is a little out of line in this situation as he is a big fat guy who outweighs Your Highness maybe a hundred and eighty pounds, but it is also agreed that if some Judy in the city of New York must be knocked down a flight of stairs it may as well be Your Highness, for she is without doubt a great pain in the neck.

And, of course, Case Ables is slightly vexed at the moment as he is just after spending plenty of moolouw in the Canary Club and when it comes on the closing hour for the drum he wishes to go somewhere else and have jolly times and he also wishes to take Your Highness with him for company and so forth, and she refuses to go.

To tell the truth, if Case Ables only thinks to ask some-body in advance he will learn that Your Highness always refuses to go out with anybody for company or anything else, unless she is sure they are in the high income-tax brackets and of excellent social position, and naturally the social position lets Case out.

In fact, the reason she is called Your Highness and is considered such a pain in the neck is because she plays the frost for all who are not well established as practically zillionaires, and she makes no bones of stating that her angle is to find a character of means who is not entirely repulsive and marry him, and when somebody asks her what about love, she says well, what about it, and, of course, there is no answer to this.

Personally, I consider Your Highness' attitude slightly unromantic, especially for a Judy who is only about twenty-two years old, but many citizens claim that it displays great intelligence, although they all admit they are glad she can never have them in mind for her purpose.

In fact, Joe Gloze, the owner of the Canary Club, states that as far as he is concerned he will just as soon marry a fire plug as Your Highness as he says he figures a fire plug will not be so cold and hard in case of a clinch. But, of course, Joe Gloze admits he is only guessing both ways.

However, no one can deny that Your Highness does very good for herself by specializing in characters of means. They are always taking her nice places and she has fine clothes and fur wraps and other odds and ends such as these characters dearly love to bestow upon chorus Judys for the asking, and Your Highness is not at all tongue-tied when it comes to asking.

Furthermore, she has quite a personal following of these characters and always brings trade to any joint in which she is working, so she gets a good salary although all she has to do is to walk around with the rest of the chorus and look beautiful, which is really no effort at all for Your Highness. In fact, many citizens say that if she is not the most beautiful Judy that ever hits Broadway, she is at least in there somewhere scrambling along close up.

The price is 8 to 5 anywhere along Broadway that Your Highness will sooner or later marry the United States Mint, or maybe the Bank of England, and 20 to 1 that she will make either of them sick of her in two weeks when she winds up in a heap at the foot of the stairs from Case Ables' slap. I remember she has on a red dress and what with this and her red hair she reminds me more than somewhat of a woodpecker that someone knocks out of a tree with a rock.

Well, while she is lying there, a bus boy in the Canary Club by the name of Little Pinks, who has a very large nose and a short forehead and who does not weigh more than ninety pounds, apron and all, runs down the stairs and begins carrying on in a way that is most distressing to hear, especially to Case Ables, as Little Pinks keep yelling that Case is a murderer and a no-good and I do not know what all else.

So naturally Case has to go down the stairs and give Little Pinks a few good clops on the chops because such talk is practically vilification of character and by no means pleasing to Case Ables. But the more clops Little Pinks gets the louder he yells and as a scene of this nature is by no means beneficial to an establishment such as the Canary Club, Joe Gloze and two of his captains of waiters go down and assist Case in the clopping, so after a while Little Pinks is very well clopped indeed.

It comes out that Little Pinks is a great admirer of Your Highness, but it is agreed that even so he is going too far in speaking so freely of Case Ables. In fact, after some discussion it is the consensus of opinion that a bus boy has no right to admire anybody and consequently Little Pinks is in great disfavour with one and all, especially when it comes out that his admiration of Your Highness is from a distance and that he never more than says good evening to her in his life and even then she does not answer unless she feels like it. And of course, everybody who knows Your Highness knows that she will very seldom feel like answering a bus boy.

It becomes plain to all that Your Highness probably never knows Little Pinks is alive, yet it seems that whenever she goes to work in a night club, Little Pinks always gets himself a bussing job there, just so he can be near her and see her. When this information is made public it is generally agreed that Little Pinks is slightly eccentric and furthermore, when Joe Gloze gets to figuring that if Pinks is so busy admiring Your Highness he must be neglecting his bussing, he gives Little Pinks a few more clops for luck.

Well, finally it also comes out that Your Highness' spine is injured, so she will never walk again and Case Ables feels so sorry about this that he talks some of paying her hospital expenses, but Joe Gloze convinces him that it will be setting a bad precedent in these situations. In fact, Joe Gloze says it may start his chorus Judys to falling down the stairs of their own free will just to get in hospitals.

There is also a rumour around that Your Highness has a right to sue Case Ables for damages, but as Case soon has thirty-four witnesses, including the cop on the beat, who are willing to swear she attacks him first and that she is undoubtedly under the influence of something at the time, nothing comes of this rumour. In fact, everybody forgets the incident as quickly as possible except Your Highness and maybe Little Pinks, who is bound to remember if only because Joe Gloze gives him the heevus from his job in the Canary Club.

Now all this is some years ago and it comes on a winter when things are pretty tough for one and all and I judge they must be especially tough for bus boys as I meet Little Pinks on Broadway one cold day and he is thinner than an old dime and does not have enough clothes on to make a bathrobe for a mouse. His toes are leaking out of his shoes and he is as blue as a toad from the cold and I stake him to four bits out of the goodness of my heart. Then I ask him if he ever sees Your Highness and he says to me like this:

"Sure, I see her," Little Pinks says. "I see her all the time. In fact, Your Highness lives in the same place I do which is in a basement over in West Fifty-second Street near Tenth Avenue. I am the only one who does see her nowadays as all her former friends give her the brush-off after she is hurt. She is in the hospital nearly a year and," he says, "she has to sell all her possessions to pay the expenses. She does not have one penny when I take her to my place to live."

"How is she now?" I say.

"She is cold," Little Pinks says. "Always so cold. There is not much heat in our basement and this is one reason why Your Highness is always slightly irritable. But," he says, "it keeps me so busy hustling around trying to get a few dibs to keep up the instalments on the wheel chair I buy her and for food and magazines that I cannot afford a better place. Your Highness must have her magazines so she can keep up with what the society people are doing. They cost quite a lot," he says.

"Are you married to her?" I say.

"Oh, my goodness, no," Pinks says. "Do you suppose Your Highness will marry anybody like me? She is too proud to think of such a thing. She is just letting me take care of her until she can get well and marry somebody with a lot of sugar. That is always her dream," he says. "When she is in good humour she talks about how she will reward me some day.

"But," Little Pinks says, "she is not often in good humour lately because she is so cold. She says she wants to go to Miami where it is warm and where there are society people like she sees in the magazines. She says she will get a chance to meet guys with money there. Yes," he says, "I think I will take her to Miami."

"Well, Pinks," I say, "that will be fine, but how are

you going to get her there? It looks to me as if you may be a little short of what it takes."

"Why," Little Pinks says, "I will push her there in her wheel chair."

"Pinks," I say, "I guess you are a case for Bellevue. It is thirteen hundred miles to Miami."

"How far is thirteen hundred miles?" Little Pinks says.

"Pinks," I say, "thirteen hundred miles is thirteen hundred miles. That is how far it is. You can no more push somebody in a wheel chair such a distance than you can roll a peanut from here to Chicago with your nose."

"Well," he says, "I must try because Your Highness cannot stand the cold much longer. Now I must hurry home to cook the dinner, and," he says, "to-night is the night I do the washing. Your Highness does not like to be without clean clothes, especially lingerie. I am a good cook and launderer now and nobody can dust and sweep or wait on an invalid better than I can. Your Highness takes a lot of waiting on," he says. "I used to forget things but now she keeps a long cane at her chair to remind me when I forget."

"Pinks," I say, "everybody knows his own business best, but what is the idea of your working and slaving for a cold, selfish little broad such as Your Highness if you are not married to her and are not even going to get married to her? What is your percentage?" I say.

"Why," Little Pinks says, "I love her."

And with this he goes on down the street and I can see that he shrinks a lot since I last see him and in fact he is now so small that I look for him to fall out of the hole in the seat of his pants any minute.

Well, it comes on the winter of 1938 and I am in Chesty

LITTLE PINKS

Charles' little grill on Biscayne Boulevard in the city of Miami thinking of very little when I notice that the character who is doing porter work around the joint seems to be nobody but Little Pinks, although he is without doubt greatly altered. So I ask Chesty if this is not who the porter is and Chesty says to me like this:

"All I know," Chesty says, "is that he is a little stirry. He comes to me with a screeve from some old friends of mine in the canneroo at Raiford. He is just after doing a three er and it seems to leave some impression on him. He talks to himself a lot. Yes," Chesty says, "he is without doubt stirr-crazy."

After a while, when the porter does not seem to have anything on his hands, I walk over to him and slap him on the back and speak to him as follows:

"Hello, Pinks," I say. "How is everything?"

He turns around and looks at me a minute and I can see that it is Little Pinks all right and then he says:

"Oh, hello."

"Do you remember me?" I say.

"Sure," Little Pinks says. "You give me four bits on Broadway one day. It is a cold day."

"How is Your Highness?" I say.

At this, Little Pinks puts his fingers on his lips, and says shush and then he takes me by the arm and leads me out the back door of the grill into a sort of area-way where they keep the garbage cans and he motions me to sit down on one can and he sits on the other and says like this:

"It is now over four years ago," he says, "since I bring Your Highness down here."

"Wait a minute, Pinks," I say. "You state you bring her. How do you bring her?"

"I push her in her wheel chair," he says.

"You push her in her wheel chair thirteen hundred

miles?" I say. "Pinks, do you think you are kidding somebody?"

"Wait till I tell the story," he says. "It is thirteen hundred miles. It does not seem like a block to me now. But let me tell it all."

It is not so difficult as it may sound to push a wheel chair from New York City to Miami (Little Pinks says) with such a tiny thing as Your Highness in the chair as by the time we start she does not weigh much more than a bag of popcorn and besides it is a very nice wheel chair with rubber tyres and ball-bearing wheels and rolls very easy, to be sure.

In fact, the only tough part of the journey is from the basement in West Fifty-second Street to the ferry that takes us across the river to the Jersey side. After that we thumb our way along, with Your Highness doing the thumbing, and we get many a lift in empty trucks, although the drivers are generally greatly surprised, indeed, at the spectacle of a Judy in a wheel chair asking for a ride.

But it is seldom an empty comes along without stopping for us and usually the driver has to get off and help lift Your Highness, chair and all, into the truck and block the wheels so the chair will not roll out on the bumps and sometimes Your Highness is so bossy about the job that she gets the drivers to asking her who she thinks she is.

She likes the open trucks best and often passes up closed vans that offer a lift to wait for one without a top so she can sit in her chair and watch the scenery on all sides and pretend she is somebody big like a queen. When she is in one of those open trucks she nearly always pretends she is Cleopatra in her royal barge scooting along the Nile which is an idea she gets from some movie and while I do not mind her pretending to be Cleopatra or anybody else I can

358

see that her conversation often makes the truck drivers very nervous.

Once in the state of South Carolina when I am pushing the chair along a road we are stopped by an automobile containing three characters who are very hard-looking indeed, and one of these characters outs with a large Betsy and requests us to hold up our hands. Then one of the others fans me to see if I have any funds or valuables, and the third character looks Your Highness over and they are surprised and slightly annoyed to find only eighty-six cents on us all told.

So they start questioning us and when I tell them all about Your Highness and me, they are more surprised than ever and one of them picks Your Highness up out of her wheel chair and puts her in the automobile. They make me get in after her and then they tie a rope to the wheel chair and tow it quite a distance behind the automobile, travelling very slow, so as not to yank the chair around too much.

They let us go at a cross-roads where they say they must branch off to get to a town off the main highway where they wish to rob a bank and, furthermore, they give me a pound note for my pocket and one of them who listens to Your Highness more than anyone else says that what I really deserve is a gold medal although he does not state why.

Another time in Georgia, I somehow lose the highway and hit a road that goes nowhere but into a swamp and the next thing we know we are in the midst of a bunch of five stove lids in striped clothes and it turns out that they are escaped convicts and are very desperate guys.

Personally, I figure we are going to have a lot of trouble with these parties, but right away, Your Highness puts them to work fixing up a camp for us for the night and ordering them around until one of them tells me he will be glad to return to the prison and give himself up, especially as every time one of the stove lids gets close enough to Your Highness' chair she reaches out and gives him a good belt with her cane.

It takes us about two weeks to get to Miami between her thumbing and my pushing and we live very good on the way. Sometimes I mooch a dookey at a kitchen door but Your Highness does not care much for Southern cooking and prefers canned goods such as I am able to obtain by climbing in the windows of country stores at night. Once I enter a henroost and sneeze a pullet when Your Highness thinks she feels in a mood for a little chicken à la king, but the pullet turns out to be very tough, and Your Highness is most critical, indeed.

However, she cheers up no little and quite some when she feels the sun and sees the ocean in Miami. In fact, she is so cheerful that she forgets to remind me of anything with her cane for one whole day and has only a few cross words for me. The first thing I do is to find a room for her in a small rooming house on Miami Beach and the next thing I do is get myself a job bussing in a restaurant not far from the rooming house.

Then every morning, before I go to work, I push her in her wheel chair over to a big hotel on the beach that is called the Roney Plaza and she sits there on the sidewalk all day long watching the people walking up and down and here and there and to and fro and, the chances are, trying to flirt with any guy that she figures has as much as nine dollars in his pockets, for Your Highness never for a minute forgets her dream of marrying someone with money and social position, but, anyway, money.

Well, to tell the truth, Your Highness is now not as beautiful as formerly, though I never before admit it to anybody. In fact, she is so thin she is almost a shadow and her face is drawn down to the size of a nickel and there is no more glint of her hair and she is by no means such a looking Judy as will attract the attention of guys, especially as the shape that once draws them her way in herds is no longer on public view.

But Your Highness does not realize the change in her appearance and when she finds that the only ones who smile at her and stop and talk to her as she is sitting there are kindhearted old Judys, and that guys never rap to her at all, she becomes somewhat impatient and one day she speaks to me as follows:

"Pinks," she says, "I know what is wrong. I do not have any jewellery. I notice that anybody who has a lot of jewellery on always attracts plenty of attention even if they are as ugly as anything. Pinks, you get me a lot of jewellery," she says.

"Well, Your Highness," I say, "this is quite an order to be sure. I do not know how I am going to get you any jewellery. I am wondering right now about the room rent."

"Oh," she says, "you can get it. You get those groceries and that chicken when you want them. Pinks, I must have a lot of jewellery. I must, I must, I must."

Then she gets mad at me and the way Your Highness gets mad at me is to never say a word but just sit looking sad and it almost breaks my heart when she does this. In fact, I can scarcely sleep when she is mad at me, so instead of trying I spend the next few nights looking around a little and casing a few big houses in which I figure there is bound to be plenty of jewellery.

One night I enter one of these houses by way of a loose window and make my way very quietly to a bedroom in which I can see somebody is sleeping and there on a bureau in plain sight is a whole hatful of jewellery. In fact, there is a big square-cut diamond ring, and a batch of diamond bracelets and a large diamond clip, so I figure that the party sleeping in the bedroom is some Judy and that she wears this jewellery earlier in the evening and is careless enough not to put it away in a safe place when she is going to bed.

Anyway, I remove the jewellery and present it the next morning to Your Highness and she is quite pleased with it, although she states that the square-cut diamond is not of first-class colour and that the mountings of the bracelets are old-fashioned and cheap. However, she says they will do very well and she puts all the jewellery on and sits looking at herself in a mirror for half an hour. She never asks me where I get it or how. One thing about Your Highness, she never wishes to know where anybody gets anything or how as long as she gets it herself.

I push her in her chair over to the Roney as usual and when I go for her late in the afternoon she is smiling and happy and says that just as she figures the jewellery attracts plenty of attention to her, although she admits she does not get much of a tumble from any young guys who look as if they may be worth getting a tumble from.

"But," Your Highness says, "they will come later. This afternoon a very fine-looking old party who says he is Dr. Quincey, of Chicago, and his wife talk to me an hour. She is old, too, but nice. Pinks, I think they are rich and maybe they will introduce me to people. Maybe they have a son. They are much interested in my new jewellery."

Well, about an hour later I can understand this interest because a gendarme comes around to the rooming house and calls me out and tells me I am under arrest charged with the burglary of the home of Dr. Quincey, of Chicago, of sixty thousand dollars' worth of swag, and while I am naturally somewhat perturbed by this announcement, I can see that what Your Highness knows about the value of jewellery is not much.

The gendarme takes me to the police station and into a room where several other coppers are waiting and also an old guy with a beard that they tell me is this Dr. Quincey and I am quite surprised to see him smile at me and to observe that he does not seem to be anywhere near as indignant as I will be myself upon beholding a guy who knocks me off for my valuables.

In fact, it is Dr. Quincey who starts questioning me instead of the cops and what he questions me most about is Your Highness and finally I tell him the whole story about us from start to finish including the part about where I finally enter his house and remove the jewellery and when I speak of this the cops are all in favour of immediately placing me in the gaolhouse without any more dickering, and then sending out and arresting Your Highness, too, and recovering the jewellery.

"One moment, gentlemen," this Dr. Quincey says. "I have a long talk with the girl to-day and observe her closely. She is extremely ill. There is no doubt of that. She is not only extremely ill but," he says, "she has strange delusions of grandeur."

"Is that bad, Doc?" I say.

"Never mind," he says. "I am not willing to condone this young fellow's crime, but let us suspend action on him temporarily. Say nothing to the girl and let her keep on wearing the jewellery a while longer under surveillance and let Pinks remain at liberty in the meantime if he promises to give himself up when you send for him and accept punishment afterward."

"What do you mean afterward?" I say.

"Never mind," he says. "We will let you know later. Do you agree?"

Well, naturally I am glad to agree to anything whatever if it is going to keep me out of the pokey but the coppers are by no means so eager. They say I have all the earmarks of a guy who will breeze off out of their reach as soon as they take their hands off me, but the old guy has them send me out of the room and has a long talk with them in private and then they tell me I can go until they want me.

Of course I do not tell Your Highness what comes off and she goes on wearing the jewellery every day and taking great pleasure in same but I notice that one of the coppers I see in the room is always around somewhere close in plain clothes, so I judge they are taking no chances on the jewellery evaporating.

In fact, sometimes the copper talks to Your Highness and as he is a young guy and by no means bad-looking, and is always hanging around, she commences to figure that maybe he has a crush on her and she plays plenty of swell for him.

When I come to get her when he is around, she gives me a large bawling out for this and that and lets on that I am just a guy working for her, although of course he knows very well who I am. Then the copper happens to let it out that he is married and after that he cannot get close enough to her to hand her a grapefruit.

Your Highness tells me that Dr. Quincey and his wife are around to see her often and she says that sometimes she thinks that maybe the old Doctor likes her pretty well himself. In fact, she says she thinks Dr. Quincey has plenty of gall to look at her the way he does right in front of his wife and I say maybe he is only admiring her jewellery.

Now for several days Your Highness is very thoughtful and has little to say and it seems to me that she is getting so she is not much more than a shadow in her chair. Her eyes are as big as dinner plates and once I think she is crying which is a great surprise to me as I never before see her shed a tear. Then one afternoon I go to the Roney Plaza to get her and I find her watching the sunset instead of the people and after a while she looks at me and smiles and says:

"Come close to me, Little Pinks."

It is one of the few times she ever calls me Little Pinks. Generally it is just Pinks and it is not often she smiles at me, either. So I go up to the side of her chair but only figuring that the chances are she wishes to get me close enough to give me a belt with her cane for something I forget to remember and she says:

"Kneel down, Little Pinks."

Well, of course, this is an unusual request, especially in such a place, but if there is one thing I am accustomed to from Your Highness it is unusual requests, so I kneel down in front of her chair and she reaches out with her cane but instead of belting me she taps me on the shoulder with it and says:

"Rise up, Sir Little Pinks, my brave and true knight. Rise up and may God bless you forever and always."

Naturally I figure this is something else Your Highness gets from a movie or maybe out of a book and I am wondering what the idea is when I see that there are real tears running down her cheeks and she holds out her thin arms to me and says:

"Kiss me, Little Pinks."

So I kiss her for the first and only time in my life and she holds me tight to her breast a moment and slowly whispers:

"Little Pinks, I love you."

Now I feel her arms loosen and her poor little body slips down farther in the chair and I do not need Dr. Quincey who happens along just then to tell me Your Highness is dead. He says she lasts longer than he expects from the first time he ever sees her.

I get her buried out here in a little cemetery in the sun where she will never be cold again and then I go to the police station and give myself up and cop a plea of guilty to robbery and take two to ten years. I am now out on parole (Little Pinks says) and this is all there is to the story.

"Pinks," I say, "I am indeed very sorry for you."

"Sorry for me?" Little Pinks says. "Say," he says, "I am sorry for you. You never kiss Your Highness and hear her say she loves you."

Well, it is a couple of weeks before I am in Chesty's drum again and I do not see Little Pinks around, so I ask Chesty what becomes of his porter and Chesty says to me like this:

"Why," he says, "they pick him up again for violating his parole and send him back to Raiford. I do not know how or why he violates it because I never think to ask, but," he says, "that guy is better off there because he surely is off his nut."

So I call up a guy I know by the name of Smiddy who works in the sheriff's office and ask him if he can remember anything about a character by the name of something that sounds like Pinks.

"Wait until I look in the record," Smiddy says. "Pinks, Pinks, Pinks," he keeps saying, so I figure he is going through a book. "Say," he says, "here is a guy by the name of Pincus who is grabbed for parole violation. Maybe he is your guy. I remember him now myself. It is a most unusual case."

"What is most unusual about it?" I say.

"Why," Smiddy says, "this Pincus makes his way into the hotel room of a winter tourist by the name of Ables and for no reason anybody can figure out he ties Ables to his bed at the point of a Betsy and bangs him across the back with a baseball bat until he permanently injures the poor guy's spine. Do you know what I think?" Smiddy says.

"No," I say, "what do you think?"

"I think this Pincus is daffy," Smiddy says. "But," he says, "of course we cannot have our winter tourists treated like Mr. Ables."

21. PALM BEACH SANTA CLAUS

··

I T is the afternoon of a hot day in the city of West Palm
Beach, Florida, and a guy by the name of Fatso Zimpf
is standing on a street corner thinking of very little and
throwing so much shade that a couple of small stove lids
are sitting on the kerb at his feet keeping cool, for this
Fatso weighs three hundred pounds if he weighs a carat
and as he is only about five feet eight inches tall he is really
quite a tub of blubber and casts a very wide shadow.

At that, he is somewhat undernourished at this time and
in fact is maybe fifteen or twenty pounds underweight as
he does not partake of food for two days, and if the small
stove lids know how hungry he is the chances are they will
not be sitting so close to him. To tell the truth, Fatso is so
hungry that his stomach is wondering if his throat is on a
vacation and what is more he does not have as much as
one thin dime in his pants pockets to relieve his predicament.

This Fatso is a horse player by trade and he is en route to
Miami to participate in the winter meetings at Tropical
Park and Hialeah, and he leaves New York City with just
enough money to get him as far as West Palm Beach by bus,
but with nothing over for food and drink on the journey.
However, he does not regret having to leave the bus at
West Palm Beach as his strength is slowly dwindling from
hunger and he figures he may be able to get something to
eat there.

Besides, the bus people are talking of charging him
excess fare because it seems that Fatso laps over on both

sides in one seat so much that they claim it is just the same as if he has three seats, and other passengers are complaining and the journey is by no means a pleasure trip for Fatso.

Well, while Fatso is standing there on the corner all of a sudden a big red roadster pulls up in the street in front of him with a good-looking tanned young guy in a sport shirt driving it and a skinny Judy sitting in the seat next to him and the skinny Judy motions for Fatso to come out to the car.

At first Fatso does not pay any attention to her because he does not wish to move around and take his shade away from the small stove lids, as he can see that they are very comfortable, and when it comes to children no kinder-hearted guy than Fatso ever lived no matter if they are slightly coloured children. In fact, Fatso is enduring no little suffering from the heat, standing there just because he is too kindhearted to move.

The skinny Judy in the roadster keeps motioning to him and then she cries "Hey, you!" in a loud tone so finally Fatso goes out in the street to the car figuring that maybe she wishes to ask him the way to some place although of course Fatso does not know the way to any place in these parts, and he can see that she is not a bad-looking Judy, though not young, and that she has yellow hair tied back with a fancy handkerchief and a blue sweater and blue slacks and a lot of bracelets on her arms and rings on her fingers.

Fatso can see that this is a party who must be in the money and he can also see that she has hard blue eyes and a bossy way about her because as he goes up to the side of the car with the small stove lids following in his shade she speaks to him in a voice that seems to scratch on her tonsils coming up, as follows:

"Look here," she says, "are you out of a job?"

Now this Fatso is always very courteous to all female characters even when he can see that they are nothing but mountain lions and he bows and says:

"Well," he says, "not to give you a short answer, ma'am, but who wants to know?"

"I do," the skinny Judy says. "I am Mrs. Manwaring Mimm."

"I am Elmore Zimpf," Fatso says, though up to this time he never before mentions his first name in public for fear of arousing criticism.

"Never mind who you are," Mrs. Mimm says. "Do you want a job or are you on relief?"

Naturally, Fatso does not want a job, for jobs are what he is keeping away from all his life and furthermore he does not care for Mrs. Mimm's manner and he is about to back away from this situation when he gets to thinking how hungry he is. So he asks her what kind of a job she is thinking of and she says to him like this:

"I want you for my Santa Claus," she says. "I am giving my annual Christmas Eve party at my place in Palm Beach to-morrow night and as soon as I see you I say to the count here that you are the very one for my Santa Claus. My Santa Claus suit will just fit you," she says. "We always have to stuff it up with pillows for my butler Sparks and he never looks natural."

At this Fatso remembers that Christmas is indeed close at hand and naturally this makes him think of Mindy's restaurant on Broadway and the way they cook turkey there with dressing and cranberry sauce and with mashed potatoes and turnips or maybe baked squash to come along and thinking of these matters causes him to sigh heavily and to forget where he is for the moment until he is aroused by hearing the young guy driving the car speak as follows:

PALM BEACH SANTA CLAUS

"This fat bum is dead from the neck up, Margaret," he says. "You better find someone else."

"No," she says, "I must have this one. Why, Gregorio, he will be a sensational Santa Claus. See here," she says to Fatso, "I will give you fifty dollars."

Well, on hearing the young guy speak of him as a fat bum, Fatso's thoughts return to West Palm Beach at once and he takes a good look at the young guy and he can now see that he has a piece of a moustache on his upper lip and that there is something about him that is quite familiar.

However, Fatso cannot place him as anybody he knows so he figures it is just the type that makes him seem familiar because of course there are thousands of good-looking tanned young guys with pieces of moustaches on their upper lips running around Florida at this season of the year, but he is greatly displeased with this particular young guy for calling him a fat bum.

In fact, Fatso is insulted because while he does not mind being called fat or even a bum he does not care to be called both at the same time because it sounds unrefined. He is figuring that maybe it will be an excellent idea to reach over and tag this young guy one on the chops, when he remembers hearing Mrs. Mimm mention fifty dollars.

So he takes this matter up with her to make certain his ears do not deceive him and sure enough she is willing to give him half a C to be her Santa Claus with two boffoes in advance so he can get across Lake Worth to an address she gives him without walking, provided he will proceed there at once, and Fatso accepts these terms and dismisses the small stove lids from his shade with a nickel apiece and the chances are they figure he is Santa Claus already

Now this is how Fatso Zimpf comes to be at Pink Waters which is the name of Mrs. Manwaring Mimm's estate in Palm Beach and this estate is about the size of Central Park

and faces on the ocean and has many palm trees and fountains and statuary and a swimming pool and a house that
reminds Fatso of Rockefeller Centre, and with enough
servants running around to form a union.

Fatso reports to the butler Sparks and it turns out that
this Sparks is very glad to see him when he learns that Fatso
is to be Santa Claus because it seems that Sparks always
considers it most undignified for a high-class butler to go
around being Santa Claus with pillows stuffed down his
pants.

Furthermore, it turns out that Sparks is a horse player at
heart and when he finds that Fatso is familiar with the gee-
gees he becomes very friendly to be sure and supplies him
with plenty of information and scandal about one and all
in the best circles of Palm Beach and several surrounding
spots.

He explains to Fatso that Pink Waters is one of the biggest
estates in these parts and that Mrs. Manwaring Mimm is
richer than six feet down in Iowa, with money that she
gets off her papa, who makes it out of the oil dodge years
back, and that she marries any time she feels like it and
that she feels like it three times so far and is now feeling
like it again. In fact, Sparks tells Fatso that she is now
feeling like marrying a young guy by the name of Johnny
Relf who also has plenty of dough or will have when his
parents kindly pass away.

Sparks says that personally he does not approve of this
marriage because there is a slight disparity in age between
the parties concerned. He says Johnny is only in his middle
twenties and not too bright for his years, at that, while Mrs.
Mimm is two face-liftings old that he knows of, but he
says she is such a determined character that he does not
think it advisable for him to mention his disapproval of her
plan.

Then Fatso remembers the young guy in the roadster with Mrs. Mimm and he asks Sparks is this the party she is going to marry and Sparks says:

"Oh, no," he says. "That is Count Gregorio Ferrone of an old Italian noble family. Mrs. Mimm meets him in New York last summer and brings him here to Pink Waters as a house guest. I understand," Sparks says, "that he is about to contract a marriage that will be most advantageous to him. I do not think," he says, "that the count is in funds to any extent."

"He is very impolite," Fatso says. "He does not talk much like a foreigner to me. He calls me a fat bum without any accent. Personally," Fatso says, "I mark him N.G."

"Well," Sparks says, "to tell you the truth I second the motion. The count is indeed a little brusque at times, especially," he says, "with the servants. He claims he lives in this country off and on for years so perhaps he loses his accent. Mrs. Mimm does not really seem to know much about him."

Then Sparks tells Fatso that he is not expected to do anything at all until it comes time for him to be Santa Claus the next night so Fatso wanders around and about and admires the sights and scenes of Palm Beach and finally he strolls along the ocean sands and there in a lonely spot what does he behold but a beautiful young Judy of maybe eighteen crying as if her heart will break.

Now if there is one thing Fatso cannot stand it is the sight of a female character in distress, so he steps up to her and taps her on the shoulder and says to her like this:

"Little miss," he says, "are you in trouble?"

"Yes, I am," she says: "who are you?"

"Why," Fatso says, "I am Santa Claus."

"Oh, no," she says. "There is no Santa Claus. I know it

better now than anybody else in this world. Anyway," she says, "if you are Santa Claus where are your whiskers?"

Then Fatso explains about how he is to be Santa Claus for Mrs. Mimm the next night and as soon as he mentions Mrs. Mimm's name the beautiful young Judy starts crying harder than ever.

"Mrs. Mimm is the whole trouble," she says. "Mrs. Mimm steals my Johnny away from me and now I must marry Count Gregorio. I hate him even if he is a count. Mrs. Mimm is an old thing and I want my Johnny."

She continues her crying and Fatso stands there putting two and two together and he can see that he comes upon another angle of the situation that Sparks the butler describes to him.

"Tut-tut," he says. "They tell me Johnny is a light-weight. Dry your tears and think no more of the matter."

Well, at this she stops crying and gazes at Fatso who observes that her eyes are a soft brown and he also observes that she has a shape that is worthy of mention, for Fatso is very observing even if he is fat, and finally she says:

"Of course Johnny is a lightweight," she says. "Everybody knows that. In fact," she says, "everybody knows he is a complete nitwit, but," she says, "what difference does that make? I love him. He is awfully good-looking and lots of fun. I love him a zillion dollars' worth. If you are Santa Claus," she says, "you give me my Johnny for my Christmas present instead of the speedboat my papa is getting me. I want my Johnny. I hope Mrs. Mimm drops dead."

Now there are more tears and Fatso keeps patting her on the shoulder and saying now, now, now, and there, there, there, and finally she quiets down and he is able to get a better idea of her story. It is a simple love story such as

374

Fatso often hears before, because a fat guy is always hearing love stories though he never has any to tell himself.

It seems that she and this Johnny have a big quarrel one night in New York because she wishes to go to the Stork Club and he wishes to go to El Morocco and harsh words are exchanged and they part in bitter anger and the next thing she knows he is in Palm Beach and Mrs. Mimm is taking dead aim at him and then this Count Gregorio Ferrone comes along and her papa and mamma decide that it will be a great idea for her to marry him and give them an excuse to have a villa in Italy.

Well, it seems that she agrees to do same while she is still sored up at Johnny but when her papa and mamma take her to their own home in Palm Beach for the winter and she learns the situation between Johnny and Mrs. Mimm is quite serious, she regrets her decision and spends all her time wandering along the sands by herself.

In fact, she says if Fatso does not happen along this particular day the chances are her remainders will now be floating out to sea, because she learns from a jeweller on Worth Avenue that Johnny just buys a square-cut diamond ring the size of a bath rug and that she knows it must be Mrs. Mimm's Christmas present and to tell the truth she hears that Mrs. Mimm picks it out herself and tips the jeweller off to promote Johnny into buying this ring. Furthermore, she hears that Mrs. Mimm is going to announce her engagement to Johnny at the Christmas party.

"And," she says, "I will have to be there to hear it because Count Gregorio is her house guest and my papa and mamma are going and it will be considered very peculiar if I fail to be present. Anyway," she says, "I will hate to have anyone know I am so downcast about Johnny and why I am telling you I cannot think except you are fat and have a kind face."

By this time Fatso is becoming somewhat impatient with tears, so he changes the subject and asks her who she is and she says her name is Betty Lou Marvel and that her papa is nobody but Junius X. Marvel, the big automobile guy.

She says everybody in Palm Beach is afraid of Mrs. Mimm because she can think up very strange things to say about anybody she does not like and that nobody dare stay away from her parties if they are invited, especially her Christmas party. Betty Lou says it is years since anybody has a private Christmas in Palm Beach because Mrs. Mimm makes them bring all their presents to her party and has them given away there by her own Santa Claus and Betty Lou says she is glad they cannot take her speedboat there, and so is Fatso when he comes to think it over.

"Well, little miss," Fatso finally says, "kindly give Count Gregorio no more thought. I am personally giving him much consideration ever since he calls me a fat bum and I will take care of him. But," he says, "I do not see what I can do about your Johnny and Mrs. Mimm and if he is such a numskull as to prefer her to you maybe you are better off without him. Merry Christmas, little miss," he says.

"Merry Christmas, Santa Claus," Betty Lou says, and then Fatso goes on strolling along the sands wishing he is younger and two hundred pounds lighter.

Well, it comes on Christmas Eve and Pink Waters is all lighted up like Palisades Park with a Christmas tree as tall as a church steeple in the middle of the patio and all the fountains going with coloured lights squirting on the water and two orchestras playing one after the other and long tables spread out in the open. In fact, it is as beautiful a scene as anybody could wish to see and very Christmasy-looking except it is quite hot.

PALM BEACH SANTA CLAUS

When the guests are assembling, Fatso is taken in his Santa Claus suit into the library of the house which opens out into the patio by Sparks the butler and given a little final coaching there.

It seems that the first part of the party is for the neighbours' children and the second part is for the grown-ups, male and female, and on the Christmas tree in the patio and stacked up at the foot of the tree are many packages containing the presents for the little ones and Sparks explains that it is the duty of Fatso as Santa Claus to distribute these packages.

On a table in the library is a pile of small packages and Sparks says that after he distributes the packages to the children in the patio, Fatso is to return to the library and put these small packages in his Santa Claus bag and go out and stand under the tree again and take the small packages out of the bag one by one and call off the names written on them and hand them out to the parties they are meant for.

"You will be very careful with these small packages," Sparks says. "They contain presents from husbands to their ever-loving wives and vice versa and from one sweet pea to another, and so forth and so on. The chances are there are many valuable gewgaws in these packages," he says.

Then Sparks leaves Fatso alone in the library while he goes out to see if everything is ready for the appearance of Santa Claus and Fatso can observe him through the tall French window that opens on the patio, bustling about through the gay scene, and with nothing else to do until Sparks' return, Fatso takes to examining the small packages and thinking to himself that if he has the money the contents represent the chances are he will be able to retire from horse playing and perhaps find some beautiful young Judy like Betty Lou to love him.

He observes Betty Lou in the patio with the young guy that he now knows as Count Gregorio and he can see that she seems somewhat depressed and then he notices Mrs. Mimm with a tall blonde young guy at her heels that he figures must be the Johnny Relf that Betty Lou is crying about and Fatso thinks to himself that from his looks this Johnny must indeed be something of a waste ball.

Finally Sparks returns and says everything is all set and out into the patio goes Fatso jingling a lot of sleigh bells and beaming on one and all and the orchestras play and the little children let out shrill cries of joy. There is no doubt but what Fatso is a wonderful success as Santa Claus with the little children and many of them wish to shake hands with him but after an hour of standing under the tree picking up packages and calling off names, Fatso commences to get a little weary.

Moreover, he commences to get a trifle vexed with the little ones, especially when some of them insist on pulling his whiskers and small boys start kicking him on the ankles to see if he is alive and by and by Fatso is thinking that maybe President Roosevelt is right about the redistribution of wealth.

In fact, Fatso finally becomes so vexed that he takes to quietly stepping on a few little toesies here and there accidentally on purpose and the childish cries of pain are enough to break anybody's heart and probably many of these children stop believing in Santa Claus.

Well, he finally gets rid of all the little children and they are taken away by their nurses and only the grown-ups are left and it is a gay gathering to be sure with one and all in evening dress and drinking champagne and dancing, and Fatso retires to the library again and when Sparks comes in to help him load up with the small packages, Fatso says to him like this:

"Sparksy," he says, "who is the most jealous married guy present at this party?"

"Why," Sparks says, "that is an easy one. The most jealous married guy at this party or anywhere else in the world is undoubtedly old Joel Brokebaugh. He is an old walrus who is married to a young mouse, and," Sparks says, "he thinks that every guy who says good morning to Mrs. Brokebaugh is after her, although," he says, "this idea will make you laugh yourself sick when you see her.

"She is undoubtedly a very low score for looks," Sparks says. "Furthermore," he says, "she has no more spirit than a gooseberry. Old Brokebaugh is so stingy he will not let her buy a new hat or a new dress more than once every few years although he has millions. He does not wish her to dress up for fear some guy may notice her. Personally," Sparks says, "I think old Brokebaugh is touched in the wind for figuring anybody else will ever want his wife, but he has a violent temper and often causes scenes and some say he even carries a pistol in his pocket at all times."

"Brokebaugh, eh?" Fatso says.

"Yes," Sparks says. "They are sitting together under the coconut palm by the big fountain, though why they come to a Christmas party nobody knows because they never give each other anything in the way of presents and take no part in the festivities. Everybody feels sorry for Mrs. Brokebaugh, but," Sparks says, "I say what she needs is some spunk."

Well, Fatso again goes out into the patio with his bag full of the small packages and by this time what with the champagne and the dancing and the spirit of the occasion and all this and that, everybody is in a lively mood and they give Fatso a big cheer and no one is any gayer than Mrs. Mimm.

In fact, she is practically hilarious and she gives Fatso a

large smile as he goes past her and he can see that she is pleased with his efforts and he can also see that she still has this Johnny with her and that Johnny looks no brighter than before, if as bright, and then Fatso spots the couple Sparks speaks of under the coconut palm and he is somewhat surprised to note that Sparks slightly overrates Mrs. Brokebaugh's appearance.

Even from a distance Fatso can see that she is a zero for looks but he can also see that the old guy with her seems to be about as described by Sparks, only more so. He is a tall, thin old guy with a red face and a bald head and eyes like a shark and Fatso observes that the servants tiptoe going past him.

Well, Fatso gets under the tree and starts calling out names once more and giving out packages and there is now great excitement and many oohs and ahs in female voices on all sides and finally he gets down to just a few packages and calls out the name of Johnny Relf and right away afterwards the name of Miss Betty Lou Marvel and in fact Fatso calls them so close together that they meet under the tree through all they do is exchange cruel glances.

Fatso does not say anything whatever to this Johnny as he gives him his package, because Fatso feels that he already does enough talking in words of one syllable to the children, but when Miss Betty Lou steps up he gives her a smile and says:

"Merry Christmas, little miss."

"Merry Christmas, Santa Claus," she says, "but I still do not believe in you."

Then she starts walking away opening her package as she goes and all of a sudden she lets out a cry and starts running towards Johnny Relf but by now Johnny opens his own package, too, and starts running towards Betty Lou.

So they meet practically head-on and start taking holds

on each other in the presence of one and all, because it seems that Betty Lou's present is a large square-cut diamond ring with a card in the box which states that it is to my beloved from Johnny and that his present is a pair of big black pearl studs with a card saying they are with all my heart to Johnny from Betty Lou.

Of course nobody bothers to look into the matter at the moment, but when somebody does so later on it is considered something of a coincidence that the writing on the two cards is exactly the same and not very neat, but one and all figure it is just an act of Providence and let it go at that, especially as an act of Providence is regarded as quite a compliment to Palm Beach.

In fact, at this particular moment nobody is paying much attention to anything much but the great happiness of Betty Lou and Johnny, except Mrs. Mimm and she is watching Fatso with keen interest, though Fatso is unaware of her attention as he walks over to where Mrs. Brokebaugh is sitting and hands her a package instead of calling out her name.

Then Fatso returns to the house figuring to get his Santa Claus suit off and collect his wages from Sparks and vanish from these parts before anybody learns that he writes these cards when he is alone in the library and swaps them for cards that will give the ring to Mrs. Mimm from Johnny and the black pearls to Johnny from Mrs. Mimm, in both cases with love.

While he is walking through a long hallway, all of a sudden Fatso gets a feeling that he is being followed, and looking around he observes Mrs. Mimm close behind him. There is something about Mrs. Mimm that causes Fatso to walk a little faster and then he notes that Mrs. Mimm is walking quite a little faster than he is.

So Fatso dodges into an open doorway that he hopes and

trusts may lead him elsewhere but he forgets that when he goes through doors it is usually advisable for him to turn sideways because of his great width. He goes at this door frontways and the next thing he knows there he is stuck right in the middle of the doorway and then he becomes conscious of great discomfort to the southward as it seems that Mrs. Mimm is forgetting she is a lady and is kicking him severely and it also seems that these evening shoes that the Judys wear nowadays with their bare toes sticking out in front are capable of inflicting greater pain when used for kicking than just ordinary shoes.

In the meantime, it appears that there is some commotion in the patio because Mrs. Brokebaugh is so startled at getting any Christmas present at all that she cannot open the package Fatso gives her so old Mr. Brokebaugh opens it for her and finds a gold vanity case with a card that reads as follows:

"To my sweetest sweet from Gregorio."

Well, of course old Mr. Brokebaugh has no way of knowing that this is Count Gregorio's present to Betty Lou and that Fatso does not even change the card but only rubs out Betty Lou's name on it and puts down Mrs. Brokebaugh's, though naturally old Mr. Brokebaugh knows who Gregorio is.

In fact, he can see Gregorio at this very moment standing near by feeling of his little moustache and looking greatly bewildered at the scene that is still going on at intervals, between Betty Lou and Johnny, and all of a sudden old Mr. Brokebaugh lets out a yell and jumps up and pulls a pistol out of his pocket and starts full tilt at the count speaking in a loud tone, as follows:

"So," he says, "you are making a play for my wife, are you, scoundrel?"

Well, of course Count Gregorio has no idea what old Mr. Brokebaugh is talking about, but he has eyes in his head and he can see that Mr. Brokebaugh is making a dead set for him and that he is hotter than a firecracker and he can also see the pistol and from the way the count turns and starts running it is plain to be seen that whatever he may be, he is no sucker.

He knocks over three debutantes and a banker worth ten million dollars making for the patio wall and trying to keep trees and bushes between him and old Mr. Brokebaugh as he goes and all this time old Mr. Brokebaugh is running after him and with surprising speed for a guy his age and waving the pistol and requesting the count to stand still and be shot.

He never gets a really fair crack at the count except when Gregorio is going over the wall and then old Mr. Brokebaugh lets fly twice and misses both times and the sound of this shooting probably saves Fatso many more contusions as it brings Mrs. Mimm running into the patio to find out what is going on and in her absence Fatso wiggles on through the doorway.

So Fatso shakes the sands of Palm Beach from his feet regretting only that he never gets a chance to ask Betty Lou if she now believes in Santa Claus and he goes on down to Miami and a year later he relates the above circumstances to me one day when we are sitting in the rocking chairs on the veranda of the Hotel McAllister hoping to catch somebody going to the races with a couple of spare seats in their car, for things are by no means dinkum with Fatso and me at the moment.

"You see," Fatso says, "to-morrow is Christmas again and this is what reminds me of these matters at this time."

"So it is, Fatso," I say. "It is strange how time flies. But, Fatso," I say, "are you not most severe on Count Gregorio in not only knocking him out of a chance to pick up a few boffoes by marriage but in almost getting him plugged by a jealous husband?"

"No," Fatso says. "By no means. You must always remember he calls me a fat bum. Besides," he says, "old Brokebaugh just spares me the humiliation of denouncing Gregorio as a former bus boy in Vincenti's wop restaurant in West Fiftieth Street and still wanted for robbing the damper of thirty-six dollars.

"I will never forgive myself if I am compelled to holler copper on anybody whatsoever," Fatso says, "but," he says, "of course I will do so as a last resort to prevent Gregorio from marrying Betty Lou. It comes to me all of a sudden why his face is familiar when I am strolling on the sands the time I meet Betty Lou. I never forget a face."

Well, at this moment a big limousine stops in front of the hotel and a small-sized lively Judy all dressed up and sparkling with jewellery hops out of the car and runs up the veranda steps with three good-looking tanned young guys with little moustaches running after her and she is laughing and gay and looks like plenty in the bank, and I am greatly surprised when she skips up to Fatso and gives him a pat on the arm and says like this:

"Merry Christmas, Santa Claus!"

Then she is gone as quick as she comes and the young guys with her and she is still laughing and Fatso is gazing at a fifty-dollar note in his hand with great pleasure and he says:

"She is from Palm Beach," he says. "Anytime anybody from Palm Beach recognizes me they stake me to something because they remember that Mrs. Mimm never pays me the fifty she promises me for being her Santa Claus. I understand," Fatso says, "that it is a public scandal in Palm Beach."

"Is this one Betty Lou?" I ask.

"Oh, no," Fatso says. "She is Mrs. Brokebaugh. I recall now I hear that ever since she gets the Christmas present that she thinks to this very day is from Count Gregorio, she decides she is a natural-born charmer and blossoms out into a life of gaiety, and," Fatso says, "they tell me her husband cannot do a thing about it. Well, Merry Christmas to you."

"Merry Christmas, Fatso," I say.

22. CLEO

+·+

Oɴᴇ pleasant spring day at the Bowie race track, there comes to me a guy by the name of Fat-Fat, who is a horse player by trade and who is called by this name because he is not only fat but he is double fat. In fact, he is very fat indeed. He has a paper in his hand and he seems greatly pleased and he says to me like this:

"Well," he says, "The Beard wants me. Yes," he says, "Uncle Sam at last calls me to join the colours. I have here a summons to report to my draft board in New York City. I understand you are seeking means of transportation there and I will be pleased to have you accompany me in my car as my guest. Why," Fat-Fat says, "I can scarcely wait to get my uniform. It is long my ambition to serve my country and besides," he says, "when Cleo my fiancée sees me as a soldier maybe she will speak to me again after giving me the back of her neck for all these months."

So there I am speeding through Delaware with Fat-Fat in his big, open automobile for at this time he is quite strong in the funds department what with putting over several nice parlays at Bowie and my presence is without doubt a great comfort to him as Fat-Fat always likes to have someone to converse with. But it seems to me he can do just as well alone, as when Fat-Fat gets sunk down behind the wheel all his chins pile up around his neck and he is never able to turn his head one way or the other to see who he is conversing with or how they are taking it. In fact, he just talks straight ahead.

He never talks about anything whatsoever but this Cleo

he is in love with, but as most of his words get lost among his chins I never hear half of what he says so I do not try to answer him and anyway Fat-Fat does not care whether you answer him or not as long as you do not try to change the subject from Cleo.

She is a brown-haired pretty who had a dancing background and at the time I am speaking of she is working for Buddy DeSylva in a show by the name of Panama Hattie and she is regarded as one of the prettiest of all the pretties in the show. To tell the truth, she is regarded by some as a gorgeous and it is generally conceded that she is by no means an intellectual, or anyway not offensively so.

I am not very well acquainted with her but Fat-Fat tells me that she is a hard-working and conscientious pretty and that after the show is over at night she hastens right to her home in the Bronx and I have no doubt this is very true, although I also hear from other sources that she generally routes herself to the Bronx by way of the Stork Club, Leon and Eddie's, La Martinique and similar detours.

Well, as we go buzzing along, suddenly we behold an interesting spectacle at the side of the road. A cow is lying on the ground quite still and a little calf is standing beside it on very wobbly pins going mah-ah-ah, like that, and a guy in overalls and a dirty shirt, who is without doubt a Jasper, is also standing there looking most depressed, and seeing all this, Fat-Fat stops the car and gets out and views the situation a while and the following conversation ensues:

"Hello," Fat-Fat says. "What comes off?"

"A truck kills my cow," the Jasper says. "I see it disappearing over the hill just as I come up."

"Why," Fat-Fat says, "this is quite pitiful. What about the midget here?" he says, pointing to the calf. "Why is it making such a row? Does it get hit too? I see many a cow in my time," Fat-Fat says, "but never before do I see a midget one."

"Look, Fat-Fat," I say, "this is not a midget. This is a baby cow that is called a calf and a fine specimen it is, too, and it is bawling because its mamma is lying here cold in death. It is now an orphan."

"Well," Fat-Fat says, "I never see such a sawed-off cow before so naturally I think it is a midget cow. I never realize there are baby cows. I always figure they come full-size. Look at its big, soft brown eyes. Who do they remind you of?"

I look at the calf's eyes but they do not remind me of anybody's except a calf's and I so state to Fat-Fat who is now squatted down petting the calf and gazing into its eyes while the calf is still going mah-ha-ah.

"They are Cleo's eyes," Fat-Fat says. "I never see such a resemblance. Mister," he says to the Jasper, "is this a boy baby cow or a girl baby cow?"

"Why," the Jasper says, "it is a cow calf so it must be a girl. If it is a boy it will be a bull calf and not a cow calf at all. Now," he says, "I must lug this calf nearly two miles to my home back here in the woods. I do not see how they wander so far away in the first place."

"Why not shoo it along ahead of you?" I say. "Or maybe we can find a piece of string and you can pull it."

"No," the Jasper says, "I will have to carry it. It is too young and it is already plumb tuckered out from walking. This is a terrible blow to me as the cow is my sole possession in the way of livestock and she supplies milk for my children. She is a Jersey and a wonderful milker. Now," he says, "I have no means of getting milk for my children or for this calf either."

"Mister," Fat-Fat says, "will you sell this baby cow to me? I will give you a hundred dollars for it. It will make

a wonderful present for Cleo my fiancée and something to
remember me by when I am in the Army serving my
country, and," he says, "more than anything else she is
sure to consider it a most touching gesture when she learns
I buy a baby cow just because its eyes remind me of her.
Cleo is really very sentimental."

Well, at this I remonstrate with Fat-Fat and try to explain
to him that such a purchase is most ill-advised. But Fat-
Fat will not listen to me, and the upshot of it is he gives
the Jasper the hundred dollars and the Jasper, who is
practically stunned by the transaction, lifts the calf into the
back seat of the car and tells Fat-Fat he must feed it milk
out of a bottle for a spell.

So away we go with the calf lying down in the seat and
going mah-ah-ah, but presently Fat-Fat finds he cannot
keep looking around at the calf on account of his chins
preventing him from turning his head and he makes me do
the driving while he gets in at the back seat with the calf and
before long he is calling it Cleo and I can see that this is
now the calf's name.

We stop at the first town we come to and Fat-Fat buys a
baby's nursing bottle with a nipple on it at a drugstore and
then he buys some milk and gets a guy in a hamburger joint
to warm it up and he feeds Cleo in a way that is astonishing
to behold. I never know before that Fat-Fat is so handy
in this respect but he tells me he often performs a similar
service for his baby brother and his baby sister, too, when
he is a kid over on Tenth Avenue. By the time we reach
New York City, I can see that Fat-Fat is greatly devoted
to Cleo the calf and I can also see that Cleo the calf thinks
very well of Fat-Fat, which is not surprising considering he
is the source of her warm milk.

We pull up in front of Mindy's restaurant on Broadway
around the dinner hour when the place is well filled with

customers and Fat-Fat lifts Cleo the calf out of the car and carries her inside in his arms and naturally it is quite a surprise to one and all to observe this spectacle, especially when Fat-Fat sits down at a table in a booth and puts Cleo on the settee opposite him. In fact, there is so much commotion that Mindy himself appears and when he sees Cleo the calf he does not even shake hands with Fat-Fat and tell him he is glad to see him back but says to him like this:

"Wrong bettors, yes," Mindy says, "Actors and newspapermen and song writers, yes. But," Mindy says, "calves no. You cannot keep these cattle in my gaff, Fat-Fat."

"This is Cleo, Mindy," Fat-Fat says.

"Cleo?" Mindy says. "Ha-ha-ha-ha," he says. "Cleo just leaves here for the theatre full of goulash with the guy with the one eyeglass she is running around with while you are absent. I think he is a nobleman refugee. Everybody is a nobleman refugee nowadays. I do not like his looks. But," Mindy says, "this is neither here nor there nor elsewhere. You must take this thing out of here, especially," he says, "as calfs are very seldom house broke."

Well, at this, Cleo the calf goes mah-ah-ah and who comes up but Ambrose Hammer, the newspaper scribe, who speaks to Mindy as follows:

"See here, Mindy," he says, "you serve veal in here, do you not?"

"The very best," Mindy says. "Veal stew, veal chops, veal tenderloin and wiener schnitzel, which is a veal."

"It all comes from a calf," Ambrose says. "You also serves calves' liver, do you not?"

"None better," Mindy says. "It is very good for nimmicks."

"You mean anæmics," Ambrose says. "Kindly do not distort the English language, Mindy. Now," he says, "what is the difference between permitting the by-products of the calf in here and the calf itself? You are being very unreasonable, if you ask me."

Naturally, Mindy is somewhat nonplussed by this argument, especially as he wishes to remain on friendly terms with Ambrose Hammer because sometimes Ambrose mentions the joint in his column, which is very nice publicity indeed, and besides by this time everybody in the place is interested in Cleo the calf and all the pretties are coming up and addressing her in baby language and Mindy can see that she is quite an attraction.

"Well," he says, "I will have to think this situation over."

So he retires to the kitchen and Fat-Fat and I have our dinner and Cleo the calf has her milk out of the bottle and Ambrose Hammer sits down with us and listens with great interest to Fat-Fat's story of how he comes to buy Cleo the calf because of her eyes and why he calls her Cleo and all this and that. In fact, Ambrose is so interested that he goes to his office and writes a very fine story about Fat-Fat and Cleo the calf and also about Cleo the pretty, but of course we do not know this until the blat Ambrose works for comes out the next morning.

In the meantime, Fat-Fat takes Cleo the calf around to the hotel in West Forty-ninth Street where he always lives in New York, figuring to register her there and then go looking for Cleo the pretty and have a reunion and one thing and another with her. But he has great difficulty convincing the night clerk that Cleo the calf is acceptable as a lodger because it seems that just a couple of weeks previously the clerk admits a guest with a boa constrictor and this boa constrictor escapes during the night and goes visiting in other rooms and causes so much unrest in the hotel that the clerk does not get a wink of sleep throughout his watch.

However, Fat-Fat is an old patron of the hotel and besides he stakes the clerk to a sawsky, so he gets his old room and by this time he is pretty well tuckered out himself so he decides to get a good night's sleep before looking for Cleo the pretty and while Cleo the calf goes mah-ah-ah most of the night, it does not seem to disturb the other guests and does not bother the clerk at all, as it seems he is raised on a farm and is accustomed to such sounds in the night.

Well, soon after daylight the next morning the hotel is surrounded by reporters and photographers from the afternoon blats because it seems Ambrose Hammer makes Fat-Fat and Cleo the calf sound very interesting, indeed, but it also seems that even before they get there Cleo the pretty has Fat-Fat on the phone and that she is sizzling about Fat-Fat telling Ambrose the calf's eyes remind him of hers and claiming that this is just the same thing as comparing her to a cow.

"Furthermore," Fat-Fat says when he is telling me about this incident later in the day, "she informs me that I am nothing but a tub of lard and that if I ever as much as look at her again she will call the cops. She says anyway she is now in love with a very high-class guy by the name of Henri something and is going to marry him. When I tell her I buy Cleo the calf as a present for her she spurns my token in words I am never before aware she even knows.

"I also have other bad news," Fat-Fat says. "I am rejected to-day by the doctors for the Army. They say I am too corpulent. They give me the elbow without even permitting me to remove my garments. Now I cannot even serve my country. On top of everything else, I blow a good bet on Air Brigade in the fourth at Jamaica. I am most despondent," Fat-Fat says. "But," he says, "I am now very glad I buy Cleo the calf or I will have nothing whatever to console myself with. I can always gaze into her eyes and remind myself of my lost love."

For a couple of days the hotel receives so much publicity in connection with Cleo the calf that the management is greatly pleased with her presence but when the blats stop talking about her she gets to be quite a bore, and they request Fat-Fat to remove her, especially as guys from the health department commence coming around and stating that it is setting a bad precedent to other hotels to have a calf as a guest.

So Fat-Fat has to get rid of Cleo the calf or find another place to live and by this time he is very fond of her, indeed, and cannot bear the idea of parting from her. Finally he finds a spot over on Eleventh Avenue along in the Fifties not far from the North River docks where an old bundle by the name of Mrs. Squamm runs a small fleabag and who is very glad to have Fat-Fat and Cleo the calf. In fact, Mrs. Squamm states that she often longs for a touch of rural atmosphere over on Eleventh Avenue and feels that Cleo the calf will provide same.

Furthermore, right next door to Mrs. Squamm's little fleabag there is a fenced-in vacant lot covering half a block which is once occupied by a house that burns down years ago leaving nothing but a big hole in the ground in the centre of the lot that is formerly the cellar, and Fat-Fat can see that this lot will be very handy for Cleo the calf to romp about in when she gets older, especially as Mrs. Squamm's kitchen where Cleo the calf sleeps opens right into the lot.

Now the summer passes by and I do not see Fat-Fat for some time although I hear of him hustling and bustling about the race courses at his trade as a horse player, and then one night I run into him in front of Mindy's and ask him how Cleo the calf is.

"Why," Fat-Fat says, "she is fine and growing like a weed. I play with her every day, wrestling and rolling about on the floor with her to strengthen her muscles and also to reduce my own weight. I never give up hope of being permitted to serve my country in the Army. She runs about the lot next door when I am at the track and is enjoying herself in a way that is a pleasure to behold. But," Fat-Fat says, "I am sorry to say that there has come up some friction between Cleo the calf and a bunch of small kids who also wish to use the lot as a playground. She detests them."

"What about the other Cleo?" I ask.

At this, the tears start rolling down Fat-Fat's cheeks and he is unable to speak, so I can see he is deeply affected and naturally I am very sorry for him, especially as I hear rumours along Broadway that Cleo the pretty seems to be crazy about this Henri. In fact, I observe them one night together in the Stork Club holding hands and gazing into each other's eyes in such a way that I can see it must be love.

Personally, I cannot blame her much as this Henri is a good-looking guy with a small moustache and is very well dressed except for a monocle and alongside of him Fat-Fat is naturally nothing but a plater compared to a stake horse but of course looks are not everything. To tell the truth, they are only about eighty per cent. I make a few inquiries about Henri but nobody seems to have any line on him except that he is undoubtedly a foreign guy and seems to have plenty of beesom but at this time there are so many foreign guys in New York with plenty of beesom that no one ever bothers to find out who they are or where they are from, or whatever.

Well, one night in the late fall, Fat-Fat calls me up at Mindy's and requests me to come over to Mrs. Squamm's house and keep him company, stating that he is not feeling well and does not wish to go out. He also states that Mrs. Squamm goes to bed early and Cleo the calf is sleeping out in the lot because she is now so big she takes up too much room in the kitchen, and that he is low in his mind and lonesome. So I go there and am playing him a little pinochle and permitting him to win to cheer him up when along towards midnight there comes a knock at the door and when Fat-Fat opens it who rushes in but a big guy and a couple of smaller guys and the big guy displays a badge in his hand and speaks like this:

"Jubble is the name," he says. "Federal Bureau of Investigation. Where are they?"

"Where are who?" Fat-Fat says.

"Kindly do not stall," Jubble says. "One of my guys hears her give this house address to the taxi jockey as they drive away from the Stork Club. They leave the cab, which is now in our custody, waiting down the street a block off and walk here and the jockey says he sees them climb over the fence into the lot next door, and as we do not observe hide nor hair of them in the lot they must be in this house because there is no other house around close. Come, come," he says, "speak up."

Now all of a sudden we hear Cleo the calf's voice out in the lot going mah-ah-ah as if she is in distress and Fat-Fat runs out the back door of the kitchen and into the lot and Jubble and his guys run after him and so do I. The street lights outside the fence throw a dim light all over the lot but Cleo the calf is not to be seen although we can still hear her. So Fat-Fat follows the sound of her voice until it brings him to the hole in the ground that is once a cellar and as the voice seems to come from this hole, Jubble and his guys all turn flashlights into the hole and we observe a somewhat unusual scene.

Cleo the calf and Cleo the pretty and Henri the foreign

guy are all down in the hole and Cleo the calf is chasing Cleo the pretty and Henri back and forth in this space which is about the size and depth of a long, narrow room, in a most surprising manner and going mah-ah-ah in a tone that indicates she is greatly vexed, and I can see that Cleo the calf is much more developed since I last notice her and in fact she is quite large.

Now and then Henri tries to climb up one side of the hole, digging his fingers in the dirt wall and Cleo the calf immediately butts him vigorously from behind and knocks him down. Once while we are gazing at this scene, Cleo the pretty also tries to climb the wall and Cleo the calf butts her in the same place she does Henri and just as vigorously and Cleo the pretty is sobbing and Henri is using the most ungenteel language and Cleo the calf keeps going mah-ah-ah so there is really some little confusion, and on viewing all this, Fat-Fat becomes slightly indignant and speaks as follows:

"See here, now," Fat-Fat says, "you must not be playing tag with Cleo the calf at such an hour in a hole in the ground. She is supposed to be getting her rest."

Well, even in the confusion I notice that the hole that is once a cellar looks as if somebody recently clears it out and does a lot of digging as if to make it deeper as there is much fresh earth around and about and there are steps dug in one wall as if to enable whoever does the digging to climb in and out and I also notice that there are light boards across the hole like a flat roof, and it is plain to be seen that these boards give way under some kind of weight in the middle so I figure this is where Cleo the calf and Cleo the pretty and Henri drop through into the hole. Furthermore, Jubble seems to notice this, too, because he says:

"Why," he says, "this is really most ingenious. I must tell our chief, Mr. Hoover, about this spy trap. Maybe we can build a few in Washington."

CLEO

"What makes it a spy trap?" I say.

"It traps this Henri guy, does it not?" Jubble says. "And he is a spy. He is Henri la Porte, alias Muller, the most dangerous secret agent and saboteur in the world. We are tailing him for months. Johnson," he says to one of his guys, "jump down in there and put the handcuffs on him, although," he says, "maybe you better wait until somebody surrounds the animal that is pursuing him."

At this, Fat-Fat drops down into the hole and puts his arms around Cleo the calf and calls her pet names and quiets her down and then this Johnson follows him into the hole and applies the darbolas to Henri's wrists and all the time Henri is putting up quite a bleat and saying he will see his ambassador and maybe the President, and Cleo the pretty is sitting on the ground down in the hole crying as if her heart will break.

We finally get them all out of the hole but Cleo the calf and go back to Mrs. Squamm's house and on the way I ask Fat-Fat if he notices the way the old cellar is fixed up and he says he does and that he is greatly bewildered by same but that it is best not to speak of this matter until we see what is what. He says there is undoubtedly more here than meets the eye, and about now a tall guy I do not see before comes into the house with still another guy that I can see is a taxi-cab jockey and the tall guy whispers something to Jubble and Jubble says like this:

"Fine," he says. "I am glad you put it in a safe place. Well," he says, gazing at Cleo the pretty who is still crying no little, "I must also put this beautiful under arrest as an accomplice, although," he says, "it is by no means the established policy of our chief, Mr. Hoover, to molest beautifuls."

Now of course here is a predicament to be sure, because anybody can see that being arrested as an accomplice to a saboteur will present Cleo the pretty in an unfavourable light before her public and Cleo the pretty begins to cry louder than ever and she looks at Fat-Fat and speaks to him as follows:

"Irving," she says, "save me."

"Why," Fat-Fat says to Jubble, "what do you mean she is an accomplice? She is my fiancée and my personal assistant. I have her stool this Henri guy into the lot so we can trap him in exactly the manner you observe, although," Fat-Fat says, "of course I do not know he is as great a scapegrace as you state. I figure he is just a fiancée thief and it is my intention to give him a going-over and this marvellous here is in on the play."

"Oh," Jubble says, "I beg your pardon, miss. I beg everybody's pardon. Why," he says, "you may get a medal for this. Now I must hasten to my office and leave my lads to follow with the prisoner. But," he says, "we must keep this capture quiet until we round up any others who may be connected with Henri."

As Jubble departs and while I am still thinking of what an exaggeration Fat-Fat is guilty of, and am also still wondering about the cellar, Cleo the pretty throws herself into Fat-Fat's arms and kisses him and says:

"Irving," she says, "forgive me for everything, I never really love anybody but you."

"Why," Fat-Fat says, "I forgive you, all right, but how do you come to be in this lot out here in the first place, not to mention being down in the hole?"

"Oh," Cleo the pretty says, "I am going away and I get to thinking of you, and I remember your address here, because I always keep track of you, and I induce Henri to make a stop. He is putting me aboard a ship that sails for South America at midnight and he is going to join me there later and we are to be married. I want to see you for the last time, but Henri has the cab stop before we reach your door. I can see now he must suspect we are being followed.

"We walk the rest of the way," Cleo the pretty says, "but Henri is evidently still suspicious as he boosts me over the fence into the lot and follows after me and tells me we must wait there awhile and what do I see in the lot but a terrible animal and for no reason this animal becomes angry and chases us around until we run across what looks like solid ground but which gives way under our feet and drops us into the hole. It is a dreadful experience, Irving," she says.

"I do not understand it," Fat-Fat says. "It is not in keeping with Cleo the calf's character to display such temper. I guess she realizes Henri is a wrongie."

"Irving," Cleo the pretty says, "you must not think Henri is as bad as these parties state. He is very kind to me and gives me a perfectly huge basket of fruits and flowers and candles for my going-away present. I leave it in the cab and, Irving," she says, "I trust you will recover it for me."

At this, the tall guy who comes in last and who seems to be questioning the taxicab jockey, steps over to Cleo the pretty and taps her on the shoulder and says:

"Sister," he says, "Henri is not putting you on a boat for South America. He is putting you on one that is going to Egypt and is loaded with war supplies. And in the basket of stuff he gives you for a present is a time bomb that will sink the ship and you with it inside of twelve hours."

"Why," Cleo the pretty says, "maybe he is a rascal after all. But," she says, "it is a beautiful basket."

Afterwards I hear this same tall guy talking to Henri in another room and he says to Henri like this:

"Muller," he says, "how do you ever come to join out with a dumb broad such as this?"

"Why," Henri says, "I need a dumb one for my purpose. But I am dumber than she is. If I do not let her talk me into making this stop for a farewell to the blubberhead I will have her aboard the Zoozoo and my work will be accomplished."

But of course I do not mention this conversation to Fat-Fat or to Cleo the pretty either as I fear it may cast a slight cloud over their happiness.

"Well," Fat-Fat says, when the guys finally leave with Henri, "everything turns out for the best. But," he says, "I am still puzzled as to how such a gentle little thing comes to commit this violent assault. Maybe I do wrong in teaching her to butt," he says.

Then Fat-Fat and Cleo the pretty kiss and hug again and their pleasure in this proceeding is really beautiful to behold and later Cleo the pretty tells me in confidence that what makes her realize that she truly loves Fat-Fat is that when she sees Cleo the calf in the lot and remembers the rumours that come to her ears of how Fat-Fat adores this creature, a terrible wave of jealousy comes over her and she cannot resist giving Cleo the calf a good kick in the slats. And Cleo the pretty says this kick is undoubtedly what stirs Cleo the calf to a passion and causes her to run them into the hole.

I drop over to Mrs. Squamm's a few days later and Fat-Fat and Cleo the pretty and Mrs. Squamm are having something to eat in the kitchen and Cleo the calf is standing half in and half out of the doorway watching them and I give them all a huge hello including Cleo the calf and sit down and Fat-Fat says to me like this:

"Well," he says, "Mrs. Squamm finds out about the cellar for me. It seems the little kids of the neighbourhood who are disputing with Cleo the calf for possession of the lot see a movie about big-game hunters in Africa or some such place and observe how they trap lions and tigers and elephants and all this and that and they are pretending among themselves as kids will do that Cleo the calf is a tiger and they make a trap of the cellar similar to something they see in the movies to snare her. Mrs. Squamm says it is called a pitfall. She thinks they are playing they are Frank Bucks. My gracious," Fat-Fat says, "when I am a kid, Jesse James is plenty good enough for me."

"Well," I say, "no doubt you will soon be passing about the neighbourhood distributing a few bootses in the pantses?"

"By no means," Fat-Fat says. "Let us say no more about this incident as I am receiving great credit for personally trapping Henri and in fact I am to be rewarded with a job in the service of the Beard. They are going to send me to a school and make an undercover guy of me to run down other secret agents and saboteurs and such. So I will get to serve my country after all."

"Congratulations, Fat-Fat," I say. "And what is to become of Cleo the pretty here and also of Cleo the calf?"

"Oh," Fat-Fat says, "I am buying a little farm up the Hudson. We are going to live there and raise a lot of little Cleos on both sides."

Then he and Cleo the pretty begin hugging and kissing again and Mrs. Squamm laughs heartily and Cleo the calf goes moo-oo-oo, like that, so I can see her voice is commencing to change no little.

23. THE LACEWORK KID

Now, of course, the war makes itself felt along Broadway no little and quite some and in fact it is a most disturbing element at times as it brings many strangers to the city who crowd Mindy's restaurant to the doors and often compel the old-time regular customers to stand in line waiting for tables, which is a very great hardship, indeed.

It does no good to complain to Mindy about this situation as he is making so much money he is practically insolent and he only asks you if you do not know there is a war going on, and besides Mindy is generally waiting for a table himself.

Well, one evening I am fortunate enough to out-cute everyone else for a chair that is the only vacant chair at a little table for two and the other chair is occupied by a soldier, and who is this soldier but a guy by the name of The Lacework Kid who is eating as if Hitler is coming up Broadway.

Now The Lacework Kid, who is generally called Lace for short, is a personality who is maybe thirty years old but looks younger and is a card player by trade. Furthermore he is considered one of the best that ever riffles a deck. In fact, he comes by his monicker because someone once remarks that his work with the cards is as delicate as lace, although personally I consider this an understatement.

He comes from the city of Providence which is in Rhode Island, and of course it is well known to one and all that for generations Providence produces wonderful card players, and in his childhood The Lacework Kid has the advantage of studying under the best minds there, and afterwards improves his education in this respect by much travel.

Before the war he is a great hand for riding the tubs and makes regular trips back and forth across the Atlantic Ocean because a guy in his line can always find more customers on the boats than anywhere else and can also do very good for himself by winning the pools on the ship's daily run if he can make the proper connections to get the information on the run in advance.

I only wish you can see The Lacework Kid before the war when he is at the height of his career. He is maybe five feet nine and very slender and has brown eyes and wavy brown hair and a face like a choirboy and a gentle voice.

He wears the best clothes money can buy and they are always of soft quiet materials and his linen is always white and his shoes black. He wears no jewellery showing, but he carries a little gold watch in his pants pockets that stands him a G-er in Paris and a gold cigarette box that sets him back a gob in the same place.

He has long slim white hands like a society broad and in fact there is no doubt that his hands are the secret of The Lacework Kid's success at his trade of card playing as they are fast and flexible and have youth in them, and youth is one thing a good card player must have, because age stiffens up more than somewhat. But of course age is a drawback in everything in this wicked old world.

It is really a beautiful sight to watch The Lacework Kid handle a deck of cards because he makes the pasteboards just float together when he is shuffling and causes them to fall as light as flecks of foam when he is dealing. His speciality is a game called bridge when he is riding the tubs and he is seldom without customers because in the first place he does not look like a guy who can play bridge very

well and in the second place he does not appear to be such
a personality as the signs in the smoking rooms on the
boats refer to when they say "Beware of Card Sharks."
In fact The Lacework Kid generally tries to get a chair
right under one of these signs to show that it cannot
possibly mean him.

I see The Lacework Kid a few years before this night in
Mindy's when he just gets in on a German liner and he has
a guy by the name of Schultz with him and is entertaining
this Schultz royally because it seems Schultz is the smoking
room steward on the liner and is The Lacework Kid's connection in winning the pools and in introducing bridge
customers to him and putting him away with them as a
rich young American zillionaire and as the trip nets Lace
two thou on the pools alone he feels quite grateful to
Schultz.

But of course this is before there is any war and later
when I see him the unpleasantness is on and no liners are
running and Lace tells me his trade is the greatest economic
casualty of the whole war, and he is wondering if there is
any use trying to ride the submarines back and forth looking
for customers.

And now here he is again as large as life and in fact
slightly larger as I can see he puts on a little weight and he
looks very good in his uniform and has a red ribbon on his
chest, so I say to him like this:

"Lace," I say, "it is indeed a pleasure to run into you
and I can see by your uniform that you are in the war
business and by your ribbon that you distinguish yourself
in some manner. Perhaps you are decorated for dealing the
general a nice hand off the bottom?"

Well, at this, The Lacework Kid gives me a most severe
look and says:

"It is a Good Conduct Medal. I get it for being a fine

404

soldier. I may get an even better award for an experience I will now relate to you."

I will omit the details of my early career in the Army (The Lacework Kid says) except to tell you that my comrades know me only as Sergeant Fortescue Melville Michael O'Shay, my mamma getting the first two names out of a novel she is reading at the time I am born, and my papa's papa bringing the last two over from Ireland.

Furthermore, they know nothing of my background and while there are occasions when I am greatly tempted to make assessments against them out of my great store of knowledge when they are playing such trifling games as blackjack, I resist the urge and confine myself strictly to the matter in hand, which is the war.

I am the waist gunner in a Flying Fortress on a raid over Germany one pleasant afternoon when our ship is so severely jostled by anti-aircraft shells that we are compelled to bail out and no sooner do I land than up comes three German soldiers with rifles in their dukes.

They point these rifles at me in a most disquieting manner and while I only know a word or two of the German language I can see that I am their prisoner and the next thing I know I am in a prison camp where I find my comrades and also several hundred other gees who seem to be British and one thing and another.

It is not a large camp and in fact I learn that it is just a sort of temporary detention spot for prisoners who are rounded up in this particular section of the country and that they are usually transferred to a larger gaff after a while. It is located in a hilly country not far from the Swiss border and you can see high mountains in the distance that I am told are the Alps.

But even with the view it is by no means a desirable place. The life in this camp is most monotonous and the cuisine is worse, which is a terrible disappointment to me as I am rather fond of German cooking, and particularly adore the apple strudel of this race, and the chow they give us makes me more violently anti-Nazi than ever and also gives me indigestion. To tell the truth, I spend most of my time trying to figure a way to escape though they tell me that if I am patient I will sooner or later be exchanged for a German prisoner.

There is a company of maybe a hundred German soldiers guarding the camp and I am only there a few hours before I learn that the officer who is in charge of the joint is a captain by the name of Kunz, and that he is also sometimes called The Butcher because it seems that in the early days of the war he is in command of an outfit in Poland and thinks nothing of killing people right and left for no reason whatever except he enjoys seeing them die.

But it seems he finally gets himself in bad with his boss and is sent to this little out-of-the-way prison camp as a lesson to him and he runs the place like the tough warden of a stir back home though he does not show up much in person around the camp and in fact I never see him myself until the time I am going to tell you about.

One afternoon a German sergeant comes into the prison yard, where I am taking a little exercise and beckons me off to one side and I am somewhat surprised to observe that the sergeant is nobody but Schultz the steward, who speaks to me in a low voice as follows:

"Hello, Lace," he says. "How is everything?"

"Schultz," I say, "everything stinks."

"Lace," he says, "what do you know about something American that is called gin rummy?"

"Gin rummy?" I say. "Why I know it is supposed to be a card game but as a matter of fact it is nothing but a diversion for idiots."

THE LACEWORK KID

"Are you a gin rummy man?" Schultz says. "I mean do you play the game?"

"Schultz," I say, "nearly everybody in the United States of America plays gin rummy. The little children in the street play it. Old broads play it. I understand there is a trained ape in the Bronx Zoo that plays it very nicely and I am not surprised, because," I say, "I can teach any dumb animal to play gin rummy if I can get it to hold ten cards."

"Well," Schultz says, "what I am getting at is do you play it as well as you play bridge and in the same way? What I must know is are you a mechanic at gin? I mean if necessary?"

Well naturally I am slightly vexed by this question as I consider it an insult to my integrity as well as a reflection upon my card playing to even hint that I do anything in cards except outplay my opponent through my superior skill. To tell the truth, I feel it is just the same as asking Joe Louis if he uses the difference in his gloves when he is meeting a chump.

"Schultz," I say, "you are undoubtedly a scoundrel to always be thinking in terms of larceny. I never swindle anybody at anything despite any rumours to the contrary that you may hear. And I never hear of any swindles in gin rummy except planting a guy who is supposed to have a piece of your opponent's play alongside him to tip off his cards to you.

"But," I say, "I consider this a low form of thievery. However, Schultz," I say, "I will be guilty of false modesty if I do not admit to you that like all gin players I think I am the best. In fact, I know of but one who can beat me consistently at gin and that is Kidneyfoot, the waiter in Mindy's, but then he teaches me the game and naturally figures to top me slightly."

Well, then this Schultz unfolds a very strange tale to me.

He says that when Captain Kunz is in the United States for some years before the war as an attaché of the German embassy in Washington, he learns the game of gin rummy and it becomes a great passion with him.

It seems from what Schultz says that after Kunz returns to Germany, he misses his gin rummy no little as the game is practically unknown in his country where card players generally favour pinochle or maybe klabriasch. It seems that Kunz tries to teach some of his countrymen how to play gin but has little success and anyway the war comes on and promoting an American game will be deemed unpatriotic, so he has to cease his efforts in this direction.

But he cannot stop thinking of gin, so he finally invents a sort of solitaire gin and plays it constantly all by himself, but it is most unsatisfactory and when he hears of American prisoners arriving in his camp, he sends for Schultz and asks him to canvass us and see if there are any gin rummy players in the crowd. And in looking us over, Schultz spots me.

"Now," Schultz says, "I build you up to the captain as the champion gin player of the United States, and he finally tells me the other night that he wishes to play you if it can be done in secret, as of course it will be very bad for morale if it gets out that the commandant of a prison camp engages in card games with a prisoner. The captain is rich and likes to play for high stakes, too," Schultz says.

"Look, Schultz," I say, "I do not have any moolouw with me here. All my potatoes are planted in a jug in England and I do not suppose the captain will accept notes of hand payable there."

"Listen," Schultz says, dropping his voice to a whisper, "I tell all my fellow soldiers here about your gin playing, and how you are so clever you can make a jack jump out of a deck and sing Chattanooga Choo-Choo if necessary, and we all agree to pool our resources to provide you with a taw. We can raise maybe fifty thousand marks. But," Schultz says, "you must not breathe a word of this to your comrades. The captain must think they are the ones who are backing you. You will receive twenty-five per cent. of your winnings, and I will personally guarantee your end."

Naturally, I figure Schultz is giving me the old rol-de-dol-dol for some reason because it does not make sense that an officer in the German army will wish to play an American prisoner gin rummy, but then I remember that gin players will do anything to play gin and I figure that maybe the captain is like the old faro bank player who is warned as he is going into a gambling house to beware of the bank game there because it is crooked and who says:

"Yes, I know it is, but what am I going to do? It is the only game in town."

Well, of course this is an ancient story to you and you will kindly forgive me for springing it at this time, but I am trying to explain the psychology of this captain as I see it. Anyway, I tell Schultz to go ahead and arrange the game and in the meantime I get a deck of cards and practise to refresh my memory.

Now, one night Schultz shows up at my quarters and tells me to come with him and he says it in such a stern voice and acts so mysterious that everyone figures I am being taken out to be shot and to tell you the truth I am not so sure myself that this is not the case. But when we get away from the other prisoners, Schultz is quite nice to me.

He takes me outside the gates of the prison camp and we walk along a road about a mile when we come to a small house set back from the road in a grove of trees and Schultz stops in front of this house and speaks to me as follows:

"Lace," he says, "in the course of your playing with

the captain kindly do not refer to our people as krauts, pretzels, beerheads, Heinies, Boches, sausages, wienies or by the titles of any other members of the vegetable or animal kingdom, and do not tell him what you Americans are going to do to us. It will only make for an unfriendly atmosphere, and his replies may distract you from your gin. He understands English, so please be discreet in every respect."

Then he hands me a roll of German marks a steeplechase horse will be unable to hurdle and leads the way into the house, and by this time I figure out what the scamus is. I figure that Schultz pegs me for a bleater, and the captain is going to try to get some information out of me and, in fact, I am looking for a touch of the old third degree from the Gestapo.

But on entering the house, which seems to be very plainly furnished, the only person present is a big guy in uniform with a lot of gongs on his chest, which is a way of saying medals, and whose head is shaved like Eric von Stroheim's in a Nazi picture. He is sitting at a table in front of a burning fireplace fooling with a deck of cards.

Schultz introduces me to him, but the guy only nods and motions me to sit down at the table opposite him and tosses the deck of cards to me. I examine the backs carefully to see if they are marked, but they seem strictly kosher in every way, and then I say to Captain Kunz like this:

"Captain," I say, "let us understand one thing. I am a non-commissioned officer, and you outrank me from hell to breakfast time, but in this game you must not take advantage of your rank in any way, shape, manner or form, to intimidate me. We will play New York rules, with gins and undercuts to count twenty each and blitzes double."

Kunz nods and motions me to cut the cards for the deal, and he wins it and away we go. We play three games at once and as soon as both of us are on all three games, we start another frame of three, with Schultz keeping score, and it is not long before we have as many as three frames or nine games going at once, which makes a very fast contest, indeed. We are playing for a hundred marks a game or three hundred marks across, which Schultz tells me is about a hundred and twenty dollars in my money, the way the Germans figure their marks.

I will not attempt to describe gin rummy in detail as you can call up any insane asylum and get any patient on the phone and learn all about it in no time, as all lunatics are bound to be gin players, and in fact the chances are it is gin rummy that makes them lunatics. Furthermore, I will not bore you with my philosophy of the game, but I say it is ninety-five per cent. luck and five per cent. play, and the five per cent. is the good card player's strength in the pinches, if there are any pinches.

The cards in gin rummy run hot and cold the same as the dice in a crap game. It is by no means necessary to go to Harvard to learn to play gin and in fact a moron is apt to play it better than Einstein. If you get the tickets in gin, you are a genius, and if you do not get them, you are a bum. When they do not come, you can only sit and suffer, and the aggravation of waiting on cards that never arrive will give you stomach ulcers in no time.

Well, I can see at once that Captain Kunz plays as good a game of gin as anybody can play and he also has good regulation dialogue, such as "This is the worst hand I ever see in my life," and "I only need one little card from the draw to get down," and so forth and so on, but he delivers his dialogue in German and then Schultz translates it for me as it seems the captain does not care to address me direct in English, which I consider very snobbish of him.

About the only word he says I can understand is *frischer* when he picks up a bad hand and wishes to know if I am agreeable to a fresh deal, which is a courtesy a gin player sometimes extends if he also has a bad hand, though personally I am opposed to *frischers*. In fact, when I get a bad hand, I play the Pittsburgh Muddle system on Kunz, which is to pick up every card he discards whether I need it or not and then throw it back at him when my hand improves, the idea being to confuse your opponent and make him hold cards that gum up his hand.

Well, I get my rushes right away and win the first frame and am going so strong on the second that Kunz gets up and peels his coat down to a pair of pink suspenders and ten minutes later he drops the suspenders off his shoulders and opens his waist band. In the meantime, Schultz kibitzes the captain on one hand and me on the next, and of course a kibitzer is entitled to present his views on a play after it is over, and Schultz is undoubtedly a real kibitzer and becomes quite excited at times in his comment.

However, once he is very bitter in his criticism of a play that costs the captain a game, and Kunz turns on him like a wolf and bawls him out and scares Schultz silly. But later the captain apologizes because as a gin player he is bound to respect the right of a kibitzer.

I keep waiting for Kunz to slip in questions to me about our Air Force and one thing and another, but he never makes a remark that is not in connection with the game and finally I can see that my suspicions are unfounded and that he is nothing but a gin player after all.

Well, daylight is coming through the windows of the house when the captain says we must knock off playing, and Schultz must hurry me back to camp, and I am somewhat startled to realize that I am four hundred marks loser which I whip out and pay immediately. Furthermore,

Schultz is terribly depressed by this situation and all the way back to the camp he keeps telling me how I disappoint him in not winning and asking me what becomes of my mechanics, and finally I get sore and speak to him as follows:

"Schultz," I say, "the guy is not only better than a raw hand at gin but he also outlucks me. And I tell you I do not know of any mechanics in gin rummy and if you do not care to trust to my superior skill to finally prevail, you can call it all off now."

Then Schultz cools down a little and says maybe I will do better next time, but I judge his disappointment is communicated to the other German soldiers as they seem very crusty with me all day though my greatest trouble is standing off the questions of my own gang about my absence.

Well, Schultz is around after me again that night to take me to the house in the grove, and in fact every night for a month hand-running I play the captain and it is not long before I am beating him like breaking sticks. And every night the captain pays off like a slot machine and every day I turn my dough over to Schultz and he pays me twenty-five per cent. and then distributes the balance among the guys in his syndicate.

Naturally, I stand first-class with all the Jerries who are in on the play and they also become more pleasant towards my comrades and finally I tell these comrades what is going on and while they are greatly amused I can see that they are also greatly relieved, because it seems they are troubled by my nightly absences from the camp and are glad to learn that it is only for the purpose of playing gin with the enemy.

At the end of the month and basing my estimate on a round ten thousand marks I have stashed away, I figure I am forty thousand marks winner on Kunz. Then one night

I beat him for a thousand marks and he does not whip it out as usual but says something in German to Schultz, and Schultz tells me the captain says he forgets his wallet somewhere, and I say all right, but that it is only fair for him to give me a scratch for the dough.

Schultz translates this to the captain, who looks very angry and seems to be highly insulted, but finally he outs with a notebook and scribbles an I.O.U., because, of course, at this stage of my life I am not trusting anyone and especially a Nazi.

He settles the next night before we start playing, but he takes a good bath this time and gives me the finger again, and while he comes alive the following night, this continues to happen again and again, and something tells me that Kunz is troubled with the shorts. When I mention this suspicion to Schultz, he seems a trifle uneasy and finally he says:

"Well, Lace," he says, "I fear you are right. I fear our good captain is in over his head. To tell the truth, your game is commencing to bore me and the other soldiers of the Fatherland no little because the captain borrows money from us every day, which is a terrible thing for a high officer to do to the soldiers of his command, and, while you win it back for us promptly, we now fear he will never replace the principal."

"Why, Schultz," I say, "do you not tell me that the captain is richer than six feet down in Mississippi mud?"

"Yes," Schultz says, "and he keeps talking of his properties in Berlin, but we are nonetheless uneasy. And the worst thing about it is that your twenty-five per cent. is eating up all the funds in circulation. It is a vicious circle. Lace," Schultz says, "can you spare me a couple of thou? I must send something to my frau and I will repay you when the boats get to running again."

THE LACEWORK KID

"Schultz," I say, "your story smacks of corn because I do not believe you have a wife and, if you do have one you will never be sending her money. But," I say, "I will advance you a thousand marks for old times' sake on your marker."

So I weed him the thousand and accept his Kathleen Mavourneen, which is a promise to pay that may be for years and may be forever, and the reason I do this is because I am by no means certain that Schultz may not incite his fellow soldiers to gang up and deprive me of my hard-earned twenty-five per cent. by force, if he can find out where I have it carefully buried. To tell the truth, I do not repose great confidence in Schultz.

Well, that night I beat Kunz for twelve hundred marks, and he pays me five hundred on account, and as Schultz and I are getting ready to leave, he says something in German to Schultz, and when we are on our way back to camp, Schultz tells me he has to return to the house and see the captain, and then I really commence to worry because I fear the two may get their heads together and plot against my well-being.

But as far as Captain Kunz is concerned, my worry is groundless as along towards noon of this same day, we hear a rumour that he commits suicide by shooting himself smack-dab through the head and this causes so much excitement that our guards forget to lock us in that night or even to watch us carefully, and all of us Americans and some of the British walk out of the gates and scatter over the country-side, and most of us reach safety in Switzerland, and I afterwards hear there is quite a scandal in German circles about the matter.

But before we go, I have a slight chat with Schultz and say to him like this:

"Schultz," I say, "tell me all."

"Well," Schultz says, "I know that when the captain asks me to return to the house after taking you back to camp, he wishes to borrow the money I get from you to play you again to-night, because when I tell him yesterday I am personally broke and cannot advance him any more, he is the one who suggests I approach you for a touch and in fact he threatens to make trouble for me over certain matters that transpire in Poland if I fail to do so.

"So," Schultz says, "when I reach the house, I first peer through a window into the living-room and see the captain still sitting at the table with the deck of cards you use spread out before him as if he is examining them, and all of a sudden, I am seized with a terrible fury at the thought that he is waiting there to take my money to gamble it away frivolously, and an impulse that I cannot restrain causes me to out with my pistol and give it to him through the window and also through the onion.

"And," Schultz says, "I will always remember how the blood drips down off the table and splatters over the nine of diamonds that is lying on the floor under your chair and how it comes to my mind that the nine of diamonds is considered a very unlucky card indeed and how fortune-tellers say it is a sign of death. It is a great coincidence," Schultz says, "considering the number of times you catch the captain with big counts in his hands when he is waiting for that very nine."

"Ah," I say, "I figure you have something to do with his demise."

"But," Schultz says, "as far as anyone but you and me know, it is suicide because I also have the presence of mind to fire one shot from his pistol which is the same make as mine, and leave it in his hand. It is suicide because of despondency, which his superior officers say is probably because he learns of his impending purge."

THE LACEWORK KID

"Schultz," I say, "you are bound to come to a bad end but now good-bye."

"Good-bye," Schultz says. "Oh, yes," he says. "Maybe I ought to state that I am also prompted to my act by the fear that the captain will finally find the nine of diamonds on the floor, that you forget to retrieve when you leave him this morning."

"What do you mean, Schultz?" I say.

"Good-bye," Schultz says.

And this is all there is to the story (The Lacework Kid says).

"Well, Lace," I say, "it is all very exciting, and it must be nice to be back on Broadway as free as the birds and with all that moolouw you collect as your twenty-five per cent. in your pants pockets."

"Oh," Lace says, "I do not return with a white quarter. You see I use all my end to bribe Schultz and the rest of the German soldiers to leave the doors and gates unlocked that night and to be looking the other way when we depart."

Then The Lacework Kid leaves, and I am sitting there finishing my boiled yellow pike, which is a very tasty dish, indeed, and thinking about the captain's blood dripping on the nine of diamonds, when who comes up but old Kidney-foot the waiter, who is called by this name because he walks as if he has kidneys in both feet and who points to Lace going out the door and says to me like this:

"Well," Kidneyfoot says, "there goes a great artist. He is one of the finest card players I ever see except in gin rummy. It is strange how this simple game baffles all good card players. In fact," Kidneyfoot says, "The Lacework Kid is a rank sucker at gin until I instruct him in one manœuvre that gives you a great advantage, which is to drop any one card to the floor accidentally on purpose."

THE LAST STORIES

24. BLONDE MINK

Now of course there are many different ways of cooking tripe but personally I prefer it stewed with tomatoes and mushrooms and a bit of garlic and in fact I am partaking of a portion in this form in Mindy's restaurant on Broadway one evening in January when a personality by the name of Julie the Starker sits down at my table and leans over and sniffs my dish and says to me like this:

"Tripe," he says. "With garlic," he says. "Why, this is according to the recipe of the late Slats Slavin who obtains it from his old Aunt Margaret in Troy. Waiter," he says, "bring me an order of this delicious concoction only with more garlic. It is getting colder outside and a guy needs garlic in his system to thicken his blood. Well," he says, "this is indeed a coincidence because I just come from visiting the late Slats and having a small chat with him."

Naturally I am somewhat surprised by this statement as I know the late Slats is resting in Woodlawn Cemetery and to tell the truth I remember I am present as a pallbearer when he is placed there to rest, but I am also pleased to hear these tidings as Slats is always a good friend of mine and no nicer guy ever steps in shoe leather.

"Well," I say to Julie, "and how is Slats these days?"

"He is cold," Julie says. "He states that it is very crimpy around the edges up there in Woodlawn especially at night. You know the late Slats always hates cold weather. He is usually in Florida by this time of year to duck the chill.

"Furthermore," Julie says, "he is greatly embarrassed up there without a stone over him such as Beatrice promises to get him. He says it makes him feel like a bum with nothing to show who he is when all around him are many fine markers including one of black marble to the memory of the late Cockeyed Corrigan, who, as you know, is of no consequence compared to the late Slats who is really somebody."

Well, of course this is very true because the late Slats is formerly known and esteemed by one and all on Broadway as one of the smartest operators in horse racing that ever draws breath. He is a handicapper by trade and his figures on the horses that are apt to win are so highly prized that one night he is stuck up by a couple of guys when he has six thou in cash money on him, but all they want is his figures on the next day's races.

He is a player and a layer. He will bet on the horses himself when he sees spots he fancies or he will let you bet him on them and he has clients all over the United States who call him up at his office on Broadway and transact business with him one way or the other. He is a tall guy in his late forties who is not much thicker than a lath which is why he is called Slats though his first name is really Terence.

He is by no means Mr. America for looks but he dresses well and he is very rapid with a dollar. He is the softest touch in town for busted guys and he will get up in the middle of the night to do somebody a favour, consequently no one gets more or larger hellos along the main drag than the late Slats.

He comes from a little burg upstate by the name of Cohoes and I hear that he and Julie the Starker are friends from their short-pants days there, although Julie is about the last one in the world you will expect to see a guy of class like Slats associating with as Julie is strictly in the muggola department.

He is about Slats' age and is short and thick and has a

kisser that is surely a pain to even his own mamma. He is called Julie the Starker because starker means a strong rough guy and there is no doubt that Julie answers this description in every manner, shape and form.

He is at one time in his life a prize fighter but strictly a catcher which is a way of saying he catches everything the other guy throws at him and at other times he is a bouncer; I do not know what all else except that he has some Sing Sing background.

At all times he is a most undesirable personality but he is very fond of the late Slats Slavin and vice versa, and they get along together in a way that is most astonishing to behold.

He is not only a handy guy for Slats but he is also a social companion and for some years wherever you see Slats you are apt to see Julie the Starker except when Slats is with his fiancée, Miss Beatrice Gee and even then you may see Julie though as a rule Miss Beatrice Gee does not approve of him any more than she does of leprosy. In fact, she makes no bones about considering the very sight of Julie revolting to her.

In addition to being the late Slats' fiancée, Miss Beatrice Gee is at this time a prominent show girl in one of Mike Todd's musical shows and she is conceded by one and all to be the most beautiful object on Manhattan Island or anyway no worse than a photo finish for the most beautiful.

She is an original brunette and is quite tall and carries herself in a way that the late Slats says is dignity, though it really comes of Mike Todd's director putting a big copy of the Bible on her head and saying she will either learn to walk balancing it or else, though he never does tell her or else what.

Other dolls call Miss Beatrice Gee a clothes horse because it seems she wears clothes with great skill, and furthermore she is crazy about them although her best hold is not wearing them, which she also does with great skill but of course only on the stage. When she is not on the stage she is always groomed like a stake horse going to the post for a big race, and no one takes greater pride in her appearance than the late Slats Slavin, except Miss Beatrice Gee herself.

While I do not believe the story that once when she has a headache and Doc Kelton puts his thermometer in her mouth, to see if she is running a temperature, the mercury freezes tight, there is no doubt that Beatrice is not the emotional type and to be very frank about the matter many think she is downright frosty. But of course, no one ever mentions this to the late Slats because he is greatly in love and the chances are he maybe thinks Beatrice is hotter than a stove and personally I am in no position to deny it.

Well, in much less time than it takes me to tell you all this, Julie the Starker has his tripe and is eating it with more sound than is altogether necessary for tripe no matter how it is cooked and to tell the truth I have to wait until he pauses before I can make him hear my voice above his eating. Then I say to him like this:

"Why, Julie," I say, "I cannot understand why Slats is in the plight you describe with reference to the stone. I am under the impression that he leaves Beatrice well loaded as far as the do-re-mi is concerned and I take it for granted that she handles the stone situation. By the way, Julie," I say, "does Slats say anything to you about any horses anywhere for to-morrow?"

"No," Julie says. "But if you have a minute to spare I will tell you the story of Beatrice and her failure to take care of the matter of the stone for the late Slats. It is really a great scandal."

Then without waiting to hear if I have a minute to spare or not, he starts telling me, and it seems it all goes back to a night in late September when Beatrice informs Slats that she just comes upon a great bargain in a blonde mink coat for twenty-three thousand dollars and that she desires same at once to keep herself warm during the impending winter although she already had enough fur coats in her closet to keep not only herself warm but half of Syracuse, too.

"Pardon me, Julie," I say at this point, "but what is a blonde mink?"

"Why," Julie says, "that is the very question Slats asks and he learns from Beatrice that it is a new light-coloured mink fur that is sometimes called blue mink and sometimes platinum mink and sometimes blonde mink and he also learns that no matter what it is called, it is very, very expensive, and after Slats gets all this info he speaks to Beatrice as follows:

" 'Baby,' he says, 'you cut right to the crimp when you mention twenty-three thou because that is exactly the size of the bank roll at this moment. But I just come off a tough season and I will need all my ready for navigating purposes the next few months and besides it looks like a mild winter and you can wear your old last season's leopard or caracul or ermine or Persian lamb or beaver until I get going again.' "

Now at this (Julie the Starker says) Beatrice flies into a terrible rage and tells Slats that he is a tightwad and a skinflint and a miser, and that he has no heart and no pride or he will not suggest that she go around in such shabby old floogers and that she will never humiliate herself in this manner. She says if she waits even a few minutes, someone else is sure to snap up the blonde mink and that she may never again meet with a similar opportunity.

"Well, they have a large quarrel," Julie says, "and when Slats and I get back to his hotel apartment that night he complains of not feeling any too well and in fact he finally keels over on the bed with his tongue hanging out and I send for Doc Kelton who says it is a heart attack and very bad.

"He says to tell the truth it is 100 to 1 Slats will not beat it and then Doc takes his departure stating that he has so many shorter-priced patients he cannot afford to waste time on long shots and he leaves it to me to notify Slats that his number is up.

"On receiving this information, Slats requests me to find Miss Beatrice Gee and bring her to his bedside, which I do, although at first she is much opposed to leaving her table in the Stork Club where she is the centre of a gay throng, until I whisper to her that I will be compelled to flatten her and carry her unless she does.

"But on arriving at Slats' apartment and realizing that he is indeed an invalid, Beatrice seems to be quite downcast and starts to shed tears all over the joint, and I have no doubt that some of them are on the level because surely she must remember how kind Slats is to her.

"Then Slats says he wishes to talk to Beatrice alone and requests me to go into the next room, but of course I have a crack in the door so I can hear what goes on between them and what I hear is Slats saying to Beatrice like this:

" 'Baby,' he says, 'reach in under my pillow and get the package of currency there. It is the twenty-three I tell you about and it is all the dough I have in the world. It is all yours except twenty-six hundred which you are to pay Clancy Brothers the tombstone makers in Yonkers for a stone I pick out for myself some time ago and forget to pay for although my plot in Woodlawn is free and clear.

" 'It is a long stone of white Carrara marble in excellent taste,' Slats says. 'It is to lie flat over my last resting place, not to stand upright, and it is cut to exactly cover same from end to end and side to side. I order it in this form,' Slats says, 'because I am always a restless soul and long have a fear

BLONDE MINK

I may not lie quietly in my last resting place but may wish to roam around unless there is a sort of lid over me such as this stone. And besides,' he says, 'it will keep the snow off me. I loathe and despise the snow. I will leave the engraving to you, Baby, but promise you will take care of the stone at once.'

"Well, I hear Beatrice promise between sobs, and also no doubt as she is reaching under the pillow for Slats's plant and when I step back into the room a little later, Slats is a goner and Beatrice is now really letting the salt water flow freely, although her best effort is in Woodlawn two days later when it looks as if we will have to send for a siphon to unflood the premises.

"But to show you what a smart strudel Beatrice is, she is around the day after we place the late Slats to rest saying that he does not leave her a thin dime. You see, she is figuring against the chance that relatives of Slats may show up and claim his estate and she even lets Slats' lodge pay the funeral expenses although of course this is no more than is coming to any departed brother.

"I do not dispute her statement because I think she is entitled to the dough as long as Slats gives it to her, and of course I take it for granted that she will split herself out from enough of the swag to buy the stone according to her promise, and in fact I am so sure of this that one afternoon last week I go out to Woodlawn not only to pay my respects to the memory of the late Slats but to see how his last resting place looks with the stone over it.

"Well, what do I see but Slats himself walking around and around a mound of dried earth with some withered flowers scattered over it and among these flowers I recognize my own wreath which says 'So long, pal' on it and which costs me a double-saw, but there is no stone whatsoever over the mound, not even as much as a weentsy little pebble."

"Just a minute, Julie," I say. "You state that you see the late Slats walking around and about. Do you see him all pale and vapoury?"

"Well," Julie says, "now you mention it, I do seem to recall that Slats is a little on the pale side of what he used to be. But he is otherwise unchanged except that he is not wearing his derby hat as usual. We do not give him his derby hat when we place him to rest, as the undertaker guy says it is not necessary. Anyway, when he spies me, Slats stops walking and sits down on the edge of the late Cock-eyed Corrigan's black marble marker, which is practically next door to him and says to me like this:

" 'Hello, Julie,' he says. 'I am commencing to wonder what becomes of you. I am walking around here for weeks trying to keep warm and I am all tuckered out. What do you suppose is the idea of not providing people with overcoats when they are placed to rest? Only I do not rest, Julie. Do you see Beatrice lately and what does she says about my stone?'

" 'Slats,' I say, 'I must confess I do not see Beatrice lately, but I never dream she does not provide the stone long before this as per her promise which I can tell you now I overhear her make to you. A solemn deathbed promise.'

" 'Never mind what kind of bed it is,' Slats says. 'It is a morbid topic. And I think you have plenty of gall to be on the Erie when I am saying my last good-bye to my baby. You owe us both an apology. Look her up right away and give her a good one and ask her what about my stone. The chances are there is a hitch somewhere. Maybe the engraving is causing the delay. I am sure Beatrice will wish something sentimental on it like Sleep well my beloved, and engraving takes time.'

"Well, I am about to mention that she already takes time enough to have George Washington's farewell address engraved on it but all of a sudden the late Slats disappears from sight and I take this as a hint for me to blow, too, and that very night I hunt up Beatrice to give her Slats' message.

"I find her standing at the bar of a gaff called the Palmetto with a couple of guys and I notice she is wearing a fur coat the colour of mist that I do not remember ever seeing on her before and I turn to a dame who is sitting at a table and say to her like this:

" 'Pardon me, little miss,' I say, 'but just to satisfy my curiosity, can you tell me the name of the fur that party over yonder is wearing?'

" 'Blonde mink,' she says. 'It is perfectly beautiful too.'

" 'And what does such a garment cost?' I ask.

" 'Why,' she says, 'that one seems to be first-class merchandise. It costs twenty-five thousand dollars. Maybe more, but not much less. It is the very newest fur out.'

"Then I walk over to Beatrice and tap her on the shoulder, and when she turns I motion her out of hearing distance of the guys she is with and speak to her as follows:

" 'Well, Bea,' I say, 'your new coat must hang a little heavy on you considering that it represents the weight of a nice tombstone. I never mention it to you before but I hear your last chat with the late Slats Slavin including your promise but until I find you in this lovely benny no one will ever make me believe you mean to welch on your word.'

" 'All right, all right,' she says. 'So I do not buy the stone. But it costs twenty-six hundred and all I have is twenty-three thousand and an odd tenner and this coat is a steal at twenty-three. If I wait another minute longer someone else is sure to snap it up and the dealer wants his all cash. Besides Slats will never know he does not get the stone.'

" 'Bea,' I say, 'I have a talk with Slats to-day at Wood-lawn. He knows he has no stone and he is upset about it.

But he is making excuses for you, Bea. He figures you are unexpectedly delayed a bit in getting it there. You have the guy fooled even yet.'

"At this Beatrice gazes at me for some time without saying a word and I notice that looking into her eyes is just the same as looking into a couple of ice cubes. Then she gives her coat a hitch and brings it closer around her and finally she says:

" 'Julie,' she says, 'I want to tell you something. If ever again you speak to me or about me I will start remembering out loud that Slats has a large bundle of cash on him that last night and I will also start wondering out loud what becomes of it and a guy with your biography cannot stand much wonderment such as that. And if you see Slats again tell him how I look in my new coat.'

" 'Bea,' I say, 'you will never have any luck with your new coat because it means leaving poor Slats up there in Woodlawn restless and cold.'

" 'No luck?' she says. 'Listen,' she says, 'do you see the dopey-looking little punk in the uniform leaning against the bar? His name is Freddy Voogan and his papa is a squillionaire out in Denver and I am going to marry the kid any minute and what do you think gets him for me? My blonde mink. He notices how nice I look in it and insists on meeting me. No luck?' Beatrice says. 'Is kicking up a gold mine no luck?'

" 'Bea,' I say, 'it is bad enough to rob the grave as you already do but it is even worse to rob the cradle.'

" 'Good-bye, Julie,' Bea says. 'Do not forget to tell Slats how I looked in my new coat.'

" Well, I will say she looks wonderful in it even though I am greatly disappointed in her because it is plain to be seen that Beatrice has no sentiment about the past. So now I am compelled to report back to the late Slats Slavin that he is on a bust as far as the stone is concerned and I hope and trust that my revelation will not cause him too much anguish."

And with this, Julie the Starker dunks up the last of the tripe gravy on his plate with a piece of rye bread and gets up to take his departure and I say to him like this:

"Julie," I say, "if you happen to think of it, kindly ask the late Slats to look over the entries at Hialeah for the next few days and if he can send me a winner now and then I can get parties to bet a little for me."

"Well," Julie says, "Slats has other things on his mind besides horses right now, but," he says, "I will try to remember your request although of course you will carry me for a small piece of your end."

Then he leaves me and I am still sitting there when a plain clothes copper by the name of Johnny Brannigan comes in and sits down in the chair Julie just vacates and orders some Danish pastry and a cup of Java, and then almost as if he hears the conversation between Julie and me he says:

"Oh, hello," he says. "How well do you know Miss Beatrice Gee who is formerly the fiancée of the late Slats Slavin? I mean how well do you know her history and most especially do you know any knocks against her?"

"Why?" I say.

"Well," Johnny says, "it is strictly an unofficial question. There is hell up Ninth Street over her. A family out in Denver that must have more weight than Pike's Peak gets the Denver police department to ask our department very quietly about her, and our department requests me to make a few inquiries.

"Of course it is not an official police matter. It is an exchange of courtesies.

"It seems," Johnny says, "that Miss Beatrice Gee is going to marry a member of this family who is under twenty-one years of age and his papa and mamma are doing handstands about it, though personally," Johnny says, "I believe in letting love take its course. But," he says, "my theory has nothing to do with the fact that I promise to make a return of some kind on this blintz."

"Well, Johnny," I say, "I do not know anything whatever about her but you just miss a guy who can probably give you a complete run-down on her. You just miss Julie the Starker. However," I say, "I am pretty sure to run into him to-morrow and will tell him to contact you."

But I do not see Julie the next day or for several days after that and I am greatly disappointed as I not only wish to tell him to get in touch with Johnny, but I am anxious to learn if Slats sends me any info on the horses. For that matter I do not see Johnny Brannigan either until late one afternoon I run into him on Broadway and he says to me like this:

"Say," he says, "you are just the guy I am looking for. Do you see the late editions of the blats?"

"No," I say, "why!"

"Well," Johnny says, "they are carrying big stories about the finding of Miss Beatrice Gee in her apartment in East 57th Street as dead as a doornail. It looks as if the young guy from Denver she is going to marry bounces a big bronze lamp off her coco in what the scribes will undoubtedly call a fit of jealous rage because he has a big row with her early in the evening in the Canary Club when he finds a Marine captain from the Pacific teaching her how the island natives in those parts rub noses when they greet each other, although the young guy claims he walks away from her then and does not see her again because he is too busy loading himself up with champagne.

"But," Johnny says, "he is found unconscious from the champagne in his hotel room to-day and admits he does not remember when or where or what or why. My goodness,"

Johnny says, "the champagne they sell nowadays is worse than an anæsthetic."

Naturally this news about Miss Beatrice Gee is quite distressing to me if only because of her former association with the late Slats Slavin and I am sorry to hear of the young guy's plight, too, even though I do not know him. I am always sorry to hear of young guys in trouble and especially rich young guys but of course if they wish to mix bronze lamps with champagne they must take the consequences and I so state to Johnny Brannigan.

"Well," Johnny says, "he does not seem to be the bronze-lamp type, and yet who else has a motive to commit this deed? You must always consider the question of motive in crimes of this nature."

"What about robbery?" I say.

"No," Johnny says, "All her jewellery and other belongings are found in the apartment. The only thing missing as far as her maid and acquaintances can tell seems to be a new fur coat which she probably leaves some place in her wanderings during the evening. But now I remember why I am looking for you. I am still collecting data on Miss Beatrice Gee's background though this time officially and I recall you tell me that maybe Julie the Starker can give me some information and I wish to know where I am apt to find Julie."

"A new fur coat, Johnny?" I say. "Well," I say, "as a rule I am not in favour of aiding and abetting coppers but this matter seems different and if you will take a ride with me I think I may be able to lead you to Julie."

So I call a taxicab and as we get in, I tell the jockey to drive us to Woodlawn Cemetery and if Johnny Brannigan is surprised by our destination he does not crack but whiles away the time on the journey by relating many of his experiences as a copper, some of which are very interesting.

It is coming on dusk when we reach Woodlawn and while

THE LAST STORIES

I have an idea of the general direction of the late Slats Slavin's last resting place, I have to keep the taxi guy driving around inside the gates for some time before I spot the exact location through recognizing the late Cockeyed Corrigan's black marble marker.

It is a short distance off the auto roadway so I have the hackie stop and Johnny Brannigan and I get out of the cab to walk a few yards to the mound and as we approach same who steps out from the shadow of the late Cockeyed Corrigan's marker but Julie the Starker who speaks to me as follows:

"Hello, hello," he says. "I am glad you see and I know you will be pleased to learn that the late Slats gives me a tip for you on a horse that goes at Hialeah to-morrow but the name escapes me at the moment. He says his figures make it an absolute kick in the pants. Well," Julie says, "stick around a while and maybe I will remember it."

Then he seems to notice the presence of Johnny Brannigan for the first time and to recognize him, too, because all of a sudden he outs with Captain Barker and says:

"Oh, a copper, eh?" he says. "Well, copper, here is a little kiss for you."

And with this he lets go a slug that misses Johnny Brannigan and knocks an arm off a pink stone cherub in the background and he is about to encore when Johnny blasts ahead of him, and Julie the Starker drops his pizzlo-over and his legs begin bending under him like Leon Errol's when Leon is playing a drunk.

He finally staggers up to the last resting place of the late Slats Slavin and falls there with the blood pumping from the hole that Johnny Brannigan drills in his chest and as I notice his lips moving I hasten to his side figuring that he may be about to utter the name of the horse Slats gives him for me.

BLONDE MINK

Then I observe that there is something soft and fuzzy spread out on the mound under him that Julie the Starker pats weakly with one hand as he whispers to me like this:

"Well," he says, "the late Slats is not only resting in peace now with the same as his stone over him but he is as warm as toast and in fact warmer."

"The horse, Julie," I say. "What is the name of the horse?"

But Julie only closes his eyes and as it is plain to be seen that he now joins out permanently with the population of Woodlawn, Johnny Brannigan steps forward and rolls him off the mound with his foot and picks up the object that is under Julie and examines it in the dim light.

"I always think Julie is a little stir-crazy," Johnny says, "but I wonder why he takes a pop at me when all I want of him is to ask him some questions and I wonder too, where this nice red fox fur coat comes from?"

Well, of course I know that Johnny will soon realize that Julie probably thinks Johnny wishes to chat with him about the job he does on Miss Beatrice Gee but at the moment I am too provoked about Julie holding out the tip the late Slats Slavin gives him for me to discuss the matter or even to explain that the red is only Julie's blood and that the coat is really blonde mink.

25. BIG BOY BLUES

✦✦✦✦✦✦✦✦✦✦✦✦✦✦✦✦✦✦✦✦✦✦✦✦✦✦✦✦✦✦✦✦✦✦✦✦✦✦✦

IT is along towards two o'clock one pleasant morning and things are unusually quiet in Mindy's restaurant on Broadway and in fact only two customers besides myself are present when who comes in like a rush of air, hot or cold, but a large soldier crying out in a huge voice as follows:

"Hello, hello, hello, hello, hello."

Well, when I take a good glaum at him I can see that he is nobody but a personality by the name of West Side Willie who is formerly a ticket speculator on Broadway and when he comes over to me still going hello, hello, hello, hello, hello, I say to him quite severely like this:

"Willie," I say, "you are three hellos over what anybody is entitled to in Mindy's even if there is anybody here which as you can see for yourself is by no means the situation."

"Oh," Willie says, "I happen to have a few hellos to spare and besides I am so glad to get back on the big street again that I feel liberal. We are here for a run."

"Do you mean the war?" I say.

"I mean *Gee Eyes*, the soldier show I am with," Willie says. "We are a riot on the Coast. We lay them in the aisles in Denver. We kill the people in Cleveland. We will do a wonderful trade here."

Then Willie sits down and explains to me that one day when he is in a camp in the desert out in California and practically dying by inches of the heat and the drilling and the victuals and the other hardships of soldier life and especially the victuals, his commanding officer sends for him and says:

"Klump," he says, for such is West Side Willie's family monicker, "they are organizing an all-soldier musical show at Santa Ana and there is a request out for the names of all enlisted men in this area who are formerly connected with show business.

"I understand," the commanding officer says, "that you are familiar with matters of this nature and you will therefore report at once to Santa Ana to participate although personally," he says, "I consider it all just so much fol-de-rol and how the hell we can win the war behind the footlights I do not know."

Well, naturally Willie does not inform the commanding officer that his connections with show business is slightly informal but he gets on a train at once and goes to Santa Ana and there he discovers that the guy who is putting on the show is nobody but a playwright by the name of Hathaway Go who is once befriended by Willie to the extent of a meal in a one-arm gaff in West Forty-ninth and who is grateful ever since.

He is slightly surprised to see Willie appear in answer to a call for show people as he is aware that Willie does not sing or dance or play an instrument but after hearing Willie's description of soldier life in the desert his heart is touched and he says he guesses he can use a sure-footed guy to take tickets although when Willie asks what about selling them Hathaway Go gives him such a long slow look that Willie never renews the subject.

However, he is greatly downcast when he thinks of the opportunities in connection with these pasteboards because he feels that everyone will want them and when Willie is in action on Broadway he is known far and wide for his skill in manipulating with tickets to theatres and prize fights and hockey games and one thing and another that everyone wants but are unable to get unless they see Willie and pay his ice, which is a way of saying his premiums.

I often hear complaints that sometimes Willie asks more ice than the face value of the tickets but this is probably only for tickets that are very hard indeed to get and naturally Willie is entitled to some compensation for saving the customers the trouble of standing in line at the box offices to buy the tickets and then finding the tickets are all gone anyway. Besides Willie frequently has to take care of others out of his end to get the tickets in the first place so life is really not all ice with him.

"Well," Willie says, "I make the best of the position to which I am appointed although I must say the spectacle of throngs of customers being permitted to buy our tickets at face value at the box office when they will be delighted to pay two, three, four, five or six slugs premium if they cannot get them any other way is most disheartening to me.

"But," Willie says, "I become a terrific ticket taker. In fact," he says, "I am known as the Eisenhower of the front door. Furthermore, this assignment comes to me in nick of time because my original outfit is sent to Europe where I understand the victuals are even worse than they are in camp and there is practically no hotel life for an enlisted man."

"Willie," I say, "I am glad to see you again and I congratulate you on your military career and hope and trust you do not sustain any wounds such as tearing off a hangnail by mistake for the stub of a ticket some night. I am sure that your engagement on Broadway will be most auspicious."

"Thanks," Willie says, "but we are all nervous and worried over a situation that develops here. Do you remember Johnny Blues? The one they call Big Boy Blues?"

"Why, certainly," I say. "I remember him as well as if he is my brother only I am thankful such is not the case."

"Do you know Big Boy Blues has a son?" Willie says.

"Yes," I say, "I know it. They call him Little Boy Blues."

"Well," Willie says, "Little Boy Blues is the star of our show. He is the greatest thing in it. He slays the customers. He is wonderful."

"Why, Willie," I say, "I am glad to hear this news. I not only remember Big Boy Blues but come to think of it I remember his ever-loving sheriff who is the mamma of Little Boy Blues, I hope. If he has any talent it must come from her because the only talent Big Boy Blues ever has that I recall is that he can crush a human skull with one blow of his fist even though the skull belongs to a copper.

"In fact," I say, "I recall the night he performs this feat on a copper by the name of Caswell. I seem to remember that Caswell is in Polyclinic hospital for eight weeks but he finally recovers and is now a captain."

"Listen," Willie says, "Little Boy Blues appears in our show as a female ballet dancer. He dresses as a dame in a short skirt and one thing and another."

Well, at this I am slightly horrified as I can see what West Side Willie has in mind. I can see that it is going to be a great shock to Big Boy Blues if he learns of the matter because it is only about a year back that he is along Broadway bragging about his son being in the Army and stating that Little Boy will undoubtedly destroy a large number of the enemy single-handed.

Naturally, everybody agrees with him as Big Boy Blues strongly disapproves of anyone not agreeing with him and it is plain to be seen that after putting his son away as a destroyer he is apt to be displeased when he finds Little Boy is not only a ballet dancer but one in the attire of a doll and I so state to West Side Willie.

"Yes," Willie says, "that is exactly what we fear. We fear Big Boy will be so vexed he will tear the theatre down stone by stone and maybe peg the stones at us. However, it is our information from Little Boy's mamma that Big Boy thinks his son is somewhere overseas and has no idea he is in our show and it is our hope that he does not hear of it until after opening night anyway.

"Then," Willie says, "we expect to be rolling so good that we can replace Little Boy if necessary, but," he says, "we positively need him for the first night because he is the best thing in the show by seven or eight lengths and it is a great pity we dast not give him some advance publicity. Well, I will bid you good night as I must catch myself a few snores. Our company gets into Grand Central at noon and I wish to be there to meet it."

Then Willie takes his departure and I remain sitting there awhile thinking of what a great surprise it is to Broadway years ago when Big Boy Blues hauls off and marries a small canape by the name of Miss Rosie Flynn who is singing in the old Golden Slipper Club in West Forty-eighth Street and how Bookie Bon goes around offering to lay plenty of 9 to 5 that Big Boy gives her at least two broken arms inside of two weeks and finding no takers as Big Boy is known to one and all as a crude character.

He is at least six feet three inches high and he weighs anyway 220 pounds and he has a loud voice that causes parties four blocks away to tremble when he lets it out and he has a record at police headquarters that consists mainly of mayhem. He is a doorman and a bouncer at the Golden Slipper when I first know him but one day he climbs on the seat of a stray truck and drives it off and the next thing anybody knows he has one of the largest trucking businesses in the city.

Now Miss Rosie Flynn does not weigh ninety pounds with her girdle on and she has red hair and freckles and is by no means a spectacular singer but she is practically famous on Broadway because it is generally conceded that she is pure. The chances are she can marry into much more genteel circles than those in which Big Boy Blues moves just on the strength of being pure and it is the popular belief that Big Boy frightens her into marrying him as no one can think of any other reason for this union.

Well, after they are married and before the stray truck comes along to provide the keystone for Big Boy's success they live in a small apartment as far over on West Forty-ninth Street as anyone can live unless they live in a canoe in the North River and it is by no means a fashionable neighbourhood but it is the best they can do on their income in those days and it is there a son is born to them who is so small that Big Boy is greatly mortified and slightly perturbed.

In fact, he brings the child over on Broadway and goes around peering into the faces of various Broadway personalities who infest the Golden Slipper and then gazing closely at the child as if he is making comparisons. I never see this child again and to tell the truth I seldom see Big Boy Blues afterwards and then only when I do not learn in advance that he is coming my way but I read now and then in the blats about him slugging his truck drivers or somebody else's truck drivers or just somebody else, so I judge he is the same old Big Boy.

But as the years go on I occasionally run into Rosie Flynn who seems to be fatting up somewhat in spots and she tells me that Big Boy by no means admires the child that she now speaks of as Little Boy Blues because he remains puny and scary but I can see that Rosie thinks very well of him, indeed. In fact, Little Boy Blues is all she talks about and as he gets older I learn from her that she has him away at school as much as possible as he is a great eyesore to Big Boy who keeps him frightened half to death by yelling at him and sometimes giving him a few clops.

From what Rosie tells me, I judge Little Boy Blues is quite a weakling and far from being a credit to a virile personality such as Big Boy but when the war comes on and Little Boy is drafted, Big Boy becomes very proud of him and wishes to be real fatherly towards him.

In fact, one day at Dix where Little Boy Blues is stationed for awhile, Big Boy approaches him with his hand extended to shake hands and Little Boy is so alarmed that he turns and runs away and keeps running until he is so far from camp that he is two days finding his way back and is put down as AWOL.

Well, I become so interested in what West Side Willie tells me about the show that I go to the Grand Central at noon myself the next day to see the soldier company arrive and it is quite an impressive scene as the members are in full marching gear with rifles and all this and that and march from the station through the streets to the theatre in West Forty-eight where the show is going to open.

West Side Willie does not march with them but joins me in following them only we stick to the sidewalk and people stop and applaud the company and the members bow right and left and smile and when I say to Willie that I consider this somewhat unmilitary, he says:

"Well," he says, "you see most of these guys are professional actors even if they are soldiers and they are bound to take bows when they hear applause even if they are sitting in the electric chair waiting for the guy to pull the switch."

BIG BOY BLUES

He points out Little Boy Blues to me and I can see that he is small and frail-looking and seems to be buckling slightly at the knees from the weight of his pack and rifle and that he has red hair like his mamma. I also see Rosie Flynn on the sidewalk ahead of me following the march so I quit West Side Willie and overtake her and say to her like this:

"Well, Rosie," I say, "I notice your offspring has your top piece but the way he does not resemble Big Boy in any manner, shape or form is really remarkable. By the way," I say, "how is Big Boy? Not that I care, Rosie, but I wish to be polite."

"Sh-h-h-h!" she says and looks around as if she is afraid Big Boy may be in earshot. "He is all right except his temper is shorter than ever. He chucks one of his own truck drivers into the river yesterday truck and all. I am so afraid of what will happen if he learns Little Boy is in this show. You see," she says, "I tell him the last time I hear from Little Boy he is with Coogan's Cobras in the Pacific."

"Well," I say, "you do not pick a soft spot for him, anyway. Coogan's Cobras are supposed to be the fightingest outfit in our Army."

"It is because I see the name in the newspapers so much," Rosie says. "It pleases Big Boy to think Little Boy is in such company. I pray he does not learn the truth before the show opens. Poor Big Boy has no appreciation of the fine and delicate and artistic. I often wake up at night in trembling at the thought of his anger if he learns of the large fees I pay for Little Boy's dancing instruction."

I commence trembling myself right then and there thinking of such a situation and at this point I unload Rosie Flynn and go on my way because I realize that if Big Boy learns of the fees she mentions he may not only wipe out Rosie but anyone who ever even knows her. To tell the truth, I am a little disappointed in Rosie as I always figure her to have

some sense and while I do not say it is wrong for anybody's
son to dance I consider it sinful to pay fees to encourage him
to do it.

Well, the day of the opening I am surprised more than no
little when West Side Willie hunts me up and gives me a
skull, which is a way of saying a free ticket for the show and
I figure it must be because business is not up to expectations
but when I mention this idea to Willie he becomes quite
provoked.

"Why," he says, "we are sold out in advance for half the
entire engagement already. This show is the biggest thing
since nylons. If you examine your ducket you will observe
that no seat is specified. That means you have standing
room only."

But standing room is by no means undesirable in a New
York theatre especially at openings because where you
stand is in back of the last row which places you in a position to leave quickly and quietly in case the show is bad and
this is where I am located for the opening of *Gee Eyes*.

I am a little late getting to the theatre and the audience is
pretty well seated when I arrive and as I am going in West
Side Willie who is taking tickets with great skill holds back
a Broadway columnist and his wife a minute and says to
me:

"What do you think we have with us to-night?" he says.
"Why, nobody but Colonel Billy Coogan, the commander
of Coogan's Cobras. He is a tall slim guy with a lot of
ribbons on his chest and he is in the third row centre."

"Yes," the columnist says. "He flies in from the Pacific
only to-day to get a new decoration to-morrow from the
President in Washington."

Naturally on taking my place in the rear of the house I
spot Colonel Coogan at once by his uniform away down
front and I am somewhat astonished to observe next to him

BIG BOY BLUES

a head and a pair of shoulders that even at long distance and from behind I identify as belonging to Big Boy Blues, and what is more he seems to be chatting with Colonel Coogan.

I am standing there wondering about this spectacle but just then the curtain opens and I dismiss the matter from my mind as I can see at once that this is a pretty good show although personally I like a little more sex appeal than it is possible to get into shows in which all the performers are hairy-legged guys with no bims whatever around.

The one thing I am looking for which is Little Boy Blues does not come on until the finale and this is a very large number, indeed, with the entire cast on stage when out comes a slim and graceful young ballet dancer in a flaring short skirt and all who can easily pass for a doll if you do not know it has to be a guy in this company unless somebody makes a serious mistake.

I can see that the dancer is undoubtedly Little Boy Blues even without looking at the programme to make sure and while I am by no means a judge of ballet dancing and in fact can do without same entirely in a pinch, I realize that he gives a great performance. In fact, I realize that he is no doubt a genius at ballet dancing and as the curtain closes on him the audience lets out a roar of applause that I afterwards hear shakes the glasses off the back bar in the gin mill next door to the theatre.

Then the curtain opens again as is always the case when there is great applause and Little Boy Blues stands there on the stage panting as if he just finishes a fast hundred yards and taking bows with one hand on his stomach and also perspiring no little and the audience applauds with even greater vigour than before and at this moment I observe Big Boy Blues jump up from his seat down front.

I notice his mouth is wide open so I judge he is yelling

something and thinks I to myself well, here it comes, although there is too much noise for me to hear what he is yelling about, and besides at almost the same instant he jumps up a guy in the seat directly behind him jumps up too and practically simultaneously with Big Boy's mouth opening a blackjack drops on his sconce and Big Boy sinks back quietly in his seat. Then I recognize the guy behind him as Captain Caswell in civilian clothes.

Well, the uproar from the audience continues but of course it is all over Little Boy Blues' dancing and no one notices what happens to Big Boy although a couple of coppers come down the aisle and lift him out of his seat and drag him away still unconscious. Furthermore, no one pays any attention to Colonel Coogan who is up on his feet and saying to everyone around him that the slugging of Big Boy is the worst outrage since Pearl Harbour though no one seems to listen to him.

By this time Little Boy Blues is panting and perspiring more from taking bows than from his dancing so the curtain closes in on him and the first act for good and nearly everyone in the audience moves out into the lobby for the intermission to smoke and gas and all they are gassing about is Little Boy's dancing. Then I see Captain Caswell talking to Rosie Flynn in a corner of the lobby and I get close enough to hear the captain say:

"Well, Rose," he says, "you certainly do the community a service by requesting police protection here to-night. If it is not for your warning and my skill with a jack we will have serious trouble although to tell you the truth we have enough already with the guy we commandeer the seat from behind Big Boy. I only hope and trust that he does not have as much influence as he claims and anyway he can have the seat now."

Then Colonel Coogan comes into the lobby still stating

in a loud voice that the jacking of Big Boy is a scandalous matter and that somebody will hear from the War Department and maybe the OPI, too, when Captain Caswell steps up to him and informs him that Big Boy is jacked because he is about to start wrecking the joint in discovering that his son is a dancer in the show.

"No, no," Colonel Coogan says. "There is a terrible error somewhere. He knows his son is in the show all right because someone calls him up this evening and gives him the information. Mr. Blues introduces himself to me and tells me about it while we are sitting there side by side waiting for the curtain. He does not seem to know just what to think about his son being in the show at first but he asks me as a special favour not to mention it to Mrs. Blues if ever I happen to meet her because she thinks her son is with my command and Mr. Blues fears it will break her heart if she learns the truth."

"Colonel," Captain Caswell says, "I distinctly hear Big Boy yell when he gets up from his seat and our experience with him in the past is that he always prefaces his acts of violence by yelling."

"Yes," Colonel Coogan says, "he yells all right, but so do I and what we are both yelling is bravo."

At this point I hear a slight gasp behind me and on looking around I observe that Rosie Flynn slumps to the floor in a dead faint consequently there is more excitement during which I take my departure without even waiting for the second act as my legs are very tired from the standing room only.

I am again sitting in Mindy's restaurant along about three o'clock in the morning still resting my legs when who comes in but West Side Willie and I am most distressed to note that he has two black eyes and swollen lips and that he seems greatly dishevelled in every respect.

"Why, my good gracious, Willie," I say. "Do you get run over by a tank division or what?"

"No," Willie says, "Big Boy Blues belts me. By the way," he says, "everybody is all wrong about him crushing the human skull with a single blow of his fist. He hits me on top of the head twice with his right and only raises a contusion and I think he damages his duke at that. However," Willie says, "it is only fair to say Big Boy comes to the theatre to find me fresh from the hospital after he is treated for the jacking he receives from Captain Caswell and perhaps he does not have all his strength. He inflicts most of my injuries with a left hook."

"Well, Willie," I say, "it shows you how Colonel Coogan is deceived by Big Boy and Captain Caswell is right all the time. I suppose Big Boy's fury over Little Boy being in *Gee Eyes* flares up anew when he has time to think about it and no doubt he assaults you as a representative of the show."

"Oh, no," Willie says. "Big Boy is still all pleasured up over Little Boy's performance, and what is more he and Little Boy and Rosie Flynn are enjoying a happy and very loving family reunion but Big Boy gets to brooding about the ticket speculator who calls him up and tells him of Little Boy's presence in the show and hustles him into buying a ticket for a hundred dollars which is about a ninety-five dollar premium."

"I see," I say. "You are the speculator, of course."

"Well," Willie says, "I am stuck with a ticket that I pay six dollars for myself and I happen to need a hundred and I know Big Boy Blues will pay anything to get in the theatre if he hears Little Boy is in the show although naturally I figure it will be only to tear the place apart. But I also know Rosie Flynn arranges for police protection so I do not see how he can do any harm even if he is there.

"So," Willie says, "I call him up and promote him. It is more than human nature can stand to let such an opportunity pass. But besides getting belted I also undergo another slight misfortune to-night. I am relieved of my job with the show and ordered to Colonel Coogan's combat unit in the Pacific."

WRITTEN IN SICKNESS

26. WHY ME?

When physical calamity befalls, the toughest thing for the victim to overcome is the feeling of resentment that it should have happened to him.

"Why me?" he keeps asking himself, dazedly. "Of all the millions of people around, why me?"

It becomes like a pulse beat—"Why me? Why me? Why me?"

Sometimes he reviews his whole life step by step to see if he can put his finger on some circumstance in which he may have been at such grievous fault as to merit disaster.

Did he commit some black sin somewhere back down the years? Did he betray the sacred trust of some fellow human being? Is he being punished for some special wrongdoing? "Why me?"

He wakes suddenly at night from a sound sleep to consciousness of his affliction and to the clock-like ticking in his brain—"Why me? Why me? Why me?"

He reflects, "Why not that stinker Smith? Why not that louse Jones? Why not that bum Brown? Why me? Why me? Why me?"

Was he guilty of carelessness or error in judgment? "Why me? Why? Why? Why?"

It is a question that has been asked by afflicted mortals through the ages. It is being asked more than ever just now as the maimed men come back from war broken in body and spirit and completely bewildered, asking "Why me?"

I do not have the answer, of course. Not for myself nor

for anyone else. I, too, am just a poor mugg groping in the dark, though sometimes I think of the words of young Elihu reproving Job and his three pals: "Look into the heavens, and see; and behold the clouds which are higher than thou."

The Book of Job may have been an attempt to solve the problem why the righteous suffer and to point out that such suffering is often permitted as a test of faith and a means of grace. They sure put old Job over the hurdles as an illustration.

He was a character who lived in the land of Uz, 'way back in the times recorded in the Old Testament. He had more money than most folks have hay and he was also of great piety. He stood good with the Lord, who took occasion to comment favourably on Job one day to Satan, who had appeared before Him.

"There is no one like Job," remarked the Lord to Satan. "He is a perfect and upright man. He fears God and eschews evil."

"Well, why not?" said Satan. "You have fixed him up so he is sitting pretty in every way. But you just let a spell of bad luck hit him and see what happens. He will curse you to your face."

"You think so?" said the Lord. "All right, I will put all his belongings in your power to do with as you please. Only don't touch Job himself."

Not long afterwards, the Sabeans copped all of Job's oxen and asses and killed his servants and his sheep were burned up and the Chaldeans grabbed his camels and slaughtered more of his servants and a big wind blew down a house and destroyed his sons.

But so far from getting sore at the Lord as Satan had figured would happen after these little incidents, Job rent his mantle and shaved his head and fell down upon the ground and worshipped and said:

"Naked I came out of my mother's womb, and naked shall I return thither; the Lord gave, and the Lord hath taken away; blessed be the name of the Lord."

Now had I been Satan I would have given Job up then and there but lo, and behold, the next time the Lord held a meeting Satan again appeared and when the Lord started boosting Job for holding fast to his integrity, Satan sniffed disdainfully and said:

"Skin for skin, yea, all that a man has he will give for his life, but just you touch his bone and his flesh and see what your Mr. Job does."

"All right," the Lord said, "I will put him in your hands, only save his life."

———

Then Satan smote poor Job with boils from the soles of his feet to the crown of his head. I reckon that was the worst case of boils anyone ever heard of, and Job's wife remarked:

"Do you still retain your integrity? Curse God, and die."

"Woman," Job said, "you are a fool. Shall we receive good at the hands of God and not evil?"

But when those pals of Job's, Eliphaz, Bildad and Zophar, came to see him he let out quite a beef to them and in fact cursed the day he was born. In the end, however, after listening to discourses from his pals of a length that must have made him as tired as the boils, Job humbly confessed that God is omnipotent and omnipresent and repented his former utterances and demeanour "in dust and ashes" and the Lord made him more prosperous than ever before.

"Why me?"

"—*Therefore have I uttered that I understood not; things too wonderful for me, which I knew not.*"

27. THE DOCTOR KNOWS BEST

A MAN has a pain in a certain spot.
It isn't a severe pain. It isn't an incapacitating pain.
But it is nonetheless a pain.

The man goes to a doctor.

"Doc," he says, "I've got a kind of a pain."

So the doctor examines him. He takes the man's temperature, feels his pulse. He looks down the man's throat. He listens to the man's chest. He tests his reflexes.

The doctor finds nothing. He gives the man some simple remedy and tells him that ought to do the trick.

The man is back in a few days, "Doc,"he says, "that pain is still there. I don't feel so good."

The doctor makes another examination. He has the man go to an X-ray fellow for a few takes of his teeth and his interior. The doctor puts the exposures on a rack and gazes at them intently. He sees nothing. He lets the man look at them. The man does not see anything, either.

Then the doctor gives the man diathermic treatments. He gives him vitamin pills and vitamin hypodermics. The needles hurt the man like hell.

"How are you to-day?" the doctor asks the man on the man's next visit. The doctor is not taking the needles himself, so he has no call to cut himself in on the man's suffering with that "we".

"Doc," the man says, "that pain is still there. I don't feel so good."

Now the doctor puts the man on a strict diet. He tells

him to stop smoking and drinking and to cease doing all the other things the man enjoys.

"Doc," the man says, "that pain is still there."

The doctor commences to resent the man's attitude. He commences to hate the very sight of the man's kisser. So do his office attendants. They look at one another knowingly when he appears for his treatments.

When the man's friends ask the doctor what's the matter with the man, the doctor shrugs his shoulders. He purses his lips. He smiles slightly. He as much as says there is nothing the matter with the man.

The man is observed taking one of the pills the doctor ordered.

"He's always taking pills," the observer remarks. "He's a hypochondriac. His doctor can't find a thing wrong with him."

Now if the man has had a good break from life and remains a bachelor, he is not in such bad shape, but if he has the misfortune to be married he is in an awful fix because his wife and family are more difficult to convince that he has a pain than the doctor. They resent his attitude even more than the doctor.

"I've still got that pain," he says to his wife.

"It's just your imagination," she says.

"You never looked better in your life. You mustn't give way to every little ache that comes along. Think of all the suffering in the world. I'm really the one that ought to be in bed."

"I don't feel so good," the man says.

"Nonsense," his wife says.

So the man finally hauls off and gives up the ghost. He ups and dies. His wife and family are astonished, and indignant.

"Well," the man's friends say. "He wasn't looking any

too well the last time he was around and he was complaining about a pain, too. Must have been something radically wrong with the old boy, at that."

The doctor is in a bit of a huff about the man dying that way.

28. NO LIFE

◆◆

You have been noticing an uneasy sensation in region of the Darby Kelly and the croaker says it looks to him like it might be——

Well, nothing serious, if you are careful about what you eat and take these here powders.

All right, Doc. Careful is the word from now on. Thanks.

Wait a minute. No orange juice.

What, no orange juice, Doc? Always have orange juice for breakfast.

No, no orange juice.

Okay, Doc. That's gonna be tough, but grapefruit is just as good.

No grapefruit, either. No acids.

No grapefruit? Say, what does a guy do for breakfast, Doc?

Cereals.

Don't like cereals, Doc.

No syrup.

You don't mean a little sorghum on wheat cakes, do you, Doc?

No sorghum. No wheat cakes. No sugar.

You don't mean no sugar in the coffee, Doc? Just a couple of spoons a cup?

Yes, and no coffee.

Now look, Doc. You don't mean no coffee at all?

No coffee.

Say, Doc, that's all right about no sugar, but you must be kidding about no coffee at all.

459

No coffee.

Not even a coupla cups a meal, Doc? Why, that's just a taste.

No coffee.

Doc, that ain't human.

No candy.

Not even a little bitsy box of peppermints at the movies, Doc?

No, no peppermints. No ice.

Yo ain't talking about a tiny dab of banana ice cream, are you, Doc? The kind that goes down so slick?

Yes, no sweets at all. No highly spiced stuff. No herring.

What kind, Doc?

Any kind. No herring.

But you don't mean a little of that chef's special, Doc? The kind with the white sauce on it?

No herring.

Not even matjes, Doc?

No herring.

Well, all right, Doc. No herring. Gefüllte fish will have to do.

No gefüllte fish. No goulash.

What kind of goulash, Doc? Hungarian?

Any kind. No salami. No highly seasoned Italian food.

I never eat that more than a couple times a week, anyway; I'll take a lobster Fra Diavolo now and then.

None of that.

Are you sure about the herring, Doc? There must be some kind that're all right.

No herring.

It's a conspiracy. Whoever heard of a little herring hurting anybody? Why, Doc, people have been eating herring for years and it never bothered them.

No herring.

NO LIFE

Well, all right, no herring after to-night and to-morrow. What's this list, Doc?

It's your diet. Follow it closely.

But there ain't anything on it a guy can eat, Doc. It's terrible. You were just kidding about the coffee, weren't you, Doc? No coffee! Can you imagine a guy trying to live without coffee—what? You can't!

And no cigarettes.

Doc, a guy might as well be dead, hey?

29. GOOD NIGHT

DIALOGUE BETWEEN RUNYON AND BED

(A Little Style Larceny from Benjamin Franklin)

RUNYON: Well, Bed, here I am again. Gosh, I feel tough.

BED: What's the matter now?

RUNYON: I ache all over. I think I've got a fever. Gosh, I feel tough.

BED: I'm not surprised. You can't stand it any more, old boy.

RUNYON: Stand what?

BED: Staying out all night and eating what you please and when you please.

RUNYON: Say, what has that got to do with the way I feel? I've picked up a germ of something somewhere.

BED: Well, that's because your physical resistance to germs is weakened from staying out all night and eating indiscriminately. You ought to know better.

RUNYON: My physical resistance is all right. This is some kind of germ that has nothing to do with staying out and eating. Say, why don't you have more covers? You haven't got enough blankets on to make a boxing glove for a bumble bee.

BED: I've got on as many as usual.

RUNYON: Well, look how I'm shivering.

BED: That's because your resistance is low, I tell you.

RUNYON: I guess I need a doctor.

BED: It doesn't make any difference whether you need one or not—you'll have him. I wish you would get one that doesn't dump himself down on me when he's looking you over. I'm a little tired myself from the way you tossed around last night and hollered.

RUNYON: What was I hollering about?

BED: How do I know? You kept hollering "take that!"

RUNYON: Oh, I remember. I was dreaming I was a prizefighter and was knocking Joe Louis out. I guess it was the knackwurst and sauerkraut I ate before I came home.

BED: Knackwurst and sauerkraut, eh? And you wonder why you don't feel good? Why, that's enough to kill a donkey.

RUNYON: See here, Bed. Knackwurst and sauerkraut don't make your bones ache and give you a fever. My chest is sore, too. I may be getting pneumonia. Gosh, I feel tough. I'm afraid I'm in for a siege.

BED: My goodness, I hope not.

RUNYON: Why, don't you like my company?

BED: Oh, your company is all right, but I enjoy it more a little at a time. Then I'm not in so much danger.

RUNYON: What do you mean—danger?

BED: Well, I have to constantly be on guard against being destroyed by fire from those cigarettes you are always smoking. When I think of the narrow escapes I've had it makes my pillows shiver. You shouldn't smoke cigarettes when you are sick, anyway.

RUNYON: Say, a fellow has to do something. He can't just lie still all day and night, can he?

BED: You certainly don't anyway. You keep me in constant torment by kicking around and getting my sheets all knotted up. Your constant groaning is most disturbing, too.

RUNYON: Say, I seem to have a lot of faults, don't I?

BED: Oh, I won't say anything about the soup stains you get on me when you are having your meals off a tray, but I wish you would be more careful about the bread crumbs. They are really most annoying. Another thing, your language is at times slightly offensive.

RUNYON: Listen here, Bed. Maybe I'd better go to a hospital and be sick if you're going to be so critical.

BED: You wouldn't like it. They would turn the lights out on you early and wouldn't let you do so much reading. You couldn't have the radio turned on all the time, either. By the way, why do you keep switching from station to station every few minutes instead of listening to one programme all the way through?

RUNYON: That's because I'm always trying to find torch music when I'm sick. It makes me feel better. I wish Ukelele Ike was always on the radio singing "It Had to Be You" when I'm sick. Gosh, I feel tough. Say, Bed, how does typhoid fever start?

BED: Oh, you haven't got typhoid fever. If you've got anything it's probably just a little cold. Is that another cigarette? And didn't I hear you groan? Well, I can see that I'm in for it again. Oh, my goodness!

RUNYON: Send for the doctor. Gosh, I feel tough!

30. BED-WARMERS

WHEN I was in a hospital for a sort of check-up, I was reminded of a medical friend of mine in Hollywood who has the biggest check-up business in all Southern California.

The hospitals out there, as everywhere else, are always pressed for space for patients, especially private rooms. My friend's clientele is strictly the private room type and he had to devise some method of holding at least one or two private rooms in reserve at all times lest some of his patients die of mortification over having to lie ill in wards.

He keeps a list of movie producers, directors, executives and even a few actors and when one of his private room patients who has been really sick is ready for discharge, he calls up some fellow on the list and says:

"Henry, I have been thinking of you lately and I wish you would pop into Gates Ajar hospital to-morrow morning for a check-up. I have a room there for you."

Naturally Henry hustles for the hospital so fast you can scarcely see him for heel dust because the chances are he is a hypochondriac to begin with and in any event the check-up is always de rigueur in Hollywood. It gives a man something to talk about when he goes out socially.

Henry takes with him an assortment of silk robes and silk pyjamas and slippers and other gear, just in case any of the nurses are attractive enough to warrant a display of this nature, and he crawls into the hospital hay still warm from the body heat of the last patient.

He does not know it but he is there just as a holder. He

does not know my friend is using him to keep the room against the coming of a patient of greater illness or importance— and especially importance—than Henry. My friend drops around about noon and takes his blood pressure and is assuming a serious expression before telling Henry that it looks bad when the phone rings.

"Doctor," the office downstairs advises him, "Mrs. Farfel has just arrived."

"Henry," my friend says, as he hangs up, "you are 100 per cent. okay just as I thought. You can get out of that bed right now and go home, and consider yourself checked up to who-laid-the-rail."

"But, Doctor," Henry says, "don't you think——"

"Henry," my friend says, "please get up. I will help you put on your clothes. I need the room for Mrs. Farfel."

"You mean the wife of——" Henry begins.

"Yes," says my friend. "Ah, here she is now! Henry, you will have to dress out in the hall."

———

Of course, I do not believe the story that my friend had three of these holders dressing out in the hall at the same time, but there is no doubt that his check-up turn-over is very rapid and very large. I fear, however, that he has lost a very good check-up customer in the person of another friend of mine, a top producer, who entered the Gates Ajar for a check-up, thinking he was going to get a good rest from his missus and was dispossessed by my medical friend in forty-eight hours.

What made the producer particularly sore was his discovery that the patient who succeeded him was that same missus who went in for treatment for a nervous breakdown. I am inclined to the opinion that my medical friend should have employed a stranger as holder, at that.

The hospital life is not for Runyon. It operates on the

theory that the day begins at about eight o'clock in the a.m., at which hour the nurse comes barging in with bright hellos that have a slightly synthetic ring to one who knows that she must have got up at six o'clock to get to the hospital from her home so early unless she lives around the corner. Even then no one can be that cheerful at 8 a.m., especially on a dark day.

The hospital regime is too upsetting to my routine. I think it was originally devised for farmers. What proof can they offer that it does a man any good to be awakened at 8 a.m., and put to sleep at 9 p.m., when all his life he has slept until noon and gone to bed at 4 a.m.? Let us be fair about this.

After a couple of weeks of hospital order I find myself dozing at gin rummy games like Jules Saranoff, the champion gin player of the Friars club, a famous man with his violin in the old days of vaudeville. When "Sary" plays gin, everyone bets on him up to the moment he heaves the ten of spades when he should have chucked the nine of clubs, which is apt to happen any minute after he has played eight or ten hours because he no longer possesses the stamina of former years.

One night I was nodding on "Sary's" left and did not see exactly what came off but it seems his opponent ginned and won the game on a bad play by "Sary" and I was awakened by his backers clamouring to be declared off the next game on the ground that he was asleep. I remarked that his eyes were open so he must be awake.

"The one on your side is," said a backer, "but the one on the other side is closed. He is sleeping one-eye."

31. SWEET DREAMS

WE think the greatest institution ever devised for human comfort is the bed. Let us talk about beds.

A man is usually born in bed, and spends at least half his life in bed. If he is lucky, he dies in bed. We used to think that the best place to die was on the battlefield, face to the foe, etc., but that was when we were much younger and more casual about dying.

Now we know that a battlefield is likely to be an untidy sort of place and much more lonesome for the purpose of dying than a nice clean bed, with the doctors and the sorrowing relatives clustered about, all wondering how soon they are going to get paid off.

However, let us not pursue those morbid reflections about beds. We prefer thinking of beds in their more cheerful aspects. We like to think of a bed as a place of refuge and rest—as a sanctuary against the outside world with its troubles and woes, where sometimes in beautiful dreams, a fellow can live a few hours in ecstasy.

Of course there may be a few bad dreams, too, but we always figured they are stood off by the pleasure derived from awakening to a realization that they are not true. Only the other night a bloke shoved us off a twenty-storey building, but we woke up just before we hit the ground and our joy on discovering that we were still safe in bed completely cancelled the few sweaty seconds we suffered while falling.

We claim to be one of the greatest authorities in the United States on beds—that is, on the sleeping qualities of beds. We have slept in beds in every State in the Union, and we must say good beds are fairly common in these days when the construction of springs and mattresses has reached a degree approaching perfection, and American housewives, in furnishing their homes, are properly placing more importance on beds than on any other items of household equipment.

We can remember when some hotel beds, and a lot in private homes, too, were pretty hard to take. Even now I occasionally run across a survivor of the times when a bed was commonly just a sort of rack with a lumpy mattress and creaky springs and skimpy coverings for a fellow to toss around on between suns, though in general Americans have become educated to the idea of complete comfort in beds.

The trouble with Americans about beds in the past was their theory that a bed typified indolence. They apparently did not realize that the better a fellow rested in bed, the livelier he was likely to be when he got up, and that the better the bed, the better his rest. It is our opinion that the energy of Americans generally has greatly increased since the improvement in beds.

We hold that many Americans owe their lack of appreciation in beds to faulty education in youth. Some parents send their children to bed as punishment. If they would reverse this procedure and send them to bed only as a reward, and keep them out of bed as a penalty, it would inspire in the kids a respect and appreciation for beds for which they would thank their fathers and mothers in later years.

It might be a good idea, too, to teach the youngsters right from taw that they should never take any worries to bed with them—that they should regard bed as a secure nest in which they should rest without giving a thought to worldly concerns. If you started on them early enough maybe they would grow up with the knack of disregarding the winds of worry rattling at the window panes, or the rain of adversity pattering on the roofs that disturbs so much adult peace of mind in bed.

We never cared much for that Spartan simplicity in beds that some fellows profess to fancy. A cot in the corner, or a crude pallet on the ground 'neath the stars is not for us. We went through all that in our army days, and you can have it.

We will take all the luxury with which a bed can possibly be surrounded—a gentle, yielding mattress, and quiet, cushiony springs, and soft, downy pillows, and snowy linen and the richest of coverings. A fellow gets little enough out of life under any circumstances without making his hours of rest too tough.

We like a bed wide and long that we can kick around in without falling out or stubbing our toes. As we have said, good beds are common enough, but a truly great bed—one that fits perfectly, and that sleeps good, is a rarity that a fellow should cherish above all other possessions. We have a bed in New York City that we think is the sleepingest bed in the whole world and would not part with it for anything, but of course another fellow might not like it. It might not just fit him. That is the thing—to get a bed that fits.

I realize, of course, that my appreciation of a bed is due largely to the fact that I am one of those fortunate chaps who sleeps fairly well, for which I am grateful to a kind providence. I can imagine nothing worse than insomnia. I am lucky enough to be able to sleep after a fashion standing up, or hanging on a hook, but in a good bed—say, that is when I really saw wood!

32. PASSING THE WORD ALONG

S INCE I lost my voice or about ninety per cent. of its once bell-like timbre, I have discovered many inconveniences as well as some striking conveniences.

The greatest inconvenience is that it involved explanations to friends on meeting them for the first time since the vocal abatement and they are grieved by the absence of my former thunderous salutations.

You see in my set warmth of greeting is rated by the size of the hellos you give and receive and I was always noted for issuing the hood rive, or top size, the good old "Hello, hello, hello, hello, the old well, well, well, hello, hello, hello."

Now that I am perforce down to the $6\frac{7}{8}$ size hello for one and all which is just a nubbin of a hello and the brush off kind you give a gee you do not like my friends are inclined to huffiness towards me until I explain about the voice.

This is a bit of strain in itself but fortunately they soon start telling me about remedies that cures other bloke they know so all I have to do is to stand there and nod my head at intervals.

I find the nod wonderfully non-committal, especially when someone is delivering a big knock against someone else because word cannot be carried to the knockee that Runyon was a party to the knock. At least they cannot quote a nod.

WRITTEN IN SICKNESS

I am occasionally distressed by strangers to whom I address myself in my low murmur answering me in imitative whisper, possibly inadvertently, possibly because they think I am kidding and possibly just because they have no sense. Sometimes even my friends do the same thing in that gentle spirit of mockery of human affliction from which many actors and others have long drawn their humour.

You have undoubtedly heard some of our public performers discoursing humorously on cross-eyed persons, on bald heads, on the deaf and the dumb and the lame and the halt. You have perhaps seen them simulate limps and other distortions of the body to point up their jokes. It is a common practice for us to apply nicknames suggestive of affliction such as "Gimp", "Frip", "Humpty", "Deafy", "Blinky", "Baldy" and the like.

False teeth and glass eyes and the toupee have long been standard items of jest among our jokesters. A person who is compelled to resort to a hearing device, one of the greatest boons to afflicted humanity ever invented, is said to be "wired for sound" which is supposed to be good for a hearty laugh.

And not only is infirmity one of our leading topics of humour but it is often brought up by men in moments of anger against the infirm, as when they say things like "That one-legged so-and-so", as if the infirmity itself was a reproach.

Of course the humour that deals with infirmities is in bad taste. Most American humour is in bad taste and growing worse under the present vogue for the suggestive and the downright obscene in the spoken and written word. But even the suggestive and the obscene is not as unkind as the humour dealing with bodily affliction.

The hale and hearty shun the afflicted and I cannot say I blame them much. I can well imagine that I am a great trial to my friends who have to bend their ears close to my kisser to hear what I am saying. Maybe it would be better for all concerned if I did not try to talk at all because everybody else is talking these days and I would not be missed.

I carry a pad of paper in my pocket and when conversation is indicated I jot down my end of the gabbing on paper and pass it on to my vis-à-vis who takes a glaum at the chirography, crumples up the slip of paper and casts it aside, nodding his head or muttering a non-committal um-hah because he cannot read it any more than I can after it is two hours cold.

The forced practice has produced a headache for me as this morning I was waited on by four guys who were all mighty belligerent. I mean they all wanted to place the sluggola on me. They wanted to bash out my brains, if any. I mean they were sizzling.

The first one to appear we will call Pat, though his name is really Pete. He had a piece of paper in his hand that he handed to me, saying, truculently:

"What does this mean?"

The paper had obviously been wadded up and smoothed out again and I could not decipher the writing, though it looked familiar.

"Who wrote this?" I asked Pat (in writing).

"You did," he said, fiercely.

Then it dawned on me that it was indeed my own writing and I read it better.

"Pat is a louse," the writing said.

I tried to remember when I had written it. It could scarcely have been at the editorial council in Joe Connolly's office because insects were not discussed, only a few heels. As a matter of fact I did less talking in Joe Connolly's office than anywhere else in town because when I walked in he had a great big pad of foolscap lying on his desk and I felt insulted. It was a hint that I talk a heap.

It might have been in Lindy's late at night when I had a meeting with Oscar Levant and Leonard Lyons, but it comes to my mind that we did not get as far down in the alphabet as the P's. We quit at the O's because I ran out of pad paper and Lindy commenced to get sore at the way I was working on the backs of his menu cards.

I was busy writing out a denial for Pat when Joe and Ike and Spike, as we will call them, came barging in and each of them had a crumpled slip, and were so hot that taken jointly you could have barbecued a steer on them. I read one slip that said Mike would rob a church, another that stated that Ike would guzzle his grandmamma if he thought it would help him while there was still another that I would not think of putting in a public print. I did not realize that I knew some of the words.

I think if there had been only one present he would have belted me but the four being there at the same time complicated matters because each one knew the others are copper hollerers or stool pigeons, which is what I had in mind in my writing, and would belch to the bulls if a murder or mayhem came off.

So they finally left muttering they would see me later and I was taught a lesson about leaving written testimony scattered around. However, I think that there is a plot for a great crime story in all this by my favourite mystery writer of the moment Raymond Chandler of Los Angeles. I mean he could have the real killer going about dropping notes that finally land him in the gas chamber at Quentin because Chandler puts all his mysteries in California as if we do not have them in Florida, too.

I notice that whipping out the pad sends most of my acquaintances to searching themselves for their specs and they invariably have some fatuous remark to make about getting old as if I did not know by just looking at them or remembering how long I have known them.

I do not pull the pad and pencil on the dames. I just shake hands and grin idiotically. Most women are nearsighted since infancy and too vain to wear cheaters but why should I embarrass them. Besides not all of them can read.

33. DEATH PAYS A SOCIAL CALL

Dᴇᴀᴛʜ came in and sat down beside me, a large and most distinguished-looking figure in beautifully-tailored soft, white flannels. His expansive face wore a big smile.

"Oh, hello," I said. "Hello, hello, hello. I was not expecting you. I have not looked at the red board lately and did not know my number was up. If you will just hand me my kady and my coat I will be with you in a jiffy."

"Tut-tut-tut," Death said. "Not so fast. I have not come for you. By no means."

"You haven't?" I said.

"No," Death said.

"Then what the hell are you doing here?" I demanded indignantly. "What do you mean by barging in here without even knocking and depositing your fat Francis in my easiest chair without so much as by-your-leave?"

"Excuse me," Death said, taken aback at my vehemence. "I was in your neighbourhood and all tired out after my day's work and I thought I would just drop in and sit around with you awhile and cut up old scores. It is merely a social call, but I guess I owe you an apology at that for my entrance."

"I should say you do," I said.

"Well, you see I am so accustomed to entering doors without knocking that I never thought," Death said. "If

476

you like, I will go outside and knock and not come in until you answer."

"Look," I said. "You can get out of here and stay out of here. Screw, bum!"

Death burst out crying.

Huge tears rolled down both pudgy cheeks and splashed on his white silk-faced lapels.

"There it is again," he sobbed. "That same inhospitable note wherever I go. No one wants to chat with me. I am so terribly lonesome. I thought surely you would like to punch the bag with me awhile."

I declined to soften up.

"Another thing," I said sternly, "what are you doing in that get-up? You are supposed to be in black. You are supposed to look sombre, not like a Miami Beach Winter tourist."

"Why," Death said, "I got tired of wearing my old working clothes all the time. Besides, I thought these garments would be more cheerful and informal for a social call."

"Well, beat it," I said. "Just Duffy out of here."

"You need not fear me," Death said.

"I do not fear you Deathie, old boy," I said, "but you are a knock to me among my neighbours. Your visit is sure to get noised about and cause gossip. You know you are not considered a desirable character by many persons, although, mind you, I am not saying anything against you."

———

"Oh, go ahead," Death said. "Everybody else puts the zing on me so you might as well, too. But I did not think your neighbours would recognize me in white, although, come to think of it, I noticed everybody running to their front door and grabbing in their 'Welcome' mats as I went past. Why are you shivering if you do not fear me?"

"I am shivering because of that clammy chill you brought in with you," I said. "You lug the atmosphere of a Frigidaire around with you."

"You don't tell me?" Death said. "I must correct that. I must pack an electric pad with me. Do you think that is why I seem so unpopular wherever I go? Do you think I will ever be a social success?"

"I am inclined to doubt it," I said. "Your personality repels many persons. I do not find it as bad as that of some others I know, but you have undoubtedly developed considerable sales resistance to yourself in various quarters."

"Do you think it would do any good if I hired a publicity man?" Death asked. "I mean, to conduct a campaign to make me popular?"

"It might," I said. "The publicity men have worked wonders with even worse cases than yours. But see here, D., I am not going to waste my time giving you advice and permitting you to linger on in my quarters to get me talked about. Kindly do a scrammola, will you?"

Death had halted his tears for a moment, but now he turned on all faucets, crying boo-hoo-hoo-hoo.

"I am so lonesome," he said between lachrymose heaves.

"Git!" I said.

"Everybody is against me," Death said.

He slowly exited and, as I heard his tears falling plop-plop-plop to the floor as he passed down the hallway, I thought of the remark of Agag, the King of the Amalekites, to Samuel just before Samuel mowed him down: "Surely the bitterness of death is past."

THE END